Moonlight Confessions

Gina Marie Martini

PAGE PUBLISHING, INC.
Conneaut Lake, PA

First originally published by Page Publishing 2020

The characters, places, and events in this book are fictional and based on the author's imagination or are used fictitiously. Any similarities to real persons, living or dead, or business establishments are purely coincidental. The information about *A New Beginning* program and the homeless shelter in this novel are fictional. Through researching homelessness in Southern Nevada, imaginary statistics were created, corresponding to the reality of this crisis.

ISBN 978-1-68456-398-2 (pbk)
ISBN 978-1-68456-399-9 (digital)

Printed in the United States of America

The Entanglements Novels by Gina Marie Martini

Moonlight Confessions
The Mistress Chronicles

For the woman who taught me to always believe
in myself and that anything is possible.
Much love and many thanks to my beautiful mother, Carolyn,
who is one of the strongest women I know.

Follow what you are genuinely passionate about
and let that guide you to your destination.
—Diane Sawyer

Acknowledgments

Family is so important and always comes first. To my sons, Joe and Anthony, your love and encouragement fills my heart and completes me. You have as much to offer the world as it has to offer you. Work hard, love with your whole heart, and live your dreams.

A heartfelt tribute to my grandparents, Elvira "Tootie" and Egisto "Chet," my guardian angels. So many loving recollections of them left a positive impact on my life. Gram was a strong, determined woman who loved unconditionally. She supported me in everything I set out to achieve, and she always had my back.

I was blessed to have had Eva and Everett "Moe" as loving grandparents. They were a beautiful couple, soft-spoken, sweet, gentle, and kind.

To my Martini cousins, for whom I love and cherish—so many wonderful childhood memories and fun times fill my head. Sunday dinners at Gram and Grandpa's house; summer picnics; holidays; the pear tree incident; the Ouija Board encounter—which really did happen! Day trips to Riverside Park; family vacations to Lake George, Ridin-Hy Ranch, and the Bahamas; weekends in Mystic; and many other treasured recollections. Cousins are our first best friends. I'm so grateful you're in my life Anna Marie, Michelle, Eddie, Robert, and Nicole; and in loving memory of my brother, Bobby, who watches our family get-togethers from heaven. He's always with us in spirit.

To Denise, my nieces, Brittnee and Amanda, and my nephew, Matthew: You are forever deeply woven in my heart. Although we live in different states, I love our exciting family adventures! We've had some sensational times in places like Los Angeles, Myrtle Beach, Mexico, France, and Ireland, inspiring me to write about some of these beautiful locations. Where are we going next?

Special thanks to dear friends and family for your advanced thoughtful review of this story, honesty, positive feedback, and overwhelming support. To Darlene Ashford, Diana Barone, Joanne Colavolpe, Sally Diglio, Paula Jandreau, Carolyn Lubitski, Stephanie Sherman, and Joan Valenti—your opinions are greatly valued.

My deep gratitude to friends, Donna Barent and Rosa Hill, for taking the time to share your experiences in setting up and managing a business, and guiding me through those important, albeit tedious, details I find terribly painful like accounting principles, taxes, and use of technical gadgets. Your patience is appreciated.

Thank you to my friend and editor extraordinaire, Pegge Dixon, for your time, your thorough review, and invaluable input.

I'd like to recognize the following books:

Brothels of Nevada, by Robert Engle, which enlightened me on the Nevada brothel culture from the era in which my story is written.

The Happy Hooker, by Xaviera Hollander with Robin Moore and Yvonne Dunleavy, which recounts authentic experiences of prostitution during the sixties and seventies. This autobiography provides details about the life of a prostitute that supports my storyline.

Chapter 1

TO BE BORN into the Meade family was once considered a fortunate circumstance as if my family was blessed by a celestial, higher power. So many wondrous memories filled my mind, reflecting upon the days from my youth—that was, before the horrendous event altered all of our lives.

When I was a young girl, Dad would toss me up on his shoulders with ease to watch the Saint Patrick's Day parade in Boston among thousands of spectators. We'd drive to Fenway Park to watch the Sox play their rival team, the Yankees, every year, rain or shine.

Hockey games were the most fun. We'd sip hot cocoa beneath a blanket, watching the Boston Bruins battle it out on the ice against the Montreal Canadiens. Whether it was the action on the ice or the blood-spattering fistfights, Dad and I would have a blast at the Boston Arena. Not because I loved sports. I didn't care who won. It was the one-on-one time with my father, the man I admired and adored. At least back then.

As the oldest child of three, all of Dad's attention was on me. A privilege, I believed, that made me special and slightly entitled.

Mom used to say, "Sadie, you're just like your dad, full of sass and spirit." She really meant I was rebellious and outspoken with a wild side, like my father.

Then Dad's injuries affected us all.

Physically, Dad suffered extensive wounds while fighting in the Korean War in 1952. While in combat, a fierce explosion from a grenade blew off his toes on one foot.

The doctors couldn't remove all the debris from his leg or his arm. He was lucky to be alive after that attack. His bravery saved the lives of a few soldiers who walked away without any major physical impairments.

Today, Dad hobbled about with a wooden cane because of his injury and the shrapnel remaining throughout the left side of his body.

Fred Meade was a war hero to his Army family. To my family, he returned a completely different person, depressed and tormented. He retired too young from his military career. The Army didn't need him anymore because he was considered damaged goods.

A job outside his military family was a challenge for him to find. Perhaps he carried deep-rooted resentment, feeling useless because of his handicaps.

Mom contemplated finding a job. She was a skilled seamstress, or she could work at the local bakery. She loved to create decadent, tantalizing treats.

A proud man like Dad would never allow his wife to work; even though no one would hire him when they saw his cane and little movement from his upper left side. We could use more money than the disability checks he received faithfully from the government.

Dad's war buddy, Rocky Cavallo, survived the blast back in '52. He and a few other soldiers owed their lives to my father. Dad kept an oak-framed photograph of his platoon hanging on the pasty-white living room wall, close to his wedding portrait with Mom. His time in the Army meant as much to him as we did.

He spoke of his military brothers with such pride. I couldn't recall him ever speaking about Lisa, Patrick, or me with as much joy and satisfaction.

Our days were routine like we enlisted in the Army ourselves. My folks were up by 0500 every morning. We couldn't sleep past 0600 without the cowbell ringing, disrupting blissful dreams, so we could complete our chores before school.

Breakfast was ready by 0700, and our school lunches were packed in brown paper bags. Dinner was promptly served every night by 1800 hours, and not a moment too late. Dad appeared at the table two minutes early with his knife and fork in hand, waiting to be served. Our lives were run by the cuckoo clock on the wall—always in military time.

Lisa was the smart one of the three of us. Her slender nose was always glued to a book, rarely blinking her blue eyes. Her brain never shuts off. She surely dreamt of algebraic equations, whereas I barely passed math class.

My sister and I shared similar features, but Lisa had a touch of reddish highlights to her long blond hair, compared to my bright, sunny color at a shorter length.

Patrick, a high school freshman, stood at a medium height with a slender build and golden hair. Dad had been more lenient with Patrick's schedule and hobbies. He was a boy, after all. Patrick was never the athletic type, yet Dad forced him to play.

Once, at the age of eight, Patrick cried in front of the whole baseball team when the ball whipped his shoulder. His back end hurt even worse after Dad whacked him with his belt for embarrassing him. No son of his would cry like a little girl because he got hit with a baseball.

"Be a man, Patrick!"

I was sick to death of hearing my father chant that. My brother probably hated to hear those words too. Instead of sports, Patrick preferred the alto sax and joined the school band.

Since the start of my senior year of high school in '64, I'd attend dances held near the military base. Dad wanted me to find a husband, preferably a soldier.

Marriage or a job? I managed to find a job at the corner market. Four nights a week I spent at Mr. Gibson's store, filling orders, pouring coffee, and exchanging money.

More importantly, I loved to have fun. My friends and I smoked ciggies and drank cheap booze; vodka was my preferred drink. And I loved the smell of a boy's flesh and the taste of his lips against mine. I had thoroughly enjoyed sex since losing my virginity at sixteen; even though my mother swore I'd go blind if I ever saw a penis before marriage, or allowed a boy to touch the special nether region of my body.

Dad knew some of the top brass and their wives who chaperoned the military dances.

One night, Pete Fiske and I were making out in the back seat of his Chevy. Pete knew how to get his hands on his father's moonshine, and he knew how to use those hands on my body.

After feeling a little tipsy from the hooch he swiped, I fixed my skirt and hair then sauntered back inside to the dance with him.

From across the room, scattered with young men in their Army uniforms dancing with vibrant, giggly girls, I recognized the cane affixed to my father's firm hand. He was checking up on me, I thought.

"Wait two minutes then ask me to dance," I ordered Pete with glaring eyes.

"Dance? Why do we have to dance now?" he scoffed, smoothing out his ash-brown hair.

"Peter Fiske, if you ever want to touch me again, you will wait two minutes then ask me to dance in front of my father like a gentleman."

"Okay, jeez. Any other orders you got for me, Sadie?"

"Fix your shirt!" I stuffed my hands inside his uniform pants to straighten his starched white shirt.

The room was bursting with girls who dreamed of meeting their future husband tonight. The Righteous Brothers "You've Lost That Loving Feeling" blared from the old speakers, adding crackles to the baritone's voice.

I turned, pushing Pete against the wall, out of viewing distance from my father. Then I grabbed his bulge that grew firmer by the second. "I'll make sure you're rewarded if you act like a good, trusted soldier in front of my father."

I went to those dances for a good time, not to find a husband.

Chapter 2

IT WAS THE summer of 1965. My best friend, Jeannie, called to tell me about a bonfire at the beach. Of course, I'd have to lie to my parents. Hanging out with hippies was prohibited.

Maybe I'd tell them about a movie I wanted to see. *Beach Blanket Bingo* was still playing downtown. It wasn't unusual for Jeannie and me to have sleepovers. I lied to Mom and Dad, saying I'd be spending the night at Jeannie's house, while Jeannie told her parents she'd be sleeping at my house.

Our parents knew each other, but they didn't socialize. Jeannie was Jewish, and my family was Catholic. Our families came from such diverse backgrounds with different religious views that they'd only talk about the weather or maintain a polite conversation about current news events when they were together at school functions.

Neither Jeannie nor I cared about having different faiths. It wasn't as if we were the overly religious schoolgirl type.

We hiked up our shorts, bikinis underneath, and thumbed our way to the beach.

Jody Atwater's older brother, Mark, picked us up in his beat-up, old Dodge. He was home from college, and maybe twenty-one to our eighteen years. Mark didn't seem to recognize who we were, exactly. He sure did notice Jeannie though. Hard not to with her massive breasts.

If my breasts were a quarter of the size of hers, I'd be happy. Unfortunately, God played a dirty trick on me with an A-cup bra.

Mark's hand kept touching Jeannie's leg since she was sitting in the middle of the front seat. Jeannie let him touch her then asked him if he wanted to party with us at the beach. He offered us a hit of reefer, threw his arm around Jeannie, and drove the Dodge toward the water.

Most of the usual crowd joined the beach party. Kids we went to school with our whole lives. Those who went to college returned for summer break, probably desperate to get back to school already.

No one ever left town unless they were deployed or dead, victims of the Vietnam War our country was fighting.

Even worse, were young men like Lee Northrop, who hadn't been seen or heard from in six months. His family had no idea if he was dead or suffering tortuous acts at the hands of our enemy. If he was found dead, maybe his family would find peace within such a tragedy. Not knowing, holding on to futile hope, must feel just as painful.

Maybe I should have considered college. At least I'd be away from this wretched town. But we couldn't afford college. Although Patrick, being a boy, would be able to go. Dad would figure out a way to send him, or he could enter the military when he turned eighteen.

With the war going strong, I hoped my brother didn't enlist or become a casualty of the draft. He couldn't handle being whacked with a baseball during a kid's ball game. What on earth would he do if he had a bomb coming his way? He might not survive boot camp. And I'd hate it if he were to end up in a state of purgatory like Lee Northrop.

"A Hard Day's Night" blasted from the radio, and I danced with the others in a circle around the warm, blazing fire with sand itching between my toes. The warmth of the flames filled my senses along with the vodka Jeannie snatched from her father's bar. He had so many liquor bottles packed up in that old bar he never seemed to miss one or two taken.

Mark and Jeannie were hitting it off. They kicked off their sandals and strolled hand in hand along the serene stretch of water.

I didn't follow them. Instead, I plopped down at the edge of the ocean and soaked my feet and legs in the refreshing, cool water. Through the glow of the moonlight, bouncing its rays off the water, he appeared in my sight.

My eyes locked with this tall blond stranger. He must be new around here, unless the effect of the vodka and reefer messed with my vision.

I attempted to stand, but it felt so much better to lie in the cool sand, mesmerized by the moon and the family of twinkling stars surrounding that large bubble high in the sky. I tilted my head to keep my eye on the fine-looking, tall blond kid until the weight of my eyelids forced them closed.

"Hey! Are you okay?"

I felt someone's hand nudging me, then my body lifted upward. The gentle breeze through my blond strands seemed as if I were flying. When my eyes opened, that cute boy was staring at me, saying something I couldn't comprehend. I turned my head and realized he was carrying me up the beach.

He placed my body down upon someone's blanket. Sand tossed through the air.

I felt the scratchiness of pebbles and shells in my bikini bottom, a rather unpleasant feeling.

"Are you all right?" he asked again, handing me a bottle of Coca-Cola. "Sip this," he ordered as he placed the glass bottle to my parched lips.

"What are you doing?"

"You were passed out in the water. You could've drowned when the tide rolled in."

I would've woken up, but I had a splitting headache. I managed to say a quick thanks to him before lying back down on the blanket.

Chapter 3

MY EYES OPENED to see a bright multicolored quilt beneath my body. Several people were passed out around me. The Drifters "Under the Boardwalk" played on the radio at a mellow tone.

Don, our school's infamous football linebacker, attempted to play the Drifters tune with his guitar, crooning to this girl, Holly, the bubbly cheerleader type. The fire was nearly out by now.

I didn't own a watch. No clue of the time, but the moon was full and straight above us, casting an iridescent glow over the calm ocean.

My head laid atop a firm, strong chest. My eyes shot up to see the face of the new kid with the blond hair. He had fallen asleep with an arm draped around me, while his toes nuzzled next to mine.

Did we do it? My hands quickly felt around my breasts and legs. My light blue bikini was still strapped and in place. Certain parts of my body didn't feel the warm, fulfilled sensations from sex.

It took a few minutes for my brain to function. The last thing I remembered was watching Jeannie and Mark glide along the edge of the beach for privacy as I cooled off in the water. I wondered where Jeannie was.

I moved Blondie's muscular arm from around me and pushed myself up to stand. My balance wasn't very steady, but eventually I caught sight of Jeannie curled up in Mark's arms, legs entwined atop a brightly striped beach towel, sucking face.

The breeze whipped along the small stretch of beach, forcing a cool shiver to run through me. If only the fire stayed lit. I looked down upon the blond beefcake whose arm kept me warm as I slept. Slowly, I maneuvered my body to lay beside him, snuggling into his thick, stubbly neck. The warmth of his breath felt soothing against my head that throbbed, thanks to my fondness for vodka. His arms wrapped around me as naturally as if we were longtime lovers.

Maybe it was the sun shining upon my face or his movement that woke me when morning came.

"Sorry, my arm fell asleep. You feeling okay now?" His voice sounded gentle and sweet.

"Me? I'm fine," I lied terribly. My head pounded, and I feared making an attempt to stand with a compromised balance.

"You weren't looking so good last night. I thought you were going to drown."

I vaguely remembered him saying that. "Did you carry me last night or was I dreaming?"

He laughed, exposing his delightful dimples. "Yeah, I carried you out of the ocean. I had my eye on you when I saw you start to doze off right down there in the water." He pointed as if that were the exact spot in the Atlantic.

"You were watching me?"

"My name's Mickey Quinn." He spoke with an accent. Maybe a New Yorker. Definitely not a Bostonian like many of the people in this small Gloucester fishing town.

"Sadie Meade. You're not from around here, are you?"

"I'm fairly new in town. My father has a fishing boat we keep docked not far from here. We love to fish."

"Where are you from?"

"Clinton, Connecticut. My dad wanted to move closer to family in Boston."

There was something about him, this Mickey Quinn. He didn't say much, but when he opened his mouth, I hung on to every word that left those delectable lips of his.

He explained that his father now owned the bait and tackle store in town.

At a closer look, his lush blond hair just about touched his shoulders like mine did. His eyes were crystal blue and soft. There were a few grains of sand trapped in the hairs of his mustache. A jagged scar on his shoulder caught my eye through the opening of his button-down brown shirt.

I stretched my fingers out and softly touched the scar, forming an outline around the edges. He watched my face as I stroked his chest.

"How'd you get this?"

"A great white got me."

"What?"

I waited for a fascinating fishing story to be told, but his eyes lit up, and a hearty laugh escaped from his mouth.

"Ha ha. Very funny. Seriously, what happened?"

"Actually, I was diving into Schreeder Pond at Chatfield Hollow from the top of a large tree branch. It was a stupid dare, really. The branch broke, and I got cut up on the way down to the water by a combination of other tree branches and some rocks. Obviously, I'm not very bright, but my body is pretty strong." He flashed his muscular arms like Popeye. "I survived the fall with just a few deep cuts and a concussion."

I felt the need to touch his head where the fall injured him. As my hands smoothed against the thick golden strands, our eyes met.

Most boys would've kissed me by now. Not Mickey. He was nice, with kind eyes and what seemed like a big heart. He pulled away.

"I hope you don't mind that I slept next to you last night. I was worried about you."

My lips formed a big smile. "I'm glad you did."

I wanted to learn more about Mickey Quinn. So much more.

Chapter 4

AFTER MEETING MICKEY at the beach, my desire to see him grew fast with intensity. Intimate feelings stirred my heart like I had never felt before. Sometimes I'd hitch a ride or take the bus up to his bait store.

He taught me how to fish and to properly bait a hook. Even though I thought it was the most disgusting thing to do to a worm, I simply craved to be near him.

Fishing was his life. He spoke of the sea like she was his lover. We often stood along the shoreline, staring out into the moonlit water, where he first held my hand beneath a billion twinkling stars.

He had hardworking hands. The calluses scraped against my fair skin when he held me. I loved the way his roughened fingers caressed my cheek before he kissed me.

Mickey's father chartered the boat to take vacationers fishing in the ocean while Mickey or his brother, Paul, ran the store. His mom worked at the local town diner.

He loved sailing. Unfortunately, I was born with a troubled belly. The continuous up and down motion of waves triggered a terrible sickness from within, so no boat rides for me.

Our first intimate moment took my breath away. I worried my vexing reputation might have caught up with me. Mickey was new in town, blissfully unaware of my previous encounters with several local boys. Some of my former lovers enlisted, stationed in North Carolina or Virginia, if they weren't deployed to the jungles of Vietnam.

I might not have wanted Mickey to know about my beguiling history, but I wasn't about to pretend and act virginal. Not my style. I kissed him hard and handled him with experienced, sensual touches.

He responded with tenderness and affection. Those callused hands glided gently over my flesh. Never had a boy treated me with such sincerity.

Did I deserve him? Did I deserve this moment of real happiness and dare I say that *L* word? I always hated that word. Feared it perhaps. Never said it. Never trusted it. At this moment, I didn't want to think anymore.

Together we removed each other's clothes and dropped them to the floor in a puddle by his bed. A real bed. Not the back seat of a car or the boys' locker room at the high school. He didn't just pounce on top of me, stick it in, and get it done. He took his sweet time, allowing this precious moment and feeling to linger. My body pulsed and tingled at the touch of his tongue. No one had ever stirred that fire, causing such an explosion within me before.

When I felt him inside me, the difference between sex and making love became evident through a mere glance from his blue eyes. For the first time, I understood there was a distinction. I loved Mickey Quinn. And I told him. I actually said the *L* word out loud while our bodies were gliding together beneath his Boston Patriots blanket.

Mickey said the *L* word back.

Chapter 5

ALMOST A FULL year passed. Mickey and I were a strong couple in 1966. No more dances. No more partying. Loving Mickey changed my life.

The bait and tackle shop made decent money throughout the fishing season. The remaining months were hard on their business and bank account. Mickey's parents mentioned moving back to Connecticut and selling their fishing boat.

If Mickey moved to Connecticut, I planned to join him. At least that was *my* plan. I hadn't mentioned it to him yet. We loved each other though. Being with him felt as natural as breathing.

After spending a full day with Mickey, I managed to be late for dinner—again. Dad would have a fit. Sure enough, as I stepped through the front door of our small yellow Cape Cod, the rest of the family sat at the oblong dining room table, stuffing their faces with Mom's leftover meatloaf, green beans, and mashed potatoes.

Dad's eyes gazed upon me, glowering with disappointment.

Lisa and Patrick's half-smiles appeared suspect as if they knew something I didn't. Maybe I was in big trouble tonight. I thought an apology would be a good way to start.

"I'm sorry I'm late. I took the bus. There was a problem at one of the stops. The driver had to…"

"You should have taken an earlier bus. You know I like to eat at 1800 hours, Sadie. I'm not going to eat a cold dinner. Your mother works very hard in that kitchen to fix a nice hot meal. The least you can do is be here on time to eat it while it's still warm," Dad said, brushing his fingers through his thin golden strands.

"Yes, sir," I said with my head lowered, hiding the disgruntled expression I couldn't help but wear.

"She's not that late, Fred." Mom came to my rescue, tossing me a wink.

"Well, now that we're all together, I'm calling a family meeting," Dad said, slamming his fork down, while still chewing on potatoes.

Oh, I hoped he didn't plan on humiliating me or grounding me from leaving the house because I was ten minutes late.

"I got a job. My old buddy, Rocky Cavallo, came through for me."

Everyone shouted with glee. Mom kissed the bald spot on the top of his head.

Lisa, Patrick, and I congratulated him.

Maybe if he had something to do every day, he'd leave us alone and be out of the house more often to give Mom and us kids some space.

"This job is a good opportunity for me. I need my family with me on this. A lot of changes are coming. The pay is more dough than I ever made before. Rocky's setting us up with a new house."

"A new house? We have a house, Fred," Mom chimed in.

"We're moving?" Patrick blurted, sounding more concerned than happy.

"You know I dread the harsh winters here in New England. My bum leg aches when it's less than forty degrees. We're going somewhere nice and warm with a lot of excitement!"

Mom clung to every word that left Dad's lips, beaming with pride.

"What does that mean, Dad? Where are we going?" I asked. Leaving New England entirely was not something I wanted. My whole life was here. My friends. Mickey.

"We're moving to Nevada. Las Vegas, Nevada!" He sprang from his seat with excitement, grabbed Mom by the hand, and performed a little dance without his cane. It was the first time I ever saw him move that quickly without leaning on that piece of wood.

The rest of the family seemed elated with this move. Everyone cheered, except me.

"I can't go. That's on the other side of the country. Why would you take a job that forces us to leave our home? You can go. You can all go, but I'm not going anywhere!" I insisted, folding my arms and stomping my left foot on the tile floor.

Dad's smile turned upside down, and he stared at me as if he were going to grab the wooden spoon and spank my ass for talking back.

"We are going together as a family, Sadie. You are my daughter. You're coming with us."

"I'm legally an adult, Dad. I don't have to live with you. I can get married."

"Married? To who? That poor fisherman? That family can barely take care of themselves. Are they going to support you too? Or will you get more hours at Gibson's store to support yourself?" He laughed.

"I can do that!"

"Until you're married, you're *my* responsibility, and you're coming with us!"

I stood to my feet and threw down my napkin into my plate of cold meatloaf. "I'm not leaving!"

"Sadie, sit down!" Mom scolded. Dad was usually the disciplinarian. Mom didn't normally say much at all. "Sadie, I said sit down."

The surprising sound of Mom's irritation forced my backside to slowly sink into my chair.

"This is important to your father. I think we should hear him out." She turned away from me and looked directly at Dad. "Fred, tell us about the job and where we'd be living. Patrick still has to finish school."

"Rocky can use someone with my military background in security. He owns a swanky hotel and casino called the Montgomery. Sinatra performs in Vegas! Imagine that. I just might meet Sinatra and other celebs!" Dad looped his thumbs around his suspenders, raising his chin with pride.

"You saved his life, Fred. If it weren't for you, Rocky could've died in Korea."

"I did my job. I served my country. That's what any good soldier would do. Rocky doesn't owe me anything. But he offered to pay for our relocation and find us a new home. My paycheck will more than cover our expenses. It's a win-win situation. And we'll be living in an exciting place."

He looked at Mom for the first time in a long time with so much joy on his face. "Suzanne, you always say I never take you anywhere. I'm taking you to Vegas, baby!"

Everyone seemed thrilled. Everyone but me. I couldn't wait to see Mickey tomorrow. Maybe we could run away together. I fantasized about how he'd propose to me. Marry me to keep me here with him.

Chapter 6

I WOKE EARLY, snuck out of the house, and met the city bus at 0600 to drive me to Mickey's store.

My heart began to harden. Hurt feelings turned to sheer bitterness. How I wanted to grab Mickey, take whatever money was in the store's register, and run far away. As long as we were together, I didn't care where we ended up. I was not hopping on some plane to move to a hot, sandy desert across the country.

There was a lot of hustle and bustle at the tackle shop at this time of day. Eager fishermen securing a head start at the crack of dawn.

Mickey appeared busy, waiting on customers. He saw me enter and returned a dazed look. I never dropped by to see him this early.

I signaled to him, rolling my fingers for him to hurry. But a lengthy line of customers waited to cash out, distracting him from my eagerness.

I grabbed a bright-orange bait thingamajig from a wire rack and stood in line with a dozen other customers, so I'd have a moment alone with him, even if it cost me twenty-five cents. Jeez, twenty-five cents for this ugly orange bit of rubber to catch a fish? I never liked the taste of fish.

Gosh, these people were so needy. Couldn't they figure out what they wanted and leave?

Patience, a trait I always lacked.

Finally, this fat, hairy man selected his pole to fish with and left the store.

Mickey smiled, removed the orange bait from my fingers, then stared at me, unclear why I wanted to buy it.

"My parents want to move to Nevada!" I belted out in an agitated tone.

His eyes bonded to the bright-orange bait, diverting him from my frazzled state.

"I don't want that." I snatched the bait quickly from his hand and tossed it off to the side. "Did you hear what I said? They expect me to go with them!"

"Are you going?"

"No, I'm not going!" My patience wore thin. He didn't understand me at all.

"What are you gonna do if your family moves?"

The line of customers became annoyed. People started asking if I was buying something or not.

A tall, husky man wearing a crazy hat with all these ugly colorful bait pieces pinned to it started yelling about needing to get back out to the pier.

"Sadie, I gotta take care of these people. We'll talk when things slow down." He kindly tossed me to the side of the line with a polite smile.

How could he be so calm when I felt shattered?

I paced in a circle around a fish tank. Live bait. I stared into the tank, watching the fish swim about, knowing this could be their last day alive. The one purpose in their miserable lives was to catch a bigger fish for sport or a meal. They had no say in the outcome of their fate. That was how I felt. My father wasn't giving me a choice. I had to make my own choices. Choose my own fate.

His brother, Paul, arrived to give him a hand behind the counter.

I charged right over. "Mickey, please talk to me now."

He held up his index finger. "One second." He waited on another customer.

My tolerance depleted completely. I yelled loud and hearty from my diaphragm, "Mickey Quinn, marry me!"

Silence. Complete silence in the entire store that a pin could be heard if it dropped.

Everyone turned their heads and stared at me, even Mickey. He glared with a stupid, dazed look emanating from his blue eyes.

Mickey turned toward his customer with an awkward gaze. "Here's your change, sir. Thank you." Slowly, he handed the man a shiny nickel.

I heard Paul mumble under his breath that he'd take care of the customers for a few minutes. Then Paul tilted his head in my direction, encouraging Mickey to talk to me.

Mickey walked straight past me, heading toward the stockroom in the back of the store. He nearly knocked over a rack that held some strange-looking fishing gear.

I followed him. Although, he didn't look nearly as excited about my proposal as I was. "Well? Aren't you going to give me an answer?" I was mostly excited yet partially frustrated.

His fingers clasped his chiseled chin, then brushed through his thick blond streaks. "Sadie, you can't come into a business and propose marriage in front of a crowd of strangers! What the hell were you thinking?"

"I'm thinking about our future. I can't move to Nevada with my parents. I may never see you again. But if we get married, I could stay here. With you."

"Sadie, a woman does not propose to a man. That's just not how it's done. Hell, that was embarrassing! If we ever do get married, it's going to be *my* idea, and *I'll* do the asking."

I crept closer to him, placed my hands across his chest, and ran them upward until my fingers reached his face. My lips were a breath away from his before I let him kiss me.

"Won't you miss me if I moved away? So far away we couldn't see each other again?"

"Of course, I'd miss you."

"Would you come to Nevada to be with me?"

"Nevada?"

"Yes, Las Vegas. It might be fun to live there…together."

"Isn't that a desert? What is a fisherman like me gonna do in the middle of the desert?"

"Can I stay here with you and your family?"

The door flew open, and his gruff father stood inside the door-frame, arms crossed, staring sharply with eyes so cold I couldn't tell they were as blue as Mickey's.

"Mickey's working today, Sadie. Time for you to go. He's working till four."

I glanced over at Mickey. His head fell, eyes staring at the hard-wood floor. He tried to walk me out, making no eye contact with his father.

Mr. Quinn placed a hand on Mickey's shoulder, forcing him to stay put. "You stay right here, son." Then those angry eyes peered at me. "Go on, now. He's got work to do."

He shooed me away, but I stood outside the door, a poor attempt to eavesdrop. Seemed his dad caught wind of my impromptu proposal.

A sharp tap was felt upon my shoulder. My head turned to see Mickey's mother in her blue and white waitress uniform frowning at me. Some might say she gave me the evil eye.

"What are you doing? That's a private conversation in there, Sadie."

"Oh, but I was waiting for Mickey."

"He's working all day. Obviously, it's very busy around here. He can't have you hanging around, distracting him. Time to go!"

With a squeeze of my shoulder from her firm grip, Mrs. Quinn personally escorted me through the maze of people in the store and outside.

I ran around to the back of the building. There was a window in the room where Mickey and I were talking. Mickey's dad started shouting, ordering him not to marry a "girl like me." My reputation hurried back to haunt me.

Then I heard directly from Mickey's own lips that he had no intention of marrying me.

Mickey said he loved me, but what he just told his father shocked the hell out of me. He acted as though my leaving town was insignificant.

All hope was gone. It looked like I was moving to Las Vegas.

Chapter 7

MICKEY CALLED ME at home when I didn't return to the store to finish our conversation. I heard him loud and clear, and I told him so. He didn't want to marry me. Maybe I wasn't the marrying kind. I was always considered the good-time girl, looking for a party.

Mickey apologized. He didn't realize I was eavesdropping, but his father was a hard-ass like mine. Neither of our fathers would have allowed us to get married.

Mickey said I didn't understand his situation with his family. He used that stupid *L* word.

I hated that word more than ever right now. I should've known not to trust it.

If Mickey didn't want to marry me, nothing was keeping me here in this town. A part of me wondered if he'd surprise me one day. Either show up on my front porch before I left, telling me he missed me and didn't want me to leave, or track me down in Las Vegas. The last words he said to me on the phone were, "I'm sorry."

I didn't speak to my father during the entire moving process. Packing, cleaning, and discarding were major tasks for several weeks. Mom and Dad worked hard to sell most of our things. We couldn't take a house full of furniture with us on the airplane.

I was so angry with my father for forcing us to leave our home. Blamed him for making me leave my life behind, friends like Jeannie, and especially for losing Mickey.

Maybe in time, we could've made it work. His parents might not have liked me much, but I knew my grandma Meade never liked my mother, yet Dad married her anyway.

We arrived at Logan International Airport for our evening flight to Nevada. Never in my life had I been on an airplane. My stomach grumbled. My nervous belly gave me trouble riding in the back seat of cars and on boats. I wasn't sure what to expect on a plane.

Our luggage was taken. Some of my most cherished possessions were packed inside, including a picture of Mickey and me fishing on the pier. Maybe it would remind me that I could feel that *L* word for someone again. I never expected it the first time with Mickey. Even if I didn't, Las Vegas sounded like a great place for a party girl like me.

Walking aboard the plane heightened my anxiety. How would this steel bubble we were trapped in keep us up in the air all the way across the country? Vicious thoughts about this contraption exploding haunted me.

Patrick thought it was pretty cool. Lisa stuck her nose in one of her books the moment her behind hit the seat.

Dad sat alone, closed his eyes, and fell asleep before the stewardess sauntered down the aisle with a big, bright smile, greeting all the passengers. The tall brunette with the cheesy grin offered reading material and cigarettes. Maybe a smoke would relax me. Of course, Mom and Dad would have a fit as if smoking once in a while was a big deal.

The captain made an announcement before the plane engine roared. The loud, obnoxious sound ran through me, surging from within my gut. Why was I stuck sitting next to my brother, who screamed with excitement nearly as loud as the engine?

The plane started to move like a car driving down the street. My stomach rumbled, hands trembled. Perspiration saturated my clothing. We weren't supposed to leave our seats, but I jumped up, ran to the tiny bathroom, and vomited the fried chicken and tater tots I ate for dinner into the toilet.

That tawdry stewardess banged on the door hard, yelling at me to take my seat. If she knew how I was defiling this bathroom, she wouldn't want me in my seat.

The lighting was dim. My skin turned a tinted shade of green as if I were celebrating Saint Patrick's Day dressed like a little blond leprechaun. I thought the worst was over. I splashed water on my face, rinsed my mouth, flushed the toilet, then attempted to reach my seat, staggering.

Mom met me in the aisle to help. She knew I was ill. We hadn't even left the ground when motion sickness kicked in. Mom believed it was another one of my panic attacks.

The stewardess brought me a bag in case I felt sick again. She offered me some ginger ale or water, wearing a sympathetic grin. But the thought of anything in my stomach made me want to heave again.

This journey became the longest night of my life. Several hours later, and somewhere over the Midwest, the captain announced turbulence. Just what my stomach needed. As if it weren't rumbling on its own already. Thank God for the bags I was given. I wouldn't have reached the bathroom in time.

Las Vegas would have to be my forever home because I'd never step foot on another plane for as long as I lived. I already hated my father for dragging me across the country. Now I really despised him for putting me through this agony.

Patrick tried to make me look out the window. I hated being so high up in the sky above the clouds like floating through a dark fog in a nightmare.

After a few more daunting hours passed with little sleep, we caught a glimpse of what seemed to be an entire city of blinking lights that sparkled through the dark hours before dawn, dazzling the passengers on the plane. We had arrived. I couldn't wait to get the hell off this plane and kiss the ground.

Chapter 8

I HOBBLED OFF the airplane, barely able to stand in the wee hours of the morning on the West Coast. The mere thought of food made me want to vomit again.

Mom seemed concerned, although the green tint of my skin had faded to pale white. She helped me walk at a gradual pace through the airport.

A tall man dressed in a black suit with a cap covering curly brown hair held up a sign with the name "Fred Meade" written in block letters.

My father approached him to announce himself. Apparently, Dad's good friend, Rocky, sent a limousine to pick us up along with all our baggage. Dad's chest puffed up, feeling like some kind of big shot because a limo driver had been hired to whisk his family away.

Mom ensured I sat in the front seat next to Buck, the driver. He had a southern accent as if he were from Texas. Motion sickness didn't hit me too hard if I sat in the front seat of a car or bus.

The bus driver back home was used to my condition. He'd sometimes ask another passenger to give me his seat. I wasn't sure if he was being kind to me or if he just didn't want me vomiting in his bus.

Fortunately, the drive to Rocky Cavallo's house was under thirty minutes from the airport. A drive in the front seat of a gorgeous black limo fared easy on my troubled belly.

The neighborhood looked beautiful before sunrise. Mansions for the rich and famous sprawled throughout the vicinity, radiating with the first crisp shot of sunlight.

The driver pulled up to a tall iron gate that magically opened. I glanced up at the colossal house. We didn't have homes this big in

Gloucester. Boston, maybe, but not in my neighborhood. Our house was probably the same size as Rocky's garage.

A man of medium height and build met us outside, wearing a colorful plaid jacket and dark-blue slacks. He brushed away his ash-brown hair with noticeable curls from his eyes. His chin was long, pronounced, as was his nose.

As he greeted my father, he sucked on a cigar that never left his lips. The two men bantered on about their war days.

Mr. Cavallo hugged my mother. I blushed at the way he hugged her. His eyes greedily absorbed her figure as if he hadn't seen a woman in years.

The driver tended to our suitcases as Mr. Cavallo welcomed us inside his massive home. He insisted we call him Rocky after my father introduced us kids to his war buddy.

Apparently, there was a holdup with the house he found for us. We couldn't move in for a few weeks, so he welcomed us to stay in his opulent mansion. Obviously, there was plenty of room. Lisa and I didn't have to share a bedroom here. I planned to count how many rooms this enormous place had.

Once inside, a screeching sound was heard. The noise grew louder when I saw a young man in a wheelchair, with a cigarette dangling from his lips, enter the parlor. I couldn't quite figure out what happened to him. Maybe he got injured in Vietnam like my dad in Korea. Rocky introduced him as his son, John.

"Did you get hurt in Nam?" I asked bluntly.

My parents glared at me as if I said something horribly wrong.

John attempted to reply, but I couldn't understand him. God, did he hurt his brain too? He didn't speak normally.

"Sadie, my son was born deaf, and he wasn't injured in the war."

John used his fingers and hands to communicate with his father.

"John says it's nice to meet everyone," Rocky informed us as he continued to use his hands and arms to speak with John. "I just told him all of your names in sign language."

John waved to us.

We waved back with an element of surprise shown upon our faces, unsure of what to say.

John was very handsome with black hair and crystal green eyes with dark lashes blinking. His arms were quite muscular for a man of slender build.

Rocky explained that John could read our lips to understand what we said instead of using his ears.

"Nice to meet ya," I said directly to John, who smiled and nodded at me in return.

Dad continued to give me a nasty look. Well, if he didn't want to be embarrassed, he should've forewarned me that Rocky had a deaf, disabled son. He hated that I brought up the Vietnam War at all, never mind my asking if John was a wounded soldier.

This war took thousands of soldiers' lives. What else was I to think?

Dad was no fan of our democrat President Johnson. He disagreed with his views on civil rights and his stance on the war that Dad believed Johnson fueled further. Violence around the country had heightened. I could tell Dad's conservative political brain was working overtime as he stared at me with that look of annoyance.

With the sun shining brightly, from the large window in the living room, I noticed a ramp that trailed along the outside of the house. I suspected the ramp was built for John to access the entrance without the use of stairs. How ingenious. Clearly, Rocky had plenty of money, which was the whole reason why we were here.

Would our new home look this magnificent? I thought about what our life would be like here as my eyes absorbed the lavish furniture and fancy artwork throughout the structure. As I gazed above, an extra-large chandelier sparkled like diamonds. An interesting mural of cherubs, clouds, and doves displayed high above us, was painted across the ceiling. I never saw anything like this except in history school books like when we read about Napoleon and the French revolution. There wasn't a cozy vibe to be found in this house. It was more wealth and glitter, something my family was unaccustomed to.

Rocky showed us our temporary rooms and allowed us time to freshen up. His cook prepared a meal for us. The smell of eggs and bacon sizzling from the kitchen made my stomach turn—not because of the aroma, but because of the residual effects from the long flight from hell.

Chapter 9

AFTER THE OTHERS ate a hearty breakfast, and we unpacked our belongings in the glamorous bedrooms selected for us, Rocky took us for a stroll outside around the property.

"Ten acres of land," he said with pride.

A few men were clipping the grass that seemed to spread for miles. Two women were plucking weeds from the gardens. Another man was pruning citrus trees with extra-large clippers. A fresh lemon scent filled the air with every breath I took. It seemed like Rocky had a lot of help to manage the property.

I asked Rocky about his wife.

That annoyed look displayed above my father's stiffened jaw; his brows curved inward. I felt his icy scowl freeze my spine. Regrettably, Rocky's wife died several years ago from a bout with cancer. Sad, yes. Was it really so wrong of me to ask? I had always been a curious soul.

The swimming pool was in sight as we continued our walk. From the corner of my eye, I noticed John rolling his chair toward the edge of the pool. He wore bright-orange shorts and a white muscle tee. I assumed he was soaking in some sun. His body seemed to lift from his chair as my eyes witnessed him tumbling into the in-ground pool.

My breath held for a moment before it occurred to me that he might be in trouble. I yelled for help, then ran toward the pool.

My parents, Lisa, and Patrick traced behind me through the grass trimmings and up a stone path.

"John!" I screamed, forgetting momentarily he couldn't hear my voice.

When I reached his wheelchair next to the pool, John's head bobbed out of the water. He appeared to be doing some arm exercises, keeping himself afloat. I sighed with relief.

"You know he can't hear you, right?" A deep, sultry voice was heard from around the corner.

I looked in the direction of the smooth-spoken sound and saw this gorgeous kid with large biceps and firm abs, wearing a rather revealing black bathing suit. He removed a pair of dark sunglasses, exposing incredible gray eyes that stared deeply into mine. He wiped away a few strands of brown hair, long with thick waves, from his tanned face.

"My brother loves the pool. Are you okay? No need to be scared."

"Huh? I thought he fell in." I worked hard to catch my breath from the sight of this man's sexy style.

"Well, it's nice that you cared enough to check on him, but John loves the pool. You must be one of our house guests."

"Yes, I'm Sadie."

"Hi, Sadie. Tommy, John's brother."

I couldn't take my eyes off his muscles. I had no intention of staring, but my mind wandered to a very racy fantasy with Tommy Cavallo and what lurked beneath that bathing suit.

He smirked at me. Did he notice me gawking at his body with lewd thoughts churning around in my brain?

John caught his attention with a wave of his arm. The two men used sign language to speak to each other.

"Sadie? Why did you run up here like that, screaming? You scared us half to death," Mom said, gasping for air.

Dad was also out of breath from the brisk shuffle with his cane. Mom saw Tommy; someone she hadn't met yet.

"Mom, I'm sorry. I saw John fall from his wheelchair into the pool. I thought he was in trouble."

Mom's eyes wavered toward the pool, seeing John's legs floating and a smile upon his face. He looked fine.

"Mom, Dad, this is John's brother, Tommy."

"Nice to meet you, Mrs. Meade. Mr. Meade." Tommy shook both of their hands.

"Tommy, how nice of you to finally come home. I assume you introduced yourself to our guests," Rocky said, appearing irritated judging by his harsh tone of voice—a tone I was rather familiar with.

"Yes, Pop," he answered with annoyance.

"You didn't come home last night," Rocky added.

"I had plans. I told you I might not be home." Tommy's irritation was evident by his eye roll.

Rocky smiled, but it wasn't a pleasant smile. I recognized a fake smile when I saw one.

Lisa and Patrick were introduced to Tommy, who then dived into the pool like an Olympic swimmer and swam some laps.

I couldn't help but watch his strong arms carry his muscular body across the length of the pool.

Rocky invited us to go for a swim, but Dad nipped that idea in the bud. "Rocky, I'd love to take a ride and see our new house. Kids, get ready to drive to North Las Vegas."

Chapter 10

THE SUN'S POWERFUL rays heated the air this morning to a balmy ninety degrees. The warmth felt good against my delicate skin and troubled belly.

Mom made sure I sat in the front seat for the drive to our new house, although my stomach started to feel better after our long, exhausting journey last night.

Rocky drove us along Las Vegas Boulevard, a glamorous stretch dominated by large, luxurious buildings. Regulars around here called it the Strip. He quickly drove past the Montgomery, his tall, extravagant-looking hotel, and mentioned we would eat lunch there later today. He wanted Dad to become familiar with the place and meet his crew.

Mom and us kids would get to explore the beautiful building on our own.

Palmer Court was a dusty dirt road. Several frames of soon-to-be houses ruled the street. Large trucks were digging and dumping sand and debris upon what would eventually transform into someone's front lawn.

Rocky mentioned this was a brand-new development. The Strip brought more residents to the county each year. He pulled into a dirt path with some gravel tossed over it at a quick pace, and stopped short in front of a decent-size home.

Our house was what I heard Dad call a split-level. It looked much larger than our Cape back in Gloucester. The house itself was a mint green color with a variety of large stones covering a portion of it and black trim. It was the first building on the street that actually looked like a house. Other homes were mere empty shells.

I hoped it wouldn't be this noisy all the time with these large trucks working and beeping, while construction men hammered incessantly.

We eagerly climbed up the steps to see the mounds of dirt that would eventually transform into our front yard. Pale flecks of grass seed blanketed the dirt. Mom appeared excited to see a few trees sprouting from the ground in the backyard. Her finger tapped her lips with that facial expression she made when deep in thought. Mom always loved flowers and fresh vegetables. She had a green thumb, tending to her hearty flower and vegetable gardens back home.

As my eyes wandered about the dry and very hot vicinity, many mountains filled the background from all angles. I remembered Mickey telling me this place was a desert. No place for a true fisherman to live. He was right. I sighed heavily, thinking about him, missing his blue eyes and gentle touch.

Chapter 11

THE MONTGOMERY HOTEL and Casino seemed to be the tallest building on the Strip. Thousands of windows sparkled along the outside walls in the sunlight. The top of the building looked as pointy as a sewing needle, presumably inches from the sun.

Rocky parked in front of the main entrance and handed the keys to a young, skinny kid with a lot of freckles across his nose. Dad's friend was a class act.

We pranced across a rich-looking red carpet to enter through the double doors of the lobby.

It was the middle of a Monday afternoon, and this place was congested with people dressed in suits or skirts, making decisions to eat, gamble, or stroll along the crowded Strip. People were coming and going with luggage, checking in or checking out.

I glanced at my blue slacks and cream-colored blouse. Not as glamorous as the women I had seen today. I might need to go on a shopping spree since Dad would have a heftier paycheck.

The lobby welcomed us with a variety of flags from other countries. I asked Rocky about them.

The flags for England, Ireland, and Scotland hung proudly. He dedicated the hotel to his mother and late wife with their heritages from these European countries. Rocky had big plans to update the look and feel of the establishment with the cultures of these three locations. A facelift would help him remain competitive with the other elaborate hotels along the Strip.

The man had quite a vision for big changes, starting with murals and sculptures representing these glorious European sites, sure to attract more guests. He mentioned working with an entertainment director to hire new acts with Irish and Scottish dancers. I never considered myself as having a strong head for business, but I could only imagine the price tag of these new features.

The hustle and bustle of activity in the casino amazed me. We crept through the razzle-dazzle of the area in search of the café for a sandwich.

My eyes became mesmerized by the blinking lights and fancy-dressed guests hooting and hollering with glee. My ears buzzed from the bells and whistles of slot machines.

I lost my family for a few minutes as I wandered about.

So much excitement from the customers. Bells were ringing, chimes were chiming, lights were gleaming, and people were shouting. The casino was amazing! Imagine, my dad got to work here every day.

From the corner of my eye, I noticed Tommy speaking with a hot chick. She looked like a showgirl, judging by her outfit, or lack of it. She was a gorgeous babe for sure. No wonder he was practically drooling all over her. I couldn't help but notice the serious curves of her body compared to mine.

Tommy stood ridiculously close to her. I'd bet they were lovers. If he stood any closer to her, he'd be inside her bustier. As close as he was to her firm body, she didn't flinch. She ran her fingers through his mop of long brown hair. Yup, they were lovers.

My family was around here somewhere. My focus drifted, completely lost in the smoke-filled room, viewing the gaming tables and the remarkable scenery while listening to exciting sounds.

"Hey, Sadie. You lost?"

I turned at the sound of my name to see Tommy approaching me. Not sure where his girl disappeared to.

"No, I'm not lost. A little distracted, maybe. Your father was showing us around then taking us to lunch. I guess I lost track of them."

"Well, this place will do that to you. Were they going to the café over here?" He pointed toward the other side of the casino.

"I'm really not sure."

"I'll take you there," he said, placing his arm around my shoulder to guide me. His touch sent shivers through me. He was a fine-looking specimen of a man, but obviously unavailable.

Between watching Tommy and all the activity around me, I didn't realize the café was upon us.

Dad and Rocky were talking at one table. Mom's eyes searched around the vicinity until she set her sights on me with Tommy.

"Sadie, I thought we lost you." She glanced at Tommy. "Thank you for escorting her here."

"It's no problem, ma'am. I'm happy to help out. They make the best sandwiches, particularly the pastrami or the corned beef, if you'd like a recommendation." He smiled, lifting only a part of his upper lip. A sexy smirk that forced a smile out of me. Then Tommy's eyes wandered to the right side of the café.

I followed the turn of his head toward this really large man who seemed to be signaling him over. Wow, this joker was huge, and a bit scary-looking.

"Pop, Nicky's here. I'll see what he needs."

Rocky looked up at Tommy, then he set his sights on the enormous man, who must be Nicky, standing near the entrance of the café. Nicky was hard to miss. Rocky nodded at Tommy, and soon Tommy and Nicky were gone.

I hoped he'd return and join us for lunch.

Chapter 12

AFTER A FEW months, my family was still settling into our new home on Palmer Court. The neighborhood construction calmed around 1600 hours every afternoon. I couldn't wait for the other houses on our road to be built so the constant banging and screeching would cease.

Despite this large paycheck Dad bragged about, we had little furniture besides the basic needs like beds, a sofa, a recliner, and a large kitchen table. He kept saying he needed to save his paychecks to build up a savings account before he spent more money.

Mom looked forward to sprucing up the yard by creating a flower garden and planting some vegetables, but Dad wouldn't let her spend the money on seeds. I didn't understand his philosophy. How much did seeds cost? The price of seeds couldn't be that expensive, and the vegetables would go nicely with dinner.

Lisa and I would catch a bus on the weekends to drive us downtown to window-shop. Window-shopping because Dad wouldn't let us spend any money on new clothes. People dressed differently on the West Coast. He wanted us to meet men, prospective husbands. No man would notice us if we looked like paupers. Dad suggested we find jobs and pay our own way.

I helped Mom bake some gingerbread cookies one afternoon. Dad saw me eating the cookies and told me I'd get fat if I sat around and did nothing but bake and eat cookies all day.

"No man will marry you if you get fat," he said.

He made me want to eat another cookie.

Clearly, Dad wanted me out of the house, so he didn't have to support me. At least that was how he made me feel. God, I needed to get away from my father and explore this amazing city!

I missed Mickey. Thought about him often. Stared at the photograph of us on the pier, my first time fishing. I couldn't help but wonder if he thought about me as well.

Lisa managed to become part of a secretarial pool and would soon start working. My younger sister secured a job before I started to look for one.

Patrick talked about college even though he was only fifteen. But Dad said we couldn't afford it. Dad used to say he had a plan for Patrick's education. All of a sudden, he began to push Patrick to enlist in the Army.

My baby brother wouldn't willingly join the Army or any military branch. If the Army was his destiny, he'd probably wind up being picked in a draft, forced by our government to fight for our country. Patrick wouldn't survive Vietnam. It wasn't that I had little faith in my brother. He simply was not a fighter. My father held the brave, war hero title in the family. That didn't mean my brother took after him. Patrick was more empathetic. He wouldn't be able to kill anyone, not even the enemy.

I'd probably survive going into battle before Patrick would. Maybe I was more like my father than I ever realized. Patrick still had a few years before he could enlist if he wanted to, or if Uncle Sam came knocking on our door for him.

As soon as Patrick told Dad he had no interest in the war or enlisting, Dad flipped. He yelled so loud, the walls vibrated. He grabbed my brother by his shirt collar and pinned him to the living room wall. Mom and I screamed for him to release Patrick. My father always picked on Patrick, but suddenly his temper flared more often than usual. He couldn't force his son into a life he didn't want.

Chapter 13

STAYING AT HOME became intolerable. I shuddered at the rattling sound of Dad's Ford parking in the driveway after work.

To escape my monotonous life, I got a job waitressing at the fountain at the drugstore on Freemont Street. The bus ride was a bit long but comfortable.

My paychecks weren't much, but I wanted to save money to buy some new clothes. I needed at least one decent outfit to wear.

After a month or so, I became familiar with the regulars and their typical orders. There was a pretty hip guy who came in a few times a week for a chocolate milkshake or a banana split. He had these dreamy brown eyes I could get lost in. He was on the thin side, but his arms were large and muscular like a weight lifter. His hands were rough and calloused like a carpenter. His name was Phil.

I had a habit of talking too much since I wasn't shy.

George, the manager, liked me to be friendly, but not overly friendly. He gave me a hard time if I spent too much time with customers, especially knowing they were good-looking boys.

These two glamorous girls, about my age, sauntered into the shop daily. I learned their names, Phoebe and Valerie. These ladies always had money and drove a blue Cadillac. An older model, but still it was a Caddy. They were big tippers too. They didn't come here for the ice cream. Usually, they ordered a cup of black coffee. They showed up around 1500 hours. I could set my watch to them—if I owned a watch.

Phoebe had long, straight black hair, dark as midnight. Medium height with large breasts, probably a D cup. Since I only wore an A cup bra, I envied her. She had a nice smile that showed off all her pearly whites. She was very pretty with a dark complexion like she had some Spanish or Mexican blood in her veins.

Valerie was more fair-skinned, medium height with light-brown hair and green eyes. She stood taller than me, but everyone was taller than me at a mere five feet. Her nose appeared to be slightly longer than an average nose size, but she looked soft, delicate, pretty.

I had never been the type to wait for a boy to ask me out. Phil seemed shy. I'd catch his eyes gazing toward me every time I bent over to pick something up. Whenever Phil was around, I became rather clumsy, dropping spoons on the floor, so he'd catch a glimpse of my assets.

So, I told him I was new in town and asked if he'd show me around. He stuttered a bit, but there was a yes in his response.

Phil took me to a reasonably priced steakhouse downtown for dinner. He was such a gentleman, I couldn't stand it. Our evening was nice. Phil didn't drink booze, but that shouldn't mean I couldn't drink. After a couple of screwdrivers in me, I suggested he drive us someplace quiet.

We took the scenic route. I, being new in town, asked Phil to show me some highlights of the area off the path of the Strip. I asked if I could drive his Dodge. I had a license, but Dad rarely let me drive the family car.

After some coaxing and a few kisses, Phil said he'd consider it. I placed my hand on his upper thigh then eased my way up to the bulge in his pants. I heard a heavy gulp emit from his throat then continued to stroke at that bulge until it was sticking out of the top of his bell-bottom jeans. He pulled the car over and parked in an empty lot. My mouth and tongue took hold of his rod.

Afterward, I got to drive his Dodge around town.

Chapter 14

PHIL BEGAN STROLLING into the fountain more often to see me rather than to drink a milkshake.

Sometimes I took my break with him in the back seat of his car. Several months had passed since I was with Mickey. I had an itch that needed scratching. The prickly feeling of his beard against my flesh heightened my desire for him. The strength of his arms around my waist, drawing me in close, added an erotic sensation to my already flustered body.

One afternoon, we were parked in the back lot of the fountain together. Phil's Dodge had a comfortable back seat. I was only allowed a fifteen-minute break, but Phil seemed to be taking his sweet time with me to Merle Haggard's "Swinging Doors." Phil loved country music, and his penchant for twangy southern songs eventually rubbed off on me.

As I exited the car, fixing my uniform and fluffing my hair, Phoebe and Valerie stood several paces from Phil's Dodge, chuckling. A teeny part of me cared that they caught us in the act, but these girls didn't give me the prim and proper vibe.

"Having fun, Sadie?" Phoebe asked with that big and bright smile plastered across her face.

Valerie nudged her arm, reminding her to be more polite.

Phil stepped out from the back seat. His face turned a rich shade of purple at these giggling girls. He kissed me goodbye, scooted into the driver's seat, then sped out of the parking lot, tires skidding over the gravel.

I approached the girls, attempting to play it cool, knowing very well what they had witnessed. Phil made a lot of interesting sounds during sex. Suddenly, I wondered if anyone else heard us in action before, but I shrugged it off. I never cared about other people's thoughts and opinions.

"Is he your boyfriend?" Valerie asked.

I never confirmed if Phil was my guy. At least nothing official. "Maybe," was my reply.

"We were thinking you should come out with us sometime."

I shrugged my shoulders. "Sure, why not? What did you have in mind?"

"We'll be around the Strip tomorrow night."

I thought about it for a moment. Anything was better than going home to my overbearing father.

"I get off work at 1900 hours…I mean seven."

Chapter 15

THE PLAN WAS to meet the girls outside the Sands hotel at eight o'clock. I packed my blue dress and heels when I left for work that afternoon. It was probably the only nice dress I owned. I didn't have enough money to buy many new clothes or shoes, but this outfit sufficed. This particular shade of deep blue always made my eyes stand out, or so people had mentioned to me.

As far as Mom knew, I would be helping George with inventory that night. George never asked me to help with inventory before, but Mom didn't need to know that.

Phoebe and Valerie appeared to be fun girls—like me.

Phil stopped by briefly to see me. We planned to see a movie together this weekend.

Seven o'clock finally arrived. The day seemed to drag. That tended to happen whenever I felt anxious about something. The clock ticked and tocked all day without moving fast enough for me.

I dashed to the ladies' room to change my clothes, leaving my uniform in my locker in the storage room. I fixed my hair and makeup. Maybe the dark red lipstick was a bit overdramatic, but it was a similar shade to the color Phoebe and Valerie wore. I wanted to fit in and not look like some square from the East Coast, even though I had to take the bus to get to the Sands.

At approximately seven fifty-five, I arrived at the dazzling hotel. The girls stood outside waiting for me. Wow, they were dressed scantily in these outfits like I had seen on television, like dancing girls on *The Ed Sullivan Show*. A lot of sequins sparkling across their tops. I suddenly felt very underdressed.

They greeted me with hugs and a peck on the cheek. I noticed their eyes wafting up and down. Damn, I knew I didn't dress right or to their standards. Valerie kept tugging at my dress, telling me I had a great pair of legs, and I should show them off. Dress lengths were shrinking with each passing day, but my father didn't care that my current wardrobe lacked style, and I didn't blend in socially. I had no idea how many hours I'd have to work at the fountain before I could afford a sequined blouse and miniskirt like the ones donned by Phoebe and Valerie.

The Sands was a gorgeous facility. I never had an up-close view until tonight. The inside of the casino looked spectacular. It compared to the Montgomery in style and excitement. There were a lot more people here. Dean Martin was performing tonight. That must be why so many people flocked to the Sands.

Phoebe took me by the hand as we scurried through the smoke-filled maze of guests. I was glad she did. I became easily distracted by the bright lights, people cheering, and slot machines chiming.

I kept minimal money in my purse. I hoped they didn't want to gamble. Maybe that was how they had the money for that Cadillac they drove and the outfits they wore. If they had luck at the gambling tables, I hoped it would rub off on me.

We found our way to the bar and grabbed one empty stool. They let me sit as they scanned the room filled with guests. A lot of couples, I noticed. Either these folks were staying at the hotel or they were here for Dean. I adored Dean Martin, especially hearing him croon "That's Amore," and I wasn't even Italian.

The bar was crowded, smoky, and loud. The noise made hearing each other difficult. I bummed a smoke off the older man sitting next to me, although the woman he was with appeared annoyed.

I noticed my friends were examining the room and whispering. Finally, I had to ask why the secrecy.

They both smiled at me like the cat that swallowed the canary.

"We're checking out the men. Seeing who's available," Phoebe whispered.

Sounded like a fun game. My eyes perused the bar. I pointed to several guys who seemed to be alone. I could detect if one was expecting someone by the way he continuously stared at the entrance or his watch. There was a man and a woman sitting at the opposite side of the bar. I could tell they weren't a couple.

Valerie wondered how I knew that, and bet me fifty cents I was wrong.

My instincts were keen. They didn't look at each other like they were lovers or on a first date. Too young to had been together so long they didn't know what to say to each other anymore. They looked more like family to me.

Phoebe decided to settle the bet and approached the man and woman. I was right. They were cousins waiting for more family members to arrive. I just made fifty cents, and I didn't even pull the handle of a slot machine.

As soon as their other family members showed, the woman left with the whole crew. However, the man stayed behind, sipping on his drink. Looked like bourbon. He tossed a couple of bucks on the bar after waving a lot of cash around.

Phoebe strolled toward him again and whispered something in his ear. He gave her a good once-over and winked. Then he shook his head, slammed the rest of his drink down his throat, and left the bar.

Phoebe returned with a shrug of her shoulder. I was so curious what she said to him, but a noisy crowd of young men entered the lounge, yelling and pushing each other. They looked like college jocks. Youthful-looking with strong builds.

Valerie grabbed my arm, spilling my drink while encouraging me to talk to these men. They looked like a fun crew and very cool. I downed the rest of the vodka in one shot and followed my friends, breaking into the circle of testosterone.

One of the men, whom they called Buddy, was getting hitched at a nearby wedding chapel in the morning. All this hollering at the bar was a bachelor party.

Phoebe and Valerie were really into it. In fact, a little too into it. I was not naive. I observed the way they danced around these boys in their miniskirts and sparkly, low-cut blouses. What did I know about these women outside their need for coffee at the fountain in the afternoons?

How did I miss this? They were ladies of the evening. Hookers. Prostitutes. Why would they invite me to tag along on an evening prowl?

"Party upstairs in my room!" one of the jocks yelled.

My friends wrapped their arms around a couple of boys in the crowd of hooting fellas and tugged on my arm to join them.

My answer should have been easy. A firm no. Why was I thinking about it? Still, I shook my head with confidence and explained I'd rather stay behind and listen to Dean Martin sing. I wasn't a prude or an innocent girl, but I also had no intention of participating in some kind of orgy.

"Come on, Sadie. It'll be fun," Phoebe said.

Valerie gently tapped my arm. "You sure, Sadie?"

"Yeah, I'm sure. I want to see if I can catch a glimpse of Dean."

The girls ensured I could take the bus home. Then they smiled, snatched up their men, and headed toward the elevator in the hotel lobby.

I wandered around the casino for a while and tossed a couple of quarters into a slot machine, thanking Valerie for the entire ten seconds of fun I had at her expense winning the earlier bet. My luck ran out at the slots.

I heard music and sounds of crooning. I followed the noise to the room where Dean was performing. I didn't have a ticket, but I sat outside listening. I found myself swirling around, holding the ends of my blue dress while he sang "Volare." When Dean was finished with his act, so was I. I caught the next bus back to my neighborhood.

Chapter 16

I HATED BEING home when Dad was around. It was his day off, and his disposition seemed miserable today, snapping at Mom, me, and especially Patrick. He didn't pick on Lisa, but the quiet bookworm never aggravated him. Patrick and I were more outspoken, and I could easily be considered defiant.

I told the family George needed me to work on my day off. A minor lie. I hoped Phil might stop in and distract me for a while.

George liked when I hung around the fountain on my days off. I'd give him a hand if it were busy. Pour coffee or whip up milkshakes for customers. It passed the time.

Phil was a no-show, but Phoebe and Valerie entered, smiles plastered on their faces. Three o'clock, practically on the nose. I smiled in response to their happy grins then waved at them. No reason not to be social.

"We looked for you last night, but you must've left," Phoebe said.

"How was the bachelor party?" I felt my lips curve into a curious smirk.

They each opened their small purses and secretly displayed a lot of dough.

My eyes grew wide at the sight. "Wow! How much is that?"

"About a hundred."

I looked around to ensure no one was within earshot and spoke softly, "One hundred dollars! For a night with those drunk jock types?"

What I could do with that kind of cash, I thought.

Valerie proceeded to explain they planned to work at one of the ranches outside of town where the work was legal. However, last night's rodeo wasn't. They took a chance to make more money with the possibility of getting arrested.

Those men were hotel guests with a room. No one stopped the girls from accepting the invitation upstairs. But hotel managers preferred their guests spend money on the premises. Food, gambling, and liquor were available on-site. Hotel owners didn't want their guests stuck in their rooms having sex with hookers who benefited financially instead of the hotel.

The legalized ranches provided girls with a room and meals. The ranches netted a piece of the money to pay for their expenses. The girls kept the rest of the money earned. It didn't sound like such a bad gig since there was some security at the ranch, and it was legal.

Phoebe overheard me complaining to Phil about needing to make more money. They wanted to help me out if I was willing to try it.

I told them no, but I guess it was nice they thought about giving me the option. Overall, they seemed really cool.

They'd be working at the Belle Maiden Ranch and might not see me for a while.

My first two friends in town besides Phil. I had no idea when I'd see them again.

Chapter 17

I HAD TO admit, the last couple of weeks not seeing the girls at three o'clock made for dull afternoons. Phil landed a better job in construction that included overtime. These three friends of mine kept me sane every day.

Boredom made me crazy. My father ignited anger from within. Without Phil, Phoebe, and Valerie around to make me laugh, I worried I'd develop a twitch or something.

Dad had been crankier than normal. For a man who was finally taken seriously for his mind instead of his damaged body, he acted miserably. Supposedly, he made a lot of money, yet we never saw any of it.

Mom wanted to spruce up the house and yard, but there was a price tag attached to her visions.

Patrick wanted to join the poetry club at school. Dad laughed at his request, saying, "No son of mine is joining some pansy-ass group."

I hoped he would help me pay for a new outfit, but I feared asking.

Lisa was the only one who never asked for anything. She'd been the favorite of the bunch in his eyes. She was sullen, quiet, worked every day, and didn't talk back to him.

I never felt so lonely in my life. As I mentioned before, boredom made me crazy. When I got riled, my mouth would start blabbing faster than Dan Gurney at the Indy Car races.

My father sat in his recliner, reading the sports page in the daily paper. The Red Sox and the Patriots didn't make West Coast headlines unless they played against a local team, or if the Sox would ever make it to the World Series again.

I stood before him, but he ignored me. Cleared my throat once, twice, but he didn't flinch.

"Dad," I said with a dour tone.

Finally, he moved. He shifted the newspaper slightly to the left and stared at me as I hovered without making a sound.

I merely watched and waited for him to acknowledge me. When he started to glance back at his paper, I was beyond frustrated. My fingers grabbed at his paper, ripping it from his hands.

"Jesus, Sadie, now look what you did!" He fumbled with the pages to put them back into a legible form.

"Can't you see I'm standing here, trying to have a conversation with you?" My left foot stomped the golden carpet.

"Well then talk already! Don't tear apart a man's paper like that. Speak up!" He wasn't looking at me. He was more concerned about the slight destruction of his newspaper.

"When we came out here as a family, you told us our lives would improve because you landed a good job with better pay."

He glanced at an article about Lyndon Johnson rather than listening to me.

"How are things better for us, Dad? We live like paupers!"

"You watch your tongue, young lady. You don't get to talk to your father like this!" He stood to his feet with help from his cane, towering over my five-foot self.

His intimidation tactic didn't work. I never backed down from an argument. Not when a situation was important and meaningful.

"I left a life behind in Gloucester. My friends and Mickey."

"Is that what this is about? That poor fisherman? You'll meet someone else, Sadie. And he better be a strong man to tolerate this loud, unladylike behavior of yours!" He let out a breath, belittling me.

"Can I borrow some money to buy a couple of decent outfits? I can pay you back in time."

"You have a job. Save your money, and you can buy whatever you want with it."

"What about Mom?"

From the corner of my eye, I saw Mom's head pop out of the kitchen, drying a dinner plate with a blue checkered dishtowel. The sour expression on her face told me she didn't really want me speaking on her behalf, but I went there anyway.

"What about your mother?" he sneered.

"You're supposed to support her, right? She can use a new dress. She wants to brighten up this place with some curtains and plant a garden in the yard. If you're supposed to be making all this money, at least take care of *her* needs." Then I went to a place no child should ever wander to in their parent's relationship. "Or maybe you can't take care of *any* of her needs anymore."

I didn't see it coming. He blindsided me completely. In my twenty years of life, he never put his hands on me.

My cheek stung from the slap. My arm felt like it had been torn from the socket. He pulled the ends of my hair so hard, I felt several blond strands tear from the roots.

Patrick came to my rescue. My brother, typically meek, mild, and compliant, charged at our irate father.

Dad struck him too. The old man unfastened his belt and began to whip Patrick's body hard.

Patrick fell to the floor, taking all the blows of Dad's anger, sparing me from the pain.

Mom raced into the den to protect him. She stood between my father and Patrick. Even took some slaps from the leather herself.

I screamed at Dad to come after me. I was the one who made him angry, not Patrick. I threw my body on top of Patrick on the floor while Mom stood in front of Dad. I felt a lash whip across my forehead, followed by a severe stinging sensation.

Dad lowered his arm and dropped the belt to the floor. He pushed Mom out of his way to stagger around her.

I heard the jingle of his car keys before the door slammed shut behind him.

Chapter 18

I WANTED TO cry, seeing my innocent brother laying on the floor with his yellow T-shirt torn from the lashing, but the tears didn't fall.

Mom stripped off his shirt to assess the damage. Cuts, scrapes, and redness with a small amount of blood seeping from his wounds, yet a stream of blood had spattered onto the carpet.

Mom looked up at me and stared for a moment. She took Patrick's destroyed shirt and placed it upon my forehead.

That was when Lisa ran in, dumfounded by the sight.

"Lisa, get me the witch hazel from the cupboard and some bandages," Mom ordered.

The blood on the floor was from *my* injuries. I got more than a piece of leather whipped at my head. The steel buckle punctured my forehead at the base of the hairline. Blood dripped down my face and into the golden texture of the shag carpet.

All I could think about was my brother's destroyed shirt and my bloodstained green and blue striped top. We didn't have many nice clothes to start with. Now we had less.

Once our wounds were cleaned and bandaged, I apologized to Patrick. It was my fault Dad attacked him.

He said it didn't hurt all that much, but he couldn't sit back and do nothing, watching our father whip me.

"This is all your fault, Sadie! You and your big mouth! I heard you yelling at Dad. Why do you always have to instigate a fight with him? It's always about you! Why are you so selfish?" Lisa scolded at an intense, loud beat.

Maybe she was right. All the madness occurred because I expected my father to help me buy new clothes. A change within my father's overbearing personality proved obvious. He became easily agitated, escalating to violent surges.

"Lisa's right, Sadie. You went too far this time. He is your father. You have a roof over your head. He provides for this family. You were disrespectful. I won't even discuss what you said about *me*. You have no right to speak for me! Don't you ever do that again!" Mom hissed, fuming and embarrassed because of my outburst about her sex life. I had never seen such an incensed look worn upon her face.

Mom turned her tall, slender frame from me as I tried to apologize. Patrick was the injured party, but he was the only one who seemed to understand my frustration with our father. Mom ordered me to my room like I was ten years old.

Chapter 19

AT TEN O'CLOCK that evening, the house emulated an eerie sense of quiet. Dad hadn't returned home yet. I didn't know where he went, nor did I care. Dad had been making a habit of staying out till all hours of the night lately.

I grabbed a suitcase from the cellar and packed up the few clothes and shoes I owned. I placed the picture of Mickey and me on the pier inside. Oh, how I missed Mickey and the life I might have had with him if we stayed in Gloucester. But he was no longer a part of my present or future. I had to secure my destiny. A future that overflowed with happiness and abundance. Life in this house wasn't happy or abundant.

All the money I earned from the fountain, I tossed into a sock and slipped it inside my purse, removing a few dollars from the sum.

After a gentle tap upon Patrick's door, I gingerly stepped inside as he was reading a Superman comic book with a flashlight beneath the sheets of his twin bed. I thought he'd be asleep but was happy to find him awake, wearing his red plaid pajamas.

As I sat beside him on the bed, his finger lifted and brushed against the bandage-covered flesh wound on my forehead.

"I'm okay, Patrick. How are you?"

He shrugged.

"Here. I want you to have this." I handed him the money I put aside. "Buy a new shirt or join that poetry club you were interested in. I hope it's enough."

Patrick stared at the money. "Thank you! Are you sure?"

I nodded, then embraced him tenderly before leaving his bedroom and quietly closing the door, not to disturb Mom or Lisa.

We kept a telephone book tucked in a kitchen drawer. I searched for an address to a place I'd be accepted to stay. At least for a little while.

I gazed around the den and zoomed in on the bloodstained carpet. Mom apparently tried to clean it up with Prell shampoo and Ivory soap. I picked up my suitcase and marched out the front door, hoping to catch the next bus out of Las Vegas.

Chapter 20

THE CLERK AT the bus station explained where I had to connect with other busses to reach my destination.

Thankfully, I managed to grab a seat up front near the driver. My stomach was already in knots. No need to add nausea from motion sickness on top of it.

The third bus I transferred to would put me within walking distance of the Belle Maiden. A part of me felt excited to see Phoebe and Valerie. Then there was that other part filled with angst, anxiety bubbling to the surface.

I never ran away from home before, but did twenty-year-old women run away? As an adult, I didn't have to stay under my father's thumb—or belt buckle.

After two connections, my stop was next. I asked the bus driver which way I should walk to access the road I sought.

He pointed to the left, suggesting I stay on the main route because it was late at night. "Holy hell," he muttered under his breath loud enough for me to hear. "It'll take two minutes off of my route to drop you closer to that road."

There were merely a handful of other passengers on the bus at this time of night. I was lucky this driver appeared generous and empathetic.

"There's only a couple of houses on the road besides the ranch at the end." His eyes glazed over for a moment, studying me. "Nah, you're not going there, right? A nice girl like you doesn't belong in a place like that."

I shook my head solely to agree with him. Phoebe and Valerie made it sound like a pretty decent place with a bed and food. I knew my way around a man's body quite well. It sounded better than living at home at the moment.

Besides, where else would I go? To the Cavallo's? Rocky would never allow me to live away from my family, even if he saw my bruised face.

George came to mind. Maybe he would have let me sleep in the stockroom, but that was his place of business, not a home. Perhaps I'd call George to tell him I regretfully quit.

That was when I thought about Phil. We were supposed to meet at the movies this coming weekend. He'd show up at the fountain looking for me. Maybe when I called George, I'd ask him to explain to Phil that I had to leave town, and I was sorry I couldn't tell him myself.

The bus driver was right. There were a couple of houses on the road. Dilapidated shacks if you asked me. Even our small house in Gloucester looked like a castle compared to these hovels.

A large sign stuck out from the ground with an arrow directing me to the Belle Maiden Ranch. I had to walk another quarter mile up the dirt road to reach the place, according to another sign.

My feet felt tired and achy. I was so grateful to the bus driver for dropping me off at the beginning of this path.

Light was scarce, but the full moon shimmered a purple pearlescent hue, seemingly painted across the black sky with thousands of stars gleaming. The shine from the moonlight allowed me to see the gravel road.

I picked up the pace when I heard a growl. A hungry coyote like back east maybe? I didn't give much thought to any vicious, nocturnal predators in the desert when I chose to leave at night.

Lights blinked up ahead. The building actually appeared pretty decent, compared to what I expected a cathouse to look like. A white structure with black trim and a strand of lights flickered along the outside.

As I approached the building, the sign on the bright red door flashed the word OPEN. The shades were lowered in all the windows, so I couldn't peek inside. The place looked larger than I expected. A long building with multiple floors that seemed to stretch out far in the back. The shingles were clean, unless the darkness of night disguised any dirt. Someone took good care of its appearance.

My knuckles gently rapped on the door.

A hefty woman of Mom's age with dark brown hair opened the door to let me inside. She displayed a happy grin at first, then a confused expression took over. Perhaps she expected a man instead of a lost, bruised young lady.

As I stepped inside the facility, the ringing of a bell chimed. A group of women, wearing short nighties or skin-tight dresses, quickly lined up.

In sauntered a tall, voluptuous woman with strawberry blond hair, wearing a twilight blue evening dress, a big smile, and a lot of makeup to conceal the deep wrinkles around her lips and eyes. Once she presented herself and eyed me up and down, jazz music began to play, and the girls paraded around the room to the rhythm.

"Hello, girlie! Where's your husband?" the glamorous woman asked.

"I don't have a husband, ma'am."

"Boyfriend?"

I shook my head.

She looked me over pretty good before ordering the music to stop with a sharp snap of her fingers.

My eyes gazed at the gorgeous women parading around. I didn't have any negligee like the ones they wore. I also couldn't fill one out the way they did. Phoebe and Valerie weren't in the lineup, I noticed.

"What can we do for you, girlie? Why are you here?"

My plan seemed foolproof until I actually stood inside this building and watched these women show off their merchandise. Were they hoping some new customer would choose them?

Then I stared downward, remembering the tiny mounds that barely sprouted from my chest. What man would pick my teeny self over any of these alluring girls with major bazookas? Maybe the bus driver was right. I didn't belong here.

"Cat got your tongue, girlie? What's your name?"

"Doris, she's a friend of mine."

The familiar voice of Valerie was heard. I glanced up the staircase that led to the second floor. Valerie strode down with a blond-haired man, maybe in his forties. He seemed to be close to my father's age, not something I cared to think about right now. She gave him a kiss on the cheek farewell. I wondered if Phoebe was upstairs, earning her pay.

"You know her, Roxy?"

Roxy? Who was Roxy? I thought. Then I realized this woman, Doris, was speaking to Valerie.

Val, I mean Roxy, eyed me up and down. Her eyes set on my bandaged forehead, as did Doris's.

"Come with us," Doris suggested with a smile. They escorted me down a hallway and into a private room. Roxy gave a friendly squeeze to my hand.

"Brandi and I met her on the Strip. She's cool, Doris."

Brandi? She must mean Phoebe.

My nerves were rattled and my heart thumped like a jackrabbit running from a fox. My fingers jingled the change from the bus fare in my pocket. I played with the coins, tossing them about.

"You looking for work?" Doris inquired.

I hesitated, then absently nodded my head.

"Ever work at an establishment like this before, girlie?"

I shook my head and managed to softly reply, "No."

"Got a name?" Doris asked.

Roxy's smile widened. "You need a new name, honey."

I fumbled through my pockets, caressed the coins, and decided upon my new name. "Penny." At least I felt like the money was the reason I was here.

"Okay, Penny. If you want to work here, I have an available room."

Doris explained how the pay system worked. With the money from my earnings, I had to pay for the room, food, and the convenience of meeting customers without the risk of imprisonment.

She asked Roxy to show me around. A "turnout" I was referred to, which meant I was a new girl.

All the girls had to be in shape. A workout room was accessible for calisthenics to ensure regular exercise.

We needed to see a doctor every week. He had to examine all the girls to check for venereal diseases. The thought made my stomach turn more viciously than normal.

"Can't the men wear rubbers?" I asked.

Both Roxy and Doris chuckled. Roxy answered, "You can't make them, but you can keep a supply available in your room."

"What happened to your face, Penny?" Doris asked with sympathy pouring from her deep blue eyes.

"I had to leave home. I had nowhere else to go. Can I stay here?"

"Roxy will get you settled. You have to clean up, and those bruises need to be covered with some makeup. Oh, and I'll contact Chip."

"Who's Chip?" I asked.

"Once the doc examines you, Penny, and approves you working here, Chip makes sure all the turnouts are ready." Doris winked before leaving me in Valerie's care.

"What did she mean by that, Val?"

"First of all, it's Roxy here. Don't use my real name. And it's Brandi, not Phoebe. That's important to remember. If you want to be called Penny, then that's what you'll be known as here.

"The doc is nice. He makes sure we're all healthy. Chip will be your first time here," she whispered. "It'll be okay. Chip looks out for us. Think of it as a test-drive. Like you're getting your driver's license. And try not to appear to be too nervous. He wants to see what you can offer the customers. Also, he needs to make sure you're ready for anyone who walks in the door.

"The johns are usually okay. Not all of them look like those fine jocks Brandi and I met at the Sands. They're usually lonely guys looking for a good time, and that's what our job is. Make them feel like studs—even if they aren't. Tell them how great they are in bed—no matter what the truth might be or how you really feel about them grunting on top of you. Sometimes it's all an act. Watch your facial expressions. You always have to look like you're enjoying their... company."

She paused and closed the door. "There are a few men who are a bit rough. They're regulars. Doris wouldn't let any turnout go with them, and you can always say no. No one forces us to be with anyone. They can't hit us. Chip and his boys watch over us for protection. They'll stop anyone if they think we're in danger."

She was brutally honest with me. I appreciated the candor, although a queasy feeling in my gut surfaced. But if Roxy and Brandi could handle this life, so could Penny.

Chapter 21

ROXY CONTINUED TO show me around after the girls paraded across the room again when the door sprang open and three men promenaded in. They wore sailor uniforms like Navy men on leave. I'd say they were on leave because they were clearly inebriated, slurring their words and stammering around with their mouths open, checking out the merchandise. Despite their drunken behavior, they were young and good-looking.

I tapped Roxy's shoulder and whispered into her ear, "I'd practice with one of them."

She giggled. "You can't do anything without seeing the doc and Chip." Then her head shook. "No need to rush, Penny. You could be seeing as many as ten to twelve men a day."

"Twelve?" My voice echoed much louder than I intended. A dozen different men every day? No wonder we had to see that doctor regularly. The money was sure enticing. I'd earn more dough in one night here than what I'd make in a week working at the fountain, even after sharing my earnings with Doris.

"When you speak with the doc, Penny, make sure you ask about birth control because most of the customers won't wear a condom."

I merely nodded at Roxy, agreeing that I'd inquire.

The three sailors chose their girls. As soon as they flew up the spiral staircase and doors were heard slamming, the remaining girls grabbed a chair, sofa, or barstool.

A skinny redhead picked up a *Reader's Digest*. The short blond, with hair flowing past her navel, was reading *Valley of the Dolls*. The others were talking over the jukebox, listening to "Love Me Do" by the Beatles. Nothing like passing the time, waiting for the next customer to march through the door.

I heard movement from the top of the staircase. As I glanced up, I recognized Phoebe, I mean Brandi, cascading slowly down the steps with a customer and another girl. The older, thin man kissed them both; then Brandi kissed the other girl beside her, long and sensuous for his pleasure.

My mouth must have flung open, watching Brandi kiss the other woman because Roxy used her thumb and forefinger to bring my lips together without uttering a word. Her eyes said plenty though. I shouldn't act surprised about anything that happened here.

Her customer continued to hang around, sitting at the bar in the corner. There were twelve barstools and a dark-haired bartender stood at an average height behind the counter, drying glasses with a white rag. I imagined this place would become pretty busy with so many seats available for customers waiting to meet the right girl to nourish their desires for a brief moment in time.

Brandi and I made eye contact. She displayed her large, gorgeous smile and darted toward me with the other woman, a petite girl with dark brown hair, short and curly.

Roxy introduced me as Penny.

The short girl with the dark, curly hair's name was Kitty. I couldn't help but admire her silver necklace with a crucifix dangling between her breasts, a surprising choice of jewelry to wear in this place.

When Roxy introduced me to Brandi, I got the feeling I needed to act as if I never met her or knew that her real name was Phoebe.

A regular staggered through the door with heavy footsteps. An older man, maybe in his fifties and very tall. He reminded me of John Wayne in *The Quiet Man*.

How could I tell he was a regular? The other girls didn't parade around for him. They acted like he wasn't worth their time or effort. His eyes gazed around the place before inching his way toward my friends. He set his sights on Roxy, calling her "baby," and picked her up off her feet completely, tossing her over his broad shoulder.

Roxy giggled like a schoolgirl, held on to his neck, and let him carry her up the stairs.

I stared in amazement.

"Sometimes he pays to have Roxy to himself for an entire day," Brandi chimed in.

"Wow, he must have money," I said.

"Yup, plus a wife and four children," Kitty added with a chuckle.

Brandi brought me into the circle of remaining women, who wore their fancy lingerie quite well. I hoped I would remember their names, seeing that I'd be living here with them. There was Monique, Tammy-Lynn, Cookie, Lana, Barbie, and Jo Jo.

Most of the ladies were welcoming to me. Two of the girls seemed to eye me up and down, Cookie and Jo Jo. Were they threatened by another woman at the ranch, competing for johns? The way they looked with their fancy hair, makeup, and big boobs, they couldn't be jealous of *me*? I didn't come here to make waves. This was all new to me. If we were back in Gloucester, I'd probably threaten to knock their teeth out in exchange for their gruesome stares. Somehow that behavior wouldn't be appropriate here at the ranch, especially on my first night.

I became settled in my small room and packed away my clothes from home in the dresser. Nothing from my suitcase was usable for this type of work.

The picture of Mickey Quinn grabbed my eyes and attention. If only we stayed in Gloucester. Life in the Nevada desert wasn't for me any more than it was for a fisherman like Mickey. If I could tolerate the long, painful flight back to Massachusetts, I'd save up enough money to return to Mickey if he'd take me. I carefully placed the photograph beneath a T-shirt in the drawer. Displaying a photo of a long-lost love wouldn't be good for business.

Roxy and Brandi lent me a couple of outfits to wear until I earned enough money to buy my own things.

Kitty shared her makeup with me. She had quite a supply of various eye shadow shades, lipsticks, and perfumes of various scents. A lot of time and effort to look pretty and alluring went into this profession.

Chapter 22

IN THE MORNING, the bell rang to wake us for breakfast. Brandi warned me the bell rang at ten o'clock. We were allowed to sleep through the early hours of the morning after the nighttime festival of men left by closing time.

Breakfast was served.

Today's breakfast included scrambled eggs and toast with coffee and orange juice. No potatoes, hash, or bacon. If we weren't in the mood for eggs, other available options included cottage cheese, yogurt, and cornflakes with skim milk.

Lunch was typically a salad or sandwich with fruit.

For dinner, in between customers, there could be chicken, pork chops, or a well-done steak, always served with some type of vegetable and salad. No burgers, fries, potatoes, chips, or ice cream.

I suddenly realized why whenever Phoebe and Valerie strolled into the fountain, they only ordered black coffee. Clearly, they didn't want any of us to gain weight.

The girls used the exercise room in shifts before showering. If we weren't doing sit-ups or leg lifts, we were to clean up our bedrooms, wash our clothes, and replenish the supplies in our rooms like extra towels, sheets, clean basins, and condoms.

The doctor made a special trip out to the ranch just for me. If he hadn't, I'd have to wait several days before his usual Friday morning examinations.

For a doctor, he was quite overweight, and he held a cigar between his lips. The top of his head shined from an enormous bald spot.

When I entered the examination room, it was already filled with smoke as if walking through a fog at dusk.

I was asked to strip down to nothing, then lay upon the table covered in a large paper towel. The doctor didn't leave the room as I removed all my clothing. I imagined I had to get used to this. Any vulnerabilities and inhibitions possessed should be relinquished.

He gave me a full examination, starting with my eyes and ears. He listened to my heart with a stethoscope. His breast exam was quite thorough as he squeezed my tiny bits. I wanted to scream out, *Yes, I know they're small!* But I watched my manners. No need to state the obvious.

His hands gently pressed my kneecaps, parting my legs as he sat at the end of the table. He stared at the goods before using that cold steel device to insert inside me, spreading me open like a turkey about to be stuffed. His hands moved around my insides, feeling his way around.

After a couple of angst-filled minutes, he removed the cold instrument and told me all was good. He planned to tell Doris I could start working. He instructed me to get dressed. Although, he stayed in the room completing paperwork while I tossed my dress over my head.

I nearly forgot to ask about birth control methods. I had no interest in taking regular medication like this pill he described that should prevent pregnancy. Although many of the girls here took the pill, I was opposed to relying on a tiny tablet to prevent becoming knocked up.

The doc tossed me a small bag with what looked like a round plastic saucer inside. He gave me a thirty-second overview of how to insert the diaphragm and clean it after each use. He also handed me a tube of some type of cream to help with any soreness or dryness. Lovely!

No sooner did I return from my checkup when Doris approached, sharing the good news that the doc approved my working at the Belle Maiden.

A tall man with black hair parted at the side stood next to her. He reminded me of Clark Gable with that thin mustache and debonair look about him. Thoughts about *Gone with the Wind* floated through my brain as Doris introduced him to me as Chip. *Frankly, I don't give a damn,* I thought to myself.

Doris sent Chip a wink.

Chip fired a sultry kiss against her pink-glossed lips before taking tender hold of my elbow and nudging me up the stairwell.

Butterflies set up residence in my belly.

Chip was kind of sexy for an older man, most likely in his forties, maybe fifty. Why did I feel nervous? Would I be graded like in school? What did I strive to achieve? An A+? Satisfactory? Exemplary? In high school I was a B student, rather average. This was a different type of test I had to pass.

We entered my room that was positioned in the middle of the hallway. Sounds echoed of girls already with customers going at it pretty wildly in the rooms near mine. Our workday began at one o'clock every afternoon. The CLOSED sign didn't light up until two in the morning.

Chip closed the door behind him and looked me over for a moment. Then he described the system of pricing and the variety of options men could choose from. A straight lay, half and half, and a full French were the most popular selections. He explained what each meant, though I had my own idea. Anything kinky and the price increased.

The Belle Maiden offered a VIP suite, complete with a Jacuzzi, mirrored ceiling and walls, and a large, plush bed with a romantic red spread tossed atop a comfortable mattress. Customers were shown that room to entice them with a longer stay and a fun time for an extra price.

Money should be handed directly to me before the men were serviced.

Before anyone touched me, they needed to be inspected. Chip explained the men must have their genitals washed thoroughly by me. The bathroom stocked basins to fill with warm water and soap. It was a part of the process to ensure cleanliness and prevent infections. The uncomfortable part was squeezing the penis to ensure no unusual discharge emitted, allowing the customer to believe that

GINA MARIE MARTINI

sharp tug was for his pleasure. That system couldn't possibly be fool-proof to ensure the men were free from venereal diseases.

Awkwardly, I practiced this process on Chip after he stripped down. Then he advised me to always wash my genitals before and after each customer.

He drew near and lowered his head toward mine as if he was going to kiss me, but he stopped suddenly. Maybe because I squeezed my eyes tightly, unsure why I was here.

What was I doing? Why were second thoughts interfering with this idea? I had no other options because I didn't want to go home.

"Well?" he asked.

"Well, what?"

"This is where you seduce your customer, Penny. Don't have a look on your face like you'd rather be watching *Gunsmoke* than be in this room with him. You always have to be interested, and act like you want his hands all over you. You're the seductress."

I got the message loud and clear. I wasn't Sadie Meade anymore. This was an act, and I was a performer named Penny.

And with that realization, Penny clasped Chip's face and brought his lips to hers. She slipped her tongue inside to dance along with his.

Penny picked up his leather belt from the floor and threw it around his neck, using it to draw him toward the bed. He sat naked along the edge, standing at full attention at a good eight or possibly nine inches long.

Penny danced before him. Bending, turning, and lifting her bare leg atop his shoulder.

Chip stroked at her toned leg, reaching above her thigh, aiming for what he wanted to touch and have at that very moment.

She pulled away, taunting him some. Sadie was always a good tease, but Penny was better.

Chip waited so patiently, licking his lips, watching her dance. He moved his body toward the table near the bed and grabbed a condom. She was grateful he did because she hadn't had a chance to practice inserting the diaphragm yet.

Penny climbed on top of him, pushing his shoulders down, forcing his back onto the bed. Her tongue massaged Chip's piece

76

before helping him place the rubber securely on. She mounted him, and took the entire thick nine inches inside her petite body, riding him steadily and in control.

Her bra remained in place until Chip lowered the front pads, exposing the small buds. He didn't seem to care of the size. He nibbled at them before flipping her over onto her back. He was an unbelievable lover, with fast and furious movements.

"I want to hear what you're thinking, Penny. Tell me you want more. I need to hear how much you want me."

"Yes, baby, I want more! You're so good, baby. Harder. Harder!" She moaned loudly as he brought her to climax.

He lasted a solid twenty minutes. When he was done, he tossed the filled condom into the pail, put his clothes back on, and left the room.

She knew she wouldn't get paid to be with Chip, but no review? No goodbye? How did Penny rank on the scoreboard?

Doris soon entered the room with a few different pieces of negligee for me to wear as I laid on the bed still naked, recovering from Chip's enormous tool. She advised I clean up, change into one of those pieces, and get downstairs for the next parade.

This would be Penny's life from now on.

Embracing Debauchery

Chapter 23

AFTER A FEW months of brothel life swirled by, I actually felt slightly homesick. I missed Mom and Patrick, even know-it-all Lisa. I picked up the telephone receiver numerous times to call home, but I fully transformed into Penny now. They might not recognize me beneath the mask of makeup and risqué attire. I didn't recognize myself.

I was certain Mom would be worried. Dad was probably grateful I left. That was what I thought, until a month or so ago.

The fuzz pulled up to the main entrance of the ranch, minus the drama of flashing lights.

One of the cops entered to speak with Doris.

Brandi knew the officer and positioned her toned figure intimately close to him, blinking her flirty eyes. Then she stepped away, tugged at my arm, and suggested I remain out of sight in the kitchen. Brandi had spied on the cop who displayed a picture of me to Doris.

Apparently, my family filed a missing person's report. The police searched all over Vegas and decided to hunt for me at all the brothels in the state.

I might die if my family found me here. They were desperate enough to contact the police. Maybe I should have called Mom to tell her I was alive and safe. She'd demand to know where I was. A nice Catholic woman like Suzanne Meade wouldn't be able to handle news like this.

Doris first asked the officer if I was in trouble with the law. The stocky officer with a colorful tattoo across his arm, merely confirmed I was a runaway.

Doris protected me and said there was no one here named Sadie Meade. Some of the other girls probably overheard her say my name aloud, learning my true identity.

After the officer sped off, despite Barbie and Monique asking if he could stay and play with them for a while, Doris took me aside in the kitchen. She didn't tell the cop the truth about my being here because she remembered my bruised face and somber disposition when I first arrived. She considered I came from an abusive home.

I never corrected her.

Although I didn't like my father much, that traumatic night was the first time he had ever struck me. Not sure his actions warranted a label like "abuse" attached to it. However, she made it very clear that if any of her girls broke the law and were wanted by the police, she wouldn't protect them. The owners of the brothel never want any negative exposure or harmful publicity. It was risky for Doris to lie to the cops about my working here.

The endless daily parade around the room in front of the customers was a tolerable routine. I had been with as many as fifteen men in one day, including a bizarre set of thirty-year-old triplets visiting from Georgia, who freakishly fantasized about sharing a woman simultaneously. Some guys only wanted a fifteen-minute party, while others paid for thirty minutes or a full hour.

Then there were the high rollers who would pay hundreds of dollars to engage several working girls in the playroom for a wild orgy. Describing the ones with peculiar fetishes was difficult. They were probably too ashamed to tell their wives they needed to be spanked, whipped, or have their genitals tied up like a Christmas package to climax.

This job was never boring.

A colored guy named Hank became a regular of mine. I had never been with a black man before Hank. Many brothels didn't cater to the coloreds, but the Belle Maiden didn't discriminate. Hank stood about six feet tall, give or take an inch. His head was shaved as if he were in the military. His face was always clean-shaven, and he had this incredible scent drifting from his virile body. From the first time he locked eyes with me, he seemed interested and genuine.

Asking the men about their lives outside the ranch was not recommended. Their lives were none of our business. But if they chose to share personal details, we would listen, and at least pretend to be interested. It was their dime to use however they preferred. I wanted to know the name of Hank's cologne. The musky scent was intoxicating.

Becoming Hank's regular girl at the ranch caused further problems with Jo Jo. Hank used to select Jo Jo before I moved in. She taunted me terribly. She and Cookie loved to hit me where it hurt, as girls often did. They'd tease me about having the breasts of a twelve-year-old. Asked if I still wore a training bra. If we were back in Gloucester, I would've knocked them on their asses by now. But I knew they were jealous.

The psychology of this business had the potential of damaging a woman's self-esteem. There was a lot of competition for the attention of these men. Sometimes, women felt sad and rejected if they weren't selected as often as others.

Chapter 24

WORKING GIRLS WERE committed to three weeks at the ranch. Then we were allowed a one-week reprieve if we chose.

Kitty and I became good friends. She'd leave the ranch and head toward the Vegas Strip on her week off. She had a boyfriend named Kenny she liked to see. At least she called him her boyfriend, but within time I figured out he was actually her pimp.

If we left the ranch on our week off, we were on our own with free time to ourselves. However, as Doris warned, she couldn't protect us if we got caught participating in illegal activities like streetwalking or any other crime. She wouldn't put the brothel or its owner in legal harm, or risk the place closing.

Kitty called the Belle Maiden from a phone booth to speak with me on her time off. The rushing sound of cars whooshing by in the background didn't conceal the panic in her voice.

Apparently, Kitty's last checkup with the doc didn't go very well. She contracted a venereal disease, gonorrhea. Jesus, I was very fortunate that didn't happen to me, I thought selfishly as she explained her delicate situation.

Kenny was angry because she couldn't work in that condition with her best customer, a man she was to meet later this evening. She was tasked with recruiting a replacement.

"He's really a harmless guy, good-looking and very nice. Big tipper too. You'll get more money from this john than working at the ranch. Kenny wants the money, and I don't want to disappoint him. Would you go in my place tonight, Penny? Please!" Desperation was evident in her voice.

"I guess I could go." Perhaps I was a little nervous, leaving the safety of the brothel versus the streets. All forms of prostitution were illegal in Clark County, which included Las Vegas. Bordellos like the Belle Maiden were located only in regions permitted by law. Doris had her hands full, avoiding the threat of being closed down as a public nuisance by the County Sheriff.

As long as Doris didn't know what I was up to, I might as well earn some more money and help my friend.

Kitty told me the motel name, address, and room number located off the Strip, where I'd have to meet Kenny.

I never worked outside the ranch before, but this was during my week off. None of the other girls would be able to help her.

Kitty was one of the nicest girls I'd met here. She welcomed me and shared her clothes and makeup. We spent countless hours fantasizing about our future with a husband and children someday. She befriended me when some of the other girls made me feel like an outcast, rivaling for the johns. I wanted to help her.

I earned decent wages working at the ranch. Kitty didn't tell me how much I'd make tonight, only that this one customer would surely pay more.

In addition to the tight black shorts and purple sequined tube top I slipped on, I added a hat with a short veil that covered my eyes. There was something dark and mysterious about that look. For the ride to the Branson Motel, I tossed a long, gray knit sweater over my body to conceal the skimpy wardrobe.

At nine o'clock, my chariot, also known as a taxi, whisked me to this beat-up motel with very few cars in the parking lot. There were more people hanging around the joint than there were cars. Several were hookers. I could easily spot them now. The motel lot was filthy with trash thrown about. As I opened the car door, the raunchy smell of debris filled my senses. This motel was a dump, not as nice as the Belle Maiden.

Room ten straight ahead. I knocked on the old, brown door.

A woman in jeans and a black T-shirt answered. Her eyes swiveled up and down my body. Then she confirmed I was Penny. Her hardened jaw and narrow brows enhanced her rough persona. Was her dark brown hair braided too tight?

A man, who I assumed was Kenny, laid on the bed in his underwear only, drinking shots of whiskey. Wild Turkey, I noticed. He had an olive complexion, dark hair, and eyes black as night as he stared into my baby blues. His upper physique looked strong, judging by his thick, bulging arms. He eyed me over without saying a word, then nodded.

I removed the long sweater. Certainly, he would rather see what was beneath all this material.

The woman in the room shoved me, demanding I take everything off and get in the bed.

I complied, expecting Kenny would want to take me for a test-drive before he sent me to see a john.

The audience, however, was unexpected.

Kenny was all about fucking. Nothing tender or romantic about him. Some of the johns were like that at the ranch. But there were many who simply wanted to be touched and told they were great in bed.

Not Kenny. He was rough with me and my body. He didn't speak. He never kissed my lips. His pointy teeth punctured my flesh, a freakish behavior I wasn't entirely comfortable with. I hoped he didn't leave any marks against my neck, breasts, and shoulders.

I heard a strange clicking sound, and a flash of light crisply blinked. The female onlooker held a camera, standing at the edge of the bed.

"Hey, what is she doing?" I shouted.

"Don't worry about her," he ordered as he held my arms down with a rough push. Then he continued ramming himself inside me while this woman took pictures of us together in various positions. Many clicks heard and flashes flickered.

Kenny moved his upper torso around so she'd get some good shots of my naked body. He directed her with action shots as if this were a photoshoot for *Playboy* magazine.

Honestly, this *boyfriend* of Kitty's frightened me. I couldn't wait for him to finish so I could leave.

When he was done, he collapsed atop my weakened body then ordered me into the shower to be clean for his good-paying customer.

Raw bite marks were left upon my shoulders from his pointy, yellowed teeth. The mirror didn't lie. My arms felt the purple bruises blooming before my eyes from his tight grip. I didn't care how much I'd be paid for this job tonight; it wasn't worth it.

Why did Kitty return to Kenny for this abuse?

After drying off from the shower with the only towel in the bathroom, curled in the corner of the floor, I quickly gathered my clothes and put them on before Kenny had any other ideas for me.

The camera woman would drive me to the hotel and collect the money from me directly afterward. He was clear how much money I had to collect for him. Any remaining cash was mine.

Chapter 25

I MADE SURE I sat up front for the drive to the Strip. My driver, "Miss Sunshine," didn't believe I might become car sick, but I warned her she wouldn't want to find out the hard way.

The Montgomery was up ahead on the left. I closed my eyes, secretly willing her to drive past it. Any hotel except the Montgomery. Much to my dismay, she turned a sharp left directly into the Montgomery's parking lot.

"Here?" I asked. "The Montgomery is where I have to meet this john?"

"There are far worse places than this classy joint for you to go. I suggest you shut your mouth and put that sweater over your body. You can't walk into this place in that outfit."

I covered myself with the oversized sweater as she told me she'd be guarding the exit. I was expected to be back downstairs in one hour with the cash, or she'd be up in the room to track me down, collecting payment from my teeth.

She was quite charming.

I was surprised she didn't follow me with her camera. But I got the message loud and clear. I was to go to the fifth floor, room 530. The door would be unlocked.

It was Tuesday. Dad didn't work on Tuesdays, at least before I left home. I would die if my father, Rocky, or his sons saw me here dressed like this. I hoped the hat with the veil sufficiently concealed my identity.

The hotel lobby was very busy with people dressed to a T. Posters hung along the walls, indicating Elvis Presley was performing this week. Wow, Rocky outdid himself managing to snag Elvis as an act.

At the edge of the casino, I recognized him through a thick layer of cigarette smoke, my father. He wasn't wearing the uniform suit he usually wore when he worked. He wore plain clothes to gamble on his day off.

The elevator seemed to stop at many floors before reaching the lobby.

I observed Dad while I waited. He wasn't looking in my direction. His eyes never left the gaming table. The way his hands moved. The dim look worn upon his face. Beads of sweat, he wiped with a handkerchief along his receding hairline. He looked terrible. Distressed.

Was this where all his money had been invested lately? Gambling his savings away? Was this why Mom couldn't plant a garden or buy curtains and furniture? Patrick couldn't participate in school activities. He wouldn't help me buy a new dress. All for another roll of the dice?

I'd think it were shameful if I weren't dressed in tight shorts and meeting a strange man for sex in exchange for a large sum of cash.

The elevator doors opened wide. I stepped inside, along with a few other patrons, making no eye contact with anyone. The elevator operator asked us all which floor we wanted before he pressed the buttons to fly us upward.

Room 530 was a short walk from the elevator. I hoped this experience would differ from my episode with Kenny. I knocked three times, then opened the unlocked door. I sucked in a deep breath before stepping inside.

The room was dark. Curtains were closed. There he lay, naked on the bed. It was hard to tell if he looked as handsome as Kitty described, peering through this veil.

"Well, hello there. I hope you're not disappointed that Kitty couldn't make it tonight. I promise to make it worth your while," I said as I eased my way to the bed, hoping not to bump into anything in this dark room. My sweater flew off, highlighting my attributes, and his rod stood firmly, demanding my attention.

He said nothing, but he was ready to go. I tossed my hat with the veil onto the chair. At a closer look, his face was familiar.

Quickly, his arms flipped the knob of the light beside the bed. He knew exactly who I was. His fingers tore at the sheets to cover himself. With the lights on, I noticed the wheelchair on the opposite side of the king-size bed.

John muttered words in his distinct voice while using sign language, but I couldn't quite understand him. His thoughts were probably along the line of *What the hell are you doing here dressed like this?*

"John? I can't tell what you're trying to say."

He opened the drawer of the night table, making a huffing sound of frustration, and grabbed some paper and a pen. He wrote to me, and as I spoke, he read my lips.

"Is this what you've been doing? Your parents are worried."

My heart pounded hard enough to burst through my chest. "I'm okay." My eyes drifted from his when I spoke.

He needed to read my lips, but I had trouble facing him, looking the way I did, like Penny.

"Please, John. Please, don't tell anyone I was here. You never saw me." Then I thought about little Miss Sunshine who'd be downstairs waiting for the money.

"Where are you staying, Sadie?"

"I go by *Penny* now."

"I'm not calling you *Penny*. That's not who you are. If you needed help, why didn't you come to me or my family?"

My shoulders shrugged, and my head lowered. "I don't know. Look, this guy, Kenny, doesn't mess around. He could hurt me. I have to give him his money, John. Are we gonna do this?" I whispered, due to the pure awkwardness.

John shook his head. Then he wrote down some information. He's moving out of his father's house soon to live independently. He handed me the piece of paper with his new address in North Las Vegas if I ever needed anything.

He offered me a drink and some food from room service. I didn't have the stomach for either. He demanded I tell him how to find me.

I shook my head.

Disappointment was evident in his green eyes. He let out a breath to compose himself from this surprise, then calmly tapped the bed with his hands, inviting me to sit next to him and relax. I knew I was safe with John. He didn't have to write that down for me to understand. My head fell to his shoulder, and I drifted off.

John nudged my shoulder to wake me from the brief nap. It was a good thing too. I didn't want Miss Sunshine banging on the door.

I wiped the sleep from my eyes then pulled the sweater over me. I hated to ask John for money when he received nothing in return, but he handed me an envelope. As I counted the cash, there was an extra two hundred dollars for me. I sat beside him on the bed and placed a soft, delicate kiss upon his lips.

He wrote on the paper that Tommy would be in the room any minute.

Crap! I wasn't sure who I'd dread to see more, Tommy or the pimp's partner in crime.

John explained Tommy got him the room to meet Kitty, at least for now until he moved into his new place. He'd be picking John up soon to take him home.

"Promise me you'll keep my secret, John. You can't tell my family or yours. No one can know."

John nodded, agreeing to the discretion I required. Using the pen, John wrote that I had to check in with him and ultimately quit the business.

I nodded before placing the mysterious-looking hat atop my head. There was no time for me to negotiate a different outcome, so I swiftly left.

As I strolled down the hallway, Tommy rushed off the elevator, nearly bumping into me. I noticed he glanced at me with that sexy smile he often wore. I kept my head lowered and prayed to God he didn't recognize me. If he had, he would've stopped me for certain.

I pocketed the extra dough John gave me, stuffing it inside my tube top.

When the elevator stopped at the lobby, that despicable woman's body was seen through the widening elevator door with her hand open.

I slipped the envelope into her palm.

She grabbed my arm, squeezing firmly until she counted every dollar inside. Then she was gone. No thanks, goodbye, or a ride home. I didn't care.

Thank God this night was over. I requested the doorman hail me another chariot for a ride back to the Belle Maiden.

Chapter 26

IT WAS SUMMERTIME, nearing the final days of June in 1967. The air became wildly hot in the desert that left me begging for a breeze. The heat differed from New England weather. The temperature grew higher here, but with less humidity.

Another Friday meant another weekly exam from the doc. It was routine for each girl to strip down in the room, climb atop the table, and allow him to examine our merchandise.

I left the ranch that one night. How I prayed my time with Kenny didn't warrant the need for penicillin to treat a venereal disease.

He had good news and bad news. The good news confirmed I had no signs of VD. However, according to the doc, I was pregnant. My heart raced feverishly. My brain crammed with clouds. It took several minutes to process that pregnancy meant a baby. An actual baby to carry for months. I was in no position to be a mother!

The doc briefly explained the adoption process if I wasn't ready for motherhood.

"Adoption? After nine months of pregnancy and giving birth? I wouldn't be able to work or earn money to support myself. I worked here because I couldn't support myself any other way. How would I support a baby?" I soon realized I was yelling all my thoughts out loud, with the doc staring into my soul, empathy pouring from his deep-set brown eyes.

"Penny, you need to calm down and relax. Let this news sink in."

All I kept thinking about were the many possibilities of who the father was.

Hank's visits were more frequent than anyone else. People wouldn't accept my blond-haired, blue-eyed, fair-skinned self having a black baby. Society didn't easily accept interracial couples or their offspring. Hank and I weren't a couple. For all I knew about Hank, he could have a wife and children.

How could I forget about Kenny? He couldn't be bothered wearing a condom. In his line of work, you'd think he would be more careful about contracting VD. The thought of creating a child with Kenny's genes horrified me.

A lot of men didn't opt to wear a condom. Many weren't regulars, and I might not see them again.

I begged the doc to help me. I'd pay anything he wanted to fix the problem for me without saying the word "abortion" aloud.

If my Catholic parents ever heard me right now, they'd condemn me to hell.

The doc's eyes turned somber. His brows curved in. In a deep, low voice, he mumbled, "No. I can't help you. You see, I had a contact who helped in situations like yours. He handled the procedure discreetly. But he's serving time in jail now. He got caught recently. The father of one of his patients pressed charges after learning about the illegal procedure that was performed on his daughter. His life is ruined, Penny.

"After that bombshell hit the news, Doris and the owner decided it was too risky to help with anything other than the adoption process right now. The Belle Maiden cannot support illegal activities that would risk negative publicity. The community may turn against the ranch," he explained.

Many members of the community, especially the church, disapproved of prostitution in general, whether it was at a legal bordello or illegal street walking. Abortion was a bigger taboo subject that feminists pushed to legalize, while anti-abortionists vehemently opposed in political forums.

I was in a bind.

I shared my dilemma with Kitty, explaining Kenny could be the father since he didn't bother to wear a rubber. So much for the reliability of a diaphragm.

Kitty remembered that Kenny knew someone in the medical profession. She heard of a girl or two who worked for Kenny in this same situation. Kenny arranged for these girls to meet with this man to have the problem taken care of.

I loathed Kenny. Hoped I'd never have to see him again. But I asked Kitty to contact him for help. I didn't know anyone else who could make this happen. My situation resulted from my time with Hank, Kenny, or any other random visitor, and the johns bore no obligation in these instances. None of these men walked out the ranch's front door with the thought that they could've gotten a girl knocked up, nor did they care. This was the lifestyle of a hooker and a hooker's problem to handle alone. The johns evaded responsibility.

A few days passed before Kitty heard back from Kenny. He agreed to help me for a hundred dollars and if I turned one more trick for him.

Sadly, I nodded, agreeing to his vile terms. I saved more than enough money to pay the fee.

I spoke with Kitty about this man she referred to as her "boyfriend." I pleaded with her to stay at the ranch. Why take chances on the street and with a man like Kenny? He didn't care about her. He only cared about the money she earned for him.

According to Kitty, if she stopped working for Kenny completely, he'd kill her. She clutched her pretty cross necklace as if praying for protection. Her fear of him was real, and I understood why. She tried to hide the bruises on her body whenever she'd return to the ranch. But I noticed them.

Chapter 27

ANOTHER TRIP TO that repulsive motel, a place I hoped to never frequent again. The outside looked dingy. Trash thrown about. Broken bottles shattered everywhere. A few rats crawled around a dumpster with an ill-fitted cover. A strong odor of garbage combined with urine filled my senses. Degenerates lurked around no matter the time of day. Naturally, this was the type of place a rat like Kenny would skulk.

I knocked on room three per his instructions to Kitty.

Kenny answered. His eyes wandered up and down my body like I was a piece of prime rib thrown into the lion's den. He called me "baby." I hated that term coming from his mouth. I hated him.

But Penny had to surface and play the part. Before I entered, Kenny wanted the cash. I handed him the money, trying hard not to roll my eyes when he wouldn't release my hand from his grasp.

Another man stood in the corner of the room. I assumed he was the customer getting the freebie from me. I'd guess he was in his fifties, judging by the mild wrinkles around his lips and more severe lines around his eyes. His thinning hair was partially gray. Not the most handsome guy I'd ever seen. Time might not have been kind to him, or he was older than I thought. Something seemed shady about this critter that made me think of a weasel.

Kenny called him "Artie."

Artie took my hand and kissed my fingertips. The formal introductions were soon over, and Artie immediately stripped off his red T-shirt and blue jeans. His body looked scrawny and out of shape. No definition in his arms or chest.

I glanced at Kenny, who didn't appear eager to leave. As much as I wanted him gone, I said nothing. Kenny wasn't someone to speak against or boss around.

Artie gave me specific directions on how to please him. He told me everything I had to do to him and his body parts. "Slower. More tongue!" he demanded before tossing my small frame onto the bed.

Thankfully, Artie slipped on a condom. As he pounded into me, I heard that clicking again.

Kenny snapped pictures after deeply inhaling the joint clenched between his lips.

"Don't get my face in those photos!" Artie shouted.

What did Kenny do with these pictures? Jerk off to these memories he collected on film? I wondered how many photos he had of Kitty.

All these thoughts ran through my mind as Artie withdrew from me, completing his mission. I was grateful he didn't last very long.

When Artie rolled off my body, I shimmied toward the edge of the bed in search of my clothes, but Kenny ordered me to stay put.

He placed the camera on the dresser, removed his pants, then slowly crawled into the bed and on top of me. "I know you want some of this," he said, grabbing himself.

"Put a rubber on," Artie commanded.

Kenny didn't wear a condom before, yet he followed Artie's direction today.

God, I hated everything about this filthy, abominable man plunging inside me. Penny's acting talents couldn't hide the disgust felt within.

Naturally, Kenny didn't care about my feelings.

Artie sat back and watched the performance along with the habitual, satanic biting. I'd love to knock this man's teeth out if I were stronger and not in need of this favor from him. If I could call an abortion a "favor."

Minutes felt like hours with Kenny on top of my body. Finally, he was done with me, but he wouldn't allow me to get dressed.

Artie kindly asked me to take a shower.

I was grateful to wash off these two from my body. I asked why he was so insistent.

"Why? Because you need to be clean for surgery," Artie replied.

In the corner of the room sat a large black bag and a larger suitcase that Artie picked up and placed upon the mattress.

I watched him open the cases to see many steel instruments, gauze pads, bottles, bandages, a long tube, and other strange-looking devices.

Artie was the doctor, or some version of one.

"Get in the shower like he told you!" Kenny grabbed my arm tightly, and threw me inside the bathroom, leaving the door wide open.

My body trembled. Hands were jittery. I started to rethink this plan of mine. Could I trust a man I despised or anyone associated with him? I sat on the floor of the tub, allowing the warm beads of water to soak my entire body that quaked with uncertainty. I was here. Who knew if I'd be able to find another person willing to perform this procedure? I doubted Kenny would refund the money I gave him for having a change of heart.

Water hissed from the bathroom sink. I pulled back the shower curtain to witness Artie scrubbing his hands and arms with soap. At least he was clean.

When I returned from the shower, clean, dry, and naked, Artie handed me a bottle of Wild Turkey, suggesting I drink.

I refused as I moved to lie on the bed, now covered with a large sheet of plastic.

Kenny wore an annoyed expression, but Artie showed gentle eyes.

"I can't use anesthesia, Penny. It would take too long for you to wake up. I don't have much time to stay here. The alcohol may ease some of the pain, or help you to fall asleep."

Pain, I thought. I toyed with the idea of running out of this motel room.

Kenny dived next to me on the bed, moaning sounds of agitation. He squeezed my mouth with his firm fingertips, forcefully parting my lips open. Then he poured the harsh whiskey down my throat, dribbling the cool liquid along my face, neck, and breasts.

I coughed relentlessly, choking on the strong liquor, then slapped his hand away. I snatched the bottle from him and drank as quickly as possible without his help. The liquor burned from the top of my throat all the way down to my stomach walls with each swig, immediately warming my insides.

Kenny sprinted from the bed and reached inside his jacket pocket, removing a small bag filled with pills. He flaunted a tiny capsule before my eyes. "This downer will calm you for sure."

Staring at the pointed objects Artie planned to use on me, tormented the restless thoughts churning about in my head. I eagerly accepted the drug from Kenny.

Instead of handing me the pill, his fingers forced my mouth open again, placing the capsule directly on my tongue. Then he grabbed the bottle and poured more whiskey down my throat to ensure I swallowed it.

Artie calmly stated, "Relax, Penny. Your body shouldn't be stiff. It will be over before you know it."

Then he removed long strips of leather pieces that looked like belts from a suitcase. As the booze filled my head with clouds, he spread my legs opened wide. He tugged at my right leg, strapping a leather bind around it, fastening it to the metal bed frame. He repeated the process with my left leg.

I attempted to kick myself free from his grasp, but Artie shushed me. "It's okay, Penny. You can't move around. This is merely a precaution to keep you still." He tightened the straps further until I was unable to move my legs.

He expected me to relax? Was he out of his mind? I saw the tools he planned to use. I began taking longer, faster mouthfuls of Wild Turkey for a while until my head was dizzy and my vision blurred. Still, my heart raced, thumping at an inconceivable rate.

The numbness took over my head, and my body lay immobile on the bed. I tried not to kick or wiggle. The sober parts of my brain chanted *It'll be over soon. Don't move. You can do this.*

Kenny placed the whiskey bottle on the nightstand next to the joint he dabbed into an ashtray. The raw, overpowering scent of marijuana, mixed with the taste of Wild Turkey, made me gag. He whisked my arms above my head. With tremendous strength, he held my arms securely to the mattress.

Beneath Kenny's arm, I caught sight of Artie's face at the opposite end of the bed, between my legs. His expression looked serious as he fiddled with instruments in his bag.

After the first brutally stabbing pain was felt, I screamed and squirmed. The security of the ties that bound my legs failed. I managed to thrust my midsection up and down, wincing in pain and fear.

Kenny jumped onto my chest, his thighs fastened my midsection down and the strong grip from his hands secured my wrists tightly. "You got ties for her fucking arms?" he yelled to Artie.

"Keep her still. I can't do this if she's bouncing around!" Artie shouted.

"This one's pretty feisty, aren't you, sweetheart?" Kenny said, taunting me. A drop of drool slipped from his lips and splashed against my cheek.

He enjoyed watching me writhe in pain.

My adrenaline rose when I felt something sharp cutting me from the inside out. I felt hot, sweaty, and panic-stricken. A lump nested in my throat. That sick feeling I got when I was about to vomit crept up.

I let out a scream in agony, then turned my head and barfed up brown, foamy chunks across Kenny's arm and hand.

"Jesus! What the hell? She just fucking puked on me!"

Artie paused and said something in return that I couldn't comprehend. My hearing started to fade as my vision blurred.

With another razor-sharp pinch felt between my legs, everything went black.

Chapter 28

VICIOUS BLOWS TO my stomach forced me awake. The cramps were unbearable. Filled with confusion, unsure where I was or why my insides ached. My eyes refused to open as if I still slept, wrestling with a nightmare in my subconscious. But the pain seemed very real.

Eventually, my lids widened to view the cold room I laid in. For a warm summer day, my body quaked with chills. My memory finally jarred.

The motel room.

The procedure.

My hands slowly moved toward my tender, empty womb. I tilted my head toward the left then the right. I was all alone, feeling grateful for the privacy, yet abandoned with intense throbs beating across my stomach.

Kenny and Artie fled the scene. A note was left for me to take some loose pills spread about on the nightstand for the pain. At least they left me these pills and a small mug I assumed was filled with water. I managed to grasp the meds and popped them into my mouth. Reaching for the mug was more challenging. I needed to sit up slightly to swallow them.

I couldn't move any further. As I tried to shift my legs, I noticed streaks of blood melted into the plastic sheet my body was glued to. My head tingled, most likely thanks to the combination of the downer and booze. I attempted to roll off the plastic layer to rest on the mattress beneath, and sobbed through the achiness. I'd think about where to go when my mind became clear and rid of the drug and whiskey remnants Kenny gave me.

I needed to call a taxi and leave this room, no matter how tired and sore my body felt. Where I'd go was another question.

There was someone who might help me. At least I hoped he'd help me without giving me a lecture. I couldn't call, but I stared at his address so many times the street name was etched in my memory.

With tender care, I propped myself up from the bed and wiped down the stream of blood drying on my legs with a towel draped across the nightstand.

Putting on clothes took more time than usual due to the constant ache in my gut. I used the phone to request a cab. In ten minutes, I'd be out of this awful room and would never see Kenny again.

Chapter 29

THE NEIGHBORHOOD APPEARED quiet this evening. The cab pulled up in front of a green ranch-style home. Lights shined brightly in the kitchen.

I asked the cabbie to park directly in front of the side entrance where the ramp was located, and flash his lights continuously inside the house to draw attention. I desperately wanted to save myself from taking extra steps.

"Do you need some help, miss?" the driver asked.

Clearly, my pain looked obvious. "Can you wait to make sure someone lets me inside?"

He nodded.

I handed him the money for the fare and a decent tip for his kindness.

He stepped outside the vehicle and opened the door for me. I took the hand he offered to help me step out. He stood outside and watched me take baby steps toward the ramp. The cab's headlights continued to flash, blinding me.

This newly built ramp structure was a blessing. I held on to the wrought iron railing as I climbed to the top to reach the door. The evening air felt warm, yet my body trembled.

The squeaky wheels of his chair were easy to recognize. Thank goodness he was home. No other vehicles were in the driveway. He didn't appear to have company. I hated for John to see me like this, but I had nowhere else to turn.

The door was framed with glass enclosures. The taxi's flashing lights bounced through the kitchen window and grabbed his attention. I waved through the window as his wheelchair turned toward the bright lights.

When the door opened, John let me inside. I signaled to the cabdriver, indicating that he was free to move on to his next fare.

John tried to say something in sign language, but I didn't know his language, and I hadn't the strength to figure it out.

His eyes swerved toward my legs, witnessing the dried stream of blood. His fingers ran down my calf, pointing and shrugging his shoulders.

"I had minor surgery. I'll be okay, but could I...do you think I can...stay here for maybe a day or two?" I hated to impose on John, especially when I had no desire to explain the procedure I just had by a weasel and a pimp.

John pointed to his sofa, directing me to sit. It hurt to bend and move quickly. He surely observed my poor attempt to stagger toward the couch.

He must have grabbed paper and a pen as I attempted to sit because he began writing furiously. "What happened? Did someone hurt you?"

I shook my head.

John held up his finger, asking me to wait. He rolled away. I heard water hissing while he fumbled with something in another room. Several minutes passed before he returned with a basin filled with hot, soapy water and a washcloth. He removed my shoes, soaked up the cloth, and gently wiped the bloodstains from my hands, wrists, and legs. I never realized my hands and wrists were stained with my own blood.

He disappeared again for several minutes, it seemed. I wasn't looking at a clock—too sleepy to pay close attention.

When I heard the squeaky wheelchair, my eyes flew open to see more notes. He placed them at eye level for me, so I didn't have to lift my head.

"There's a guest room around the corner. It's yours for as long as you need." He handed me a clean, oversized shirt to sleep in.

Moving at that moment was not a priority.

Chapter 30

I AWOKE TO the sun's rays shining through the living room window. Still feeling sore and weak, my body shivered. John sat over me in his wheelchair, exposing a concerned look. He wore the same green knit shirt and tan slacks from yesterday. He might not have gone to bed last night.

Another man squatted beside me.

My body charged upright, uncertain who he was or what he planned to do to me.

"Sadie, I'm Dr. Clark, a friend and neighbor of John's. He was worried about you. I dropped by to meet you."

Once I heard he was a doctor, I relaxed. I had become programmed to men wanting to have sex with me, no matter my condition. My head hit the pillow of the couch again, still in a haze.

"Sadie, you have a fever. I can prescribe you something, but first I have to understand what happened to you."

"It was just a simple surgery."

"Who's your doctor?"

"I don't remember."

"Which hospital did you go to?"

"I...I don't know."

"Can you tell me what kind of surgery?"

I shrugged, unable to say the words.

"Sadie, you can trust me. I want to help you. If you can't tell me what happened, I'll call an ambulance and have you taken to the emergency room."

To put my trust in a perfect stranger was unlikely. I had learned not to trust many people lately.

I felt John's hand clench mine. He nodded his head at me with a worried expression.

John was someone I trusted. I closed my eyes because I couldn't look at either of them when I said the words aloud, "I had an abortion."

Dr. Clark ordered prescription pain medication and an antibiotic that should help with the cramping and fever. I had no idea what those pills were that Artie left for me in the motel room. Could have been baby aspirin for all I knew.

John's friend examined me and commented on the butcher job Artie did. He offered to check in on me regularly. He'd want to confirm there was no evidence of a life growing inside me still, and to ensure I showed signs of improvement with no infection or hemorrhaging.

By the end of that day, the fever subsided and the pain lessened.

I thanked John for his quick thinking. The doctor explained I could have died without medical assistance. They saved my life. I could have become a casualty of a procedure that took the lives of many desperate women in this country.

Chapter 31

SLEEP WAS ALL I wanted. After a couple of days of rest and feeling very safe in John's house, I called Doris. Although, I wasn't anxious to return to the ranch.

I didn't know what to expect from Kenny's weasel of a friend when I agreed to this arrangement. How I'd feel afterward or what my recovery would be like, were not questions I thought to ask in advance.

Doris sounded grim when she heard my voice. Apparently, some grave excitement occurred at the Belle Maiden.

Roxy had been beaten by a john and sent to the emergency room. This guy hit her face so hard, her eyes were blackened, lip was split, and her nose was broken. The hospital released her so she could rest comfortably in her room now.

The john was arrested after Chip took him down and beat the crap out of him. No one knew why this man snapped, or why he attacked poor Roxy.

I'd bet Cookie and Jo Jo were happy they'd have more business this week with Roxy and me out of the way.

What would I do now for work? Where would I stay? After hearing what happened to Roxy, Kitty's battle with VD, and my own situation, returning to the ranch was not enticing.

John was kind enough to let me stay here for as long as I needed. He wasn't expecting any company this week. Rocky and Tommy traveled to the East Coast to conduct business in Philadelphia.

For a deaf man, John was a good listener. Easy to talk to. Although he mainly encouraged me to return to my family, the Meades. Not my family at the Belle Maiden.

Going home to Mom and Dad scared me as much as returning to Doris and the girls.

I opened up to John about a lot of things. Why I left home and how I met Roxy and Brandi, who told me about the ranch. At the time, living at the ranch made sense. But now, I wanted to run away from there too. Maybe it was time to stop running.

He didn't want me working at the ranch. And now that he knew where I had been, if anything ever happened to me, he'd feel responsible because he didn't stop me. Maybe he'd snitch to my parents.

Chapter 32

BUCK, THE DRIVER with the Texas accent, picked John up and helped him into a red Chevy van. I watched as Buck lifted John and placed him in the front seat while his wheelchair was stored in the back. I had no idea John maintained a part-time job. He continued to surprise me.

The air felt breezy yet warm. I had adapted to the typical hot Nevada temperatures. My mood felt positive. This day seemed full of hope.

The tasty smell of meat roasting from a barbecue in the neighborhood caused my belly to rumble. I hadn't eaten much since my procedure. After enjoying some fresh pineapple and sliced apples, I stepped outside onto the patio with colorful cement blocks to feel the sun against my fair skin. Breathing in the fresh air heightened my senses. In an instant, I felt my lips curve into a genuine smile.

My eyes closed as I relaxed on a lounge chair in John's tranquil yard among the potted pansies.

The sound of a car parking, followed by a door opening and closing, caught my attention. John's family was out of town, and he wasn't home. Maybe his neighbor had company. My eyes closed again until a shadowy figure appeared, standing above me.

"What the hell is this?" The horrible, fearful sound of Kenny's voice resonated.

My eyes burst open, staring into his cold, dead eyes. My body froze. How did he find me? I couldn't speak through the web of panic exploding within my brain.

"Where's Johnny? What did he do, take up with you exclusively? You're not working for my customer without paying me my share," he demanded.

"I don't know what you're talking about!"

"John's brother told me he's not doing business with me anymore. Since he met you. That's no coincidence! I came here to see John directly to work things out, seeing he can't use the telephone. We had such a nice deal going on between him and Kitty until *you* came along. Now I find you soaking up sunshine in his yard. You don't take business away from me, bitch!"

He grabbed my arms, jerked my body up from the chair, and brought me in close to him. Close enough to feel his foul breath against my lips.

"He's not paying me, I swear!"

"Bullshit! A whore like you doesn't hang out here on prime real estate like this for free." His laugh sounded sadistic.

"I have nothing to do with whatever arrangement you had with John. He's just my friend."

"You're gonna get me a finder's fee. And if you don't, I'll be back. Your sweet ass will make me a lot of money."

He took great pleasure seeing the terror sweep across my face. That was the only time he smiled. I never took guff from anybody before I met Kenny.

"Come here, baby." Suddenly, he acted as if he cared, giving me a peck on the cheek then my lips, while I trembled. Maybe this was his game with Kitty, convincing her he cared. The emotional baggage she carried served his purpose.

I quivered, afraid to stop him.

His slippery tongue licked the side of my face as his hands wandered around my body. "Seeing that you recovered from your procedure the other day, let's go inside and have a party, baby."

I pushed him off me, but he didn't release my arm. He held on to me tighter, kissed my neck, then bit my shoulder with those sharp vampire-like teeth.

"Stop! I'll get you your money. But I need a couple of days. Now let me go!"

His fingers grabbed my face forcibly, then kissed my lips with a hard and wet smack. "Now that's what I want to hear. I'll be back here in two days."

"No. Not here."

"Ahh, you wanna come see me at the motel?" His brows raised, actually believing I enjoyed having him on top of me, panting and biting.

The motel. Not a place I'd ever want to frequent again. I mentioned the first place that jumped into my mind. "At the end of this road is a flower shop. I'll meet you there, outside the shop, with the money. But with the condition that I'm done doing any work for you."

"You are in no position to bargain with me. Besides, I don't know if you have the kind of money I want for you to walk away from all our fun times."

"I'll get you enough money."

"And if you don't, I'll have to visit your new boyfriend here and collect from him directly." He grabbed me by the roots of my hair and pulled me in, glowering into my eyes, anger exuding. Then he calmly kissed my forehead. The man ran from hot to cold in seconds. "You got two days. I'll meet you there at midnight."

Finally, he released me and slithered off.

Chapter 33

MAYBE I WAS in over my head. I understood why Kitty feared Kenny. Did he really show up here to talk to John, or threaten the disabled man? I didn't want John to get hurt because of me and *my* bad choices.

Kenny mentioned that Tommy discontinued services with Kitty. She told me John was a regular of hers. I could see how that would anger Kenny, losing a wealthy regular customer like John.

John should know about this. I did nothing but bring him trouble when all he did was try to help me. Not only did I have to warn John that Kenny might have come here to hurt him, I needed enough money to pay Kenny off, so he'd leave us both alone.

A distraction from this madness was in order. If I kept thinking about Kenny and what he could do to John or me any longer, I would surely fly off the deep end.

The refrigerator was stocked with food. I became a decent cook, thanks to helping Mom in the kitchen many times. I managed to broil chicken legs, bake sweet potatoes, and toss a salad for dinner.

All the doors in the house were locked, and the shades lowered, fearing that Kenny could be outside lurking. My body jumped at any noise heard outside or a creak within the walls of this house.

The drumming sound of Buck's van parking in the driveway was detected. Suddenly, I felt safe, relieved to have John home. Once Buck helped John into his wheelchair and inside the house, I somehow managed to describe to John about Kenny's intense visit and the threats he made. I ensured the pad and pen were at his fingertips because I knew he'd have a lot to write to me.

He explained that when I visited him at the Montgomery that night as Penny, he saw the fear in my eyes. Frightened of Kenny. John wanted no part of that association anymore. He seemed to like Kitty a lot, but he didn't want to work with a pimp who terrorized his girls. So he asked Tommy to cut ties with Kenny and to ensure Kitty was safe. But Kitty wouldn't leave the street life or Kenny.

Obviously, Kenny didn't like John and Tommy trying to take his girls from him.

John handed me the name and contact number of an ex-Marine, a tough security guard at the Montgomery. He was also a good friend of Tommy and John's. His name was Jim.

I wasn't comfortable talking to anyone who knew the Cavallos. However, John confirmed that Jim wasn't the type who asked questions or gossiped.

All I had to do was invite him over, tell him Kenny had been harassing me, and John wanted him stopped. Jim wouldn't need to know who Kenny was, or who I was for that matter.

John would pay him to secure our safety. He believed Jim was trustworthy. And I trusted John.

A gorgeous black Pontiac Firebird pulled into the driveway the next morning. A man of medium height with short brown hair and extra-large biceps knocked on the door.

John let him inside, and they shook hands.

Jim knew sign language and exchanged a few words with John, using precise hand movements.

I should really learn a few words in sign myself to communicate better with John. Lately, I wasn't in the right mindset to learn a language.

Jim puffed away on a Marlboro as he gave me a once-over.

All we shared with Jim was that a dangerous man was shaking me down for money. Jim didn't need to know who or why. He only needed to know the time and place. John offered Jim money to ensure my protection.

I couldn't tell what else was said in sign language between John and Jim, but Jim's eyes exhibited compassion.

In a sincere, kind voice, Jim said, "Don't worry, miss. I'll see to it that this man never bothers you or John again." Jim offered us each a smoke. Although John said he was cutting back on his smoking habit, he lunged for that cigarette. Given the intense circumstances we faced, I accepted too.

After Jim left, John told me he was doing this on one condition and one condition only. I needed to leave this business completely and go home to my family. If I stayed in this line of work, I could wind up dead.

That was a good possibility.

Chapter 34

JIM ARRIVED AT John's home fifteen minutes before the meeting with Kenny. He was a quiet man who didn't say much during our short drive up the road, except to rehash our plan, which basically was to pay off Kenny quickly and quietly to ensure my safety. If the situation looked ugly, Jim would be waiting in the wings to protect me.

Jim's Firebird was parked across the street with the lights out, so he could observe the payoff with a pair of binoculars.

I stood beneath a streetlight in the empty parking lot to ensure Jim's view wasn't compromised, observing the pretty floral design painted across the flower shop walls. The stream of the bright light produced a feeling of security. As if I could feel safe meeting this animal.

The envelope I clutched contained five thousand dollars. I never held so much money in my life. Kenny didn't ask for a specific amount, but John wanted to be sure he never bothered me again.

As I waited for this evil man I despised, I thought about how much money I held tightly in my palm. Maybe Kenny would take four thousand. My back faced Jim. I crouched to the ground, leaning against the streetlight post. I counted ten one hundred-dollar bills, removed the money from the envelope, and stuffed the dough inside my pants pocket.

Kenny took his sweet time getting here. The wait was agonizing. My pulse rattled and thumped through my temples, instigating a headache.

A dark pickup truck pulled in and flashed its headlights my way. Kenny had one of his goons with him. A husky man with long, wavy black hair. I'd never seen him before, but if he was an associate of Kenny's, he was no good.

Thank God, Jim wasn't far away. They could slit my throat, steal the money, and drive off.

The way they laughed and eyeballed me was maddening. Kenny didn't introduce me to his friend. He inspected the empty parking lot, continuously shifting his head back and forth.

His friend sucked on a Tootsie Pop. I could smell the sweet chocolate-flavored lollipop from where I stood.

The street, unnervingly quiet at this time of night. No sounds to be heard other than our own voices. I thought for sure my quick-paced beating heart could be heard by anyone within a few mere inches of me.

"You got my money, Penny?"

"You never said how much you wanted, but I have four grand in this envelope."

The look on both of their faces displayed sheer surprise. "Four thousand dollars? Where the hell did you come up with that kind of cash, girl?" He smiled and laughed with excitement.

As he reached for the envelope, I stepped back with it.

"Our deal was, you leave me and John alone from now on. Our business is completely done."

"Shit, for four thousand, I can move to Mexico and start a new business there with Junior here." He patted the back of his friend, Junior. That menacing laugh of his sent chills up my spine.

"Come on now. Give it to me."

I thought I should have offered him two thousand and kept the rest, but I handed him the envelope.

Kenny placed the cash inside his jacket. "We'll give you a ride home," he offered.

"No thanks," I answered.

"I'm being polite, Penny. Don't be rude."

Junior laughed through his lollipop in a sadistic manner that triggered a queasy feeling in my gut.

"Take your money and leave. That was our deal," I reminded him sharply. My heart throbbed vigorously.

In an instant, the two of them grabbed me by my arms. I fought back but slipped and fell to the ground.

They pulled my body by my hands, dragging me behind the flower shop over the rough gravel. I could feel the flesh shredding from my back and legs from the crushed stone they yanked me through.

My eyes closed to prevent the dust wafting around my face from blinding me as it swept up from the rocky ground. My arms felt like they'd be pulled from the sockets from the force of their upper body strength. I tried desperately to wiggle myself free from them.

That was when I heard a loud thud.

One of my arms released.

I opened my eyes that stung from the debris to observe Jim whacking Junior in the head with a baseball bat.

My other arm was freed as Kenny started to run, leaving his injured friend behind.

Jim chased Kenny, shouting that he'd be dead if he ever came near John or me again. Jim got in a few good, hard whacks with the bat against Kenny's back and leg.

Kenny yelled in pain, attempting to run from Jim. He appeared wounded, limping from the last blow to his side.

Junior laid still on the ground. His dark, cold eyes widened and the chocolate pop was still attached to his lower lip with blood seeping from his head. I wished Kenny's head had been beaten in.

Kenny managed to escape Jim's grasp, punching him hard in the gut. He sped off haphazardly in his Ford truck. Jim wounded him and his truck, beating the door and a headlight with his bat.

Jim raced toward me to ensure I wasn't hurt. Outside cuts and scrapes from the gravel, I was in better shape than the man lying on the ground unconscious, inches from me.

Jim grabbed Junior's wallet and took out a few dollar bills. Then he tossed the worn brown wallet into the bushes. "Police will think it was a robbery gone wrong."

He reached for my hands to help me stand. "Hurry, let's get to my car! Avoid the bright streetlight, and I'll drop you off at John's."

Complete silence on the drive back to John's house. I sprang from the car. My body quivered terribly. I couldn't remember if I thanked Jim for saving me. He watched me step inside the house before he moved along, keeping a safe pace, not to bring suspicion upon himself.

The next day, the evening news highlighted the murder of a man known by the police as a street pimp named Hector "Junior" Morales. The owner of Gallagher's Flowers in North Las Vegas found his bludgeoned body in the parking lot early this morning. Police believed it was either a robbery or a scuffle related to his criminal history. No witnesses or suspects.

Chapter 35

I OFFERED JOHN the thousand bucks I put aside from the envelope for Kenny. Despite his fear that the cops might connect Jim and me to Junior's death, he was grateful Jim helped me. He let out a slight chuckle at the thought of petite me shaking down this dangerous pimp.

Once the humor was gone, he reminded me of how risky that would have been if they found that money on me. Precarious was how my life became since I left home earlier this year.

John expected me to return home and make peace with my family. The time had come for a fresh start.

John told me to keep the cash I removed from Kenny's extortion fund.

I never expected to keep this money, and I argued with John about it. This wasn't my money to keep, but he insisted I put it aside as an emergency fund for when I settled in at home. He was quite adamant about my reconnecting with my family; and he was not allowing me to procrastinate initiating a family reunion.

John requested Buck drive me to Dr. Clark's office a few blocks away for what should be my last checkup.

As nice as the doctor appeared, my fingers trembled at the thought of seeing him again. I worried he'd find another medical issue or a baby still growing within me. My fears caused me to be late for the appointment, but the doctor's secretary kindly asked me to have a seat upon my tardy arrival. My delay did not facilitate a canceled appointment. Why was I so anxious, desperate to hightail it out of this room and bypass Buck in the parking lot? I took in some deep breaths in an attempt to calm my shaky disposition.

Dr. Clark stepped into the waiting area and smiled sincerely at me. "Good morning, Sadie. So nice to see you," he hummed in a happy tone. Then he offered me a stick of Wrigley's Doublemint gum.

My fears suddenly subsided.

Upon examination, Dr. Clark explained my insides were as good as could be expected after the work Artie did on me. There were no signs of a viable pregnancy. I needed to continue taking the antibiotic he gave me until the bottle was empty to prevent infection. He shook my hand, stating I was welcome to contact him if I had any questions, and especially if any pain or excessive bleeding occurred.

After I dressed, Buck drove me back to John's house to say a heartfelt thank you and goodbye to my friend. If John didn't help me, what would have become of me?

A part of me liked staying with my friend, John, but I had some wrongs to right.

I visited the Belle Maiden to collect my things and officially retire from the business. Doris appeared understanding and kind.

Saying goodbye to the girls proved harder than I anticipated. I told Roxy, Brandi, and Kitty I'd miss them, and if they ever decided to retire from this business to look me up.

I pleaded with Kitty to stay away from the streets and Kenny. There was something severely broken in that man that couldn't be fixed. I worried she was in too deep with Kenny already. So deep she might not be able to dig herself out. I hoped all my friends managed to avoid danger.

Roxy's face still wore bruises and a gouge on her nose from the damage the crazy customer caused.

I left the girls my makeup, lingerie, and risqué clothes. I packed only the type of clothes my family would recognize me in.

Before I strode out the ranch door, Cookie and Jo Jo approached and hugged me goodbye. Maybe they didn't hate me as much as I thought. Maybe their rivalry and taunts were a way to release their own personal frustrations.

My time at the ranch was short-lived, but it felt like a lifetime.

Chapter 36

I WOULD ALWAYS remember this day. The day I left the ranch and returned home to make amends with my parents—July 31, 1967, a few days before my twenty-first birthday on August 3.

I'd been gone for eight months. Eight months of selling my body to strange men. Eight months of living in fear, without understanding the danger I put myself in. Eight months of putting my family through hell.

My hair had grown to an unusually long length for me, but I liked it long. I entwined the blond strands into a neat braid, enhancing the appearance of innocence. I wore a pale blue dress with a Peter Pan collar and beige pumps with a low heel I purchased. No makeup except for some pink lipstick.

Penny was safely tucked away, tamed and camouflaged by my proper, domesticated identity.

When I approached the green split-level on Palmer Court, the first thing I noticed was the absence of Dad's car in the driveway. Maybe that was a good sign. The last time I saw him, he looked like he was losing his shirt at the casino.

I tapped my shaky knuckles against the door.

Mom answered. The glow to her face, that I remembered fondly, had extinguished. She simply stared at me for a moment. Sadness exuded from her blue eyes. She looked tired and wrinkled as if she had aged over the last eight months. No smile to be seen until her brain made the connection that her oldest daughter stood before her.

"Hi, Mom," I muttered softly, unsure what her reaction would be.

When the shock faded, her frown vanished. She smiled and quickly wrapped her arms around me as if she'd never let me go.

She didn't ask me where I was or what I had been doing with myself. She asked only two questions. Was I okay? And will I be staying at home? My answer was yes to both.

Patrick looked thrilled to see me, excitement shown upon his face. The sensitive soul he was cried when he hugged me. Even Lisa embraced me and said she missed me. Missed someone bossing her around.

I wasn't much of a crier or emotional wreck like the rest of them, but my heart felt warm and full again.

I forgot how much I liked to hang out in the kitchen with Mom. We baked chocolate chip cookies. Something that once seemed so mundane now felt precious.

As the chips were added to the flour mixture, she asked me where I had been. I expected that question in a harsher tone than the melancholic melody she used.

I merely replied that I needed to escape for a while and stayed at a friend's house until I was ready to return. I apologized for causing her to worry.

She nodded, sufficiently satisfied. Perhaps she didn't really want to know the truth about how I spent my time away. I certainly didn't want to explain it to her.

Mom cooked up a celebratory meal for dinner, Irish stew and homemade soda bread, one of my favorites.

When Dad came home from work, she greeted him with a big grin, beaming with happiness.

From what Patrick told me, Mom hadn't smiled much since I left.

Dad thought Mom had gone mad, suddenly radiating with glee.

I stepped out from the kitchen, holding my breath. I could barely look Dad in the eye.

When he saw me standing before him with my head lowered, he inched toward me, cane in hand, in a manner that made me question if he'd slug me. Instead, he pulled me in and squeezed me tightly before sobbing. My father, the toughest SOB I knew, cried with tremendous ferocity. Then he apologized to me for losing his temper that night. He swore it would never happen again.

Chasing Serenity

Chapter 37

I HAD SAVED about twenty-five hundred dollars, including the money John let me keep. Lisa and I hopped on a bus that drove us downtown to enjoy a shopping spree together. I bought her some new slacks and a few blouses. She helped me pick out several outfits for Mom and Patrick as well.

We stopped at the garden store. I purchased some seeds, soil, and gardening tools for Mom. I requested they deliver the supplies by the weekend. She would be thrilled!

Lisa questioned where I got so much dough.

I told her I won it gambling. I hoped she and the rest of my family never learned the truth. Lisa was the smart one. Hard to fool her, but she didn't challenge my response.

Although I had this money, it was a security blanket only. I needed a job to make sure I never felt scared or penniless. I couldn't say I picked up credible talents working at the brothel. At least nothing I could tell a prospective boss.

We arrived at the Montgomery. I handed Lisa a few dollars in coins to play the slots to distract her for a while.

I climbed the stairway to see my father first, but he wasn't in his office. Rocky was nowhere to be found either. I approached the front desk where a line of people stood to check-in and waited for several minutes before it was my turn.

The staff wore matching uniforms of burgundy and gray. The brunette's name tag read "Greta." Greta welcomed me to the Montgomery and asked if I was checking in.

"No. I'd like to see Tommy Cavallo if he's available, please."

She eyed me over with her brown eyes beneath chocolate-brown strands.

"May I ask what this is concerning?"

"Please tell him Sadie Meade is here, and I'd like to speak with him."

Greta picked up the phone and requested the operator connect her to Tommy's office. After some back-and-forth conversation with someone on the other end, she asked me to have a seat in the lounge area and wait.

Patience, a weak characteristic I had been trying to improve. Nearly fifteen minutes passed before Tommy himself sauntered toward me, looking snazzy in a black suit and plaid tie.

He smirked at me in a way that made my heart dance. Then he asked how I had been and proceeded to tell me how worried my father had been when I was away.

That surprised me. My father actually opened his heart and inner fears with others outside our family.

After a rather simple response, I got right to the point. "I can really use a job, Tommy."

A surprised look appeared across his face. "What kind of a job? What can you do? Can you type?"

"Sure," I said, completely exaggerating. I could get by on a typewriter. Typing was Lisa's perfected skill, not mine.

He thought for a few minutes. "I believe we need cigarette girls if you don't mind the skimpy outfit." His eyes scanned my body, surely envisioning how I'd look in the scanty attire.

I was truly sick of wearing revealing clothes that made men drool.

"Oh, we need a girl to check coats. The pay may be low, but it's something to start, and maybe you'll work your way up. There are enough opportunities here," he said with great pride, arms outstretched, pleased with the family business he helped manage.

"I'll take it!"

Chapter 38

WORKING AS A coat check girl was slightly boring unless people received the wrong numbered tag and coat. We'd have to take time searching for the right coat, which meant someone else had the wrong numbered tag and coat too. So far after a few weeks, that only happened a few times. I guess I wasn't much of a coat checker, but it gave me something to do, and the pay was better than I expected, plus tips, unless I misplaced someone's coat.

I could tell Dad was in trouble. As much as he worked, he gambled. I spotted him at the roulette wheel and blackjack table. I tried to talk to him about it. He told me a daughter shouldn't get involved in her father's business.

Things at home were bad between Mom and Dad. Dad was hardly ever around. I noticed Rocky stopped by—a lot. I remembered the first day we met Rocky and the Cavallo boys. The way Rocky looked at my mother and greeted her sent sirens blasting off in my head. I shouldn't make assumptions or accusations, but their friendship seemed awfully suspicious.

Besides the issues with my parent's marriage, it felt good to be home again. My nightmares diminished. I could actually sleep. A restful, heavenly kind of sleep. It had been months since I experienced a normal, sound sleep. Hard to relax after being up all night, letting strangers have their way with my body. Meeting Kenny, possibly carrying his demon seed, and watching Jim beat a man to death, was enough to send an ordinary woman over the edge. Ordinary, I wasn't.

One night, I caught Jim monitoring me at the coat check counter. Our eyes met, but he turned away without saying a word. I almost waved to him, but it would probably be best if no one knew we met before. How would I explain that to anyone? *Oh yeah, Jim and I met the night he rescued me from a couple of pimps, who were blackmailing me and tried to rape me, before he split open one of their heads with a baseball bat.* As grateful as I'd always be to Jim for that night, I couldn't act like I knew him.

My shift was about to end on a Friday. My feet ached from standing all day. I noticed Tommy talking with that showgirl. The same one from last year, and her stern facial expressions told the whole world that she was mad.

Although I tried not to stare, I couldn't help observing the two of them. His hand gestures were sharp and highly animated as if he were also angry.

The woman stormed off, arms crossed, shaking her head. Tommy stood still, running his hands through his thick brown mop. His eyes glanced in my direction.

I didn't want him to catch me staring or appearing nosy.

He wandered toward me.

I tried to look busy, fussing with the numbered coat tags. What else could I do in this small room I had been stuck in all day?

"Hi, Sadie! How late are you working tonight?" he asked with a smile, showing off his perfectly straight teeth.

I bit my lip, curious. "I'm just waiting for my replacement."

At that moment, Margie, an eighteen-year-old college student, arrived. She studied by day and worked as a coat check girl a few nights a week to help pay for her school expenses. Nice young girl.

"I have an extra ticket to Sinatra tonight."

My eyes widened.

"You like Sinatra?" he asked.

I smiled, unable to contain my excitement. "Of course, who doesn't?"

"Well, the person I was going to take can't make it. I know it's short notice, but..."

"Yes! I'll go with you!" I didn't wait for him to officially ask me. Frank Sinatra! Who wouldn't want to see him?

"He's playing at Caesars Palace."

128

"Do I have time to go home and change?"

Tommy scanned me over. His eyes drifted past the slight curve of my hip.

I wore a red dress that just about reached my knees, with tall black boots. Coat check girls didn't have a uniform, but we had to dress neatly and wear a name tag.

"You look nice. We don't have time for you to change, but I'll drive you home after the show."

I wasn't thinking of this as a date, but I could certainly do worse in the man department. Tommy was not only sexy and handsome. He was rich.

I couldn't wait to tell my mother about this. I called her at home to explain I'd be late so she wouldn't worry. She was happy to hear I was spending time with Tommy and seeing Sinatra with him. I hoped she didn't get the wrong idea. My coming here with Tommy was a spur of the moment, right place, right time, sort of coincidence.

Maybe I was the first person he saw after whatever argument happened between him and his dancer girlfriend. If another cute girl was working this shift, she might be sitting with Tommy tonight, listening to Frank sing "Fly Me to the Moon" and "That's Life."

After Sinatra's amazing show ended, Tommy told some funny stories on the drive back to my house in his sports car. He had such a great sense of humor and love for his family, especially his brother. I understood why. John was a great person, but Tommy couldn't learn how close John and I became.

As his hot red convertible sped into my driveway, he turned toward me and stared. His eyes looked deeply into mine as if he wanted to kiss me. An expression I was familiar with.

Was I supposed to do or say something other than a genuine "thank you"? I had become programmed to exchange sex with a man for money, favors, and an abortion, so why not Sinatra tickets?

I hoped he didn't know about Penny. Would John have told him after promising me he wouldn't?

"Thank you, Tommy. I really appreciate you thinking of taking me with you tonight."

He nodded as his eyes drifted from mine.

I opened the car door and stepped inside my house, without a kiss or any other type of exchange besides a mere thanks.

Mom stayed up, waiting for me. Did she do that when I was gone for so many months? Waiting and hoping I'd walk through the door. The thought of her fearing for my safety tore at my heart. I would never do that to her again.

Chapter 39

AFTER SEEING SINATRA with Tommy, he made a point to stop by every day at the coat check booth to say hello to me. If I didn't know any better, I'd think I was developing a crush on him. My stomach actually felt jittery whenever he floated by.

It was payday on a warm day in the fall of 1967, and I wasn't scheduled to work. I stopped by the Montgomery to collect my pay for the week. I had the need to strut through the casino to see if my father was gambling while he worked.

Anytime my brother or sister needed something, they came to me to borrow from my "casino winnings." I became the family fixer and provider, a powerful role in the family dynamic.

Patrick started a paper route each morning to make some money for himself.

Lisa was a go-getter in that secretarial pool. She managed to earn a steady job, working for an attorney's office with ties to city hall.

Mom considered finding a job, but Dad was too proud of a man to allow her to work. Frankly, I believed he wanted her home, so he'd know where she was, and to assure she cooked him a nice breakfast and dinner every day. He didn't say those words, but I knew my father.

Lisa once called me selfish. She wasn't wrong, as much as I hated to admit that. To think I was a lot like my father was not entirely good for my self-esteem. My anger for the man ran deep. Although, I learned to tolerate him more since I returned home. Perhaps I saw parts of my father in me that I didn't like about myself.

I breezed my way through the casino. Not much activity occurring. Few patrons around, risking their savings accounts to line the Cavallos' hefty pockets.

Eleven o'clock in the morning and the lounge looked dark as I strolled by, yet the figure of a man I recognized sat alone in a corner booth. He seemed to be hiding from the world.

As I approached him, his shot glass was filled to the rim with whiskey. A bottle of Jameson sat on the table within quick reach of his fingers. The Jameson made me think of Kenny and the whiskey he poured down my throat on that awful day I sometimes still had nightmares about.

Tommy sat back, head leaning against the brown-paneled wall, legs and feet up, lying across the red cushion of the booth. He poured a shot of whiskey down his throat with ease.

I didn't have to say a word. He asked me to join him.

I sat on the opposite side of the booth.

He stood up, walked behind the bar, and grabbed me a glass.

My hand waved, stopping him. "I don't drink that stuff," I said.

"What's your poison?"

It was eleven o'clock in the morning. Granted, I had no plans on my day off, but getting trashed this early never occurred to me. One drink would be okay, so he didn't drink alone.

His eyes were glazed over and rather sullen. His hair, recently cut, but he had a tousled look as if his hands had been running through the thick brown strands.

"Vodka, neat," I requested.

He shrugged and looked around the bar, eventually finding Smirnoff among the many bottles lined up in rows.

When he returned to the table, he sat next to me, pushing my body toward the wall, our outer thighs touching.

"What's eating you?" I asked.

He simply poured, ignoring my question.

"Is it that girl?"

"What girl?" he asked as if he were absolutely clueless I had spotted him with that showgirl the night we saw Sinatra.

"I've seen you with one of the dancers in the show."

"Nah, that wasn't anything serious."

He didn't flinch when I mentioned her. I guess she wasn't his girlfriend. Just a lover maybe. I slammed back the shot of vodka.

Tommy snickered, surprised I knew how to drink like that.

"If it's not about a girl, why are you drinking like this in the morning?"

He sucked down another shot before he considered responding. "Pop had to bring in a business partner. He needed money for the expansions we're making here. We have to stay competitive. Too much competition with the hotels and entertainment along the Strip."

He filled both of our glasses again. "He wants the entire hotel decor to have a European look, representing England, Ireland, and Scotland to match the flags hanging in the lobby. It will cost a lot more dough than expected."

I listened, still unsure why he looked so unhappy. "Why are you concerned if your partners are fronting the money?"

"These guys from Philly are pretty demanding. They have a lot to say. And they have a lot of power behind them."

He stopped talking and kept drinking.

I managed to keep up with him on my fourth vodka shot, feeling pretty good now. My head was woozy though.

His eyelids lowered. A solemn look took over his chiseled features. I brushed the top of his hair with my fingers then gingerly trailed downward.

He groaned as my hands gently massaged the nape of his neck, appreciating the pressure against tense muscles. He started to relax to the point where his eyes closed as if he'd fall asleep right there in the booth.

I nudged his shoulder. "You can't fall asleep here, Tommy. No more whiskey, okay?"

"I'll go upstairs and sleep it off."

"Upstairs?"

"Yeah, there's a suite I use when I'm here late and need to rest." He flashed me the gold key from his pocket before attempting to stand with no luck.

"Let me help you," I offered, but my legs were a bit wobbly too. I hadn't had that much to drink in a while. Not since the night Kenny drowned me with booze in that filthy motel room.

Fortunately, the casino was fairly empty. Rocky wouldn't appreciate seeing his son sloshed before noon. Surprisingly, he managed to stay on his feet okay, even though he wobbled a bit around the slot machines.

We staggered to the elevators. The elevator operator acknowledged Tommy's presence, despite his physical condition. He pressed the button, knowing which floor to let us off.

Mere moments passed before we entered the corner suite on the twentieth floor without anyone in management spotting us. The suite was similar to the one Penny met John in a couple of months back. The curtains were closed so darkness filled the room, but the bed had been made.

Tommy found his way to the king-size bed and flopped his body down, removing the crisp white dress shirt, exposing his muscular build with definition in his arms and abs.

"Wow, how did your arms get so...so huge?" My big mouth worked in overdrive. If only I could think without speaking my thoughts.

He smiled confidently, knowing he had a sexy, solid body. "The boxing gym. Weights."

"You're a fighter?"

"Damn straight." He let out some punches into the air, jumped off the bed, then proceeded to approach me, pretending to give me a one-two move across my chin.

All I could manage was a silly schoolgirl giggle.

"Your hair looks nice long," he said before delicately playing with my blond locks. Then he touched my chin with his thick fingers and pulled me in for a kiss.

Maybe it was the alcohol. Maybe it was his fantastic manly physique. Maybe it was the smoldering erotic kiss. God, he was a great kisser.

His hands found their way around my body, caressing and squeezing. He knew exactly where to touch.

I became putty in his firm grip, allowing him to tear off my clothes. My skin tingled from his strokes.

I couldn't wait to feel what swelled within his slacks. With expert hands, I reached inside, satisfying him with delicate tugs. I was not disappointed with my findings.

His arms embraced my petite body, pulling me off the ground and carrying me to the bed. It had been so long since a man tried to please *me* in bed. That was *my* job, making sure the customer had a pleasurable experience. They never thought about me or my needs and desires. Why would they? They paid for a service by the minute.

As drunk as Tommy might have been, the sensations his mouth, tongue, and large instrument offered sent me swirling—multiple times.

He passed out afterward. He couldn't possibly have anything left in him after the amount of whiskey consumed and the energy burned up on me in this bed.

I nodded off myself, albeit briefly.

How many women had he brought up here? I wondered quietly. Thinking about that was one thing. I'd never ask him. It could never compete with the amount of men I pleased at the ranch.

When I awoke, Tommy was still out cold. I felt the need to check his neck for a pulse. He laid so still without a sound or a breath leaving his lips. I never killed a man from incredible sex before.

He let out a soft snore.

My head was still a little foggy from the vodka. I slipped out of the bed, flung my clothes back on, and left the suite before he woke.

Chapter 40

THE NEXT DAY, Tommy strolled into the coat check room while my back was turned. I jumped out of my skin when I bumped into him inside this small space.

My heart fluttered at the sight of his rugged good looks and sexy smile. I began to fantasize rolling beneath the sheets with him again. Tommy was a magnificent lover when drunk. I couldn't help but wonder if his performance magnified when sober.

"Hey. You took off yesterday." His voice sounded soft, practically whispering.

I avoided eye contact with him and shrugged my shoulders, playing it cool.

"If I was out of line, I'm sorry. I'd hate for you to think I took advantage of you."

Ha! If he only knew that maybe I took advantage of him.

"I didn't think that, Tommy. Look, it's complicated. You own this place, and I'm just a coat check girl. My father works here. I don't want people talking." Really, I didn't care about other people and the infamous grapevine.

"I was a little drunk and stressed."

"Yes, you were." I chuckled.

"I didn't want you to be upset with me, or think..."

"Think what?" Jeez, it was just sex. Wild, impetuous, mind-blowing sex. Maybe he was used to girls making a big deal about sex. Did he think I'd expect a marriage proposal? I tried not to roll my eyes in front of him as these thoughts churned through my brain. At least I wasn't speaking my thoughts aloud as I often did.

He shook his head. "I don't know. You held your booze better than me."

"Well, you had a head start. Not sure how long you were drinking before I saw you."

"So we're okay?"

"Of course." I managed a smile.

Since that afternoon in Tommy's suite, he made a point to speak with me every day I worked in the coat check room. He hadn't asked me to see another show with him, or any version of a date. But I'd like to think we were friends.

Chapter 41

THE HOTEL STAFF worked vigorously to assist in setting up the banquet hall for a ceremonial event for law enforcement. I was asked to work extra hours to help wherever needed. Tommy asked me personally to work. The extra money was welcome.

The coat check room would certainly be busy later on. Before guests arrived, he wanted me to help set up the tables in the hall. It was something different to do than tagging and hanging expensive coats and hats.

I asked Tommy if Patrick could work parking cars. He was driving Dad's car long before he had an actual license, so he acquired a lot of practice. Of course, since this was an event for law enforcement, I suggested Patrick bring his license with him, just in case.

Patrick took a shine to Tommy and his magnanimous presence. Tommy was attentive and gracious with him. Attention our father hadn't taken the time to give him. Dad remained upstairs, watching from the glass rooms high above the crowd, managing security detail.

Personally, I was grateful to Tommy for letting Patrick help tonight. I threw him a wink and a smile when Patrick arrived and greeted Tommy with a handshake.

I started to see Tommy differently, I must admit. Maybe my feelings were growing beyond a casual friendship. I toyed with him, using my feminine charms. Maybe Penny began to surface. After all, she was a part of me. I couldn't shut her off completely.

Everyone was working hard tonight. The cooks were cooking. Waiters were taking orders. Cigarette girls were selling tobacco products. And I was checking coats. Margie called in sick. I worked the coat room alone, and a lengthy line had formed with people waiting to check their items.

My arms and legs throbbed. My back screamed for a bed to lie down on.

The end of the long line of people with coats neared. My eyes glanced upward at a colored couple with coats and a hat to check. The man's dark brown eyes stared steadily at me.

The connection was made.

He recognized me without the heavily applied makeup and seedy outfits. Hank, one of the possible candidates for impregnating me a few months ago, stood before me.

When our eyes met, I had difficulty looking away.

So did he.

The woman at his side kindly asked me for her coat tag, breaking the silence and awkward moment.

Hank gazed at my name tag. "Thank you, *Sadie*," he said with a sincere smile, not acknowledging the fact that he knew every inch of my body, and I knew his—very well.

I noticed his uniform and caught a glimpse of his wedding ring. Hank, my regular at the ranch, was a cop. A married cop.

Although I moved on to the next couple in line, I couldn't help but watch Hank dash off with his wife. She was a very pretty lady, dressed elegantly in a turquoise dress, and seemingly proud to be on her husband's arm.

I took a much-needed break and stood outside the coat room, leaning against the counter.

Tommy stopped by, offering me a chair to sit. My body appeared weary enough for him to sense my exhaustion.

My hands continued to rub the lower part of my back. I must look a fright since he went out of his way to find me that chair to rest my aching parts. But I was so happy to sit, even for a brief moment. The patrons who dropped off coats would soon return to retrieve them at the end of the ceremony. I'd be busy again and back on my feet.

"I was outside with your brother. He did a good job helping the valets. No dents or damages yet," he teased with a laugh. "Seems like a good kid. Smart too."

His fingers firmly massaged my neck, relieving some of the tension in my tender muscles.

"He is a good kid," I replied.

"You held your own in here, considering how busy it was. Sorry Margie couldn't make it tonight."

I managed a smile.

As the event concluded, people began leaving the banquet hall, approaching either the bar, the casino, or the coat check counter. The rush and madness continued.

Most people stuck around, which was what Tommy and Rocky hoped. Stay and gamble. Just because they were cops didn't mean they couldn't be entertained by some cards or a roll of the dice.

The counter slowed down enough for me to sit.

My eyes wandered around for Hank. His coat hung next to his wife's. All those nights he came to see me, he never mentioned a wife or his job. Not that he owed me any of that information.

Another hour passed. Every so often, a steady surge of guests stood before me to claim their coats. The next quiet moment I had was when Hank returned with his tickets and not his wife.

He placed the stubs on the counter for me.

As I reached for the tags, he rested his hand on top of mine. It was difficult to look at him. I wanted to leave Penny and her world behind me. Hank no longer belonged in my world.

"Is Sadie your real name?" he asked.

"Is Hank yours?" I rebutted a bit angrily.

He held out his hand for me to shake. "Officer Henry Dubois, but my friends call me Hank."

I accepted his hand. "Sadie." No need to tell him my last name.

He cleared his throat and looked around the area to ensure no one was within earshot. "When I learned you left the ranch a few months ago, a part of me was glad you retired."

"A part of you was glad? What about the other part?" My jaw stiffened when I asked.

His dark eyes drifted down. Silence filled the space between us.

"You have a lovely wife, Hank," I said with bitterness lurking in my tone.

"You sound angry."

"I retired from that life. Penny doesn't exist anymore. Besides, what's a cop doing visiting a ranch?" I asked softly, hoping no one around could hear our discussion.

"I wasn't committing a crime. Neither were you."

"So who's your girl now? Seeing Jo Jo again?" I asked, although it shouldn't matter. My big mouth blurted my thoughts aloud before I had time to stop myself.

Hank smiled without offering a response.

I handed him two coats and a hat.

"It was a pleasure meeting you tonight, *Sadie*." His pearly whites showed through his brief wavering smile as he placed a few singles in the tip jar for me.

Would my past come back to haunt me? Hank was someone I saw often at the ranch. For all I knew, other johns could've come here and seen me as "Sadie." Maybe they thought I looked familiar but didn't recognize the real me beneath the painted face and lingerie. Would I have recognized them? Penny didn't study their faces. It was business. Nothing personal. Looking into their eyes and heart could have made it personal. There was no room for feelings or schoolgirl crushes on those men.

Hank was different. I considered him a friend.

Chapter 42

EVER SINCE I saw Hank that night at the Montgomery, I couldn't help but pay more attention to the people around me. I'd watch them, but avoided eye contact directly.

I thought I recognized a couple of men who strode into the Belle Maiden, but I wasn't sure. Maybe they were there to see one of the other girls. Lots of men switched things up. Maybe they chose Monique one night then Lana the next time. Not many were faithful to one particular girl, like Hank was with me. Using the word "faithful" to describe a married man in a whorehouse was comical.

Distracted by these lurid dreams, I made more errors tagging coats and handed out the incorrect numbered tags to guests. I couldn't imagine Tommy or Rocky firing me over it. I always found the customers' coats. Nothing was ever stolen or misplaced for very long.

Since I started working here, Dad spent less time in the casino. He also didn't hang around here on his days off. Perhaps knowing I might witness him rolling the dice struck a nerve. Hopefully, he was saving his money now in lieu of blowing it on the fantasy of luck.

Margie arrived to relieve me. Time to head upstairs to the accounting department to collect my paycheck for the week.

I promised Patrick I'd give him money for drama class. My brother really liked the arts, and he was good at it. Much more talented in music, theater, and poetry than athletics. My father didn't support him in these activities, so I did. Dad wasn't around much to notice how Patrick spent his time.

The elevators in this place flew up and down pretty quickly. As I returned to the main lobby, the doors opened, and two clearly recognizable faces entered. When they saw me, I froze. The remaining guests on the elevator exited to the lobby. That was when he pushed his way in, trapping me in the corner.

Kenny shot an icy glare through cold black eyes with one hand cuffed firmly around Kitty's arm. I could see him squeezing her to the point of bruises appearing soon enough. His body leaned against me, pinning me to the cool steel of the elevator. He released Kitty from his grasp. His face rammed against mine, drooling with contempt.

Was the elevator operator on his break? I wondered.

"I ought to kill you right now for murdering my boy, Junior, you little bitch!" His hands took hold of my neck, and he began to strangle me until he noticed my name tag. "Hmm. *Sadie*, is it?"

I coughed and gasped for air when he released his secure grip.

With each step he took, he favored his left leg, limping. Was this the result from the beatdown Jim gave him? Good, I thought. But he blamed *me* for his injuries and his friend's death. Visions of Jim cracking that man's head open surged through my mind. So much blood. My hands began to tremble. My jittery fingers raised, and I pushed him away.

Kenny didn't like that. He slapped my face hard enough to leave a mark.

"Baby, stop. Leave her alone. You don't want to get arrested again," Kitty said. Her voice sounded rattled, yet calm.

Somehow Kitty knew what to say to make him back off. She seemed twitchy, skittish. Her eyes looked sad, glazed-over, and unfocused. I wished she stayed away from this maniac. I warned her. I wanted to help her break free from Kenny, but she had to make that leap on her own, like I did. Of course, John and Jim helped me. If it weren't for them, my life might have turned out differently. Maybe I'd be dead.

"I know where to find you now, *Penny*." He emphasized that name, reminding me of who I was to him, belittling me, controlling me, creating terror from deep within me. I knew his threat was real.

The doors opened and a family of four stepped onto the elevator on floor nine.

I jumped off as quickly as possible.

Kenny and Kitty remained on the elevator.

Kitty's sad eyes gazed upon me, seemingly begging for help without a word uttered.

Kenny pointed to his eyes then pointed his fingers at me as the elevator door closed. He'd be watching me now.

I was no longer safe here.

Chapter 43

KENNY DISCOVERED MY real first name. All he had to do was ask another employee for Sadie's last name. I suspected Kenny could be despicably resourceful. Maybe I gave him too much credit. If he had half a brain, he could tell someone how much I helped him, and he wanted to reward me with a generous tip if only he knew my last name. Any worker here would fall for that line and offer him as much information about me as they could.

My body stood as still as a calm summer day, until the rickety sound of a maid's cart startled me enough to jump, feeling panicked. I had to get out of this place! The stairwell was my only way out of the hotel since I feared using the elevator. My hands gripped the railing as I anxiously hobbled back down to the lobby. Since Kenny learned my name, he could harm my family or me. Meade was a common last name, but not too common for him to locate me.

What exactly could Kenny do to me? He couldn't force me to work for him anymore. I wasn't some lonely girl without a place to live, but he was dangerously unpredictable.

He could beat me.

Rape me.

Murder me.

Then a more frightening notion came to light. He might harm my family solely to make me suffer. Oh God, what a horrendous thought! Making me watch him rape my mother or sister. What if he murdered Patrick or Dad as payback for Junior's death?

I enjoyed working at the Montgomery, but I shouldn't work here anymore. I couldn't be anywhere Kenny might find me. How could I return to my home with my family? People I loved might suffer because of my history with that psychopath.

My head spun viciously. Nausea set in like on my flight from Boston to Vegas. After reaching the lobby floor, my legs froze. The walls within the spacious area began to close in. The people and the furniture spiraled around in continuous circles. I couldn't catch my breath.

Then darkness emerged, conquering my fragile stability.

Chapter 44

VOICES WERE HEARD in frantic tones.

A woman's voice echoed that she called for an ambulance.

I felt someone's hand brush against my forehead. My eyes flew open. Fingers were running through my blond strands. As my vision returned, I was able to focus on Tommy, wearing a worried look, staring down at me.

I laid on the lobby floor with my head in Tommy's lap. He was speaking, but my hearing hadn't returned in full quite yet.

My brain shifted to overdrive, reorganizing my thoughts. Memories of Kenny and Kitty came to mind. That wasn't a nightmare. Kenny found me and threatened me. How quickly he forgot about the four thousand I gave him to leave me alone. Jim murdered his friend and injured him. All bets were off. Desperation strangled my rational judgment. Another one of my panic attacks must have caused me to faint.

I lifted my head and asked Tommy to help me stand.

"Sadie, stay still. Help is on the way."

I knew I didn't need help. Not by a doctor. I needed a hit man. I needed Jim. "I'm fine, Tommy," I said before leaning against his muscular arm to steady myself. He held on to me, ensuring I was stable before releasing me.

"What happened? Why would you faint? Do you want me to call your father?" So many questions spewing from his mouth added to my confusion.

The only answer I could give him left my lips. The only answer that would make sense. Maybe the only answer that could somehow protect me.

"I'm pregnant."

I couldn't quite translate that unfamiliar, anxious look on his face. Was it an *oh shit, am I the father* look? Or was he trying to remember how long ago we had sweltering, passionate sex upstairs in his room? Did he remember he neglected to wear a condom? Those thoughts would still lead to the *oh shit, am I the father* question that must be thrashing about in his brain.

Chapter 45

WHY DID I tell such a tale? Yes, I was desperate and terrified of what Kenny might do to me. The look in his eyes said enough. He'd harass me until I either returned as Penny to work for him, paid him a boatload of money, or I was dead.

I didn't want to bring John into any of this. He did enough for me. Kenny was *my* problem. A problem I now involved Tommy in.

Tommy just stared at me at first, then without a word uttered, he prodded me to the elevator at a careful pace. I took a step back before entering, making sure there was no sign of Kenny or Kitty. There must be a john in one of the rooms, waiting for Kitty to work her magic while Kenny snapped illicit pictures.

Tommy nudged me inside the elevator, and we rode upward to the twentieth floor. The same floor we stopped at the night he was drunk. The night we lost all inhibitions and ravished each other with blazing intensity.

Yes, it was the same room in the corner at the end of the hall. The day shined brighter than the last time we were here. The drapes were open to display an incredible sunny view of the Strip. I couldn't let the beauty of this room distract me from the conversation I was about to have.

He kept staring at me. Then the pacing across the dark green carpet began. He reached inside a drawer and pulled out a bottle of Jameson, then searched for a glass. When one couldn't be found, he drank directly from the bottle, a long, hard slug.

"Are you sure? That you're...uh..." He pointed to my stomach. "A doctor confirmed this?"

I instinctively rubbed my belly with both hands. "Yes."

He appeared distressed, hands on hips then back to the bottle. "You know, I have to ask you…was there anybody else? Besides me, I mean?"

I shook my head back and forth. God, when did I become such a good liar? How long could I keep up this wicked hustle?

"Were you going to tell me?"

"I wasn't sure how. It's not like we were dating."

"Well, you said it was complicated between us because I own the hotel and your father works here." He studied my every movement, holding on to my stomach as if I'd blow a baby out of me at that very moment. "Here, sit down. I mean, you just passed out. Did you hurt yourself from that fall?"

"You look like *you're* going to pass out, Tommy. I'll be fine. Banged my head a little," I said cleverly, realizing the strike Kenny gave me across the face might bruise. I sat beside him, tenderly touching his hand.

"What are we going to do now?" he asked. His concern was evident, shown through his somber gray eyes and curved brows that softened when he looked me square in the eye.

"We're going to be parents, Tommy. What do you think we should do?"

Chapter 46

THE FIRST THING Tommy and I discussed was explaining to our folks the shocking news that they would be grandparents next summer. He wanted to tell Rocky himself first. He had a good relationship with his pop, although Rocky had this untamed desire to control Tommy's life.

Telling my parents would be a struggle, and I wasn't ready to tell them the big news because it was a big lie.

I had no idea how Tommy's conversation went with Rocky. But Tommy came to my house, and in front of my parents, he handed me a lovely round diamond ring in an eighteen-karat, white-gold setting.

He didn't propose on bended knee. We sat across each other at the dining room table, not the most romantic moment. He simply asked with a wavering eye, "Will you marry me, Sadie?"

"Yes," was my sharp reply. There was an awkward hug between us afterward. The kind of hug you'd give your pal.

Mom was surprised yet happy. So were Lisa and Patrick.

Dad grunted suspiciously. "I had no idea you and my daughter were dating. When did this start?"

"Dad, please. We didn't advertise it," I responded with a harsh tone.

"Oh, I knew this was possible after you brought Sadie to see Frank Sinatra!" Mom chimed in.

Dad glanced at Mom as if she were insane.

"Now we have a wedding to plan!" Mom added, beaming with enthusiasm.

Dad appeared nervous. The wheels in his balding head were turning, probably thinking about how much a wedding would cost him.

I neglected to tell them the facade of becoming grandparents. I didn't have the heart, but I'd have to say something eventually.

Tommy didn't want me to work anymore. Because I passed out in the middle of the lobby, he thought the stress of the pregnancy and standing on my feet in the coat check room all day would be overwhelming.

I didn't argue with him.

If my scheme to avoid Kenny was to be successful, I couldn't work at the Montgomery.

Our wedding was planned for February 3, 1968. A simple service at St. Francis Church, followed by dinner in one of the banquet halls at the Montgomery. We could have whatever style wedding we chose at the Montgomery. I hated taking a step inside the hotel, afraid to run into anyone from Penny's world, especially Kenny. He could be there right now, asking questions about me.

February 3 was a couple of months away. A typical pregnant woman would be showing evidence of a baby by then. I also needed to separate myself from my family at their house, in case Kenny found my home address. Once Tommy and I were married, I'd change my name to Cavallo, so Kenny might have difficulty finding me. At least that was my intention.

Given the circumstances of our engagement, I told Tommy there was no reason for an engagement party or a notice in the newspaper. His father was insanely rich. Wealthy people often broadcasted celebratory events occurring in their glamorous lives. I wasn't prepared for that. Tommy released a breath of relief. No announcements.

Rocky's wedding present was a new house near the Vegas Strip. As generous as his gift was, I suggested to Tommy that we move a little farther from the Strip. Somewhere I'd feel safe with a baby and less noisy. Also, somewhere Kenny would not find me, but naturally, I never revealed that tidbit. I added the Strip could entice undesirable people, and that was really no place for a baby to grow up safely. Tommy agreed with my thought—for the baby's sake.

A good liar and master manipulator. New talents of mine.

I moved into the Cavallo mansion until our new house in Henderson was ready for us to live in.

My mother was not thrilled that I chose to live with Tommy before the wedding. I still hadn't told my parents I was "pregnant."

There was definitely an attraction between Tommy and me. Despite the "pregnancy" and the fact that we weren't in love, our lust for sex was fierce. I could keep up with him in every insatiable aspect.

We hadn't told anyone besides his pop about the bundle of joy expected in July. I allowed him to believe I felt too ashamed to tell my parents I got knocked up before the wedding.

He scoffed when I said that.

If he only knew my virtue was long gone, a thousand times over at least.

Chapter 47

TOMMY BOUGHT ME a 1967 Ford Galaxie 500. I hadn't driven a car much since we moved to the desert, except for that one night with Phil. I wondered how Phil was momentarily. Thoughts of my love for Mickey Quinn dissipated as well. My life prior to the Belle Maiden felt like a completely different existence, led by a stranger.

Tommy took me out for a couple of test-drives. He thought about trading the car in and finding me a driver instead. Yes, my driving was that horrendous. I begged him to let me keep the car and practice. He didn't want me driving alone in my condition. I wasn't entirely sure if he cared about *my* safety or the baby's.

He arranged for a line of credit at J. C. Penney and Sears, and added my name to his accounts. I could walk in there at any time, purchase whatever I wanted, and the clerks would add the dollar amount to Tommy's account. He would pay the bills off for me each month.

For Christmas, my whole family received expensive gifts from Tommy and me from these beautiful department stores. A girl could get used to this life.

Dad didn't appear too upset about the marriage after we gave him tickets to a Raiders game on the fifty-yard line. A game in which they were playing the Patriots. He was beyond thrilled.

They all realized the benefits of my marrying into money. So did I.

We celebrated Christmas as one family at Rocky's house. The Meades and Cavallos breaking bread together. I liked this future I created. But unless I actually became pregnant, I needed to endure an accident in which the baby wouldn't survive.

I was really excited to see my friend, John. I hadn't visited him since our engagement was announced.

When John's chair soared through the house, excitement bubbled within me. I raced toward him, but he made no eye contact with me, intentionally turning his head in the opposite direction. The circumstances of our friendship were certainly unique. Was he playing down our alliance, attempting to keep my mischievous deeds a secret? He and Tommy were very close. My mind deviated to an ugly state. Was he angry about the upcoming wedding? With me?

I approached him with a glass of champagne in preparation of Rocky's toast.

John's eyes stared me down as if he were ashamed. He didn't look at me that way when I introduced him to Penny the night I showed up at his hotel room in Kitty's place. He didn't look at me like this when I confessed to having an abortion, or when I needed money to pay off Kenny. Why glare at me with immense contempt?

Tommy was distracted with a phone call from the Montgomery, a part of his typical routine as a hotel manager.

While everyone else discussed the wedding menu and guest list, I followed John down the hallway to the den. He parked his chair in front of the window that overlooked the colorful gardens and fruit trees. For privacy, I closed the door of the room and handed John some paper and a pen, knowing he had something to say to me.

His chair swirled around to avoid me. He was definitely angry.

I grabbed the handles of his wheelchair to keep him steady and asked him point-blank why he was upset.

"You're lying!" He angrily scribbled across the paper.

Maybe my eyes gave it away. Lying to John was much harder to do, although I tried. "What am I lying about, John?"

"He's marrying you because you're pregnant. That's a lie!" he stammered in his own muddied voice.

I shook my head, unsure if my demeanor was convincing. I thought I had my devious skills down pat, but lying to John was difficult.

John wrote, "Dr. Clark told me that butcher who terminated your pregnancy damaged your body. The odds of you being pregnant this soon are slim. Maybe there were other men. Don't make my brother marry you out of some false sense of obligation. If you want money, I'll give you money, but don't force Tommy into marriage."

His look was cold and bitter instead of his usual sweet, caring way. He was protecting Tommy now. Protecting him from me. The fact that he knew about Penny changed our friendship. He no longer trusted me. But I couldn't share this lie with anyone. Not even with John.

"I don't want your money, John. Tommy is the only man I slept with since I left the ranch," which wasn't a fib. I avoided answering the question about really being pregnant. I'd only lie to him. I had to lie now, and I needed to be convincing. "Did you tell Tommy about…Penny?"

John shook his head in frustration and wrote that he kept his promises. He didn't have to keep that secret anymore. If Tommy knew about my life as Penny, he might cancel the wedding. John tore up the papers with his handwriting on it and handed me the pieces to discard. Then he rolled away.

Chapter 48

TOMMY APPEARED IRRITATED because I still hadn't told my family I was pregnant. Lying to him was strenuous enough. Buying baby clothes to act like an excited, expectant mother was another challenge. There was no baby.

My lies were overpowering me, but I needed to get through Christmas and the wedding to legitimize my marriage to Tommy.

The holidays were stressful, especially knowing John could blow me out of the water. I hoped to rekindle my friendship with him again. I wouldn't forget how good John was to me when I needed him.

Because our sex life was pretty damn amazing, Tommy and I began to actually date. It seemed he was making an effort to get to know me better. Our relationship was being built totally backward.

Tommy made plans for us on New Year's Eve day. 1968 was upon us, and I was learning more about my fiancé.

Evel Knievel, a fearless daredevil, prepared for a hair-raising stunt with his motorcycle. Tommy ensured we were front and center for the action. He was really excited about seeing this celebrity.

This risk-taker planned to jump over the water fountains at Caesars Palace! Tommy told me the jump was well over one hundred feet.

There was a lot of fanfare about this crazy act. People were filming the crowd, attempting to capture the jump on camera. Tommy and I waved into one of the cameras, hoping we'd be seen on television. We enjoyed ourselves and had a lot of laughs while we waited for the big moment.

The sound of his engine roared before Knievel, dressed in red, white, and blue, gathered up sufficient speed as he raced toward the long ramp in front of the fountains.

I held my breath, watching his bike, as if in slow motion, lift off the ramp and fly through the air.

The crowd gasped. Screams were soon heard.

We couldn't see how he landed on the other side. Tommy and I raced through the maze of people to discover Knievel had landed awkwardly. The man had slipped off his bike and tumbled across the parking lot next door at the Dunes.

We watched as medics tended to the injured man, who laid still on the ground. He was lucky to be alive, but it looked like he was in rough shape.

I thought for sure I witnessed a man die before my eyes for the second time in my life.

After the new year began, Tommy introduced me to a few friends from college and their girlfriends. Another opportunity to get to know Tommy better, through the eyes of his friends. Still in awe of Knievel's life-threatening jump, he bragged about seeing the incident in person, watching the man's broken body roll across the pavement. Tommy was quite a storyteller, instigating a gasp by everyone who had already watched the event on the evening news. Somehow, his charismatic mannerisms always amplified a story, no matter the actual level of excitement.

Tommy's friends were great and acted thrilled to meet me. However, I didn't seem to fit in well with the women for some reason. They'd smile and nod in my direction, but I obviously wasn't welcome into their clique.

Veronica, the exotic-looking ringleader of the women in this circle, intentionally touched Tommy in an intimate way. I caught a strange glimpse between them as if they had history. Lovers during their college days maybe. An eerie vibe gnawed at my gut. My trusted intuition screamed in my ear.

This Veronica woman wanted Tommy, judging by the way her sultry brown eyes constantly gazed upon him.

If I attempted to speak, Veronica ignored me as if I were invisible. The other girls followed her lead. She actually talked over me, bragging about collaborating with Tommy to promote the Montgomery since she earned a college degree in marketing. This woman was trouble. Smart. Beautiful. Career-oriented. A threat to my upcoming nuptials.

Veronica sashayed to the ladies' room, swiveling her shapely hips like the swing of a pendulum.

I followed her.

While she was in the stall, I washed my hands and refreshed the frisky crimson shade of lipstick against my lips until she stepped out toward the sink, ignoring my presence completely.

With good intention, I faked a tumble in my six-inch heels and spilled my dirty martini over her silk dress.

"You stupid child! Look what you've done!" she screamed as the gin and olive juice combination drenched the white silk across her lower half as if she peed herself.

"Oh, I'm so clumsy." My smirk grew, unable to control that delightful feeling of payback.

Steam fizzled from her ears as she released another shriek of irritation, staring down at the ruined fabric. "I don't know what Tommy sees in you!"

"I suggest you show some respect, Veronica. I'm about to become Mrs. Thomas Cavallo, and I'll have his ear on some business decisions." I completely exaggerated, but my potent advice was clear.

My smile remained plastered as I made strides with the other girls in the group through our fascinating dinner conversation about wedding plans, while the men talked business. Veronica sat quietly with her mink stole atop her lap, hiding the embarrassing stain that wrinkled the sheer fabric.

The drive home turned into a reenactment of World War II. Tommy and I argued hard about Veronica while Johnny Cash was calling June Carter a big-mouthed woman in the popular "Long-Legged Guitar Pickin' Man" tune.

Tommy insisted Veronica had only been a friend, now involved with his buddy, Jude, and that nothing ever happened between them.

I strongly recommended he hire someone else to manage the ad campaign for the hotel, or he'd be forced to listen to my constant nagging.

According to Tommy, there was another ad agency in the running for the job. Ultimately, he hired Veronica's competition. I would never know for certain if this other agency was a better choice, or if he wanted to prevent my continual badgering.

Chapter 49

WITH JOHN ONTO me, I needed some insurance. Someone to back up my claim about being pregnant and losing the baby. If Tommy ever learned I wasn't pregnant, I'd be back at square one, minus a job. At least my square one initially included a paycheck.

I found Dr. Rudolph Ivanov in the phone book. His office wasn't too far away. Despite my miserable driving skills, I managed to locate his establishment. The woman at his office supplied very good directions.

Dr. Ivanov, a.k.a. "the doc" from the Belle Maiden.

When I arrived, several women were waiting to be seen. I approached a woman with a short dark bob, maybe in her thirties, sitting at the reception desk and drinking a steaming cup of coffee.

"Name?" she asked.

"I don't have an appointment, but I need to see Dr. Ivanov today."

"Are you a patient?"

"Yes."

"Name?"

Now how do I answer such a simple question? He only knew me as Penny. No last name.

"Honey, I need your name."

"Penny…Smith."

The woman wrote down my name and asked me to have a seat. She explained the doc was very busy today, and without an appointment scheduled, he might not have time to see me.

To occupy my time while waiting, I read *Reader's Digest*, then found various objects in the hidden pictures puzzle in a *Highlights* magazine. *Good Housekeeping* published a quiz to see how good of a housekeeper I was. My score reflected the same ranking as the type of driver I was. I should read this magazine more often to sharpen up my wifely duties since I'd be married soon.

I should ask Mom to show me how to make some of her best recipes. I must admit, I wasn't thinking about being a married woman. I needed to think about my life as Tommy's wife now.

Women came and went into the doc's office. I had been waiting a long time. Long enough for my patience to wear thin. Big deal, I didn't have an appointment. I needed to see him today.

I charged up to the woman on the phone and chimed the silver bell for service. She held up her index finger, asking me to wait. I continued to ring the bell until she resentfully asked the person on the line to hold.

"Miss, you need to wait your turn." She took the bell and placed it behind the counter, out of my reach.

"I need you to give the doc a message for me. You tell him Penny is here. I'm a friend of Doris and Chip's. He'll know who I am."

"Miss, I told you he's very busy today. You may not be able to see him at all."

"Well, if you tell him I'm Doris and Chip's friend, I know he'll see me." My voice sounded confident, firm, and demanding. I was not leaving without seeing him today, even if I stalked the parking lot for him.

The woman stood up and marched through the door, which I imagined led to the doc's office. She disappeared for a few minutes. When she returned, her expression looked stern. Her lips were squeezed tightly, brows curved inward. "Right this way, friend of *Doris and Chip*." She punctuated their names heavily. Attitude. I liked her.

I followed her to a smoky office with an ornate desk made of dark wood. Shelves filled with many thick books and an encyclopedia collection were built into the wall. Stacks of paper were piled high atop the desk. File cabinet drawers were open with several folders sitting on top. The doc wasn't a very neat or organized man.

He kept me waiting a good ten minutes before he entered. Still fat and bald with a cigar glued between his teeth.

"Penny?" He gave me a good scan as if he didn't recognize me in my adorable mini tent dress with pink and orange vertical stripes. A different look than laying naked on a table for him every Friday. "My girl out front told me you were here. Last I heard, you left the Belle Maiden. What brings you by? This couldn't wait until Friday's appointment at the ranch?"

"I didn't return to the ranch, Doc. I'm here for another matter. I hope you'll help me."

He nodded. "I can try." He lifted some folders from his chair onto the desk, so he could plop his heavyset body down in his seat to face me.

"I want my medical records. In particular, the one that showed I was pregnant."

"That I can do."

"Suppose I need that record to be adjusted?"

His brows raised. "Adjusted? What exactly are you asking?"

"You must know my real name is not Penny."

He nodded without uttering a sound.

"I need that record to show my real name and a date change."

"A date change?" A hearty gasp escaped, displaying his surprise and confusion with my request.

"Yes, instead of my records showing I was pregnant in June. It needs to show I was pregnant in October."

He shook his head at me. "Why would you ask me to do that?" His finger tapped his chin. "No, wait. I don't think you should tell me anything more."

Hmm, plausible deniability. "Well, what if you gave me a medical record without a date or a name on it with all the specifics about that pregnancy, and I added in those extra details myself?"

"You're asking me to lie within medical records." He shook his head, lowering his eyes. Then he glared at me as if I asked something completely immoral of him. The man who treated the women at the Belle Maiden was also a regular customer. He'd gone through all the women there. Even me.

I should receive something in return for having his pudgy, sweaty body grinding on top of me. The suffocation I felt laying

163

GINA MARIE MARTINI

beneath him sparked my memory. His massive belly scrunching me to the mattress with each visit to satisfy his itty-bitty gland.

"Look, I'm asking you to give me my medical records with some…blanks. You don't need to know anything more."

"My name is associated with your records."

"I am asking you as someone who knows about my past and all I went through, and as a *friend*. These are my medical records. I need them to say Sadie Meade instead of Penny, and leave the dates blank. I'll take care of the rest."

He simply stared into my desperate eyes, presumably deep in thought.

"Please do me this favor, Doc. I'm getting married, and I don't want my husband to know about my past."

"Come back tomorrow. Let me see what I can do."

"I can't come back tomorrow. This has to be done today. I'll gladly wait out in the reception area for you all afternoon if necessary."

He scratched his bald spot, uneasy with my request. I didn't see what the problem was. Why would the date of my pregnancy matter to him and his record-keeping?

At approximately three thirty that afternoon, the doc gave me a typed-up report with details about my pregnancy with the date of service and estimated due date left blank. I could easily type this information in myself.

Before I left, I asked him to describe the symptoms and treatment for a miscarriage.

Again, he shook his head in disbelief, but he answered my questions.

"One more thing." I paused. "How much do you charge for a house call?"

He gulped.

Chapter 50

MY MOTHER PLANNED most of my wedding. She had become quite close to Rocky, a friendship that pierced at my gut for some reason. She offered me suggestions and opinions. All I had to do was give my blessing regarding the church ceremony, dinner menu, and entertainment. Mom had everything under control in a few short weeks.

Rocky agreed to pay for the affair. Either because he had the money to spend, or he knew my father had empty pockets, throwing down chips at the casino.

I spent more time selecting our house than planning the wedding. We settled on a lovely five-thousand-square-foot English Tudor in Henderson on a dead-end street with many acres sprawled throughout the backyard. Tommy thought it would be perfect for a child. I agreed, if there were an actual child in the near future. The place needed some new appliances and a good paint job. Otherwise, it would be ready for us to move in after the wedding.

Picking out the wedding dress was almost as much fun as a root canal. Mom offered me her gown to wear, but it was much too old-fashioned for my taste. I recommended she let Lisa wear it when she got married. Wearing Mom's wedding dress was something Lisa actually wanted. My sister was far more traditional than me.

I had a small amount of time to find a gown I liked before the wedding. My options were limited. But I did like one with a scooped neck and beaded straps. The bodice had a floral pattern in ivory with clear beads.

The seamstress referred to it as an A-line layered gown with tulle. It felt a bit itchy at first, but a slip would prevent the need to scratch.

The back of the dress looked pretty with many buttons flowing upward. An optional sash could be worn with the stunning gown. Some women might not like the sash because it added some weight around the bride's waist. Perfect for me!

People should see my waist looking a little thick. I started eating a lot of ice cream, thinking I'd add a few pounds around my midsection to play the part of an expectant mother.

The altar at Saint Francis Church looked beautiful, filled with yellow and white daisies and lilies. The traditional roses and carnations were not my cup of tea. Yellow exuded happiness, I thought. I needed to be happy on my wedding day instead of feeling like a nervous wreck.

Tommy was a dreamboat, rich, and great between the sheets. Why wouldn't I be happy to be his wife?

Then I thought about John, who suspected I wasn't really pregnant. He couldn't have shared my secret with Tommy. If he did, the wedding would surely be off. Tommy didn't strike me as the marrying kind before I told him I was pregnant with his child.

Lisa wore an emerald-green-colored dress as my maid of honor. Mom wore a lovely floor-length gown in mint julep. All the men wore black tuxedos.

Dad walked me down the aisle across a white carpet draped along the floor with a stream of yellow daisies tossed along the lacy runner.

A sheer silky veil covered my eyes, shielding my view of the guests and my groom. As I drew near the altar, Tommy's fingers ran through his brown waves. His left leg shook every now and then as if it fell asleep and he was trying to wake it. I wondered if the guests noticed his blatant jitters.

Then there was John. His lips formed a smile, but his eyes displayed an icy glare, seemingly unsure of me.

Butterflies invaded my stomach. A war zone surged from within me. I lied and manipulated myself into this marriage. I could definitely fall in love with Tommy. My hope was that Tommy would fall in love with me too. I felt certain there would be other children for us in the future.

After reciting our vows as directed by Father Flanagan, we kissed to seal the deal.

Besides my immediate family, every other guest at the wedding were friends or relatives of Tommy's. He paraded me around, introducing me to so many people. I was as polite as I could be, but I'd never remember everyone's name.

Veronica and Jude declined the invitation. In fact, Tommy hadn't heard from Jude since the night drinks were on Veronica; at least my drink was on her.

There were a few interesting people Tommy wanted me to meet. Men his father conducted business with. Italians, judging by their last names. They spoke with accents like the criminally charged Al Capone in *The Untouchables*.

One of these wise guys was very familiar to me. Too familiar. Tommy introduced him as Benny DeLeone.

Penny knew him as Mr. D.

I looked at his wife, the demure, quiet type. No wonder Mr. D. had to visit a whorehouse. He definitely recognized *me* upon our handshake. Talk about an awkward moment.

Mr. D., I mean Benny, had a bizarre foot fetish. I had to soak and scrub my feet when he was finished. Did he ever punish his wife's toes the way he punished Penny's? Did Mrs. D. know about his peculiar fetish or the parts of his body he begged me to stick my big toes in?

Doris explained Mr. D. was a VIP at the Belle Maiden, meaning he was a gangster who should be treated with respect. The ranch was owned by gangsters. As if it were an honor he chose *my* feet to violate on a regular basis.

Benny's intense glare advised me to keep my mouth shut. I felt exactly the same way. There was an unwritten rule at the ranch. We knew to never discuss who our johns were with outsiders. But we could never be sure if they talked about the girls. I gleaned from Benny's stance that his wife had no clue how he spent some of his evenings. He wouldn't dare tell Tommy about Penny. If he did, I could ruin his marriage. And he knew it.

Chapter 51

FOR OUR HONEYMOON, Tommy made surprise arrangements he wouldn't divulge. He drove us in his gorgeous Camaro with our suitcases squeezed in the limited space in the back.

When we arrived at the airport, my face began to turn a mild shade of green. I wasn't even onboard yet, and my nervous stomach bounced up and down. I thought he knew I couldn't fly. It was my fault for not informing him of this important detail. My mind had been preoccupied, plotting a faux pregnancy and miscarriage.

"Why are we at the airport?"

"I told you I picked out a special place for us to go on our honeymoon."

"I can't fly."

"What do you mean you can't fly? You flew to Vegas all the way from Boston."

"Yes, and I was deathly ill the entire way!"

"Deathly ill?" he scoffed as if he didn't believe me. "Sadie, come on. You'll be fine. The night is clear. Shouldn't be a rough flight."

He had a way about him, my *husband*. A way to talk me onto this death trap, enticing me with the first-class accommodations he arranged.

I let Tommy have the window seat. I couldn't look outside. I closed my eyes and squeezed his hand hard the moment the engine started to roar.

He winced from the strength of my fingers. "Jesus, Sadie, relax."

The plane didn't move ten yards before my anxiety heightened. I couldn't catch my breath. I suddenly felt excessively warm and sweaty. My heart thumped wildly. Then I barfed up the steak dinner Rocky paid for. And there was no bag or a bathroom close enough for me to access. The aisle floor suffered the blow along with my pumps.

Tommy called out to the stewardess to request we exit the plane. He used my pregnancy as an excuse. He went as far as saying he thought I should see a doctor.

The passengers were in an uproar because the pilot had to turn around to let us out at the gate. I vomited again as the plane swirled in a circle to head back. I doubted the other passengers who witnessed the event wanted me to stay. My symptoms would continue the entire trip unless I passed out.

We would have traveled to Hawaii. So much for a Hawaiian honeymoon. I noticed the disappointed and somewhat frustrated expression on Tommy's face. But I had no business flying.

Instead of a tropical vacation, we stayed at the Montgomery. Tommy managed to snag tickets to sold-out shows like Liberace and Wayne Newton. He asked his secretary to cancel the Hawaiian hotel and all the activities he had planned. I overheard him mention chartering a sailboat in Maui. My stomach churned just thinking about it. Anyplace we were to travel needed to be within driving distance.

Hawaii would have been a fabulous vacation, but I couldn't handle the motion of a plane. A boat would be far worse.

Thoughts of Mickey Quinn entered my brain. When the water was rough back home, my legs shimmied, challenging me to stand on the pier with him when he fished. Just watching the water float up and down instigated an ache in my belly.

The first night of our honeymoon was ruined because of my agitated stomach. I didn't feel right again until morning.

Because driving was our only mode of transportation, we took a day trip through the dry, yet lovely landscape of Arizona to see the Grand Canyon. Its beauty was astonishing! Miles upon miles of natural earthy colors, mixed with a thin layer of light pink, decorated the canyon buried below a brilliant blue sky freckled with white fluffy clouds. The canyon looked incredibly deep. I feared moving too close to the edge without a barricade. If I had another panic attack, I might stumble and fall off, becoming a meal for carnivorous beasts living below.

We weren't prepared to camp, but we trekked through the territory to catch other sights and spectacular wonders the desert's beauty offered. I fared well until a rattler slithered quickly away from our heavy steps.

Tommy said my shrieking scared him off. He assured me the snake was more afraid of us than we were of it.

Somehow I doubted that.

Tommy became a little frisky on our hike, but there were too many spectators around to consummate our marriage against the rocky terrain. He was full of surprises.

That evening, Tommy brought me to a club called Spritz. We sauntered into the joint and witnessed this scrawny bit of a man on the stage, attempting to belt out the Rolling Stone's "Satisfaction." His performance was not satisfying, but awkwardly memorable.

People took turns upon the high stage with the microphone. They jammed with their own guitar or cello. One chick played the violin. Some performances were better than others. No one should expect to be the next Mick Jagger though. It was entertainment for us that passed the time.

Tommy took me by the hand, and we crept around the bar. He knew the man who stood tall in the back, monitoring the crowd. Tommy approached him with a shake of the hand and a friendly pat on the back.

"Tommy, how are you? Is this your lovely bride?"

"This is Sadie. Sadie, Vince Russo. He owns Spritz."

Vince Russo looked like a shady character to me. His jet-black hair was slicked back. Eyes as dark as the evening sky. Good-looking though for a man probably in his forties. He gently took my hand and kissed the back of it.

"It's a pleasure to meet you, Mrs. Cavallo."

"Thank you." I felt a smile form on my face, despite my unwavering suspicion of this man.

"I apologize for not attending your wedding. Did you receive my gift?"

"Thank you, Vince. We appreciate your generous gift. I understand why you couldn't make it. And allow me to express my condolences on the passing of your brother, Frank," Tommy said, grabbing his hand to shake again.

"Thank you." Vince nodded without making eye contact.

"What happened to your brother?" I asked with great curiosity.

Tommy whipped his head toward me as if I shouldn't have asked such a question.

"Burglary at his house," Vince answered, displaying a half-smile. "My niece moved in with me last year. She's a sensitive soul, you know. Misses her dad. But I'll make sure she's all right. Frank wanted me to take care of Angie."

"I'm sorry for your troubles," Tommy responded.

"Me too," I added, not knowing what else to say. Seeing that I asked him about his brother's death, a reply from me was warranted.

Vince requested the bartender send a bottle of champagne to our table on the house.

Tommy poured us each a glass, and we toasted to our future together.

Chapter 52

THE TIME HAD come for Tommy to resume his management responsibilities at the Montgomery. It was difficult for him to sneak away entirely from work on our honeymoon when we were staying at the hotel.

When we entered our new home for the first time, it was everything I hoped it would be.

The crafty painters added a remarkable flair to the walls in earthy tones. The in-ground pool in the yard was filled with crystal clear water. The outdoor patio was recreated with a new cement floor and outdoor furniture of burnt orange and wicker. I loved to be outside in the sunshine, smelling the purifying aroma of chlorine. We didn't have a pool in Gloucester.

Tommy and I roamed around the inside. He equipped the place with modern-day appliances in the kitchen, a television set, and an eight-track player with tapes of some of my favorite country singers like Jim Reeves, Conway Twitty, and Loretta Lynn.

He took pride showing me an empty room across the hall from what would be our bedroom—the baby's room.

"What do you think about the pale-yellow color on the walls? I hope you like it. You never said what color scheme you had in mind. If you hate the yellow, we can have it repainted."

It was sweet of him to be so interested. A smile brightened my face. "I love it, Tommy! Yellow is perfect."

"We need to buy a crib and a high chair still." He smiled, eyes beaming enthusiastically.

My heart overflowed with guilt.

Tommy seemed really excited about fatherhood. Perhaps someday I'd give him a child. Unfortunately, not right now.

He took me by the hand and headed toward our bedroom, complete with the furniture I picked out, all in oak. The curtains and bedspread were golden with a dusting of red flecks. Very rich-looking.

I thanked him with a sensuous kiss that led to making use of our brand-new bed. I could definitely fall in love with Tommy.

As we laid in bed, staring at the antiquated light fixture above us, catching our breaths from the afternoon amusement, he turned toward me with a serious look. "You need to tell your family about the baby now."

He must have recognized the displeasure in my sour expression, but he didn't understand why. A yellow room, soon to be filled with baby furniture, would be a dead giveaway when family visited.

"Sadie, we're married now. It doesn't matter if they find out you were pregnant before the wedding. Pop is so excited about becoming a grandfather, he's going to spill the beans to them soon enough. They need to hear it from us, not Pop."

"You're right."

"Maybe your mom can help us. I mean, what do either of us know about having a baby? He or she will need clothes, diapers, and food. I don't know what kind of baby food or clothes to buy. How do you change a diaper? I was thinking about that, you know. All those pins to hold that cloth in place. What if I stick him and make him cry?"

A million parental thoughts emerged from his brain. Normal fears about becoming a first-time daddy. What had my lies done to him?

"Okay. I'll tell them. Mom will be a big help, I'm sure." I rested my head upon his chest, running my fingers through the prickly hairs. "Don't worry, Tommy."

Chapter 53

ACCORDING TO THE doc, some type of accident would most likely be the main reason for a miscarriage to occur, considering I should be about four months pregnant at this time.

I wandered around the inside and outside of my new house. A tumble down the basement stairs? Car accident?

I sat in a lounge chair, woven with colorful plastic strips, absorbing the sun's magical rays as my brain worked in overdrive to solve this dilemma. There was a cool breeze in the air, but still a warm enough day for February, compared to Massachusetts weather. I imagined how lovely the pool would be in a couple of months.

A cup of hot tea was on my mind. As I crept up the few steps to enter the kitchen, I lost my balance slightly on a wobbly cement block. We should add a railing here to ensure no one would get hurt. But this would be a good spot for an injury. This loose block of cement was the perfect catalyst to promote a bad fall.

Tommy was at the hotel as per usual during the day. According to the grandfather clock in the living room, the doc should be finishing up his rounds at the Belle Maiden by now since it was Friday. I dialed his office phone. No answer.

As I waited for time to pass, I stood atop the outdoor steps to figure out exactly how this would happen. How would a pregnant woman trip down these few steps? Would there be blood? I'd need some scrapes and bruises, evidence of a traumatic experience to my body.

I took my time inching down the steps to find the weakness in that block. If I stepped on it a certain way, could I lose my balance?

Maybe I should be carrying my lunch, I thought. Walking abruptly down these steps with a glass and plate in both my hands might make it difficult to remain steady.

Before the wedding, Tommy added my name to his bank account and checkbook, thinking I might need to access money for the baby. I considered withdrawing money to pay off the doc, but I didn't want to explain my purpose for taking such a lofty sum. Instead, I took a generous sum from my remaining stash from the Belle Maiden.

Two hours passed before the doc answered his phone and agreed to do this final favor for me. He stressed the word "final."

Once I confirmed he was on his way, I stood on the top of the outdoor steps, holding a glass of milk in one hand and a turkey sandwich on a glass plate in the other. Admittedly, I was hesitant to take such drastic lengths. When I felt the loose block beneath my toes, I closed my eyes and flung my body down the few steps.

The glass pieces shattered across the cement floor. I intentionally landed on my stomach. Some glass fragments became tangled in my hair, and my hands suffered minor flesh wounds. There wasn't much blood, but my ribs took a beating from falling face first. As I moved my body to sit up, the sting against my knees felt sharp. The right side of my face was scuffed.

I stood up, wobbled into the house, leaving the mess outside on the ground, and waited for the doc to show.

He arrived at my house, surprised by the luxury someone like me, a former brothel whore, married into. He never questioned why I needed people to think I was pregnant. However, he might suspect now that he had seen where I lived. He probably pegged me for a gold digger.

It was better he didn't know any of the details about my fear of Kenny and using Tommy as a safety net.

"How'd this happen?" he asked, pointing to my face.

"Do you really want to know?"

"Yes, Penny." He coughed then cleared his throat. "I mean *Sadie*. If I'm the doctor treating your injuries and making a house call to tend to you, I need to write this up in your patient file."

I nodded before encouraging him to follow me through the house and out the kitchen door toward the patio. "See? Loose block." My toes rocked the block up and down. "I stumbled and fell on my face…as you can see." I pointed to the scrapes against my cheek and chin.

He pulled out his medical bag and tended to the abrasions. The bandages were large and a bit overdramatic. I liked that effect.

"Because you're *pregnant*, under normal circumstances I'd send you to the hospital to confirm the condition of you and the baby. A trip to my office will have to do. I can't risk having another doctor in the emergency room examine you. My reputation is at stake."

At the doc's office, I waited patiently for him to properly scribe the details in my medical chart. He pulled my records from the ranch, and altered them with my actual name to show that I had been his patient previously.

Aside from the cuts and probable bruising that would occur later, he advised me to act more like a grieving mother. Most women cry, feeling heartbroken to lose a child they carried for several months.

"My credibility is on the line. You better be a good actress, Sadie."

I tried to think of sad things. Really sad and horrible things to make me cry or feel empathy. I remembered the hurt I experienced when I had to leave Mickey behind. I recalled the first time I met Kenny and was obligated to have sex with him. The way his teeth tore at my flesh for his own sick pleasure. My fear of Kenny came to light, thinking about what he might do to me if he found me.

Then I considered the baby I had actually carried before Kenny's weasel friend, Artie, terminated him. For the first time, I recognized that pregnancy as a human life that I discarded. Was it a boy or a girl? I'd never know. I was in such a terrible state at that time. It was a circumstance that required immediate attention. I never thought of that situation as "human life." An innocent baby didn't ask to be created due to my promiscuous circumstances. Whoever the father might have been was irrelevant.

I had never been much of a crier, but suddenly, my heart felt heavy and tears plopped over the thick bandages glued to my cheek.

At that painful moment, the doc made the call to explain the devastating news to Tommy.

When Tommy arrived, the doc escorted him into the examination room where I sat waiting, fully dressed and ready to leave.

His face bore no expression when he approached me. He stared at me for a few moments without a word uttered, sensing my sadness between the bandages.

"I'm sorry," was all I could say. And I sincerely meant it. But I was sorry for bringing him into my web of destruction, orchestrating such a dubious plot.

"How do you feel?" he asked.

"Tired, sore, sad," I replied, thanks to the doc's coaching.

Tommy placed his arms around me, bringing my head toward his shoulder.

I felt his smooth lips brush against my forehead, warming my heart.

"Can I take her home now?" he asked the doc with sheer remorse detected in his gray eyes.

Chapter 54

AS TIME PASSED, Tommy's heart seemed to heal. He had difficulty walking by the room with the pale-yellow walls. He shut the door and kept it closed. A constant reminder of losing his son or daughter was too painful to view each day.

Tommy hired a painter to change the baby's room to a cream color. The room was transformed into a guest bedroom, adding a full-size bed, dresser, mirror, and end tables. I picked out the drapes, sheets, and bedspread in various shades of blue with a floral design that complemented each piece.

In an attempt to ease Tommy's mind, I advised we could have another child in the future. He seemed to be grieving this child still. Too soon to discuss future offspring.

Pop was furious with the construction crew. He threatened to sue for the loose block that made me fall.

That was the last thing I wanted to have happen.

I couldn't go to court and tell a judge a big, fat lie! Then my doctor might be required to speak as well. I wasn't convinced the doc would lie for me under oath, no matter how much money I'd offer him. I begged Rocky not to sue them. It was a terrible accident. I wouldn't want to relive this nightmare in court.

Rocky finally agreed at the sound of my distress.

The construction crew returned and tore apart the steps. They replaced the stairs with a ramp and affixed a railing. This was not only a safer option to prevent injuries, but convenient for John's wheelchair when he visited. If he ever came to visit.

The fact remained that John hadn't visited recently. Perhaps that was for the best. It had been hard enough to keep up this act with Tommy. John might see right through me. He already had doubts that Tommy was the father of this baby, or if I were pregnant at all.

The timing was suspect. A miscarriage shortly after I married into a wealthy family. Information this juicy could leak out to employees at the Montgomery, igniting vicious rumors. Another reason why I asked the doc to give me copies of my medical records. Proof of a pregnancy and miscarriage should I need it.

Rocky told my parents the news. They came by to see us and pay their respects. Mom fussed over me, of course, ensuring I was resting and eating well.

Tommy allowed them to think the pregnancy was new. No need for them to believe I was supposed to have been four months along.

Even my normally rigid father appeared melancholic when he cuffed my chin with compassion upon greeting me. His face splashed with redness, eyes somber.

Tommy and I acted like newlyweds again after the lengthy period the doc suggested we wait, recovering from the faux miscarriage. Sex had never been a problem for us.

He wanted me to start taking medication for birth control. He practically demanded it. Most of the girls at the ranch took the infamous birth control pill. Taking a prescription medication was not something I wanted to start and maintain on a regular basis.

I was taken aback. I thought Tommy wanted a child, considering his sadness for losing this baby. And even though I showed him the diaphragm, as if I had to prove I was being responsible, he began to wear condoms any time he touched me.

Lack of trust? Added insurance to prevent an unexpected pregnancy?

I wanted to love Tommy, and I hoped he'd return that sentiment. But without trust, love might not be possible.

Chapter 55

A NEW SHOW was opening at the Montgomery. Magicians, comics, and dancers, all of what the Vegas Strip offered tourists.

I avoided the hotel as much as possible since my run-in with Kenny. For all I knew, he could show up at any time, looking for me to torment if he had nothing better to do. He really hated me for his injuries, losing John as a customer, and the death of his friend, Junior. Those incidents were not my fault, but I was the root cause of them.

Tommy asked me to join him at the first performance tonight. The premiere was a semiformal event, which meant we needed to look formal since we were the owners.

I pinned my hair up into a bun, threw on the pearl necklace Tommy bought me as a wedding gift, and wore an ivory gown with lace and beading along the trim.

The men wore white tuxedo jackets and black slacks as if the style was a uniform.

Mom wore the mint-colored dress she donned at my wedding. Had I known she needed a new dress to wear, I would've taken her shopping. Perhaps I should have assumed she'd need something new to wear.

I had become the bank for Mom, Lisa, and Patrick whenever they needed anything major that Dad wouldn't approve of purchasing.

Mom required household items more than clothing. She never asked me outright for anything. If I saw her wearing the same clothes repeatedly, or if she struggled with a toaster that burned the bread, I'd gladly buy her what she needed.

Tommy didn't seem to mind my spending habits, but I always explained how the money was spent. He understood and respected my need to take care of my family.

Lisa desired an education. She loved her secretarial duties for an attorney, but she was interested in the law field.

Dad wouldn't approve of her taking college classes because *we can't afford it*, his famous words. He also didn't believe Lisa could become a lawyer solely because she was a girl.

I reminded him times were changing. Career-minded women were making strides, thanks to the women's liberation movement, a cause my father disagreed with wholeheartedly.

Patrick loved art and the theater. I'd been paying for his drama classes. Tommy offered him a part-time gig, working backstage after school to prepare for shows at the Montgomery. He hadn't been cast to appear on stage, but he craved the experience and all the drama.

Apparently, a lot of drama existed among the performers and crew. Who was sleeping with who, as well as ferocious competition and backstabbing.

I hadn't seen the showgirl Tommy used to date. Whether she left on her own, or Tommy let her go, I'd never know.

Patrick was considering colleges to attend. Dad claimed he'd help pay for it, but I'd believe that when I saw it.

Since I married into a wealthy family, Dad wished the same for Lisa. But she really wanted to learn. Lisa had one of those brains that constantly absorbed information. So, I offered to help her with college expenses. Most likely, I'd also help Patrick.

The show was amazing from start to finish. The guests stood to their feet and applauded, demanding an encore. Tommy and Rocky were thrilled. Reporters were present, and a five-star review was expected. I glanced at my mother, who didn't get out too much. Her face beamed with joy and enthusiasm.

I wanted to see my brother.

Tommy directed me backstage and signaled to a burly man with a thick black beard guarding the door to let me enter the private area for employees only.

Backstage, many people raced around feverishly in flashy costumes or carried stage props. I didn't know anyone in the show personally, but I asked several people where Patrick Meade was.

Most people shrugged, either not knowing who he was or where I could find him.

Finally, a woman in a bright red leotard, with breasts at least ten times larger than mine, pointed to a room where she saw him enter.

When I opened the door, darkness filled the space. This couldn't be the right room.

Faint sounds were heard. Muffled moans.

My fingers drifted along the wall in search of the light switch. When the lights turned on, there stood Patrick, looking pretty turned on himself. His hands and lips were all over one of the performers.

Chapter 56

NORMALLY, I DIDN'T surprise very easily. But this was a surprise. Not because my little brother was making out behind a closed door with one of the lead performers of the show. The actor his hands were fondling was Leo Drake.

Leo, a thin yet well-constructed man, judging by his toned figure highlighted by his clingy costume. Golden hair with light green eyes. Very handsome, but considerably older than my seventeen-year-old brother. My gay brother. Why didn't I see this coming? Had I been too consumed with my own underhanded schemes to pay attention?

After I picked my jaw up from the floor, I managed to say a quick hello and hoped there wasn't much surprise in the sound of my voice.

"Sadie! What are you doing back here?" Patrick asked, tucking his white button-down shirt back into his unbuttoned slacks.

Leo adjusted the collar of his brown costume. I was too absorbed in this moment to pay attention to his unique costume and his role in tonight's performance.

"I hoped to say hello and catch up, but I see I'm interrupting. You can carry on, Patrick. I'll leave." My hands were wildly animated as I spoke, unsure what to do with them.

Yes, I was surprised by this turn of events, but I loved Patrick. My concern was the obvious age difference. My brother appeared to be a willing participant in this embrace. As long as this man did not coerce my brother to do anything against his will, I would support his decision and life choices.

Hell, after living in a cathouse for several months, nothing should surprise me.

"Sadie, wait!" Patrick nodded at Leo, apparently to give us some privacy.

I tossed Leo my version of an evil eye as he stepped outside the room, still waiting for my brain to decipher what my eyes spotted, and to determine what game Leo might be playing. I wouldn't want this obviously more experienced man to hurt my brother.

"Patrick, is this…" I paused, attempting to find the right words to continue my sentence, "what you want? He didn't force himself…"

"Sadie, no. I don't need Dad's voice coming from your mouth."

Oh God, did I sound like my father? "I'm not our father's puppet. I'm surprised. You never shared this with me."

"It's not something I wanted to talk about."

"You can talk to me about anything."

His eyes drifted away, and he turned his back.

"All I care about is your happiness. Leo is older and surely more experienced. Patrick, people talk about this kind of thing. Being a homosexual can't possibly be an easy life. I want to make sure you're safe."

"Safe?"

"Gay men are often ridiculed. You've seen the news. I don't want that for you."

"You act like this is a choice I made."

"Isn't it?"

He shook his head, seemingly disappointed in me. "All I ask is you don't tell anyone. Can you do that for me?"

"Of course. If my reaction sounded like I disapproved, I'm sorry. I can't apologize for being caught off guard. I promise, I can keep your secret."

Chapter 57

MY BROTHER'S SITUATION weighed heavily on my mind for the days that followed. Had he ever been with a woman? Did he have the desire for a woman, or were his interests always in men? I wanted to understand his feelings if he'd let me. News like this needed to sink in, especially because of the way his secret was exposed to me.

The house phone rang, disrupting my thoughts. Tommy left some important papers on the dining room table. This became a common occurrence when he brought work home with him. He asked me to bring those documents to the hotel before his meeting with some important people.

Normally, I didn't care about his business, but I snooped a little at the papers. Looked like contracts with the Heavenly Tea Emporium. Big deal, he was changing his beverage distributor, I thought. Carmine Toscano's name had been tossed around between Tommy and Rocky. He was the new investor of the hotel from Philadelphia, paying for the renovations to give the place a facelift to resemble parts of Europe.

The hotel lobby was quite busy with guests coming and going. Construction for the remodel began. I waved to one of the girls at the reception desk, but she looked busy. She tossed me a quick wave back once she noticed me.

The elevators were equally busy with many people waiting. Since Tommy's office was only a couple of flights up, I chose to leap up the stairs.

Mrs. Arden, Tommy's secretary, greeted me with a cheerful grin across her pudgy face. I felt comfortable with her. A middle-aged, overweight, married woman who took care of my husband's business needs. Had she been a youthful beauty with large breasts, I might be jealous.

"Thank you, Mrs. Cavallo, for bringing him this folder."

"Where is Tommy?"

"He's in the conference room. I'm afraid you can't go in there right now. I'll bring these to him immediately. Have a nice day." Her eyes squinted as she smiled and stood to carry the paperwork behind closed doors.

Angry shouting could be heard from across the hall in Rocky's office. Through the partially closed blinds, I saw my father taking a verbal beating from his old war buddy.

"What is going on?" I whispered.

I hadn't seen my father gambling at the Montgomery while I was working in the coat check room. Apparently, it didn't prevent him from gambling at other casinos.

Rocky was outraged about a debt my father owed. He hollered, "You don't want to owe any money to those people!"

Dad was still gambling hard.

Sadness overwhelmed me when I heard my father actually use the, *but I saved your life, Rocky,* card.

Yes, he saved Rocky's life more than fifteen years ago during a war. With all that Rocky had done for him with a new home and new opportunities, it was shameful that he'd say that, as what? A defense for a terrible habit he developed? The nightlife in this city enslaved my father.

"This is the last time I'm bailing you out, Fred! I mean it. Not only will I throw you out to those animals you owe money to, but you'll lose your job!" Rocky screamed angrily.

"Thank you, Rocky. I won't let this happen again. I swear!"

I left the hallway quickly, not to be seen, and used the stairwell to return to the lobby to exit the hotel. My father had little dignity left. He didn't need to know I learned his gambling habit now bordered the line of addiction.

Chapter 58

MOM SHOWED ME how to bread chicken properly for a crispy coat. I fried up a nice chicken dinner with mashed potatoes and green peas.

Tommy had been coming home late every night. So much happening at the Montgomery with his new investors and the reconstruction of the hotel. His pop had been placing more responsibilities on him. In a way, I believed he was happy for the challenge. He craved his father's respect.

He barely said two words to me as he dug into his dinner. I tried not to take his distraction personally.

"Tommy?"

He looked at me from across the table without saying a word.

"How is my father doing? I mean, as an employee. Your father gave him this job out of a sense of obligation. Is he satisfied with my father's work?"

He swallowed a large chunk of chicken hard. A slight coughing fit began. After a drink of water, he composed himself and asked me to repeat the question. Was he stalling?

"I want to know if my father is pulling his own weight at the hotel."

The silence was maddening.

"Tommy, my relationship with my father is difficult. I'd like to think we're making progress, but it's far from perfect. You know this. Don't lie or tell me something you think I need to hear. I want to know the truth."

"If you want the truth, I'll tell you the truth. Pop owes your dad for saving his life. For that, we are all grateful. He's good at managing security detail and developing a plan for the men to work with."

"I sense a *but* coming."

"*But* your father is a bigot. Complaints pour in about his hiring practices and unfair treatment of some employees. Unless applicants for his unit are white Catholics, they don't stand a chance to be hired at the Montgomery. We can't afford a bad reputation like that. So I talked to Pop, and we had him pulled from the hiring process. My father or I have final say in who we hire, and your father needs to change his tune."

My father's prejudices were not news to me.

"Did he say something to you? Complain that we took that responsibility away from him?" Agitation was evident in Tommy's voice.

It was one thing for me to be irritated with my father. Hearing the disdain Tommy felt for him hurt a tad.

"No. I was just curious. Are you going to fire him?" I asked softly, hoping he would tone down his detest.

"If it were up to me, I would've canned his ass months ago! But it's not up to me, Sadie. That's my father's call. If he doesn't straighten himself out, he'll be out of a job, and no one will hire him in this town if they know we fired him."

Gambling was not the only issue my father had. He was not well-liked. But it hurt to hear this from Tommy. Hurt to know Dad was failing in life. Failed his wife, children, and employer. The dice were his only friends. No wonder he seemed so miserable all the time. A vicious cycle he might not be able to break from.

"Maybe I should talk to him."

"Stay out of it! I told you this in confidence. He can't know I shared this with you," he snapped.

"I understand, but he's my father. Maybe if I talk to him…"

"And say what? How are *you* supposed to know any of this if I didn't tell you?"

"Tone it down. Don't raise your voice to me. I was only trying to help." Bile filled my throat, angered by his unnecessary frustration toward me.

Tommy didn't know what hit him when I challenged him, judging by the surprised brows and widened eyes he displayed.

"He's my father, and if I want to have a discussion with him, I will! And don't worry, I won't bring up anything you said to me." I picked up my plate, threw it into the kitchen sink from my chair, smashing it into several pieces, and left the room for him to eat the rest of his dinner alone.

He didn't come to bed that night.

Chapter 59

THE YEAR 1969 snuck up on us quickly. Tommy and I had been married for a full year. Rocky and my mother coordinated a nice anniversary dinner at Rocky's estate.

My father claimed he wasn't feeling well and didn't attend. I worried he was sitting at a blackjack table somewhere with only the dealer and random gamblers to keep him company.

I tried to speak with him about life in general. I kept my promise to Tommy by never allowing Dad to know that I learned his secrets and difficulties on the job.

Dad needed to stop gambling. I mentioned the name of a financial advisor to Dad. I never said this advisor was a friend of Tommy's. My hope was if he spoke with someone about his finances and budget, maybe his life could improve.

He merely looked at me with a snarky grin then strode off. He didn't want his daughter advising him about his finances.

Dad had a gambling problem, and he needed help.

My mother and Rocky laughed together—a lot. I'd catch him staring at my mom when she wasn't looking, to the point where I wanted to blush, and I wasn't the blushing kind. Being married to my father must be difficult and lonely, especially when he was distancing himself from everyone except casino dealers and loan sharks.

Rocky was a wealthy, good-looking widower. My mother, an attractive woman without putting in much effort. Couldn't my father see he was wrecking his whole life, including his marriage?

Patrick looked well and happy. Privately, he shared with me that he and Leo were a couple, but no one else in the family was aware of his love life. Leo was always introduced to others as his friend and mentor in show business.

Patrick's dream was to be accepted to UCLA. Los Angeles offered a lot of opportunities for students interested in the theater.

Leo was already established as an actor, engaged in a large production in Las Vegas. Leo hadn't made a commitment to move to Los Angeles with my brother yet. He might not find a better venue than the Montgomery.

I smiled, knowing Patrick seemed very happy right now. But Leo was far more mature and wiser. Would he give up his stint in Vegas for my lovesick brother?

Chapter 60

TOMMY WAS LATE coming home—again. He'd been working so much more than usual. I worked at the Montgomery. I saw firsthand what a serious businessman he was. That hotel meant a lot to his family. I felt safe and secure when he was home. Whenever he came home really late, I wondered if he had a girl in that suite of his.

Jealousy was an emotion I'd never experienced. Maybe if I were in love with Tommy the way I loved Mickey Quinn, I'd identify with it more. I loved the life Tommy offered. For that, I tried to be understanding when dinner was ruined because he wasn't home on time.

Bitchiness, however, came naturally. Another trait I inherited from Dad. I looked like Mom, but my personality was all Dad. I'd been working on keeping my emotions in check. Sometimes I made people feel uncomfortable with my uncensored mouth.

I wasn't a pushover, but I couldn't give Tommy a reason to throw me out on my ass either. He didn't love me any more than I loved him, yet I was still his wife.

The phone rang. A frantic tone in Tommy's voice was evident. There was a reason he was late tonight, and it wasn't work-related. He received an emergency phone call from the hospital.

Rocky had been admitted, and the situation seemed dire.

I grabbed my purse and keys, hopped into my Ford, and found my way to the facility. I often drove by the Sunrise Hospital when in this area, but I never needed to pay attention to the entrance or parking lot. I drove around the block several times before I detected the signs with arrows offering direction.

My mind was cluttered with terrible thoughts about what could have happened to Rocky.

After stopping at the information desk, I learned where Rocky had been taken. The elevators seemed to take forever to reach the intensive care unit.

When I arrived on this floor, signs were displayed, instructing me which direction to turn. My eyes caught sight of a rogue wheelchair roaming the hallway. I sprinted toward him and locked eyes with a melancholic John, who pointed toward the room where his father laid.

As I peered inside, Tommy was speaking with the doctor. They stood over Rocky, who was either sleeping or unconscious. A tube dangled from his mouth. Several wires, blended in with his chest hairs, were affixed to his upper body and attached to a noisy machine.

I waited outside with John and asked if he knew what was happening.

He shook his head. His eyes were unfocused, barely making contact with me.

While alone with John, I took the liberty to attempt to make peace. I wanted so much for John and I to be friends again. I grabbed his attention and silently formed the words, because John could read my lips, asking if he was still upset about my marriage.

He shrugged at first, then expressed a slightly suspicious smirk.

"You're important to me, John. I know you have your doubts about my marriage to Tommy. I really want this to work, and I'm trying to be a good wife."

He raised his hand and gently brushed his fingers across my stomach. "No baby," he mumbled clearly enough for me to understand without writing it down.

I shook my head. "Not anymore." I sighed as the words left my lips.

"Hmm," was the only sound he made before rolling toward Tommy, who finished his conversation with the doctor.

Tommy's eyes found their way to me, seemingly welcoming behind despair. I held out my arms and embraced him with tenderness.

John studied us as a couple, I noticed.

Tommy spoke and used sign language so John and I would both understand what had happened. "Pop might have had a stroke, but they have more tests to run."

"What exactly does that mean?" I asked.

"He was found unconscious, and he's still unconscious. Right now, he's in critical condition. Only one of us at a time to see him, and we can't stay long." He signaled to John to have a turn with Pop.

John nodded and rolled his wheelchair inside the room. I watched him tap Rocky's hand before holding it.

"Where did this happen? How did this happen, Tommy?"

"He was home. Pop left the office early today. Said he had a headache and was tired. I'm not sure if he called for help or if anyone was with him. Probably Stella, the housekeeper."

He looked so worried, pacing the hallway and running his fingers through his brown waves.

"Is there anything I can do?"

He wrapped his strong arms around my body and squeezed me tightly. I hadn't seen him this nervous since I told him I was pregnant.

"Thank you for coming."

"Why don't we go to the cafeteria and have something to eat?" I suggested.

He nodded then checked in on Pop and asked John to join us.

John declined and waited in Pop's room, staring at this bull of a man, once a powerful soldier who now looked weak, frail, and older than his years.

Chapter 61

I USED THE payphone at the hospital to call Rocky's house and speak with his housekeeper.

According to Stella, Rocky sent her out on a variety of errands that afternoon. When she returned, the ambulance was already at the house. She had no idea what happened in the moments before his episode.

She was grateful I thought to call and tell her how he was, although the news was grim. Stella agreed to continue managing the house for him.

Later that same evening, Tommy waited by Pop's bedside, unable to leave him.

I encouraged him to come home with me. Staring at his father wouldn't make him wake up at a quicker pace.

Apparently, I was wrong.

When Tommy returned home around five in the morning, he tapped on the bedroom door and shared the good news that Pop woke up. Unfortunately, he was very confused and couldn't speak clearly.

The doctor explained he might be in a state of confusion for a while, perhaps permanently. Some other symptoms of a stroke were fatigue, loss of balance, communication difficulties, facial paralysis, headaches, and blurred vision.

Rocky was scared and disturbed, unable to communicate. Tommy said he desperately wanted to speak, but his brain and tongue were out of sync. Would he die? Would he have to live with these awful symptoms for the rest of his life? What would his quality of life be? All good questions no one could answer. More time was essential to determine if Rocky would recover fully from this episode.

Tommy appeared distraught. Even my feminine charms didn't work to get him into bed with the hope of distracting him from his worrisome thoughts.

I envisioned his stormy contemplations churning wildly in his brain. He was thinking about the hotel and casino. He didn't speak out loud, but I knew he worried about his business partners. Would he be able to manage the business without Rocky to mentor him? He was barely home enough, a slave to that place. How could our marriage survive this turmoil? My question, not necessarily Tommy's. I wasn't sure if our marriage was a priority to him.

Tommy realized he needed extra help running the Montgomery. He hired a couple of managers to handle the day-to-day activities and report to him. This way, he could manage the bigger business details and keep the partners at bay. Not to mention, he constantly checked in on his father.

Rocky made small improvements over time. Every inch of improvement was progress. He could speak a few words, but his confusion lingered. All he talked about was the hotel when he could speak a full sentence.

Tommy worked out all the legal aspects of taking over the family business. Pop had a power of attorney in place that legally gave Tommy control of Rocky's care, all the money, and the business.

Tommy's eyes showed relief as he shared that information with me. He was very concerned the partners would try to take over the business. These men were to be silent partners, but they weren't very silent. Despite the fact that he had extra help at work, Tommy spent more time at the hotel than with me.

Chapter 62

ON JULY 16, 1969, the whole country watched the Apollo 11 spacecraft blast off to the moon! Everyone talked about this amazing venture, amplified by the media to boost ratings.

Children's toys geared toward spaceships, astronauts, and aliens. Reruns of Lost in Space, and Star Trek, starring William Shatner and Leonard Nimoy, played throughout the summer, allowing everyone to believe the theory that life might actually exist on other planets.

Patrick had stopped by to see Tommy and me, and to watch Neil Armstrong and Buzz Aldrin land the spaceship on the moon on July 20. Hearing Armstrong say "one small step for man, one giant leap for mankind" sent chills up my spine. It was worth staying up most of the night to watch. The United States won the space race, leaving the Soviet Union in the dust! Our nation waited and prayed for our heroes to return home safely.

Patrick visited us often. I felt immensely proud of my little brother, who was accepted into UCLA, his dream school. When he moved to Los Angeles permanently, I'd miss him. Tommy would miss Patrick too.

Patrick admired and respected Tommy.

Tommy was kind to him and became his role model, unlike our father. He made sure Patrick was respected at the hotel. They had lunch together in the hotel café. People knew Patrick had connections at the Montgomery. He was the boss's brother-in-law. With Tommy totally in charge of the hotel and its amenities, other people working in the entertainment division paid more attention to my brother. He needed that self-esteem boost.

As for Leo, well, I wanted Patrick to be happy. I wasn't sure if Leo's interests were as genuine.

I hadn't told Tommy about my brother's relationship with Leo. I waited for the imminent moment for the phone to ring, pulling Tommy away from home again for hotel business before I questioned Patrick about their relationship.

"What did Leo say about UCLA?"

My brother became quiet and very still as if contemplating how to answer my question, which wasn't a difficult one. "Leo is such a talented actor. California is the place for him to be." Patrick spoke as though he was determined to believe his own statement.

"Is that what Leo wants?"

He shrugged.

"Patrick, you need to do what's best for *you*. UCLA is your dream! I'm so happy for you and so proud!" I approached him with my hands outstretched and carefully placed them upon his shoulders. "Whatever you do, don't make decisions based on Leo and his happiness. You're young. Much younger than he is…"

He cut me off mid-sentence with a raised tone. "I'd appreciate it if you wouldn't talk as if my going to UCLA means Leo and I are finished."

Patrick never raised his voice to me before. My brother was scared. He looked everywhere except directly into my eyes. Deep down, Patrick must know Leo wouldn't be happy about this situation, or want to be a part of a long-distance relationship.

At Leo's age, and with his experience, my brother was a good time for him. Not that I thought he completely took advantage of Patrick's naivety and innocence. I believed Leo cared for Patrick.

But Leo was Patrick's first love. My brother seemed to be in denial that a broken heart was in his future. I could see it from miles away.

Chapter 63

MOM SPENT THE day with me, giving me a lesson in pie-making.

She insisted, "Every woman should know how to bake for her husband."

I would have rather gone to Sears with her, but I humored her inclination to transform me into a perfect housewife.

We drove to the market to buy fresh fruit. We left the fruit stand with a combination of blueberries, peaches, and apples.

Mom taught me how to roll out the perfect crust for a pie. I had fun with her amongst the flour dust that glued to my hands and face.

The hardest part was peeling the fruit. The blueberry pie was less tedious without any peeling involved.

In the end, we had two blueberry, one peach, and two apple pies. Now who would eat all these pies? Mom said she'd take a couple home to Dad. I was too tired to eat.

Baking was much harder work than I anticipated. A pretty good bakery dwelled a few blocks away. I decided I was much better at buying pies than baking them. Still, it was a nice day to spend with Mom.

Mom seemed concerned about Rocky and his condition. She and Dad visited him recently. She said he recognized them, but he had difficulty speaking. It was a heart-wrenching visit for her.

Tommy equipped Pop's house with round-the-clock nurses and all the necessities to live there, preventing him from staying at a convalescent home permanently.

After Rocky's fall down a flight of stairs and injuring his knee, followed by a slip in the bathroom, slamming his eye against the pointy edge of the sink, Tommy and John had to make the painful decision to keep Rocky in the nursing home for his own protection.

The chime of the kitchen telephone made me jump. The loud, erratic voice of my father was heard on the other end. He was yelling and rambling to the point where I had to tell him to slow down.

"That sonofabitch husband of yours!"

Mom placed her ear on the phone next to mine to listen to Dad trash-talk Tommy.

"He fired me, Sadie!"

"What happened?"

"He just fired me! His father is practically on his death bed, and that man you married is taking over."

Dad continued with his rampage, but I knew Tommy had solid reasons to fire him.

Mom snatched the phone from me and said she'd meet him back at home. When she hung up the receiver, she looked at me with the saddest blue eyes I'd ever seen. "Can you do something for him, dear? Please. If he has no job, he'll go crazy being home all day."

"Mom, I can't get involved. Do you realize what he's been doing?"

I nudged the chair toward her to sit for an uncomfortable discussion.

"Dad doesn't know this, but I overheard Rocky giving him a warning. Tommy told me he's been spoken to about his poor work habits."

My feet began to pace across the kitchen floor, picking up puffs of flour the broom missed. "He's been gambling a lot, Mom. Did you know that? That's why Dad never has any money."

Her expression told me she needed a moment to process this information. Her hand pressed her forehead as if she willed herself to prevent a migraine.

"Will you speak to Tommy and ask if he'll give him another chance?"

I nodded, hating to give her false hope because I knew the outcome would remain unchanged. I couldn't force Tommy to give him another chance. I didn't have that kind of power over my husband, not where the business was concerned. This was a far cry from when I demanded he not hire Veronica for that marketing job.

Dad had many chances by now because Rocky was in charge. He used the Korean War and saving Rocky's life as leverage. It wasn't fair, but I promised Mom I'd try.

I called Tommy's office several times.

Mrs. Arden said he had been in meetings all day, but she'd have him return my call.

He called the house once, and we spoke for maybe thirty seconds. As soon as I mentioned my father's phone call, he cut me off.

"We'll talk about this when I get home, maybe eight o'clock." Then he hung up sharply, without saying goodbye.

My approach would be different than normal. Whenever I grew upset about something, my mouth would take over before my brain kicked in. Then we'd fight. We both knew how to fight hard.

Tonight, I dressed up wearing a lovely royal blue dress I found hidden in the closet. The neckline was a bit low, and the length was short. My legs were my sexiest asset, so I thought I'd wear something to show them off.

Before Tommy would have his choice of pie for dessert, I prepared a pot roast with wild rice and broccoli.

It wasn't unusual for Tommy to be late. Eight o'clock turned into eight thirty. Then at eight fifty-five, he strolled inside the house.

Johnny Cash's "Ring of Fire" softly played on the eight-track player.

Rather than greeting him with complaints about being late and ruining supper, I wore a smile and slipped my husband a kiss on the lips that lasted at least ten seconds.

He smiled at me, ridding his face of the frown he darted in with.

I grabbed my potholders, opened the range door, and removed the roast and vegetables that were kept warm in a low-heated oven.

"What did you do with my wife?" he asked, chuckling.

"I cook all the time. You're never home to eat with me."

"I don't want to fight," he said with a soft voice.

"Me neither. I made this nice-looking roast for dinner, and I cooked it at a low temperature, knowing you'd probably be late. You've had so much going on between your pop and the hotel."

He grasped onto a sharp knife from the drawer and began to slice the roast, placing a thick portion on each of our dishes.

The broccoli and rice seemed a little dry, but edible. I added some of each to our plates before we both sat down. So far, the night was peaceful. I hated to bring up my father and spoil the pleasant mood.

We didn't talk much, but the energy between us radiated positivity.

"Do you have a favorite pie?"

"Pie?"

"Mom and I baked today. She's a wonderful baker."

"What kind did you make?"

"Apple, blueberry, and peach."

"If I had room, I'd have a bite of each."

His look was sexy, and he knew it. That sensual grin he tossed me melted my heart every time.

"I'll try the blueberry."

Two blueberry slices were easily cut and placed upon dessert plates. I poured him a shot of Jameson to relax him further. For a few minutes, Tommy seemed at peace and happy to be eating a meal I prepared. And the pie was both sweet and tangy with a flaky crust that melted in my mouth, thanks to my mother's skillful baking abilities.

Then I opened my mouth about Dad, and the peace and happiness between us dissipated.

"Is that what all this fuss is about? Do you really think a hot meal was enough to rehire your pathetic father?"

"Don't call him pathetic, Tommy. I want to understand what happened. Did you really have to fire him?"

"Sadie, the man has been on warnings since he was hired. He's prejudiced, incompetent, lazy, and he spends more time at the gaming tables than performing his damn job. There are laws now that clearly state business owners can't discriminate against the coloreds. Your father wouldn't hire anyone unless they're white and Catholic. And he treats everyone else on the job brutally. He left me no choice! When is he going to take accountability for himself? He always points his finger at everyone else, but he's the real problem. I told him he can keep the house my father bought for him if he can afford it."

"The house?"

"He mortgaged it, Sadie. Your father is in way over his head in debt. He's got to figure it out and stop throwing it all away at the casino!

"You can't help him either. I mean it! I know you help your family out with some expenses, but you can't pay his mortgage with *my* money!" His wide nose flared from anger. He reached for his car keys and left the house, leaving more than half his pie slice on the plate.

So much for having a nice evening together.

So much for my father having any chance of getting his job back.

Chapter 64

DAD THOUGHT I could help him. Pure disappointment flaunted across his face. Melancholic eyes and a frown so deep I expected tears to be shed. He hated to ask his daughter for a favor, but he thought I might be able to reason with Tommy. I explained that I tried, but Tommy's decision was final and there was nothing more I could do.

Mom posed cheerfully, wearing a prominent smile. She told Dad the job was just not for him, and he'd find something else.

How she could be so encouraging toward my father, I didn't know. Why didn't she get angry? If Tommy gambled all his earnings away, leaving us broke, I'd be as angry as bees whose hive was poked with a stick.

As soon as Mom stepped out of the room, my anger released.

"If you didn't gamble with your paycheck every week, you wouldn't be in this position!"

Dad's head swerved angrily. "What did you say to me?"

"You heard me loud and clear! That woman in there loves you and stands by you even when you can't pay the bills or hold a damn job. Unless you want to lose her and the respect of your family, you better clean up your act and put your family first for a change."

He said nothing. His eyes glazed over, seemingly unfocused. I had never seen this dismal, disgraced look worn upon his face.

By the end of the summer, a FOR SALE sign stuck out of their lawn.

Dad's unemployment checks wouldn't cover the amount of money he owed on the house plus expenses. He gambled away their entire savings, bankrupting them financially and emotionally.

Tommy wouldn't allow me to help them pay their bills. I still had some of my own money left from the Belle Maiden. I used it to help them move into a small house in Bakersfield, California.

Mom hated to be that far away from me, but Dad had to steer clear of casinos and the Vegas Strip. Bakersfield was far enough away to tame Dad's itch for the dice and cards, yet close enough for me to reach them by car. Had they moved back to Massachusetts, I'd never step foot on an airplane to see them. My mother knew that.

Mom learned about a group called Gamblers Anonymous that met regularly. She insisted Dad join. She planned to attend with him to hear what information was shared in a group setting and ensure Dad benefited from the experience.

Patrick earned a scholarship and was packed for UCLA, where he would live on campus. Our parents moving didn't upset his plans. He had no intention of living with them.

As I predicted, Leo ended their relationship, tearing at my brother's heart. Patrick wouldn't speak about it. He quietly mumbled that it was over, and his tactic to deal with the pain was to focus on his education.

Lisa, on the other hand, was torn. She didn't want to leave our parent's home, but she also didn't want to leave Las Vegas and her job. It wasn't because she couldn't find another job in California with her brains and skills. She met a man, Al Collins, a lawyer at the firm she worked for.

I remembered how I felt when Dad uprooted us to move to Nevada, and I had to leave Mickey Quinn and my love for him behind. My sister finally understood how I felt about that and why I was always so bitter about the move. That wonderful feeling of bliss and butterflies didn't happen too often. But when it did happen, losing it seemed unbearable, like losing a piece of yourself you didn't know existed.

For my sister's sake, I asked Tommy if she could stay with us for a while until she could make her own decision about moving to California, or seeing where the relationship with Al might lead.

Tommy approved.

Chapter 65

TOMMY'S BAD HABIT of coming home from work late worsened. Issues constantly arose at the hotel. Granted, he took over all responsibilities from his father since the stroke. Not to mention, the pressures from his silent partners, whom he never liked to discuss with me.

I wasn't sure why I bothered to cook anymore, so I stopped planning large meals. He didn't seem to notice or care, and he had hardly been around. As my husband, I had certain expectations of him. One expectation was that he spent his nights at home with me.

This morning, I awoke in our bed alone. Sometimes when he returned from the hotel late, he would sleep in the guest room, which I assumed was to not disturb my beauty sleep. His bed had not been slept in last night.

I hated for him to sleep in another bedroom while Lisa lived with us. I didn't want her to question our unique style of marriage.

Lisa had been spending a lot of time with Al. She confided in me that they had premarital sex. She literally blushed and quickly braced her fingers against her mouth, expecting me to be as surprised that it happened as she was. I didn't mean to chuckle. She seemed horrified.

If my innocent sister only knew about all the premarital sex I had with hundreds of men. Somehow, informing her that we were amidst a sexual revolution, and women didn't have to wait until they were married to have sex, didn't make her feel better.

Lisa was far more religious than me. She and Mom attended Sunday Mass together every week before our parents left Las Vegas. Lisa still attended Sunday service. I feared if I stepped inside a

Catholic church, I might be struck by lightning, taking out half the parish with me because of my past and deceitful ways.

With both Tommy and Lisa out, I made a small pot of coffee and considered scrambling an egg. Unexpectedly, I heard the front door spring open over Tammy Wynette singing "D.I.V.O.R.C.E." on the radio.

Tommy strolled into the kitchen and mumbled, "Good morning," looking rather disheveled.

"Where were you last night?"

"Where I always am. Working." His tone was cold.

"I am sick of sleeping alone every night, and you don't bother to come home or call."

No response.

"Did you hear me?" My voice rang at a high octave.

"It's hard *not* to hear you."

"What the hell is going on with you? You're distant, inconsiderate, and frankly, nasty!"

He sneered then quickly switched to a very uncomfortable subject. "Was the baby really mine?" He approached with a stern expression.

I gulped then prepared for a good fight to defend myself. Calmly, I answered him the best way I knew how. "Of course. I wasn't with any other man for a few months before we were together."

He stared at me with no emotion. For a split second, I wondered if John blew my secret past out of the water.

"I'm not sure how to know for certain that I was the baby's father. How do I know if I was the only man you had sex with?"

"You're asking these questions *now*? You didn't question me when you proposed. I never asked you to propose. That was your idea." I pointed my index finger right at his nose. "What triggered this behavior?" My defensive instincts kicked in.

"Why wouldn't you say yes to my proposal? Marry into all this money. Money you seem to be pretty comfortable spending. I've been paying attention to the bank statements."

"Oh, I'm sorry. Was I supposed to follow some type of budget?"

His body slinked closer to me, then he firmly squeezed my shoulders with his strong hands. His voice was low and resentful. "Maybe I need to. I work my ass off, and all you do is spend money and complain that I'm not home early enough!"

I wrenched myself from his grip, picked up the pan that waited for the egg to fry, and whacked the hot metal against his arm, singeing the hairs on his skin.

He screeched from the burn then fought me physically for the pan.

When my fingers released the handle, he tossed it across the room, taking out the coffeepot. He pinned me to the wall with the force of his powerful arms. Suddenly, his eyes softened and he released me, taking two steps backward.

"I'm outa here! I'm not living like this. I'll get a lawyer, and will take whatever I can get from you and this marriage!"

I left him standing in shock in the middle of the kitchen. His eyes were large. One hand rummaged through his hair, the other on his hip.

Why would I walk away with nothing? We were married for more than two years, and he rarely came home at night. He was probably having an affair. Had Veronica slithered her way into his life without my knowing?

My closet was filled with clothes, shoes, and accessories. For many years I did without such beautiful things, and now I had them. Did I really want to leave? I grabbed a suitcase from the back of the closet and started to pack. I'd need more than this one suitcase to carry all my belongings.

While I continued to resolve the lack of space in my suitcase, Tommy calmly stepped into our bedroom, drawing in a deep breath before speaking.

"Where are you going?"

"Why do you care? You're never home. You don't trust me. I won't live like this!"

"Stop. Just stop. I'm overtired, and I was out of line." He grabbed the green blouse I was folding and tossed it onto the bed, away from my suitcase.

"You make these accusations that I'm using you for your money. And you bring up the baby's paternity. Now?"

I fumbled through the bottom of my dresser, pulled out some papers, then handed them to him.

"Here. I have copies of my medical records that show when I was pregnant. You picked me up from the doctor's office after my...*injury*. I'm afraid I can't actually prove you were the father. Unfortunately, you have to take my word for it. Or not. I don't care anymore!"

His eyes perused the forms briefly. "I admit, I was out of line. I'm sorry. You don't have to leave."

"Why would I stay? You're never here. Obviously, you don't want me around!"

"That's not true," he whispered calmly, appearing sincere.

Why would he stop me from leaving if he didn't want me here? I felt his hands caress my back with a tender touch. He brought me into his chest and held me.

"I have a lot going on right now. I stay at the hotel to get some sleep, and sometimes I just can't make it home. Cut me some slack, huh. I'm under a lot of pressure with Pop's condition, his power of attorney, and my business partners."

"Well, you need to come home. I want you home *every* night. If you want me to stay in this marriage, you need to be here. I didn't marry you to live alone! If you need help managing the hotel, hire more people!" My anger took over, and I pushed him away from me.

"I will." He moved closer, forcing an embrace with raw affection until I relaxed.

"We didn't get married for normal reasons, Tommy. We didn't love each other, but I thought we could try."

"You don't have to leave," he muttered before kissing my cheek.

When I stopped fighting him, his lips touched mine. Somehow the argument ended when our bodies hit the sheets.

Chapter 66

LIFE WITH TOMMY didn't change much, except that he made a point to come home each night after my insistence. He worked so hard, very dedicated to the business to ensure its success.

He never said the L word. Neither did I. But our arrangement seemed to be mutually beneficial. He wanted a pretty wife on his arm and a family someday. I hadn't been using the diaphragm. That was, when he scheduled time to have sex with me. And when he had a few too many drinks in him, he neglected to wear a condom. Maybe I could give him a child, an actual baby to bear.

The money coming in was more than I expected to see in one lifetime. He bought a bright yellow Ferrari with black stripes. Sometimes we'd go tooling down the freeway looking for a drag race against other hot cars with thrill-seeking drivers.

I was living the life of luxury, shopping wherever I wanted. My red Porsche sat next to Tommy's Ferrari in the garage.

Tommy filled our bank account with a ton of money, and I spent it. This was a glorious situation.

It was Friday afternoon. I bought some poppy flower seeds, one of Mom's favorite flowers. She gave me some pointers for gardening. I thought I'd try to beautify the yard and add some color.

Tommy hired a groundskeeper to take care of the lawn and trees. However, I wanted to give this a shot myself. If I failed, I'd ask the professionals to make improvements.

My clothes and shoes were covered in dirt. My fingernails were desperate for a manicure. But after all this hard work, we might have some lovely red poppy plants.

A severe screech was heard, calling my attention to the driveway where I witnessed a blue Cadillac pull in with squeaky brakes. When the doors opened, I recognized the gorgeous ladies stepping out, dressed in proper attire for this neighborhood—dark-colored pencil skirts, blouses with a respectable neckline, and heels.

I heard myself scream with enthusiasm.

"Sadie!" they yelled in stereo.

"Phoebe! Val!" I ran toward them, arms widened for a hug until I realized I was far too filthy to touch them. A chuckle escaped my lips as I pulled myself back, keeping at least a foot length of distance from them until I showered. "I can't believe you're here! Wait. How did you find me?"

"We left the Belle Maiden, Sadie," Phoebe replied with a half-smile showing.

"The doc mentioned seeing you awhile back. When we told him we were quitting, and we wondered how you were doing since you left, he said he saw you," Valerie added.

My first thought had me questioning if the doc gave them more information than they needed or if he merely told them where to find me.

"Yes, we did run into each other once. Why did you quit? What's been happening?" My eyes lowered, observing the dirt affixed to my body. "Come inside. I'll take a quick shower, then we can catch up."

They paused, eyes widened as they stared up at the enormity of my house that sat upon a couple of acres stretched out, seemingly for miles in the back.

"Whoa. You really live here?" Valerie asked. "Where did you meet your husband, and where can I find one for myself?"

Phoebe poked her in jest.

I showed my good friends around the house then brought them outside by the pool. They were pleased to lounge in the colorful chairs, soaking up the sun.

I made fresh lemonade after a quick shower to scour off the mud and grime from my gardening activities.

"So, where is this husband of yours? How'd ya meet?" Phoebe asked.

"He's part of a family my father knows. We were friends at first. Things between us naturally progressed after I left the ranch." I smiled brightly, neglecting to reveal the real reason Tommy and I were married, or that our sex life had taken a downward turn, and the small fact that we weren't in love. A girl could have some secrets, right? I certainly held many.

The girls told me they shared the second floor of a three-family house in Whitney and started to work full-time at "respectable" businesses. They saved a sufficient amount of money to break free from their previous profession.

Because Phoebe dropped out of high school, she worked hard to earn her GED certificate so she could find stable employment. She managed to snag a job as a bank teller. One of her johns, a bank manager, gave her a break, despite her previous work experience. Phoebe always seemed intelligent, and she had a knack for numbers.

Valerie started waitressing at an upscale restaurant in Paradise.

Doris and Chip retired and left the ranch, moving to Sparks together.

The new madam had extreme rules and expected a bigger cut of the girls' wages. They didn't feel safe anymore. Everything had changed. Drugs were readily available and passed out like candy for the johns, and for the girls to take the edge off. Some of the girls got hooked on hardcore drugs, while others suffered the hazardous effects of the business from an outbreak of crabs and other social diseases.

I was lucky to leave that life when I did.

I treated the girls out to a nearby pub for dinner and drinks. A local band was playing that night. I hadn't been out with friends in a long time. I considered these ladies my friends, no matter if they were Phoebe and Val from the fountain on Freemont Street, or Brandi and Roxy from the ranch.

Joel, the lead singer of the band, was positively adorable.

Phoebe had her eyes on Max, the edgy-looking drummer.

Of course, I was married, and my large diamond ring confirmed my status. A little flirting didn't hurt, especially since Tommy barely touched me.

We were just having fun. The fun would continue every Friday evening at the pub with Joel's band, the Renegades.

Chapter 67

CHRISTMAS CAME AND went fast in 1970. My mother, Patrick, Lisa, and Al joined Tommy and me for dinner. Lisa was practically living with Al, but since she hadn't told Mom and Dad yet, she stayed with Tommy and me while they visited.

John was always invited for the holidays. This year, he chose not to come for Christmas dinner. Tommy felt disappointed his brother didn't join us, but he made a point to pick up John later that afternoon to visit Rocky with a decorated tree and presents.

Another missing party was my father. He was still angry that Tommy fired him. As if avoiding him at Christmastime was punishing Tommy. Now Dad spent his time sitting on the couch, staring at the television all day and night. He refused to come here—ever.

Where was his pride when I tried to convince him to stop gambling? He shouldn't blame Tommy for his deficient work habits. Rocky gave him so many chances. Why couldn't he take accountability for his own actions instead of blaming others? That was the stubborn side of him.

At least Mom convinced him to leave the Strip and start fresh elsewhere. With his physical impairments, he hadn't found another job.

The hatred between my father and Tommy needed to end. New Year's was here. A new year, a time for new opportunities. At least that was how this day should be considered. In spite of the fact that my father was a grouchy, stubborn man, I wanted to give him a Christmas present in person.

I begged Tommy to come with me. "Be the bigger man. He's your father-in-law," I pleaded.

Tommy became furious, and we fought. It seemed fighting and sex were our strong points. Where was the in-between? A common ground? Almost three years of marriage, and we still hadn't developed those basic fundamentals required in a good relationship. Love being the first and foremost missing ingredient to the recipe.

Phoebe and Val were attending a New Year's Eve party at the Flamingo on the Strip. I felt an obligation to visit my dad, especially since he wouldn't come to my home for Christmas.

Lisa joined me, but Patrick wanted nothing to do with our father. He headed back to school early.

Patrick's life revolved around meeting a man and feeling that special chemistry to ignite a real relationship. He only talked candidly to me about his love life, keeping the rest of the family in the dark.

I found the chemical psychology that connected to love fascinating. Patrick's experiences were really no different than a heterosexual relationship. Finding the right chemistry and connection with another person. When that magical moment occurred, meeting "the one," you would travel adventurous journeys, exploring all possibilities until L swept into your soul.

Tommy was sick of my asking him to join me in California for New Year's. There was nothing keeping me here when he said he'd be working, so I chose to spend New Year's in Bakersfield. Yes, I gave him attitude, but he didn't care.

I often wondered why he hadn't thrown me out or asked me for a divorce. He barely touched me. Most evenings he slept in one of the guest rooms.

When my family visited, Tommy would sleep in our room, in our bed. Maybe we both liked to put on a show for outsiders. Maybe it reminded us of the wild, passionate lust radiating within us both.

Chapter 68

ONCE THE HOLIDAYS were over, Tommy began traveling more often, using the new company jet. Tommy bragged about this beautiful aircraft. It was a shame my stomach couldn't tolerate a harmless flight to a fascinating destination. Every month he took business trips, meeting other hotel and casino owners throughout the country and the Caribbean. As busy as he was just managing the Montgomery here in Las Vegas, he planned to expand the business and purchase other entities on the market, of which were in financial trouble. He hired a few managers to oversee the hotel and casino operations, which allowed him the freedom to travel.

Rob Lubitski was Tommy's right-hand man and trusted friend here in Vegas. Rob stood tall at six feet with a stocky build. His delightful smile radiated across his handsome face, highlighting lively brown eyes. I overheard Tommy telling him a joke one day. His hearty laugh seemed to make everyone around him smile.

Tommy knew I hated to fly, although seeing a tropical oasis might have been beautiful. Knowing Tommy, he'd probably leave me alone most of the time while he worked. A slacker, he wasn't. And we had the bank account to prove it. Even if we divorced someday, I'd be set for life financially.

With him gone, I felt a breath of relief. He wasn't around to argue with me about anything. We quarreled about silly things like the kind of toothpaste I'd buy. I preferred Close-Up, whereas Tommy favored Pepsodent. I, apparently, couldn't fold the laundry properly either. Tommy was a bit persnickety, and he had a thing for punctuality. I always made him late.

Since he was away a lot, I hung out with my friends and saw Joel's band wherever they played. And I folded the laundry however I wanted.

Phoebe started dating Max, the drummer of the Renegades. Valerie flirted relentlessly but hadn't met anyone too special.

Phoebe and I reminded her that a *nice* girl wouldn't jump into bed or a back seat of a car with a potential new boyfriend easily, no matter how tempting he might be.

I was having fun for a change. Fun—something I had forgotten how to do.

The girls and I were back at our Friday night haunt, The Pub on Main.

The Renegades played an Elvis song, "Love Me." Joel sang a lot of Elvis songs, but this song he crooned directly to me. He sauntered off the stage as soon as the music started, took the empty seat next to me, and threw me a wink as he belted out the melodious tune.

Chills swirled through me. A rush of heat combatted the cool feeling as my cheeks blushed. Women in the crowd were screaming, jealous he was giving me all his attention.

Joel reminded me of James Dean. There was something very rugged about his look, despite the clean-shaven, youthful face. His hair was a dark golden color with sparkling blue eyes. He wasn't very tall, but he still towered over my five-foot height.

When the song ended, reality set in. Those fireworks I heard rumbling through my ears, tickling my senses, faded.

"That man is sweet on you," Phoebe said with a wicked smile before striding to the bar for another martini.

I couldn't help but smile back.

Valerie gently nudged my side and changed the subject. "When was the last time you heard from Kitty?"

Seeing Kitty with Kenny in that elevator triggered my marriage to Tommy, although I wouldn't discuss that.

"I saw her a few years ago at the Montgomery with her pimp. Why?"

"No one has seen her in a couple of weeks. I keep in touch with some of the girls still. Monique called me. She and Kitty were tight.

Kitty was close to you when you were at the ranch. I wondered if you saw her recently or heard from her. She'd been hitting the drugs pretty hard before we left the ranch. Hard-core stuff."

My heart raced with empathy. I had no idea Kitty got caught up in serious drug use.

"I'm not sure if she'd know how to locate me now, Val." I chose not to reveal the fact that Kitty knew my real first name and that I worked at the Montgomery. "I heard her pimp is a pretty scary guy. Do you know if she was still working for him?"

"I'm not entirely sure what she did when she left the ranch. Normally, Kitty would've checked in with Monique by now. Monique is very worried."

I was equally concerned.

Chapter 69

TOMMY HAD BEEN away more often than usual. I could be a suspicious soul and knew men cheated on their wives. With legalized prostitution at the brothels, infidelity was as routine as brushing your teeth.

I checked with the airport to confirm Tommy was using the company airplane. If I ever found out his plane was sitting here in Las Vegas and he wasn't home, I'd instigate a dirty, ugly fight. I often thought about what I'd do should I end this marriage. It didn't really feel like much of a marriage anymore. When he was home, he never touched me.

For dinner, I made a ham-and-cheese sandwich with lettuce and tomato. Not much on television to keep me company, so I turned on the news and read a *Good Housekeeping* magazine.

A journalist on TV mentioned that a woman's body was found inside a dumpster not far from the Strip. Numerous police officers were shown on-site.

"The young woman has been identified as twenty-six-year-old Rachel Snow," the CBS reporter stated.

Poor Rachel Snow, I thought.

He displayed a police mug shot of Rachel. This poor young woman was discarded like trash. Her somber expression was easy to recognize.

Rachel Snow was Kitty.

Quickly, I ran to the phone in the kitchen and dialed Phoebe and Valerie's phone number.

Fortunately, Phoebe answered. I heard Max's voice in the background, singing along to "Lola" by the Kinks.

I asked Phoebe to turn on CBS and watch the events roll out. As she listened to the reporter speak, I described the picture they showed. The picture of Rachel Snow, who we knew and befriended as Kitty.

This reeked of Kenny. If not Kenny, maybe a john roughed her up and dumped her, hoping her body would disappear as if she never existed. Society might not care who killed her once her profession became exposed. But she was my friend.

Phoebe sobbed on the other end.

I shed a few tears myself. I wanted Kitty to break free from Kenny. I warned her. Why didn't she listen to me? If only I could have helped her.

One person came to mind. Someone who might be able to help and understand the discretion I required.

Chapter 70

THE TELEPHONE BOOK listed the main phone number of the station. I couldn't speak to just any police officer. My conversation had to be off the record, and my name needed to be out of it—completely.

I left a message with the desk clerk. A couple of hours, that felt like days, passed before I heard from him.

Hearing Hank's deep, husky voice on the other end of the phone triggered fond recollections of the moments we spent together at the ranch. He was a regular, gentle and compassionate, who treated me with kindness at thirty-minute intervals. I always felt safe when Hank came to my room, my bed.

My voice surely sounded frantic when we spoke. His shift was ending. I gave him my address, requesting we meet in person.

Officer Henry "Hank" Dubois. Tall, clean-shaven, all but a few whiskers of hair across his upper lip. A rich chocolate brown skin tone and sleepy brown eyes. When I saw his smiling face on the opposite side of the door, the fresh, musky aroma brought me back to when he held me in his arms. I loved his scent.

I greeted him warmly as I opened the door wider for him to enter.

"I must admit, I'm surprised to hear from you after seeing you that night at the hotel." He took cautious steps through the door without making an effort to step farther inside.

"Sorry about that. I have no desire to blend my past in with my present. I didn't mean to be rude that night."

His words cut me off. "I get it. I'm a little confused why you sounded so desperate to talk to me. White cops serve and protect your neighborhood." He stretched his neck out, looking around the house. "Nice place, Sadie." His smile was infectious.

"Please come inside." I opened my arms, inviting him to follow me down the hall. "No one else is home."

"No one else?"

I flashed my wedding ring. "He's out of town on a business trip."

I led Hank to the kitchen and held up the coffeepot, offering caffeine.

He shook his head. "A glass of water would be great."

I fetched a glass from the cupboard and poured him a drink from the faucet. "Do you remember Kitty from the ranch? She was short like me, only with dark curls."

His eyes stared into space while his thick fingers caressed his chin as if he were trying to remember her. "I can't place her. Why?"

"Kitty is Rachel Snow. The woman whose body was found in the dumpster."

"I was questioning some people in that area earlier, assisting the detectives. I'm familiar with the case. Why was she on the streets and not at the Belle Maiden?"

"She had a pimp. A crazy guy named Kenny."

Hank offered no reaction.

"Do you need to write this down?"

"Sadie, the detectives know she was a prostitute because of her record. I'll suggest they talk to the women at the Belle Maiden though. Maybe someone has more information that will help."

"Kitty was my friend, Hank. Kenny is a monster."

"What do you know about him, other than he's bad news? He's a pimp. They're all no good."

"He stays at the Branson Motel."

"The one on Claremont Street?" he clarified.

"That's it."

"Not a pretty place. Should I ask how you know these details?" he questioned.

"Kitty told me about him and where he'd meet his girls to prep them for business."

I didn't lie. I just omitted the fact that I was one of those girls for a very brief moment in time. A time I wished never happened and hoped to forget.

"Do you know Kenny's last name?"

"No. Sorry. Maybe this isn't much help. I can't help but think he may have had something to do with her death."

"Well, anything's possible. If he didn't do it, maybe he knew who she was supposed to meet that night. I'm not on the case, Sadie, but I know the detectives."

"Please, I called you because I trust you, Hank. I can't have my name associated with this. If my husband found out about my time at the ranch..."

"I won't say a word," he stated, and I believed him.

"Oh, one more thing." A thought jumped into my cluttered mind. "Were there bite marks?"

Hank's eyes raced upward to meet mine. "Bite marks?"

"Kenny liked to bite. Left actual flesh wounds, or so I've heard." My cheeks warmed, ashamed to know such intimate firsthand knowledge.

Hank was silent for a moment. "Can you prove that?"

I hated thinking about how I'd have to prove it. Admit I turned a couple of tricks for him and had been with him sexually. If Tommy found out, I'd lose everything.

"No, I can't. Why?"

"Because I overheard that Rachel's body had fresh bite marks against her shoulders and breasts. Several punctures, in fact. The detectives didn't release that detail to the media."

"Well, now that's a clue, right?"

"I'm not sure we can prove that Kenny gave her those marks. Unless maybe you know someone who could testify that this was a *ritual* of his."

I said nothing. As much as I hated Kenny and wanted him to go to jail, I couldn't tell a judge and jury how I knew this was a part of his standard fucking practice.

Chapter 71

IT WAS A breezy Saturday in October. A welcome kiss of fresh air for a hot day in the desert. I drove to the market for some groceries to broil T-bone steaks and bake potatoes.

When I returned, Tommy's Camaro was parked in front of the garage. He didn't normally come home for lunch in the afternoon.

As I strolled up the porch steps and inside the house, I heard voices. Much to my wonderful surprise, Patrick stood in the kitchen, his hand around a can of beer and shooting the breeze with my husband.

Tommy helped me manage the two paper bags I was juggling to prevent a head of lettuce from rolling out.

Patrick's face whipped toward me, displaying the darkest black eye I'd ever seen. Cuts and scrapes outlined with traces of blood smeared along the left side of his face. His nose wore a bandage.

A look of anguish must have washed across my face at the sight.

He turned his head away.

"Your brother had a bit of a scuffle at school yesterday. He's all right though, right, Pattie?" Tommy stated as if it were normal for a college-aged man to be in a fistfight. Tommy tousled Patrick's hair a bit, teasing him.

Tommy's foolishness launched a quick giggle from my brother.

"Are you okay, Patrick? What happened?"

"It's nothing, Sadie. He's fine. We're off to the gym," Tommy answered for Patrick.

"The gym?"

"I'm gonna give him some pointers. Show him how to properly defend himself." Tommy punched the air with his muscular arms, bobbing and weaving as if he were in a ring, preparing for a match.

Somehow that frightened me. Naturally, if I knew who cracked my brother's face like an egg, I'd want to wallop him myself. Tommy and I were both good fighters. Fighting wasn't a skill of Patrick's.

Both men stared at me, clearly recognizing angst in my expression.

"I know you're worried about me, sis. It looks worse than it is. It'll be good if Tommy teaches me how to box."

"We're just going sparring, Sadie. I promise not to hurt him." Tommy laughed, but he understood my concern. "Pattie, take this." He handed my brother a gym bag. "Put it in the car and wait for me outside, okay?"

Patrick left as Tommy instructed, leaving a soft kiss on my cheek.

The moment the front door slammed, I released my frustration. "My brother can't fight, Tommy."

"That's the problem. He needs to learn how to defend himself. If he lets those guys at school whip his ass all the time, he'll be bullied for the rest of his life. I'm helping him. He needs to build up his confidence."

Sadly, I knew Tommy was right.

"Sadie, maybe you don't realize it, but your brother has a target on his back."

"A target?"

He hemmed and hawed before pacing several steps around the kitchen. "Patrick is gay," he whispered.

My eyes widened. Of course, I wasn't surprised by his news flash. I was shocked that Tommy knew.

"Did he tell you?"

"You knew?"

We both chuckled.

"He and I talked about it. I didn't tell anyone else. He doesn't want our parents to know."

"Sadie, I could tell years ago. He hasn't told me outright, but I think he knows that I figured it out. And for the record, I don't care.

225

He's a good kid. We can't be there for him when he's at school. He needs to learn to stand up for himself."

"Thank you." I gingerly placed my arms around his neck. I didn't understand this awkward sensation when attempting intimacy with my husband. When receptive, the warmth of his touch felt so nice.

Chapter 72

LISA AND AL got engaged!

Mom visited a couple of times each month. Lisa pretended she still lived with Tommy and me. She wasn't a virginal bride, but it was important to her that our parents thought she was.

Lisa loved the holidays, especially Christmas, so their wedding was slated for Christmas Eve morning, 1971.

A couple of weeks before her big day, and I felt overwhelmed with the remaining tasks. Mom had been a huge help, but she wasn't able to drive to Las Vegas every week.

Mrs. Collins, Al's mother, was a bit flighty and forgetful. She continued to add more names to the guest list at this late date. The Meade side was very small, plus some of Lisa's friends from the office. The Collins family initially invited fifty guests. Just before the invitations were to be mailed, the total number of guests suddenly jumped to eighty.

I had to explain to Mrs. Collins that we wouldn't have enough room to squeeze another person inside the small banquet room we reserved at the Montgomery. This had to be the last of her guests, or they'd be sitting outside the hotel. She didn't like my remark, but I wasn't the woman marrying her son. Lisa couldn't possibly be the bad guy in this situation. She didn't have it in her to be rude. As matron of honor, it became my job to take care of these details, even if I ruffled a few feathers.

Lisa was expected to meet me here to review the seating chart one more time before she shared it with Al's parents. We worked very hard to make sure Al's Aunt Josephine didn't sit near Aunt Esther and

Uncle Grant. Of course, I needed to ensure Dad sat separately from Patrick and Tommy too. Honestly, way too much drama planning this shindig.

The doorbell rang. I was relieved to rest my eyes from staring at table numbers and names for the last hour.

Although I expected my sister at the door, who normally let herself in, the man on the other side wore an ugly, crooked grin. His black eyes chilled my bones, and his muscular arms pushed the door open with such tremendous force that my small frame fell backward onto the tile floor. I could barely speak. But he gave me little chance to try.

His hands picked my body up by the nape of my neck then pinned me to the wall. "Did you really think I'd let a bitch like you get away with what you did? Junior is dead because of you!"

Kenny's face pummeled close to mine. I could taste the salted beads of sweat against his cheek. I hoped Lisa wouldn't walk in on this.

"I don't know who that guy was who attacked your friend."

"He came after me! Messed up my leg. I live in pain every day because of you!"

"I had nothing to do with that! You ran when he hit your friend. I ran in the other direction."

"No, he told me to stay away from you and John. He knew you!"

Kenny's twitchy hand released me, but I was too afraid to move from this spot against the wall. I wanted to run. But no matter where I ran, Kenny would find me now that he knew my name and address. I studied his mannerisms as he gazed around my home. His eyes looked everywhere while his head continuously nodded.

"You moved up in the world, Penny."

"What do you want?" I asked. My voice sounded shaky as my eyes monitored the door, and my ears listened for Lisa's car, hoping to not endanger my sister.

He clicked his tongue over and over, thinking as he limped in a circle, constantly holding on to his arm and leg as if he were in agony. Sweat gushed from his pores. He looked ill.

"What do you want, Kenny?"

"I think I'm overdue for a settlement from you, seeing that your friend killed Junior and practically crippled me."

He picked up an antique vase that belonged to Tommy's mother. I prayed he wouldn't smash it.

"Seems you've got access to some serious dough, Penny." Carefully, he placed the vase back in its spot atop the console table.

"I gave you four thousand dollars to let me walk away. That was our deal."

"That deal is null and void since Junior died!" His fingers squeezed my mouth firmly. His eyes stared into mine then looked at my lips as if he were going to kiss me.

I'd rather he murder me here on the tile floor than press his lips against mine. He released me before his hands intentionally brushed across my breasts. Then he staggered into the living room as I trailed a safe distance behind. His eyes caught sight of an enlarged wedding picture of Tommy and me hanging above the fireplace.

Kenny snickered at the sight of the framed photo. "Your husband's a pretty rich man, Penny. I know a lot about you, girl. A lot more than he probably does. Remember all our fun times? See, I have photos to capture those fond memories we shared."

Those damn pictures he took of me. Compromising photographs I'd rather not think about. Kenny wasn't original, but his extortion tactics were effective. I couldn't let Tommy or anyone else see those pictures.

"How much do you want for them, Kenny?"

"I'm not sure I can part with those photos of us, Penny." His laugh turned sadistic.

"You came here for a reason. If you don't want money, what do you want?"

"I want a *shitload* of money!"

"We don't keep money in the house. For me to get a thousand bucks will take some time."

"Oh, one thousand won't cut it. I was thinking more along the lines of twenty grand."

A look of surprise must have swept across my face. "Twenty thousand dollars? I can't get ahold of that much money, Kenny."

"Twenty G's is pocket change to your rich husband! You're pretty creative, Penny. I know you are. You've got two weeks or those pictures will land in your husband's lap."

Taking twenty thousand from our account would raise Tommy's eyebrows. On the other hand, if I didn't give Kenny what he wanted, he'd release those disgusting pictures and destroy my life.

"I need three weeks."

His body came barreling toward me, pinning my back to the wall again with ferocity.

"I'll give you till New Year's Day. You come to the motel to deliver it this time. And you damn well better come alone...at midnight." His wicked grin widened. "I know where you live. I know where your husband works. And I know your sister's getting married soon. She's a looker like you. I wonder if she's as good a lay as you." He closed his eyes, fantasizing.

I couldn't hide my surprise or fear that he threatened Lisa, and he knew about her wedding. "You leave my family alone. I'll give you the money for the photos, the negatives, and my freedom."

He released me when he caught sight of my purse that hung on the railing leading upstairs. His broken body jumped at it, tore through it, and pulled out the fifty dollars stuffed inside. He smiled as he crumpled the bills into his pocket. There was something even more frightening about him than I remembered.

"Midnight on New Year's, Penny. Don't make me come back here and remind you what you are, what you'll always be, and where you come from. Once a whore, always a whore." He snickered as he strode out the front door.

My body suddenly trembled.

How could I be sure his blackmail would end?

Chapter 73

TOMMY PLANNED TO work through the holidays this year and miss Lisa's wedding. We had such an argument about that. I didn't care about the bad blood between him and my father. He needed to attend my sister's wedding on Christmas Eve morning.

He had managers running the hotel operations. He bought more hotels to manage. The company jet had been earning its keep, accumulating miles, thanks to all the traveling Tommy scheduled.

The money was great, but if he had so much extra help managing the business, why couldn't he be free for Christmas? Other holidays were less important to me. Christmas was nonnegotiable. I put my foot down, and he eventually caved.

Dad was less than thrilled to be back in Las Vegas. Another blow to Dad's pride was that Tommy paid for Lisa's wedding reception, giving him some say and control of the details. Dad didn't realize Tommy had no interest in the details. Still, Dad refused to stay at my house with that "sonofabitch husband" of mine. Mom and Dad stayed at the new house that Al recently purchased for him and Lisa to live.

Mom planned the entire meal, flowers, and music. She tried her best to stay on budget and keep the total sum low, knowing Dad couldn't afford the bill.

Lisa was far more traditional than me. She chose to wear Mom's wedding dress, as I predicted. Mom helped by taking in the waistline slightly and fixing the hem so it properly fit her. She was quite handy with a needle and thread.

I paid for my hairdresser to spruce up Lisa's poker-straight blond hair and to polish her nails. Being that it was Christmas Eve morning, she charged me thirty dollars for the personal service on a holiday. Reluctantly, I paid her outrageous fee since it was the morning of the eve of Christ's birth.

Paying a thirty-dollar salon bill was peanuts compared to the twenty thousand I had to withdraw to rid my life of Kenny. Tommy had been so distracted lately, and he rarely came home these days. But he was bound to notice a substantial amount of money removed from our account.

A plan began to formulate in my head, but my safety was a concern. Kenny could've killed Kitty. What if he tried to kill me? Or he could continue to blackmail me for the rest of my life. It had to end. Under normal circumstances, I wouldn't go down without a damn good fight.

But the one advantage Kenny had over me was fear.

Chapter 74

LISA'S BEAUTIFUL WEDDING proceeded smoothly. A Mass at Saint Francis church, followed by dinner and dancing at the fabulously renovated Montgomery in the Ireland wing, Ring of Kerry banquet hall. Her wedding colors were pale pink with hints of yellow shades blended in. I wore an A-line pink chiffon dress with ruffles along the hemline. Three of Lisa's friends from work were bridesmaids, wearing the same style dress.

Mom and I went shopping when she visited last summer. I insisted I buy her a new gown to wear. She would have been perfectly happy to wear the mint-colored dress she wore to my wedding. However, a lovely sapphire blue gown with a pretty lace pattern caught my eye. As soon as she tried it on, her blue eyes twinkled with delight. She looked gorgeous wearing that stunning gown.

Patrick, Tommy, and I dined with Al's two brothers and their wives. My parents sat with Al's parents. This seemed to be the best way to divide up the drama between my father and Tommy. Patrick avoided Dad as well.

Tommy seemed itchy. Something had been off with him. I had been too caught up in my own mess with Kenny to figure out what was eating him. The bond he shared with Patrick helped.

Whenever Patrick returned from school to stay with us, Tommy's personality improved. I loved when my brother visited because of the positive effect he had on Tommy.

From the corner of my eye, I observed a figure standing in the doorway of the banquet hall. I shook my head slightly, hoping for a clearer view among the sea of Collinses dancing to the band's version of "Daydream Believer" by the Monkees.

It was Kenny. Here at my sister's wedding.

My legs froze.

He smiled that creepy grin at me before he exited the hall.

My feet moved before my brain had a chance to stop them. My hands shook as I attempted to open the door. Carefully, I peered out of the room, staring into a vacant hallway. Kenny was not within eyesight. He wanted me to see him to torment me and prove he could find me anywhere and anytime.

I tried to inhale, but the air around me suddenly became thick enough to slice. My breath caught in my throat as my heart thumped wildly in my chest. If I hadn't heard the shouting, I might have fainted. Somehow my panic attack was interrupted by an argument across the room.

Dad was yelling about something. I couldn't make out his words. Tommy wasn't around my father, thank goodness. But Patrick stood near Dad, vigorously raising his arms in frustration.

I raced to the table and arrived at the same time as Tommy, who stood next to Patrick with a hand placed gently upon his shoulder. Tommy had a way of calming my brother down and reasoning with him, like with teaching him self-defense.

"I'm not like you, Dad!" Patrick shouted. "I'm not joining the Army to follow in your footsteps."

"What is going on here? Why are you causing a scene at Lisa's wedding?" My question was directed at Dad.

"All I asked, calmly and quietly, was if he was joining the Army after he finishes college."

"You forgot to mention what you said about my *pansy-ass* theater hobby."

"Can't we discuss this at home after the wedding without an audience?" I pleaded, slightly embarrassed.

Although the band slowed the vibe down with their version of Conway Twitty's "Hello Darlin'," the Collins family gathered around to hear what the commotion was all about.

Patrick realized Al's family was listening in, and Lisa seemed agitated that the few Meades in attendance started a ruckus. "I'm sorry, Lisa, Al." He briskly marched away from the table.

"Why is he so touchy-feely? He's not a man!" my father shouted.

"Maybe it's time for you to go home, Fred. And I mean back to Bakersfield," Tommy ordered. The first words he said to my father since he came to town.

Dad kicked the chair that sat between them and leaned his body against his cane. "Who the hell are you to speak to me like that? This is my daughter's wedding, and if I want to have a discussion with my son, you can't stop me. And if I want to visit longer, I don't need your permission!"

Tommy's face displayed anger exuding from within, but he maintained control.

I quickly stood in front of Tommy. "Please check on Patrick for me."

After a moment of nasty eye exchanges with my father, Tommy left the banquet hall in search of my brother.

I turned to the crowd and plastered the biggest, fakest smile across my face that I could muster.

"Time for the bride and groom to cut the cake!" I affixed myself between Lisa and Al, and nudged them to the table where the three-layer, tiered cake sat. The lovely white cake was adorned with pink roses around the large bottom layer for decoration. Ribbons of pink frosting swirled around the delicate edges of each layer, with candied flowers placed perfectly along the top, surrounding a glass figurine of a bride and groom cake topper.

The cake was cut and served, a useful distraction from the embarrassing argument.

Chapter 75

CHRISTMAS DAY WAS nerve-racking. I negotiated the entire Christmas holiday with Tommy. He wanted to escape after the incident with my dad at the wedding, but I wouldn't allow it.

Lisa and Al left for their honeymoon in San Francisco. Dad decided he'd spend Christmas Day alone, having the entire house to himself while the newlyweds were away.

Mom and Patrick joined Tommy and me for dinner.

On December 26, Tommy went back to his usual habit of working a lot. He forewarned me about a business trip he was taking to France to look at a hotel there. He wouldn't be home for New Year's.

New Year's at midnight. I'd have to pay Kenny off. Maybe it was best that Tommy was out of town. I could obtain the money, then think up some extraordinary lie when he returned and reviewed the bank statement. A fee for Lisa's wedding, perhaps. Jesus, a twenty thousand sum would be close to impossible to explain.

Mom told Dad Tommy wasn't home. She put up a fuss about him making amends with Patrick, who always stayed at my house when he came to town.

I could tell Dad begrudgingly showed up on Mom's orders. If I noticed, Patrick saw it too.

"I already apologized to Lisa and Al for the argument at their wedding," Dad stated.

Mom nudged him to continue.

"Patrick, I'm sorry for making fun of your acting hobby, calling it *pansy-ass*."

It was a start. Maybe a rough start, but still a start.

"I only want what's best for you, son. And the Army may do you some good. That's all I was trying to say."

"Do me some good, how?" Patrick asked.

"I don't know. Toughen you up some."

"You mean, make me a man? I am a man, Dad. I'm just not the man you expect me to be. The Army won't change who I am."

"The Army is a fine institution."

"The Army won't take me…because I'm *gay*."

Both Mom and Dad's eyes bulged simultaneously. Speechless, they were.

I stood in front of Patrick, facing our parents. "Okay, let it sink in."

They stared into thin air, without blinking.

I snapped my fingers crisply in front of their faces a couple of times, then glanced back at Patrick.

Dad looked at me with angry eyes. "You knew?"

I nodded.

"You are *not…that*! It's that pansy-ass theater program you're in, trying to change you into something you're not!" Dad yelled with great insistence.

"I am gay. And I'm glad it's finely out in the open."

Dad popped Patrick right in the jaw, splitting his lip. A thin spot of blood dripped down his chin.

Patrick didn't fight back. Dad might have respected him more if he tried to fight him.

"Fred, please! Stop it!" Mom shouted before turning to Patrick. "Are you hurt?"

"My lip will heal, Ma. But the words coming from this man's mouth my entire life won't. He's always saying I'm not a man. I don't play sports. I like the arts and theater, so I'm not a man. I expected no more from him when I told him *I am gay*." He exaggerated the last three words of his sentence to force the fact down their throats.

"Patrick, please. Let them absorb this. Even I needed some time to understand, and you know I support you."

"How could you support this, Sadie? He's an embarrassment to the family! I can't even say I have a son anymore. I've got three *girls*!" Dad stormed out.

Mom followed him before turning to Patrick. "You are my son. I love you, no matter what." Her fingers gently touched his cheek. Tears cascaded from her eyes, and her tone sounded genuine.

Patrick merely nodded, accepting her sincerity.

That night, Patrick slept on the sofa in the den, although there were two other bedrooms available for him to choose. He liked to watch TV. He said it drowned out the noise in his head. Noise our father put there. Patrick felt safe with Tommy and me. And if the TV allowed him to relax and sleep better, he was welcome to keep it on all night long, even the snowy, static channels through the night.

Chapter 76

SEVEN MORE HOURS on this New Year's Eve 1971, and I'd be at the Branson Motel to pay off Kenny.

With Tommy's continuous traveling, he hadn't been paying any attention to me or my activities.

I had no trouble withdrawing cash from the bank. I feared the teller would need to contact Tommy to approve the large transaction. There was so much money in the account, an account with my name on it, she didn't deem it necessary to bother my husband.

This wouldn't be the last I'd hear from Kenny. As long as he had those photos or the negatives, he could knock on my door at any time to blackmail, threaten, or kill me.

A spiteful woman I could be at times. Outspoken. Loud. Harsh in tone. But I honestly never despised anyone, felt true hate with venomous thoughts and wishes for death on anyone, until I met Kenny. I knew he either killed Kitty himself, or he was responsible for her death in some way. I expected him to pay for that.

Our medicine cabinet in the bathroom was stocked with a variety of drugs. I wondered if Tommy used this stuff recreationally. A container labeled "Benzodiazepine" also known as Valium was half full. I crushed the pills into a powdery substance, then poured the dusty particles into a pint of Wild Turkey. I mixed the contents sufficiently to prevent any residue from the drug to be seen.

My hair slicked back into a bun. The evening felt pretty cool for desert weather, so I borrowed Tommy's long, tan trench coat, which was swimming over my small frame. I wore a vintage black Fedora

Tommy had hidden so far back in the closet he probably forgot he owned it. I looked like a pint-size Dick Tracy.

The bottle of Wild Turkey was snug in the front coat pocket. The cash filled a paper grocery bag.

I cautiously drove the Ford to the motel about twenty minutes before midnight. A taxi was considered, but if I had to bolt, I wouldn't want to be standing around waiting for a cab, and the Porsche would call a lot of unwanted attention in that neighborhood. My stomach ached the moment I pulled into the rundown parking lot. Only a few people in sight. The purity of night, stained by lust, at this broken-down motel.

A few deep breaths were needed before I knocked upon the tarnished door.

Surprisingly, it took him a minute or longer to open the door. But there he stood, wearing his tighty-whities and nothing else. A vile sight.

My head swerved as I discovered he wasn't alone.

She was a young girl. Really young with tangled light-brown waves. She sat upright in the bed with a piece of the bedsheet covering her bare breasts. Her face looked pale, hazel eyes glazed. Her trembling fingers gripped the white sheet tightly.

"Hello," I said kindly to the young girl. My god. She looked much younger than eighteen.

"Don't talk to her," Kenny ordered. "You got my package?"

My plan was to drop the bottle of whiskey and attempt to hide it from him so he'd want it even more. Then I suspected he'd drink from it and eventually pass out from the bits of tranquilizer crushed within. At least that was how I fantasized this night would go.

But vivid thoughts of him pouring booze down my throat when that weasel, Artie, terminated my pregnancy, sparked my mind. I didn't want him to share this with the young girl who sat upright, seemingly frightened in his bed.

The end table beside the bed appeared filthy, laden with dirty silverware, needles, specks of white dust, and a couple of cigarette lighters. The foul sight nearly distracted me from my purpose.

"I want the pictures, copies, and negatives first," I demanded.

Kenny snickered.

I noticed the girl wiped a tear from her eye with shaky fingers.

"Are you okay, honey?" I asked her gently.

She stared in my direction, then glanced at Kenny as if she needed his permission to speak.

"Of course, she's fine. She's in good hands here with me, aren't you?" He directed his question at the girl, who instantly turned her head from him.

"If I give you the money, I'm taking her with me too." I pointed to the young girl quivering at the head of the cheap metal bed frame.

Kenny smiled crossly before I felt the sting of his hand against my cheek.

I doubled back, and the whiskey bottle fell from my pocket and onto the floor.

The young girl gasped and held her mouth, clearly distraught by the violence exuding from Kenny.

He picked the bottle up and placed it upon the end table beside the bed. "I'll take this!"

He laughed, watching my fingers caress the cheek he whacked with great force. A welt was sure to appear at any moment.

"You don't get to take any girls away from me. She's just fine. Not for you to worry about. Now I want my money."

"I told you I'd give you the money for the pictures, copies, and negatives. That was the deal."

His head shook, grinning from my demand, then he stepped backward toward the bureau. His secret stash was inside a dresser drawer, contained within a shoebox. There seemed to be a lot of pictures and numerous envelopes in that box. He lifted an envelope. I could see the outside was labeled "Penny." He waved the envelope around as if to fan off his warm flesh before handing it to me.

"My money, Penny."

I snatched the envelope from his fingertips. There were numerous negatives and pictures of me naked with him and Artie on top of me. Disgust and shame overwhelmed me.

I glanced at the girl in his bed again, too frightened to move. What had he done to her? Did he take pictures of her? Was he grooming her for a life on the streets and a dumpster as a grave like Kitty?

"You don't need her. You've got a lot of girls, Kenny. Let me take her home." I turned to the girl. "How old are you?"

Kenny pushed my body to the wall then wrapped his large, strong hands around my neck. He reached for his pocketknife, clicked it open, and pierced its tip into the side of my temple. The scratch of its sharp point pricked at my flesh. A warm, thin streak of blood drizzled down my cheek.

"I told you not to speak to her!"

The paper bag with the money fell to the floor.

He released his hold on me slightly to bend and pick up the dough.

My fingers stretched outright, desperate to reach the whiskey bottle from the table. I managed to shift the bottle within my grasp. Instantly, I struck him hard on the back of his head, causing his body to collapse at my feet.

The young girl screamed and jumped from the bed. She ran into the bathroom and slammed the door closed.

I could hear her cries from the other side.

Kenny's body wiggled. He reached for me with hate in his eyes until he flopped to the floor, out cold. God, I hated him even when he laid there unconscious.

As much as I wanted to run out and take that young girl with me somewhere safe, I wanted something on Kenny, so he'd leave me alone forever. I moved the pocketknife away from his body and tossed it to the other side of the room. I stormed to the dresser and scrambled through his belongings.

Keys, ticket stubs, and a lot of photographs of women like me were contained in a large shoebox. He had multiple envelopes with names written on the outside. Then there it was, staring me in the face. An envelope labeled "Kitty."

Something jiggled within the packet. As I peered inside, Kitty's silver cross necklace was curled in the corner. Did Kenny rip it off her cold, dead body after he murdered her? Without forethought, I placed her most cherished possession inside my pants pocket. I wouldn't leave her cross with her killer.

The envelope also held more pictures of her than I cared to see. Photos of her naked, having sex with a variety of men. Other pictures of her tied up and handcuffed to a bed. Her body wore bruises. Track marks along the inside of her arms were visible to my eyes, along with bite marks on her shoulders and neck.

I never cried much, but I shed several tears for my departed friend.

Next to the shoebox sat a metal canister. I opened the large tin can, purely out of curiosity, and to ensure there were no other pictures of Penny. I wasn't an expert on drug paraphernalia. Although, I experimented at the Belle Maiden. Sometimes the urge surfaced to take the edge off in order to tolerate that lifestyle. There were many vials and small packages with pills, powder, and needles inside this container. Kenny wasn't just a pimp. He must be a drug dealer. And a user, given the condition of his room, the puncture-like wounds on his arms, and his twitchy appearance.

Since Kenny was an addict, his blackmail would never end.

Suddenly, I felt his strong, muscular arm around my neck, choking me. Kenny came out of his stupor. He lifted my body off the floor by my neck, squeezing tighter and tighter.

My legs kicked at the dresser, knocking the shoebox and all of its contents over. I squirmed, grabbing at his arms to free myself from the pain for as long as I was capable.

The room started to fade when for some reason, he released me. Dropped my body hard on the floor. His torso slumped on top of my legs.

I gasped for air and attempted to crawl away from him as quickly as my tired body allowed before he could catch up to me. But he wasn't trying to chase me down.

Kenny collapsed on the filthy motel room carpet, facedown with blood oozing from his back. His entire body began to shake as if seizing.

When I looked above him, the young girl stood trembling with a towel loosely covering her body. She held the pocketknife in her hand, blood dripping to the floor. Kenny's blood.

My legs moved, pushing my body upright to stand. The main threat was in agony and incapacitated. However, the young girl holding the blade, staring down at Kenny, might be a loose cannon.

She kicked his legs violently as tears raced down her face.

What torture did he put this poor girl through in this motel room? I recognized his teeth marks on her shoulders. I wouldn't put rape past his long list of crimes.

The first thought I had was to ensure the door was locked so no one would enter. Who knew how many visitors Kenny expected tonight?

"What's your name?" I asked her calmly, wearing the sweetest smile I could gather.

She simply stared into thin air, scared, shaken, and in shock.

"It's okay. I want to help you. You saved my life. He's a bad man." Slowly, I took a few steps toward her. "Can you lower that knife please? I promise I'm going to help you, and get you out of here safely."

With petrified eyes displayed, she dropped the knife to the floor, splattering a few drops of blood along the white bed sheets.

Kenny's body continued to twitch. So much blood. I'd be damned if I helped him. I picked up Kenny's knife, darted to the bathroom, and washed away the blood. The irony, him being killed by his own blade.

"Where are your clothes?" I asked.

She didn't answer, but I noticed a pair of jeans and a blouse thrown sloppily over a dingy golden chair in the corner.

"You need to clean up."

Her eyes were glazed over with apparent streaks of blood on her arms and hands. A few bloody specks were splashed against her cheeks.

"Jump in the shower quickly and wash up," I ordered.

She didn't move.

Cautiously, I drew near her to take her attention off a very bloody, wounded Kenny. I nudged her by the shoulders into the bathroom, then turned the knob in the shower for a steady stream of warm water to flow. She had no blood on her feet from the pool surrounding Kenny's body.

"Get in the tub, wash off, and get dressed. Hurry!"

She started to come around and nodded before releasing the towel from her body and stepping into the tub.

"It's Renee. My name," she stammered.

"Hi, Renee." I tried to manage a smile for her. "It's going to be okay. He's not dead. You didn't kill him." A lie I wanted this young girl to believe.

While Renee was in the shower, washing Kenny's filthy hands, blood, and saliva off her, I carefully approached his lifeless body. I picked up the shoebox from the floor and left it sitting on top of the dresser with Kitty's envelope at the top. I placed some of Kitty's pictures, particularly the one that showed the bite marks, inside Kenny's wallet on the dresser.

I swiped every bill he had in his wallet, like the night Jim rescued me from Kenny and Junior. Maybe the cops would think he was robbed.

Renee tiptoed out of the bathroom, showered and dressed. She saw Kenny's body then began to cry and quake. She inched near him, wincing with hate. I thought she was going to kick him again.

"Don't go near him! I don't want his blood on you." I directed her to crawl over the bed toward me on the other side to avoid stepping over his limp body.

At a snail's pace, she crept on to all fours atop the messy bed. Her knees guided her across before she flew into my arms.

"Shh. It's going to be okay, but we have to get out of here. Is there anything here that's yours?"

She shook her head.

"Are you sure? Once we leave this room, we can't come back. I don't want you linked to this *incident* in any way. No clothing? Handbag?" I paused, thinking. Then the camera on the nightstand caught my eye. "Did he take photos of you?"

She nodded.

I crawled across the tangled sheets on the bed and lifted up the camera to open it from the back. Then I whipped out the wiry strand of film, exposing the negatives, ruining any photographs taken of Renee.

The paper bag sat on the floor with the money in it. I tossed in the contents I stole from Kenny's wallet, the knife that debilitated him, and the exposed film.

When Renee and I started to leave together, I remembered the bottle of Wild Turkey I laced with sedatives. I couldn't leave that behind. I threw the bottle inside the paper bag too.

"Renee, we're going to walk out of this room very calm and cool. Okay? No running or crying. We can't attract any attention to ourselves. My car is parked on the other side of the motel."

She nodded before wiping away residue from her red, swollen eyes.

I made sure the lights were off, windows in the room locked, and the cheap orange curtains drawn. I opened the door and peeked outside to ensure no one else was around.

A junky-looking vehicle drove up, bumper hanging down on an angle beneath a broken headlight.

Quietly, I closed the door and locked it, praying the driver didn't notice someone was in this room.

I placed my finger across my lips, signaling Renee to be very quiet.

As I peered carefully through the curtain, I saw a large black man approaching.

He rapped on the door to the sound of a song I couldn't recognize in that instant.

I nudged Renee to sit atop the bed, and I covered her mouth, fearing she'd burst out crying any second.

The knocks turned to thunderous bangs. "Kenny, you in there?" The incessant banging was maddening. "Come on, man, we need to talk!" He waited and continued violating the door for a few more minutes.

I worried the cheap motel room door would burst open. Renee and I both flinched with every loud thump he made.

"Shit!" the man said before I heard the clunky sound of his car door opening and closing. The loud surge of the engine rumbled. The sound dissipated as he sped off.

I was trying to keep Renee quiet, but who was there to keep me quiet? I wanted to scream, cry, or run as fast as I could away from this scene. I stood to my feet, taking baby steps around the bed.

Kenny laid still on the floor, facedown with his eyes stiffly widened. He had to be dead, but I wasn't going to touch him to be sure.

I feared he'd jump up and kill us both with his bare hands. Although the puddle of blood around his body swelled.

After a few agonizing minutes of silence in this sadistic room, I found my way to the curtain and scoped the outside lot. The area seemed quiet except for a couple of homeless men sitting on the ground, resting against the broken fence aligned with the structure. On the inside doorknob hung a white DO NOT DISTURB sign.

I took Renee by the hand then grabbed the paper bag with my money, the film, the drug-laced bottle of whiskey, and the murder weapon, assuming Kenny was, in fact, dead. We swiftly escaped.

The room looked dark from the outside, and the door locked. I placed the DO NOT DISTURB sign on the knob outside the door.

With any luck, it would be a couple of days before Kenny's body was found.

Chapter 77

MAYBE IT WASN'T the brightest idea to bring Renee back to my home, but I couldn't very well leave her on the street.

Neither of us spoke a word in the car. She didn't question me about anything. Not where we were going, how long she could stay, was Kenny really dead, or would we become suspects in his murder. I didn't know the answer to any of those questions if she had the wherewithal to ask.

Before reaching Henderson, I took a long detour, stopping at Lake Mead, a reasonable place to dispose of a murder weapon.

"Wait right here. I'll be back," I told Renee, who barely made eye contact with me.

I grabbed Kenny's knife from the paper bag. No trace of blood visible to my eyes. I dropped it in the dirt and massaged grains of sand around the sharp blade. Then I marched toward the water and hurled it as hard as I possibly could into the lake.

The silent journey to my house seemed to take forever. An overwhelming surge of relief flew through me the moment I parked inside the garage.

Renee was a slight kid, but rather tall. I offered her a nightgown to wear to bed and showed her to one of the guest rooms.

"Are you hungry?"

She shook her head.

"When was the last time you ate?"

Her shoulders shrugged. Then the tears started to fall again.

This girl clearly had no business being on the noisome streets. I wanted to hold off asking her questions about her life, but I couldn't wait.

"How old are you?"

"Um, fifteen," she whispered. Her delicate voice rattled through chattering teeth.

I tried to hide my surprise about her age. "Why were you with Kenny tonight? How did you meet him?"

She didn't answer me.

I poured her a glass of cola and whipped up a turkey and swiss sandwich as she gathered her thoughts.

Through tears and a crackled voice, she explained that she ran away from home after an argument with her parents. A friendly man found her at the bus station and offered her a place to stay. That friendly guy brought her to Kenny, who said he'd take care of her.

Kenny's idea of taking care of a woman was bedding her then preparing her for a life of hustling.

"What kind of fight did you have with your parents?"

"It was stupid. I was so stupid to leave. They were angry because I got a D in geometry. They grounded me and wouldn't let me go to a concert. I ran away. Took the bus into Las Vegas to see the show. That's all I wanted to do. Then I met that guy, and…"

"You're safe now. And you weren't wrong to hurt that awful man." I hugged her to try to reduce the tears, never using the terms "murder" or "dead."

"I know what he's like. What he did to you in that motel room he did to me too. And I want you to know that sex is not always like that if you're with a nice boy. And when you're much older. I'm sorry you were brought to him."

Renee merely nodded, agreeing with every word I said.

"At home with your parents, did you have food to eat?"

"Yes."

"Did you have a bed to sleep in and clothes to wear?"

She nodded.

"They only punished you because you didn't do well in school, right?"

Another nod.

"Why'd you get a D in math?"

She shrugged. "I missed a couple of homework assignments and didn't study for a test."

"Your life sounded pretty good until you were grounded. Trust me, life at home is far better than any life you could have on the streets. If you do well in school, maybe you could go to college and get a good job, so you're never in that kind of position with a man like Kenny again. I have a feeling your parents are worried sick about you. Maybe tomorrow, after you get some sleep, you can call them. Tell them you're safe. I'll make sure you get home."

She nodded through the tremors.

Really, she should contact her parents now. I thought about relieving any stress her parents felt if they realized she had snuck out of the house. But Renee was not in the right state of mind to talk to them. She needed to settle down before making that call.

She finally calmed enough and asked if she could sleep. Whether or not she actually slept, I wouldn't know.

I lit a fire in the living room. As the red and orange flames filled the pit, I tossed in all the photos Kenny kept of Penny. The film I took from Kenny's camera hit the flames next. I poured a shot of vodka, tossed it back easily, and watched the fire crackle and pop away any evidence of Penny and Renee's association with Kenny.

My fingers lifted the pretty silver necklace from the pocket of my jeans and clasped it securely around my neck. With a tender touch, I placed my lips upon the crucifix and said, "You can rest in peace now, my friend." If only my soul could feel a similar version of tranquility.

I poured the bottle of whiskey with the added sedatives down the kitchen drain. As soon as the bank opened after the holiday, I'd return the twenty thousand to our account. Tommy would never know it was gone.

In the morning, Renee's hands weren't shaking as severely as last night. She didn't have much of an appetite still. I eavesdropped on her conversation with her frantic mother. It was easy to sense the worry and relief in her tone, hearing Renee's voice. Her father drove to the police station, filing a report because she had gone missing. Renee was fortunate to have a loving family to return to.

I tapped on the guest room door, where Renee had slept, the room I referred to as Mom's when she visited. Upon entering, Renee sat cross-legged on the bed, clutching Mom's rosary beads in her hand.

"You're Catholic, Renee?"

"I went to Saint Anne's through the eighth grade," she whispered before setting the rosary beads on the nightstand. She managed to display a hint of a smile.

I lifted the beads and gently placed them back in her palm. "You can pray if you'd like."

She shrugged her shoulders then nodded. "Will you pray with me?" she asked with melancholic eyes that melted my heart.

Maybe she assumed these beads were mine. It had been many years since I prayed with rosary beads, but I gripped Renee's hand with compassion and an optimistic smile then sat beside her on the bed. Together, we chanted the prayers I remembered from my youth.

Once the last Hail Mary and Glory Be were complete, Renee smiled in a way that secreted solace, which helped calm my rattled nerves. Praying provided me with some consolation too.

I gave her a few minutes alone and stepped outside for fresh air. Keeping the rhythm of prayer going, I said the Act of Contrition as best as I could from memory for atonement. Although, reciting a few prayers might not compensate for all of *my* sins.

Later, I prepped Renee before driving her to the bus station where she'd meet her folks. She had to tell her parents she spent the night in the bus station, had a change of heart, and wanted to return home. I suggested she apologize for worrying them and to never tell anyone what happened in that motel room. If she talked about it, she could be arrested, and a horrible man like Kenny was not worth her getting into trouble with the law.

Kenny was found and probably at the hospital recovering, I lied to her. It was in her best interest not living with the cold, hard truth that she most likely killed him, and his body would soon be in the morgue. A cross I would bear for her.

Renee hugged me tightly and uttered a sincere "thank you" before I dropped her off at the bus station.

I stayed and watched as her parents dashed toward her with open arms, thrilled to have their daughter with them, safe and sound.

Her emotional scars would heal in time. At least that was what I whispered to convince myself of the possibility. That was my hope for Renee.

Chapter 78

AFTER A HIGHLY stressful week, I looked forward to my usual Friday night out with Phoebe and Valerie. Tommy was expected home Sunday night.

Kenny's death didn't make the news, which made me anxious. If his body wasn't found, did he survive? He couldn't have. Too much blood was drained from his body. I hoped to hear about the death of a pimp and drug dealer on television or in the newspaper. Any news to ease my mind and assure that he was not still breathing, telling the police I attempted to murder him, or bringing Renee into it.

Between the holidays and Lisa's wedding, I hadn't been out in weeks. Nor had I seen Joel. I missed his flirty winks, swaying to his songs, and the strumming of his guitar.

The girls told me all about their Christmas and New Year's parties. I wished I was with them. They had a lot more fun than I did.

We reminisced about life at the Belle Maiden when we were alone. Fun times. No sad or painful memories.

Talking about the ranch led to Kitty and how her murderer was out there roaming free somewhere. Only I knew who her murderer might be, if my instincts were on target, and he was most likely no longer roaming free. Something about that thought gave me satisfaction, even if I was an accessory to Kenny's presumed death.

We raised our shot glasses and toasted to our friend, Kitty.

By the end of the night, we all had a few too many drinks. The vodka shots flowed down my throat smoothly. I stopped counting after the fifth shot. I was in no condition to drive. Max would take home the girls. I intended to call a cab.

The final song of the night was Frankie Valli's "Can't Take My Eyes Off You." Joel sang the romantic tune in his melodious voice directly to me. How I loved when he did that.

At the end of the song, his face was so close to mine, I thought he was going to kiss me. Instead, his lips gently caressed my forehead. His eyes were serious, yet comforting as he stared deeply into mine.

I stuck around after the others left. I hadn't called a cab. In fact, I no longer planned to. Joel stepped into the back room to collect the rest of his things, and I followed him.

His back faced me. My arms wrapped around him snugly, surprising him. His head quickly whipped around. I didn't give him a chance to think or say a word. I reached up and met his lips with mine.

He grabbed my waist firmly, pulling me in close. Our tongues entwined playfully. Then he stopped suddenly.

"You had a lot to drink tonight, sweetheart."

I knew it wasn't the alcohol. God, I loved that he called me "sweetheart." My own husband didn't call me that. Tommy never called me anything endearing.

"Maybe I should call you a cab."

"Not till morning. Take me home with you, Joel."

The passion between us sizzled. I missed that glorious feeling. The feeling of actually being wanted, desired.

None of those emotions came naturally with Tommy anymore. I was no fool. I saw the signs. Maybe he took on a lover himself. Another dancer at the hotel perhaps? He barely touched me or acknowledged my existence.

I didn't want to think about any consequences tonight. I needed to be held and kissed.

The affection Joel had for me was evident in the way he loved me. His kisses brought me comfort and warmth. His thin yet powerful arms offered me security. His eyes were thoughtful, kind, and loving. When he entered me, a raging stream of bliss and pleasure filled my senses as I released all of my stress and anguish through an incredible, pulsating charge. Joel made me feel incredibly sexy. A sensation no man had allowed me to feel in a long time.

Chapter 79

HANK CALLED THE house late the next morning after Joel drove me home. He requested we meet in person, which was odd.

If he wasn't in uniform, I didn't think he should come to my house. A colored man knocking on my door in this neighborhood in broad daylight while my husband was away would fire up the grapevine.

He suggested a diner not far from his precinct as our meeting spot.

I followed the directions Hank provided because I wasn't familiar with the area. The drive took longer than anticipated, but eventually I made it to the Hawthorne Diner and parked along the gravel stone lot.

Upon entering the joint, the waitresses and customers' heads all turned in the direction of the small pasty white girl with blond hair. Relieved, I was, when Hank's hand waved at me from the back-corner booth. The crowd settled down after seeing I was welcomed by their tall, handsome neighborhood cop.

I walked through the thick haze of smoke, breathing in the combined fragrances of tobacco, coffee, and maple syrup.

My body plopped down on the red cushioned seat across him. The aroma of maple syrup overpowered the scent of Hank's cologne I enjoyed. His smile was welcoming and pleasant as always.

"Thanks for meeting me here."

"You wanted to meet in person. Here I am."

A very tall, dark-skinned waitress appeared with a pot of coffee and a mug.

I nodded for a cup.

She took her time, slowly pouring the beverage while her eyes wavered back and forth at Hank and me. Eventually, she had her fill of studying our faces and stepped away. Or maybe my mug was filled to the brim with the steamy hot brew, and she moved on to other customers.

"Do you have any new information about Kitty?" I blurted out before taking in the caffeine.

"I heard about a possible lead."

My heart began to throb so hard I felt the thumps pounding in my throat. "And?"

"The detectives found her pimp, Kenny Perez."

I could taste the bile building in my mouth from the tremendous thuds. I swallowed the hot brew that burned my throat on its way down. "Was he questioned?" My eyes wandered from Hank's.

"Kind of hard to question a *dead man*." He watched my reaction as he sipped his coffee.

My eyes closed, relieved that his body was found, and he really was dead. "He's dead? How?"

"All I know is he was meeting one of his *ladies*. Can't locate her, but he was lying in a pool of his own blood on his motel room floor."

"What does that mean?"

"Well, he didn't die from natural causes. Someone stabbed him from behind."

"Are you saying you can't prove he killed Kitty?"

"The evidence found at the motel had explicit photographs of Kitty. And he had some pictures of her in his wallet. Strange."

"Strange, how?"

"The pictures in his wallet were placed there very recently."

I tried to keep a straight, clueless face. "What does that mean?"

"He had items in his wallet for a long time. There were heavy creases and fading of his belongings. The pictures of Kitty seemed new, untainted, as if someone planted the photos there to try to associate him with her."

Damn, I thought to myself. I tried to be so clever.

"Of course, we really don't know. Maybe Kitty's real killer is trying to pin the murder on a dead man. Maybe Kitty's killer murdered Kenny too."

I offered no reaction. "I suppose ridding the world of one more pimp isn't a bad thing."

"Except the detectives can't question him. We'll never know of his whereabouts when she died. I wanted to meet you in person to tell you her murder may go unsolved. We have no other leads right now. I'm sorry." His eyes lowered, accepting the disappointment my face surely displayed.

"From what Kitty told me about Kenny, I bet a lot of people wanted him dead."

"You're probably right. The detectives are still questioning people from that area. Maybe somebody saw something. We really don't know if his death is in any way connected to Kitty's."

I placed my mug filled with coffee carefully on the table, then folded my hands in my lap, hoping Hank wouldn't notice them quivering.

Chapter 80

MY AFFAIR WITH Joel continued. One night with him wasn't enough. Tommy was gone so much that Joel and I managed to see each other several nights a week. He had an apartment across town. The neighborhood looked a little sketchy, but he didn't have a roommate. We had a lot of privacy at Joel's place.

It didn't take long before Phoebe and Valerie noticed something intimate sparked between us. My cheeks blushed when they asked. I couldn't hide it. Joy and contentment poured from my heart when I was with Joel. My friends didn't judge me. Our relationship seemed more real than my marriage to an absentee husband.

Naturally, Joel asked about my marriage and why I stayed married to a man who was never home. When Tommy was home, he barely talked to me. He didn't sleep in our bed anymore unless my mother or brother were in town for a visit.

Could I leave Tommy? Yes. But what would happen to me? Tommy wasn't a great husband, but he was a great provider. I enjoyed the luxury of helping my parents with expenses, and Patrick with college. We paid for Lisa's wedding. I'd never be able to help my family financially if I left Tommy. I might not be able to support myself.

I hadn't said the L word to Joel. I wasn't sure if I felt it, or if I just liked the attention he gave me. Right now, the situation worked for both of us.

Besides the Pub on Main, Joel booked this dive bar away from the Strip called AJ's. The block seemed pretty rough with older buildings in need of a makeover, and a few small businesses and liquor stores lined the street. The bar drew in bikers and street gangs. His talent as a musical artist was appreciated by the tough crowd. Often fights broke out among the patrons. Tables thrown, glass bottles shattered, chairs smashed against the backs of oversized drunken men.

The Renegades played at AJ's a few times in the past, but the owner hired them to work every Friday night. The guys needed the work, even if the atmosphere was on the rough side.

From a different perspective, there was an evangelist group trying to save us all from ourselves. They'd stroll pleasantly into the bar, hoping to sell what they were preaching.

I had witnessed them dust a man off and pick him up, literally. They literally picked him up from a barstool, drunk as a skunk, and carried him into their Volkswagen van. They promised him shelter for the night and possibly a job, depending on his skills.

They were trying to clean up the area and help those in need. A worthwhile cause, provided people actually wanted their assistance. The drunks at this bar might not want to clean up their act.

This became the mix of people to share space with on Friday nights.

Phoebe nudged my arm and glanced over to the door. A couple of young girls sashayed in, wearing miniskirts and tight tube tops, revealing their belly buttons and cleavage. Prostitutes? Probably. A little on the young side, which concerned me.

I was legally an adult when I made the decision to turn tricks at the brothel. Young girls like Renee might not understand this life they were entering—if it was a choice. Some might be forced into this career with no place to go and no one to turn to.

The men surrounded these girls, buying them drinks while fondling their waistlines and curly blond wigs. After a couple of rounds of alcohol had been washed down these girls' throats, the fellas became more touchy-feely. Enough to make me uncomfortable. Their advances seemed acceptable to these young girls, but I was afraid for them. This was a sketchy place with a rough, stoned crowd. I had never seen them in here before.

I shot back the remnants of vodka in my glass and charged over in front of the two girls, pushing numerous hands off their bodies.

Moans and groans from the male patrons of AJ's started, followed by insulting remarks and angry growls.

"Back off!" I shouted. I turned to the girls and said, "You don't want any of this action."

They were silent, but their surprised brows and glazed eyes almost seemed appreciative of my effort to save their bodies from potential assault.

That was, until their pimp strutted in. A solid, stocky, fair-skinned man wearing a bright red jogging suit. He towered over all of us. He was hard to miss, and he wasn't happy with me.

As soon as this pimp put his hand on my arm, cursing excessively at me, Joel plummeted off the stage during his Three Dog Night "Joy to the World" number and pounced upon the tall, menacing man.

Joel was very strong for his small stature, but no match for such a large street guy like this pimp. The two brawled with the entire bar as spectators egging them on.

Barstools were thrown.

Beer bottles smashed.

That pimp used a sharp piece of glass and sliced Joel's right hand and arm. Blood streamed from his wounds.

Max and the other band members ran to Joel's aid, fists throwing lefts and rights. They went at it until noses were bloodied, lips were split, and body parts were swollen and bruised.

The two hookers ran over to their pimp, ensuring he was all right.

The pimp pushed them both away, calling them expletive names, grabbing their arms, and shoving them out the door.

"Don't go with him!" I screamed. "You're not safe on the streets!"

"Stay away from my girls, bitch!" the pimp harshly warned me.

By this time, the police arrived. Both the pimp and Joel were arrested for fighting.

The two hookers ran from the cops unscathed.

Chapter 81

VALERIE, PHOEBE, AND Max offered to ride to the police station with me, but I assured them I'd take care of Joel and pay his bail. It was my fault he got into this mess. If I didn't challenge that pimp and mind my own business, Joel would still be up on stage singing me the Jerry Reed song I requested. Instead, he was in need of a doctor and bail money.

And if I didn't get involved, who knew what those men would have done to those young women? Yes, they were hookers, but their profession didn't necessitate a monopoly of gangbangers holding them down and taking turns violating their bodies—probably without paying.

No one from this crowd knew that Phoebe, Valerie, and I worked at the Belle Maiden. And I wanted to maintain discretion. We were all out of the business and planned to keep it that way. No one needed to know about the poor choices we made at a vulnerable time in our lives.

I wasn't entirely sure how to explain to Joel my rationale for helping those young girls. Feeling passionate enough to start a brawl that landed him in jail. Of course, I never asked him to protect me.

When I arrived at the police station, Joel still wore cuffs during an interview with a couple of officers. He shot me a sweet look and a wink, indicating he was okay.

From a distance, I mumbled, "I'm sorry" to him.

In response, Joel blew me a gentle kiss through the air. Not a bit of spite or anger in that man.

The arresting officer asked me for a statement. Apparently, a witness told this cop I was the instigator, a rabble-rouser.

I explained the crowd was ready to assault the young girls in the bar. I was worried about their safety and spoke up to those men. Then I pointed to the pimp in holding, still in handcuffs, and told the officer that he put his hands on me. Joel was merely protecting me. "How would I have known what he did for a living, or that those girls were prostitutes?" I was in high acting form, a talent I picked up from my brother.

"Save it for the judge," he said.

"When will that be?"

"Monday morning."

"Wait, does Joel have to stay here all weekend? Can I bail him out?" I pleaded.

"Nope, not tonight. Afraid it's got to wait till Monday, ma'am."

"I'm okay, Sadie," Joel muttered as he was escorted off to a six by nine cell.

"He needs a doctor!" I yelled as I witnessed the officer hauling him away, still in cuffs.

An officer sat at the main desk near the entrance of the station. I approached him with sad eyes, appearing distraught. I worried about Joel spending the whole weekend in the slammer.

"Do you know if Officer Dubois is working tonight?"

"Hank? Yeah, he's walking a beat."

"Is there any chance you can get him a message? Pleeeeeze?" I begged, forcing a tear to fall, which was rather difficult for me to fake.

I could only imagine what a jail cell looked like in this place. The gray walls were dingy, and my shoes stuck to the tacky floor with each step taken. If this was what the cops had to work in daily, I wouldn't expect the prisoners to have a comfortable bed with clean linens to sleep on.

My feet paced along the cracked, sticky tile floor. It took nearly ninety minutes before Hank arrived with a prisoner in tow. He escorted a thin man with wide-rimmed glasses wearing handcuffs. A part of me was curious what this man, who looked like a bookworm, did to get arrested. My impatient side desperately needed Hank.

His eyes raised at the sight of me. The officer at the desk gave him a message via the radio that I was here, waiting to speak to him.

He expected me, but he was curious as to why. And it had nothing to do with Kitty's death.

Once he completed booking and processing his suspect, he dashed toward me, no smile to be seen as he normally wore.

"What are you doing here, Sadie?"

I encouraged Hank to follow me into a corner for some privacy.

"I had a *situation* tonight."

"What kind of situation?"

"My friend was arrested. But he was protecting me from a pimp."

"What are you doing hanging around a pimp?" His arms crossed. "Does this have anything to do with Kitty?" Irritation in the undertone of his voice was easily detected, showing concern for my safety.

"No. I was out with friends listening to a band. Two hookers walked into the bar. Well, without sounding like the start of a bad joke, or going into too much detail, I was only trying to defuse a bad situation. Then their pimp put his hands on me. My friend stepped in, and there was a fight."

"Who is this friend?"

"He's in lockup. They won't release him on bail."

"He won't get a bail hearing until Monday morning now. What do you want me to do?"

"Can you make sure he's okay. Keep an eye on him for me."

"Who's this friend of yours, and how good of a friend is he?"

I offered Hank the details he requested without telling him Joel and I were lovers. Naturally, Hank was uncomfortable with babysitting duty. Joel would hate that I asked Hank to look out for him in the joint.

I felt so helpless right now. Helpless, yet responsible for stepping into a situation that didn't concern me.

My concern for these young girls, who made poor choices that led them to the streets, ran deep. If John didn't help me, I could have died, winding up like Kitty in the bottom of a dumpster at Kenny's hand. I helped Renee escape Kenny's clutches. I wanted to help others on the streets, at least the girls who would accept help.

In church, Father Riley gave a sermon stating, "God helps those who want to be helped. God can give us direction, but we have to listen for his message and take action." I didn't possess his almighty power, but perhaps I could somehow be a vehicle to drive a wedge between street pimps and innocent girls who got caught up in the hustle. Girls like Renee.

A hundred thoughts floated through my brain at once. I shared my vision with Hank. As a police officer, he would know the streets where some of these girls worked. Not everyone could be saved, but maybe there was a way to offer them shelter. Help them find a normal job, or convince them to go home to their families if the environment was safe.

I remembered those do-gooders from the Evangelical church who walked the neighborhood around AJ's bar in search of souls to save from sin. Maybe they weren't the affable yet peculiar group as I suspected. Perhaps this organization consisted of really good people who wanted to make a difference in the world.

A New Beginning
1973

Chapter 82

A CONSTRUCTIVE PLAN was put in place after a solid year forming collaborations, developing proposals, and creating agendas. Once I partnered with the leaders of the Evangelical church, my vision came to life.

There was a shelter affiliated with the church and within close proximity. The facility was meant to be a religious school that didn't get off the ground due to insufficient funding. The church accepted people who needed God and prayer in their lives, while the shelter offered them safe refuge.

We called the program *A New Beginning*.

Government funds were available but limited. That was where I came in. I offered to support and finance the program, if the church representatives agreed to help me try to rid the Strip from underage prostitution in particular. Of course, if any woman wanted to leave the streets to find a job and a place to live without hooking, she could partake in this program. But these women had to leave their pimps and street associates behind for good.

Tommy wasn't around much these days. When he was, I could tell he was high, drunk, or both. He was pretty much useless to me except for his bank account. If I asked him about his condition, he'd get angry. Sometimes he got physical, pushing me away from him. Throwing furniture. Punching walls. His whole demeanor changed when he was home as if he hated being home with me. I couldn't talk to him about it without a fight ensuing.

One thing about Tommy and me—we loved to fight. Admittedly, I was the instigator. Why did I stay in this marriage? I didn't need him, but I needed his bank account. So did *A New Beginning*.

This mission gave me a purpose. Every day brought new challenges and new people looking for something better than what they had at that very moment in time. A lot of these women reminded me of myself. There were many homeless men without a solid support system, a good family, or a job who needed assistance too.

Joel escaped the charges from the brawl that night at AJ's. We remained romantically entangled. Sometimes I felt like I was betraying Joel whenever Tommy slept mindlessly in my bed when my family visited. Joel never asked about my sex life at home. There wasn't one. He knew Tommy traveled out of town a lot.

I rarely spoke about Tommy to Joel, and I took off my wedding ring. I wore it around the family only. Wearing a large diamond at a shelter wouldn't be wise. I thought Joel believed I stopped wearing it because my marriage was over. An odd notion since my marriage never really started. Tommy and I never had a chance to fall in L. But Joel didn't need to know the background information about Tommy and me.

From time to time, Tommy would leave empty vials with some type of powdery residue in it. Cocaine maybe. I hated picking up after his mess.

The guest room farthest from my bedroom became Tommy's room. It was a pigsty. He used to be such a stickler for cleanliness. When my mother and brother came for a visit, he'd stay in my bedroom. His sleeping patterns were different.

Even Patrick noticed something seemed off about Tommy. I attributed his behavior to the stress of the hotel business. Yet he continued to buy more hotels. His visits to his pop diminished as well.

Thousands of dollars supported the funding of improvements at the shelter and expansion efforts to allow for more people to sleep there. A kitchen was added to cook large meals. The shelter was not meant to be a permanent home for anyone, but cots were full every night.

My friends all pitched in to help with the cause.

Tommy's bank account helped substantially, and he hadn't questioned me about the money. He might not have been reviewing the bank statements carefully, if at all.

Community service did us all good. It also reminded us where we came from and where we had been in life.

The restaurant Valerie worked for donated food to stock the shelter's pantry. She managed to find some of our visitors jobs at her restaurant or other local businesses.

The church often needed people for maintenance work.

Phoebe managed to help those with regular jobs be approved for loans to buy a vehicle, and in some cases, a home. She moved up at the bank because she had a gift for numbers. She was actually quite brilliant.

The bank manager insisted Phoebe take college classes to sharpen her skills. After one class, she started promoting the need for education to some of the people at the shelter. If they had a high school diploma, there were grants and funds available for people with limited finances for college. If they didn't have a diploma, there were state tests to earn an equivalent.

Joel helped me post signs around town to collect decent clothes in good shape that others could use. Some locals in the community donated checks, knowing the money supported a church and its cause to reduce homelessness in town. I had a closet filled with clothes I didn't need.

Joel was pretty handy. He fixed leaky pipes, built furniture, and painted walls when the band wasn't playing.

I knew I couldn't ask Tommy for much help, so I connected with Rob Lubitski, the manager at the Montgomery, and asked him to consider helping some particular people out by interviewing them for jobs like in the coat check room where I started, maid service, maintenance work, or a higher-level position if the applicants had the proper skills. Rob was happy to help my cause.

Hank had a pivotal role. Instead of busting hookers and other street people, if he believed they didn't deserve jail time, or it was their first offense for solicitation, he'd bring these people to the church directly. Some people stayed and tried to use our resources to improve their lives. Others fell back into the familiarity of street life.

We couldn't save everyone who walked into the shelter, but we tried. They had choices and opportunities. We could only help those who wanted to be helped. A frame of mind I had to grow accustomed to, without physically shaking sense into those who chose to remain on the streets.

Valerie reached out to the doc from the Belle Maiden. After what I put him through, falsifying medical records, I wasn't comfortable asking him for another favor. However, he agreed to drop by the shelter once every two weeks to check on the people's health and treat anyone in need. He discontinued services at the Belle Maiden shortly after Doris and Chip retired. His Fridays were wide open for volunteering.

Some of the visitors at the shelter were down on their luck. Many teens were runaways. Several men who returned from Vietnam suffered from serious injuries to their bodies and minds.

Nixon had announced on January 23, 1973, the news that an agreement was reached to end the war, citing to "bring peace with honor in Vietnam and Southeast Asia." Unfortunately, our brave brothers in arms experienced so much plight and scourge in the insufferable Vietnam jungles, many developed severe problems like drug or alcohol dependencies and a cornucopia of mental illnesses.

Alcoholics and drug addicts needed help we couldn't offer. First of all, they needed to *want* to clean up their act. If they didn't want to change, they wouldn't. If they truly aspired to get clean, the doc facilitated treatment in a mental hospital for them to dry out. Those with serious psychiatric disorders often required a lengthier stay at a facility to treat their complex issues.

Despite our efforts to help people with a wide variety of difficulties and health concerns, some members of the community challenged us, saying we were doing favors for whores who didn't deserve it. Those anti-war activists took out their frustrations with the government on the vets. The men who fought hard and were blessed to survive the war should be revered, not dishonored. Society had no idea how we were working hard to improve the lives of these brave soldiers, and building women up.

The women's liberation movement was well underway. Some of the women we tried to help needed a major self-esteem lift. They had to realize their importance and self-worth. Simple attributes like self-respect, dignity, and pride needed to be instilled.

Women could compete with men for similar jobs and become assets to employers and the community once they believed in themselves and their abilities. The mindset of society often became a barrier to our success.

Another important event that occurred in January 1973, was the Supreme Court ruling in favor of legalizing abortion after the Roe versus Wade lawsuit was highly debated.

Had it been legal when I was in dire straits, maybe I wouldn't have had to go through the tortuous situation with Kenny and Artie. Legalizing abortion shouldn't warrant irresponsibility. If you didn't want to have a child, protection was key. With that thought, I worked with the doc to ensure birth control was available.

The doc was able to supply condoms only, but it was a start. We had to battle with the evangelists for condoms to be distributed. They disliked the idea of abortion more than promoting protection from pregnancy. We won that debate.

There was a young pregnant woman who asked about the abortion procedure. Her name was Jenny, with a soft personality, crystal blue eyes, and hair the color of fire. She couldn't look me in the eye when explaining her intentions, knowing we were on church grounds.

The church was not a supporter of the procedure, despite legitimacy. She was a seventeen-year-old rape victim. She wasn't a prostitute. Jenny's parents were drug addicts, and their home was not safe, so she ran away. She lived on the street with no place to go until Hank found her, and he brought her to me for help.

I told Jenny I'd never judge her for whatever decision she made and asked the doc to explain all her options.

Jenny chose to continue with the pregnancy. I found a home for girls for her to live at throughout her pregnancy. She gave birth to a healthy girl that she held one time after she was born. As distraught as Jenny was, she chose to give her baby girl up for adoption, ensuring she would have a good home and a nice life. A stable future Jenny was unable to provide for her.

The point was, Jenny had numerous options that she was entitled to make. Every woman now had a choice.

Chapter 83

A MAJOR DIFFERENCE was noticed in Tommy's persona lately. He appeared more alert. His eyes were clear and focused. He spoke coherently, and he wasn't falling down drunk. The change was drastic, and this didn't happen overnight. Clearly, I didn't notice his appetite for Jameson and whatever cocktail of drugs he chose diminished.

He arrived home around eleven o'clock one evening, an early night for him. I parked my Porsche in the garage at the same time.

"Why are you out so late? Another church function at this time of night?" he asked.

"What are *you* doing out this late? Don't tell me, hotel business," I rebutted, sarcasm whirling.

He held the door open for me. A hint of a smile, that sexy smirk he used to warm me over with, no longer worked.

I breezed through the door, beneath his arm, annoyed that he finally seemed interested enough in my life and whereabouts to question me.

"Tell me about this church you're involved with again."

"Hmm, you never seemed to care before," I bitterly replied.

"Well, maybe I have a right to know, considering all the money you're pouring into this church. Your family is Roman Catholic, yet you're working with some Evangelical church? It doesn't make sense."

"I'm not there to pray under that particular faith, Tommy. They're making a difference in the community. So far, we have helped numerous people get off the street in a short time frame. We give them shelter, food, and resources to find a home and a job."

"Yeah, Rob told me you hit him up to find steady work for some people at the hotel."

"It's not like I could've come to *you* for anything." There was so much more I wanted to say to his face. Like tell him what a sloppy drunk he was. But I didn't have to.

"I know I haven't been *myself* for a while, but I'm...back."

"Am I going to find empty containers of God knows what in your room?"

"No, that's over. I swear. I've been under so much pressure lately. I was partying a little too much."

"A little?"

"Okay, a lot. My mind and body are functioning again, and I can't help but notice how much money you're investing in this church." His tone was much calmer than I anticipated.

"Yes, I'm investing in this church and its services for the community. We're really making a difference out there. And it gives me a purpose. I'm not just sitting by the pool or planting flowers in the yard."

He nodded. "I'm glad you found something to be passionate about, but I need you to take it down a notch. Why does this church require thousands of dollars?"

"I'm finding homes for the homeless. I've taken some prostitutes off the street for good. Vietnam Veterans have resources for assistance to improve their lives after the war brutalized their minds and bodies. Drug addicts and drunks are sobering up." I had to stop after I said that, choking on the irony. I spent so much time, effort, and money helping strangers when my own husband had a problem with drugs and alcohol that I completely ignored.

Chapter 84

TOMMY AND I had been married for seven years on February 3, 1975. I didn't acknowledge the date, nor did he. I had become such a different person since our wedding day. For the better, I'd like to think. Our marriage was a convenience for me. I wasn't certain how Tommy benefited.

AJ's Bar was demolished and rebuilt into a bookstore a year prior, so Joel's Friday night gig ended. The Renegades still played a couple of nights every week, wherever they could perform.

They were playing at a nice restaurant this evening called Palmieri's. Chandeliers, dim lighting, cloth-folded napkins on bright-colored tablecloths, and a lovely white-stone fireplace glistened with miniature lights atop its mantel, charmed the guests. Palmieri's was definitely a step above a dive bar that attracted gangs, pimps, and violence. After all this time, I still enjoyed listening to the guys play a combination of rock and roll and country tunes.

It was time for my crew of friends to be away from the shelter, the people, and their issues or drama. We drank, laughed, and played. It was our own personal time to unwind.

Since Tommy was more alert these days, I couldn't leave my wedding ring home unless I would be working at the shelter. It was easy to explain that I shouldn't promote the life of luxury I lived to the people I tried to help. I had to relate to them on some level and not appear high and mighty because of the money in my bank account.

Going out with my friends at a nice restaurant was no excuse to leave my wedding band sitting on top of my jewelry box in the bedroom. Although, I slipped the ring off my finger and placed it inside my purse whenever Joel was with me.

During the band's breaks, Joel always sat at my side. I'd have a bottle of Bud waiting for him as soon as their rendition of the Allman Brothers "Ramblin' Man" began, ending their set.

I had to be cautious in a fancy place like Palmieri's. No one Tommy associated with would be hanging out at those dingy places where Joel once played. But Palmieri's was the type of establishment Tommy would take business associates to. He was in town this week, but not home.

I explained to Joel that I couldn't show off our relationship here. A part of him appeared perturbed, but he merely shrugged, knowing I'd be going home with him later for a brief interlude.

Tommy and I had an arrangement. When he wasn't traveling on business, I expected him home every night. Even when he was a drunken mess, he came home, albeit around two in the morning sometimes. He might have slept in one of the spare bedrooms, but he was still in our house. I had to go home too, at some point.

During Joel's break, a short man with thinning brown hair, wearing a business suit and dark-rimmed glasses, approached him at our table. He wanted to speak with Joel privately.

There was an entirely different class of people at Palmieri's than what I was used to associating with. People-watching had become a hobby. Spectating for potential folks in need of guidance that *A New Beginning* could help them with. If anyone in this restaurant needed saving, it was from the IRS or a jealous spouse. Patrons donned evening dresses, business suits, furs, and gorgeous, sparkly jewelry. No hookers or indigents here.

Joel returned to the table at the end of his break. He took a long swig of his beer before jumping back on stage. He never had a chance to tell me what that man wanted. The man my eyes spotted scurrying out the front door.

Later that evening, on the drive home with Joel, his silence prompted me to ask him what that man wanted during the break.

He shrugged. "A potential gig out of town."

"Wow, where?"

He didn't respond.

"If not in the Vegas area, Reno?" I asked.

"Outside the West Coast actually."

Surprise was evidently displayed across my face.

"Would you come with me, Sadie?"

My eyes shifted away from Joel, out the window, watching a stretch of prominent buildings fade as we raced by.

"Sadie, do you love me?"

My head whipped toward him. "How long would you be gone?" was all I could ask. I didn't know how to answer his question.

He stared straight ahead, but he wasn't focused on the road. He nearly blew a red light, screeching to a halt, causing our bodies to fly forward, nearly hitting the dashboard and window. He seemed annoyed with his pouting glare.

"What is this *thing* we have if you don't love me?"

"I didn't say I don't love you, Joel. I guess I have a hard time saying that word. I struggle to know for sure if it's real."

"You're married. And I know you're not happily married. Do you plan on leaving Tommy? We've been screwing around for a long time now. I have no idea where I stand with you."

"Joel, you know how much you mean to me."

"No, Sadie, I don't. That man tonight thinks I've got what it takes to make it big in New York. He wants me to cut a record. He works with musicians and writers, and he's looking for someone like me to sing."

"New York? You'd leave your whole life behind to go to New York?" I asked with surprise.

"What am I leaving behind? A married woman who doesn't love me? A band that will go nowhere? Community service because it's important to *you*? New York may be a good thing for me."

Within a month's time, Joel packed his bags and left town.

Max told me where Joel could be reached if I ever changed my mind and wanted to visit him. I took the information, but I knew I'd never get on a plane and fly to New York. Not even for Joel.

The Renegades called it quits. The rest of the band members attempted to find a new lead singer, but no one clicked. They found regular jobs. Working a regular job kept them away from the shelter.

Max and Phoebe remained a strong, positive couple.

I felt lost.

Chapter 85

LOUD CRASHING OF pots and pans disrupted my sleep. I sprang from the bed, barely alert. My eyes attempted to focus on the clock that told me it was two fifteen in the morning.

Footsteps sounded heavy. More banging rang loudly through my ears. I didn't hear Tommy come home because I was sound asleep after a long, hectic Monday in May. Memorial Day, in fact.

My feet tracked across the golden shag carpet to the large closet. A wooden baseball bat sat upright in the corner; a momentum saved from the time when I feared Kenny. I wrapped my fingers tightly around the base as if I was going to aim and swing for a home run.

The bedroom door was slightly ajar, but I couldn't see anyone from this angle.

I stepped into the hall with my fingers clamped firmly around the bat as my body hugged the edge of the ivory-colored wall. When I reached the bathroom with a full view of the kitchen, I spotted Tommy leaning against the counter.

"Tommy? Oh my god! You scared the hell out of me. What are you doing?" As I neared him, I assessed the situation. The kitchen looked a mess with pots and pans tossed about. The light fixture in the ceiling had been smashed with broken glass shattered across the tile floor.

Tommy was sobbing. He wiped his nose and sucked in a deep, lamenting breath. "It's John. He's dead."

The bat escaped my grip and dropped to the floor, hitting my big toe. I barely felt the pain because my mind was busy absorbing the ache in my heart. Did I hear him right?

"John? No."

Tommy approached me, arms outstretched. I let him wrap those strong arms around me and cry on my shoulder. After a few moments, he gathered his thoughts and wiped away the tears from his lids. Then he explained to me what he knew.

Some lady friend of John's was with him. Tommy referred to her as a "lady friend," but I was well informed. I knew he saw prostitutes on a regular basis. This lady friend called for an ambulance because John started to feel chest pains. He died in her arms before help arrived. She drove in the ambulance with John's body to the hospital, then notified Tommy.

Tommy contacted the emergency room before I woke and was told he could go to the morgue in the morning to claim his brother's body. He demanded an autopsy. He needed to know why his brother died at such a young age. This made no sense.

I couldn't help but reminisce about the night I arrived at the hotel room with John waiting in bed for Kitty, but he got Penny instead. What a surprise it was to him when I showed up that night. He was so disappointed in me many months later. Although I never came clean to him, he suspected I wasn't really pregnant when Tommy thought we were having a child. Despite everything that happened, John kept my secret. I'd always remember that.

Guilt consumed me. He didn't come around here at all anymore, nor had I visited him. John had this innate ability to see through my lies. He had to know my marriage to Tommy was a sham. If I visited him at his house, he'd certainly call me out.

Tommy was a mess. As much as we argued, he was my husband. I had to be supportive of him.

I wasn't sure if he stopped drinking completely, but I offered him a shot of Jameson, of which he declined. I grabbed some aspirin from the medicine cabinet and filled a glass with cold water from the faucet.

He accepted the pills and swallowed them down in a single gulp.

We walked to the bedroom, and I invited him into my bed, our bed. We didn't have sex. I just held him, allowing him to tell me stories about their childhood, or to simply cry on my shoulder. Some stories he told broke my heart. He shared a lot of information with me about his brother and their distressing past, growing up with John's handicaps. I had no idea of the challenges they endured as children and the guilt Tommy preserved.

Tommy refused my assistance to plan the funeral. My mother called, wanting to help as well. He insisted he had it covered. He wanted to take full responsibility for burying his older brother.

After the arrangements were made for the service, the doctor informed Tommy that John died from a heart attack. John refused to take medication to control his blood pressure, and he didn't stop smoking completely as advised. Apparently, John didn't tell Tommy he had hypertension.

The funeral was on Saturday, May 31, 1975. Tommy never told Pop he lost a son.

Rocky was still confused, and he had difficulty comprehending information. How could he grasp the idea of losing his child? This was the first time Tommy felt grateful his father had been incapacitated. News like this might kill him.

Tommy arranged for a lovely service at Saint Francis Church. The casket was loaded with red and white roses. Wreaths and crosses made from exquisite, fresh-smelling flowers that stated on sashes across the decor "Son," "Brother," "Friend." Numerous flower arrangements were sent from family, friends, and business associates. I didn't know many of the people who sent the arrangements, nor most of the guests in attendance. I felt so out of touch with my husband's world.

Father Flanagan expressed beautiful sentiments about John during his sermon after the readings from saints Matthew and John, read by friends I never met.

At the end of the service, my father approached Tommy, offering his hand to shake in sympathy. The first time he had been at eye level with him in years. My stomach ached, worried there would be friction. But at a time like this, Dad was on his best behavior, and Tommy accepted Dad's condolences.

Patrick, Lisa, and Al were all supportive during this difficult time. Lisa whipped up a few meals for us to eat during the week. If she only knew Tommy rarely ate at home. Still, we appreciated her thoughtfulness.

Mom and Dad stayed at Lisa and Al's home.

My younger sister was pregnant with her first child. Our folks were thrilled to become grandparents, as was I to become an aunt. For some reason, I thought I'd have a child first. Logically, Tommy and I were not in a good place in our marriage to have a baby.

Patrick was staying with us. He and Dad glanced at each other during the funeral, but they didn't speak.

Although Mom visited faithfully, this was the first time Dad returned to Vegas since Lisa's wedding. He was not here necessarily to pay his respects to Tommy. Rocky was his good friend and military brother.

I had every intention of building a bridge between Patrick and Dad at some point. Maybe I could extend that bridge to foster a peace treaty between Dad and Tommy too.

Chapter 86

THE CROWD DISSIPATED after the brief cemetery service. It was difficult for Tommy to walk away, knowing he'd never see his brother's smile, hear his laugh, or sign in perfect rhythm with him.

His cold steel wheelchair sat next to the coffin. One of the few things Tommy said during the service was, "John can walk now. His legs work wherever he's at. He doesn't need this chair anymore."

With a sudden rush of revulsion, he kicked the side of the wheelchair several times hard, releasing his anger. The chair tipped over as Tommy continued his torment against the steel. He hated that John was confined to that contraption.

I worried he'd break his foot, so I tugged at his arm, drawing him in intimately close, attempting to calm him. He wiped his eyes then stormed to the car.

Before returning home to a house filled with guests still wanting to pay their respects to Tommy, we stopped at the convalescent home to visit Rocky.

We walked through the cold corridor, but Tommy stopped, deep in thought.

"I need to make a call. I'm going back to the lobby to use the payphone."

"Now? Can't you wait until we're leaving?"

"No, I really need to make this call. Please go in and see Pop. Tell him I'll be there shortly."

I visited Pop a few times by myself. Some days he knew me. Other days he'd ask me who I was. It was like a roll of the dice. Not sure the kind of reception I'd get from him today. As I turned the corner around some elderly people, slowly striding by with canes and holding on to railings built into the walls, I heard voices emanating from Rocky's room.

When I approached closer, I recognized the silhouette of my mother sitting with him, enjoying a reasonable conversation. They were laughing about a fire that started within the outdoor grill, making extra-crispy fried chicken. I had no recollection of such a memory.

Dad left the cemetery with Lisa and Al, yet Mom showed up here to visit Rocky alone.

When I entered the room, Mom's hand left Rocky's. He was fully dressed in a green polo shirt and blue jeans, sitting atop a made bed with a light blue spread. He glanced at me and called me by name. A good sign.

I bent down to kiss his cheek. Facial paralysis set in on the right side, an effect from the stroke.

"Hi, Pop. How are you feeling today?"

"I need to get outa this joint, Sadie. Do you know they do experiments here? We're all guinea pigs for the C. I. A."

My initial analysis was wrong. He might have known me, but he was still very confused.

"Really, Pop? Well, if the CIA experiments on you, they'll learn how sharp you are, right?"

His brown eyes molested my mother. His smile grew much wider than I'd ever seen. Somehow, her presence grounded him.

A flash of light gleamed brightly in my head. She looked at him with adoration, and he returned the sentiment. Were they lovers? Did my quiet, prim mother have an affair? All these thoughts rushed through my mind without confirmation.

Her upper lip raised, staring practically through my blue eyes. Her brows curved upward as her fingers twirled the ends of her blond hair, witnessing the wheels turning in my head. I didn't have a good poker face with her.

"So, I heard you two talking about a grill fire or something? When was that?"

Mom sharply replied, "When you were away from home several years ago, Sadie. Your father and I often had dinner with Rocky and his sons. Where's Tommy? Isn't he with you?" She quickly changed the subject. I noticed.

"He'll be up soon."

Her smile looked shaky, and she suddenly avoided eye contact with Rocky. But that didn't stop his eyes from groping her. Those blue eyes of hers focused on me and the spinning wheels zipping in my head as I tried to make sense of their game.

Tommy arrived, acting happy to see Pop. I knew it was an act. Not that he didn't want to see his father. His heart suffered from this tremendous loss. A loss he couldn't share with Rocky.

I nudged Mom to step outside with me while Tommy spent time alone with Rocky.

"Were you with him, Mom? When he had the stroke, I mean. Were you the one who called the ambulance?"

Her eyes glanced to the left of my figure.

"Mom, we always wondered if he called the ambulance himself. It *was* you, wasn't it?"

She nodded haphazardly then shed a tear.

"I'm not upset, Mom. And I'm not one to judge. No one has to know."

"If you figured it out, your father might too." Her hands covered her eyes.

"I know Dad is difficult. Your marriage can't be easy."

"I can't talk about this, Sadie. I just can't."

"You fell in love with Rocky."

Her complexion glowed when they were alone in his room, even with the damage to his brain. I unsuccessfully tried to recount the last time she looked at my father with such devotion.

"I blame myself. He wanted me to leave your father, but I couldn't. I'm all he has. He's my husband. Rocky and I argued that day at the house. Then he developed a migraine and became dizzy. His symptoms worsened as the day passed. When he fainted, I called for help. I waited with him for as long as I could. Once I heard the sirens approaching, I left him alone in the house. What excuse would I have for being there *alone* with him? I rushed down the block, then waited and watched him being carried into the ambulance."

I hugged her tightly, then coaxed her farther down the hallway so Tommy wouldn't notice her tears.

"It's not your fault, Mom."

For the first time, maybe I recognized a little bit of my imperfect mother's untamed emotions within myself.

Chapter 87

CHRISTMAS CREPT UP quickly. A whirl of vigorous activity circled around me with the demands of the church and shelter.

Mom and Patrick were in town for the holiday. They offered to help serve food at the shelter Christmas morning. A holiday meal with ham, mashed potatoes, and apple pie for those without families or the necessary funds to feed their families.

I managed to convince Tommy to join us. Rarely did our worlds collide these days, but since his money had been the primary reason the shelter's doors stayed open, it was advantageous for him to see its operation. He complimented me, impressed by my vision and hard work.

Mom stayed with Lisa, Al, and my niece, Abby, who was born just before Thanksgiving. The fuzz atop her head lightened to a bright blond. Her large, round eyes turned a brilliant shade of blue like mine and Lisa's. She was definitely favoring the Meade side of the family.

Dad drove up with Mom last month for the birth of his granddaughter, but he wouldn't return for Christmas. He loathed Tommy, and he hadn't made amends with Patrick yet. I needed to do something about that. I had to step in and make an attempt to mend their broken father-son relationship.

Bakersfield for New Year's became an annual trip to celebrate Christmas with Dad. Patrick never came. Lisa and Al joined me faithfully, but this year with Abby in the mix, the drive would be too much for them. I was determined to make this New Year's special and convince Patrick to take the drive with me before he returned to school.

Patrick shared numerous stories about his love life. It amazed me to learn how many men were hidden in the closet. The main reason why my brother wasn't in a relationship was because the men he fell for preferred to stay hidden.

Los Angeles offered clubs for gays to engage in liaisons or chance encounters. He met a lot of men and had had his share of affairs. Unless anyone became publicly outed, they remained concealed, attempting a life of normalcy.

Most recently, Patrick had fallen for Garrett, a man he met at college. Garrett was involved with a woman, pressured by his parents and compelled by familial opinions, instead of fighting for the ability to choose a partner he really loved. He'd never live the life he craved if he didn't stand up for himself. Society's influence hindered him from coming out.

The problem between Patrick and Dad wouldn't end unless Dad accepted Patrick's lifestyle. Patrick couldn't change who he was, nor should he.

As for Tommy, I didn't expect him to like my father, but it would help if they could be in the same room together without World War III starting. They managed to be civil at John's funeral. Tommy wasn't thinking about anything except missing his brother and keeping the disheartening news from his pop.

Still, I tried to convince Tommy to drive to Bakersfield with me instead of another business trip to Paris.

"I don't know why you need to travel on New Year's. What is so special about Paris? You don't even own a hotel there. Put it off for a week," I suggested.

"I'm working on future business opportunities and relations in Paris. Besides, nothing between your father and me will change, Sadie. His beliefs are so different from mine. I can't tolerate the way he treats Patrick."

"Tommy, I'm trying to bring the family together."

"This is *your* family, not mine."

"You're my husband. You are a part of this family."

His eyes rolled.

"Do you see what you do? I really thought after all the years we've been married that maybe we could actually grow to love each other. But you don't even like me!" I yelled so loud I felt the walls vibrate.

"Oh, here we go! I'm going to the office," he said with annoyance, rattling his car keys.

"Sure, run and hide in your office. Whenever anything gets heated around here, you hide at the office, or to France, Italy, or wherever the hell else you disappear to. Why are you still here at all? If you can't stand me, why stay? Just leave!"

"You have no idea how much I want to," he mumbled beneath his breath. But I heard his stinging words.

I picked up the Poinsettia centerpiece and tossed it at his head. My aim was slightly off, and the pottery smacked against the back of his shoulder.

He let out a groan before charging at me, pinning me against the wall. The force of his strong arms holding me tightly was nearly erotic.

After a moment filled with rage, he collected his emotions and released me before meandering toward the door.

Perhaps he feared such intimacy with me, but his arrogance angered me.

"You want to leave? Go! It's not like we have a real marriage anyway!" I shouted.

"You always have to fight about everything. Why can't you accept that I don't want to sit around your father's house and listen to his gripe against the fucking world? I'm done with his bullshit. I'm done with yours too."

"Why don't you leave for good then?"

"I'm honoring my commitment."

"Commitment?"

He snickered, "Till death do us part." And he was gone. Out the front door and off to the extravagant city of Paris. Probably to some foreign babe, one of which he undoubtedly had at every hotel he owned.

I was too surprised by his chilling comment to speak or stop him. Tommy was not a religious man. I couldn't believe he stayed in this marriage solely because we said "I do" in a Catholic church.

Till death do us part.

Chapter 88

PATRICK REFUSED TO drive to Bakersfield with me for New Year's. I hoped to convince him to join me. He was as stubborn as Tommy, only less cruel about it. If it weren't for his money, I would have left Tommy and this marriage a long time ago.

I spent several days visiting with Mom and Dad, gossiping about their neighbors, but it was time to get back to my life and the shelter.

We were beefing up our marketing of the program, preparing to hit the streets again, campaigning for those in need. We didn't want to come across as a strange cult of fanatics, trying to force a bunch of religious mumbo jumbo down people's throats. We wanted to share the number of people we had helped find jobs and homes. Show off our success stories. Let people know it was possible to improve their lives if they trusted us and had faith in themselves.

The program launched more than three years ago, although the first year was a trial-and-error process. In the early stages, we weren't carefully tracking the number of people who stepped through the door. Once Phoebe compiled numbers, producing a regular report, we became more accountable for the records we kept.

Granted, we wouldn't always know if anyone who left the shelter went back to the streets. Some found their way back to the shelter a second time. We began counting the number of people who returned for assistance and determined what they needed to start a new life and maintain a state of permanence. What failed the first time that put them back on the streets? For some, they lacked income. For the addicts, it was the high they craved and couldn't live without.

Valerie told me that she and others in our group were physically attacked by an angry pimp for talking to his girls. Fortunately, they managed to escape unharmed. The pimps were negatively affected by our program if we kept taking their girls off the street.

As I was driving home from Bakersfield, my fingers turned the dial of the radio to find a good song to distract me from random thoughts about Tommy, who had yet to return from his overseas trip. Sometimes, I called the airport to keep tabs on his whereabouts.

A catchy new love song played. Something oddly familiar about the lyrics. Perhaps I heard the song before.

The radio announcer said he received a lot of requests for the new Joel Sinclair song.

I couldn't believe what I just heard. Joel made it in New York! He cut a record. It was a good song from what I could tell. Maybe the familiarity of the song wasn't the lyrics, but the voice. Joel emitted a distinctive raspy tone in his voice when he sang.

I smiled from ear to ear, knowing how hard he worked for this moment. I also missed him. Hearing that song, now stuck in my head, engrossed me enough to nearly miss a red light. I slammed on the brakes—and got nothing.

The brakes were gone.

Fortunately, there was no traffic at that intersection, and I skated through with ease. Both my feet slammed on the brake pedal over and over as the Porsche flew down the street at a speedy pace. Horns were honking. People were waving angrily, thinking I was intentionally driving recklessly.

Suddenly, I noticed a gigantic, long truck was taking a wide turn from the right up ahead of me.

I had nowhere to turn and couldn't stop.

Chapter 89

MY EYES OPENED to a bright light that stung my pupils. My hands went mad, swinging everywhere to dim that light.

"Whoa, wait, Mrs. Cavallo."

His voice sounded calm and soft, but I had no idea who this man was, flashing a light in my face. Where was I? Who was the man with the gleaming light?

That insufferable, luminous sphere defused, and a very handsome blond-haired, blue-eyed man stared back at me, wearing a long white jacket. A doctor.

"Mrs. Cavallo, I'm Dr. Solinsky. You were brought to the Desert Springs Hospital. Do you remember what happened to you?"

I tried to answer his question, but I shook my head. No memory to be found within my brain.

"You were in a car accident. You're going to be okay, but you have some cuts and bruises, plus a concussion. Do you remember driving?"

My mind desperately searched for a response to his question but got nothing. Zero recollections. I turned my head, allowing my eyes to circle the room. Bleeps and buzzes were heard from a machine with multiple wires dangling. Those wires trailed over the bed rail and were affixed to my chest and arm. What happened to me? Did this doctor say *car accident*? I wanted to shout but couldn't.

At some point, I recalled driving the Porsche. "Yes," I managed to say with a dry, scratchy throat.

"Can you tell me what happened?" he asked.

Why did my mind play such a dirty trick on me? My memory was shot.

A nurse brought me a glass of water with a straw.

Carefully, I raised my torso for a much-needed sip.

He must have sensed my struggle to remember.

"It's all right. We need to run some tests. Is there anyone I can call for you?" His words suddenly sounded garbled, and his voice distorted. I watched his lips move, but I couldn't comprehend his remarks anymore.

The room faded to black.

Chapter 90

THE NIGHTMARES SUFFOCATED my brain. I couldn't remember falling asleep. I heard voices talking over me, but my eyes wouldn't open.

Visions of an enormous eighteen-wheeler in front of me on the road. My beautiful sporty Porsche crashing. Glass smashing. A sound like thunder deafened my ears. The smell of burning oil filled my senses. And my skull felt like it had been cracked with a hammer. This nightmare replayed throughout my lengthy nap like a horror flick marathon.

When the bad dreams finally ceased, my eyes opened at the encouragement of that handsome blue-eyed doctor. Or maybe it was the bright light he flashed in my eyes again.

"Welcome back, Mrs. Cavallo. How do you feel?"

It took me a moment to comprehend his question. A simple question I had no reply to. My stomach rumbled.

"I'm hungry."

"That's a good sign. There's someone here to see you."

When the doctor moved out of my line of sight, I noticed Tommy standing in the back of the room. His eyes looked so serious. I couldn't recognize the expression, but my chaotic memory flashed, *till death do us part.* As he approached me, I heard myself scream. Goose bumps crawled across my porcelain skin.

"Stay away from me," I managed to yell with a dry mouth.

"What? Sadie, it's me. I flew home as soon as I could to make sure you were all right."

"No, you wanted this. You want me dead!" My legs pushed my body upward in the bed, trying to move myself away, but he continued to approach me.

"Mr. Cavallo, please wait outside," the doctor politely insisted.

"Why? What is wrong with her? I'm her husband!" he yelled at the doctor, who scrambled to push Tommy outside my room.

My heart raced angrily, barely keeping up with my frenzied mind, processing information. The accident became fresh. Flashes of memories slowly returned a bit jumbled. I remembered visiting my parents in Bakersfield for New Year's Eve. Tommy and I argued. It was a bad fight. *Till death do us part*, the last words he spoke.

After Tommy left, the doctor took baby steps toward me before he cautiously sat at the edge of the bed.

"Mrs. Cavallo, you were admitted by ambulance from an accident scene. You have a concussion. You're healing, but you've been asleep on and off for a couple of days now. Your husband was in Italy. He flew home right away."

I had no response. I kept thinking of those cruel words Tommy said to me. Words that chilled me to the bone. Italy? That didn't sound right to me.

"Why would your husband want to hurt you?"

"Keep him away from me. I don't want him near me," I said in a low tone, frightened of Tommy. Although, I wasn't the type who scared easily.

"Okay," the doctor answered, a bit of skepticism in his tone.

"There's someone I need you to call for me," I asked. "Sergeant Hank Dubois."

Hank earned a promotion to sergeant. He built quite a record with the number of arrests made. I trusted Hank. If he could tell me exactly what happened, according to police reports, maybe I'd remember more. I envisioned that large truck in front of me. Then ramming into its side. The crash and glass breaking around me haunted my mind.

Tommy might not want a divorce, but a dead wife would mean he'd be free from our marriage, commitment, vows. And he wouldn't have to pay me off with alimony if I unexpectedly turned up dead.

Hank snuck into the room as I was finishing up a dish of green gelatin. I felt at peace when I saw his smile. He approached and gave me a friendly hug.

"How are you feeling?"

"Clueless. I hate feeling like this. I don't trust my memory. Small, quick flashes of that truck are surfacing."

"According to the doctor, you had a concussion. You were out of it for a long time. I came by to see you."

My eyes raised to meet his. "You did?" Why was I surprised? Hank had been a loyal friend of mine for about nine years since we met at the Belle Maiden.

"Of course, I came. As soon as I heard about the report of your car, I made sure you were okay. Phoebe and Valerie know about your progress. Every time they stopped by the hospital, you were asleep. I talked to your husband. I told him we met through the shelter. I wanted to tell you that in case he mentioned our meeting to you."

"You spoke to Tommy?"

"Yeah, he seemed worried."

"Worried how?"

His brows curved. "What kind of question is that? He sat in this chair." Hank pointed his finger toward the turquoise-colored chair in the corner of my room. "He was just sitting there, watching you. I'm a cop, Sadie. I can tell when someone is concerned."

I shook my head. I might never figure Tommy out. "Tell me what you know about my accident, Hank."

"I read the report. You were driving erratically. Witnesses said you ran lights before hitting that truck. It's a miracle you survived."

Empty thoughts lingered. Why would I drive recklessly? Then I recalled stepping on the brakes.

"Hank, I lost my brakes. They didn't work. I tapped them constantly and got nothing."

"What was left of your car got impounded. I can ask for an inspection to see if there was anything wrong with the brakes."

"Yes, please. I think Tommy may have tried to kill me."

"That's quite an accusation, Sadie. From what I know, he was in Venice. I'm the one who told the officers on the scene to call the

Montgomery to find your husband. His secretary said he was traveling overseas."

I said nothing, but Hank could always read me.

"Look, I'm no fool. I don't know anything about this guy or your marriage, but I know you aren't the happily married couple you want people to believe. Wanna give me a reason to worry about you and your safety? Has he hurt you before?"

I shook my head. "We had an argument before he left the country. I thought he was in Paris, but he was in Italy. What if he wants me dead?"

Later that day, Tommy was brought in for questioning.

Chapter 91

HANK KEPT ME apprised of the investigation. Tommy adamantly denied tampering with my brakes and attempted murder. The Porsche's remains were going through an inspection. My beautiful car was destroyed. More memories of the crash returned.

I recalled hearing Joel's song on the radio. I tried desperately to remember the words and the melody, but I could only remember it was a love song and hearing his name announced. I felt immense pride for his accomplishment. If he stayed in Nevada, he might not have made the big time.

Imagine, I was involved with a famous singer! He'd be a wanted man by millions of girls. Maybe as famous as John, Paul, George, and Ringo! I knew him when he was simply my Joel, the rugged-looking songbird, jamming in dive bars, singing to me personally. I missed those times.

When the investigation concluded, Hank returned and advised that Tommy had been released. They couldn't hold him any longer. Not only did he have a solid alibi, being out of the country, but the Porsche's brakes were shoddy. There was insufficient evidence of alleged tampering.

Apparently, Tommy flew from Paris to Venice to meet with his business partners at a hotel in the serene city of canals. That explained his location in Italy.

Tommy called my parents, who were headed this way to see me, according to Hank. Hank spoke to Tommy directly. He seemed pretty convinced Tommy didn't attempt to harm me.

Hank said he asked Tommy about the argument we had before he left the country.

Tommy admitted that we fought because he didn't want to visit my father. He explained to Hank that he never drove to California with me. He had business in Europe, and I gave him a hard time. He snapped and said some *unpleasant* things to me, but he'd never try to hurt me.

As more memories fluttered about my head, the more I realized I might have been wrong to make such an accusation. When I talked to the doctor, he blamed the concussion. My brain had been bruised. Memories were unclear. I felt frightened and confused. But I was ready to face Tommy, so Dr. Solinsky contacted him.

Tommy arrived with Mom and Dad trailing quickly behind. He was excited to share that he bought me a brand-new Cadillac to replace the Porsche.

After Mom fussed over me, and Dad seemed relieved that I was healing, I asked to speak with Tommy alone.

He stood in the back, seemingly concerned, while Mom and Dad stepped out into the hallway to allow us privacy.

"I asked your parents to come with me because I didn't want to scare you or upset you, coming here alone."

"I'm sorry. My mind has been cluttered. So many visions and unclear memories. It's taken me some time to translate it all."

"I swear to God, I didn't do anything to your car. I'd never try to harm you."

I nodded, believing his sincere plea.

"Look, our marriage isn't normal. But you're my wife. I come home every night when I'm in town because it's what you want."

"I'm sorry you had to be questioned by the police. When I regained consciousness, I was so afraid. I kept thinking about what you said to me when we argued, *till death do us part*. Maybe my imagination ran wild."

"I'm sorry I gave you reason to fear me."

The next day, I was released from the hospital and drove home with Tommy in the new black Caddy.

Chapter 92

DAD STAYED WITH Lisa and Al while in town, visiting his grand-daughter and ensuring my recovery progressed properly. Mom preferred to stay with Tommy and me, so she could take care of me.

I was feeling better. The swelling in my head lessened. My memories returned. If they hadn't returned, I imagined I wouldn't know. I considered taking a drive to the shelter, but Phoebe and Valerie had everything covered. They simply expected me to rest and heal.

Much to my surprise, Patrick drove up from Los Angeles. These days he worked at a community theater for the mere pleasure of it. For steady work to pay the bills, he wrote articles for a local newspaper. He shared an apartment with two friends he met through the theater after earning his bachelor's degree in journalism. I promised him if he ever got a part in a play, I'd be sure to watch from the front row.

Mom was thrilled to see Patrick, although it had only been a couple of weeks since she saw him for Christmas. She stepped away to make some tea, leaving us alone.

"Hey, how are you feeling? I thought I was supposed to be the only *drama queen* in the family." He laughed.

I couldn't help but release a hearty giggle. "I'm feeling better. You didn't need to come out here for this. I know how busy your life is."

"You could've been killed. At least that's what Mom said."

"She exaggerates."

"Maybe I needed to see how you looked for myself. Besides, I wanted to visit our beautiful niece again. You and Lisa aren't the only women I drive to Vegas to see anymore." He tugged at the bandage on my forehead. Then he stared at the scrapes and bruises across my face, arms, and shoulders, with gashes from the broken glass.

"My body really took a beating from that crash. Thank God I have a hard head. I wonder how that big ole eighteen-wheeler looks." I laughed. "Probably not nearly as pathetic as me."

Patrick wore a grim expression. "You can cry, you know."

"What?"

"You never cry. My entire life, I don't think I've ever seen you cry. You were always the strong, brave one. You could take on the world with that tough attitude. A little bossy maybe."

"Hey!"

"Well, you can be bossy. But you're not invincible. You don't have to take on the world and all its problems."

"Is this a lecture about how much time I spend at the shelter?"

"No. I think it's great you found a worthwhile cause to be involved in. If everyone cared about things the way you did, the world would be a better place."

That was probably the nicest thing he ever said to me. Maybe the nicest thing anyone had ever said *about* me.

"Don't scare me like this again," he demanded.

I nodded.

"I love you, sis."

I smiled big and bright.

Mom roamed into the room, carrying a tray with a teapot and some cups. I heard the front door open and close quickly. Maybe Tommy came home from work early, I thought.

I was wrong. Lisa bounced in with Abby in her arms beneath a pink knitted blanket. Shuffling behind them was my father. His face showed his surprise to see Patrick sitting beside me.

Patrick looked away from our father and started to tickle Abby's little feet.

The tension in the room swelled as thick as LA smog.

Everyone focused on Abby or my bruised skull. Anything to prevent Dad and Patrick from acknowledging each other. I had had enough.

"Dad, you drove up here because you were so concerned I was badly injured. I could've died! It was a stupid car accident. And you thought about how awful it would be to lose your daughter. Accidents happen at any time to anyone."

I pointed to Patrick. "What if it were Patrick lying in this bed? Or worse! What about John? He was far too young to die, but it happened. The two of you need to patch things up and remember you are family."

"I appreciate you saying that, Sadie, but Dad doesn't accept me."

"Don't speak for me," Dad bellowed.

All our eyes were upon him. The room became quiet except for Abby's baby coos.

"Sadie's right. You're my son. I don't want anything bad to happen to you." His hands stroked the top of his balding head, deep in thought. "I don't understand how you see everything in the world so differently than me."

"I'm not the son you wanted, but I'm what you got."

Dad shook his head. "Look, I may not agree with how you live your life. I can't help it. I was born into a British and Irish Catholic family. I'm old-school. I see on the news how people like you are treated. Beaten up. Bludgeoned. I don't understand it."

"If I lead my life based on your expectations, I'll be miserable. And I can't live like that."

I chimed in to keep the tension at a minimum. "I think Dad is saying he's going to make an effort to *try* to understand." My eyes caught Dad's, hoping he'd agree with my sentiments. "And be *supportive*," I force-fed him.

"I…I need time, but I want to try." Dad held out his hand to Patrick. The first attempt ever at reconciliation.

Patrick stared at his hand, then looked at my father's face, sincerity shown through regretful eyes. He accepted his hand; then Dad brought him in for a long-overdue hug.

Chapter 93

THE DOC RECOMMENDED a psychologist friend of his to assist at the shelter. Having someone offer guidance to people with social issues and mental health concerns was desperately needed. I was introduced to Louise Massaro.

Louise, a lovely, petite woman with dark chocolate hair enhanced with blond hues, emitted positive energy and kindness. She wore a dark gray pinstripe business suit and practical pumps. Fresh out of college or an internship, judging by her youthful skin tone and sparkling brown eyes filled with ambition and promise.

After speaking with her for a few moments, I understood why the doc thought she'd fit in well. Those of us who worked here must relate to our visitors while displaying compassion without judgment; a way to earn their respect without showing any evidence of wealth to establish trust.

Louise made a good, professional impression. She jumped right in talking with people. She seemed to have an easy way about her that made our guests comfortable enough to open up about the drama or unfortunate circumstances in their lives.

Those with a detrimental military background or substance abuse issues typically required extra guidance. Even prostitutes who returned to the shelter more than once needed some direction to help stay off the streets. Unfortunately, many girls went back to those dark and desperate streets permanently, or fell victim to the tragedies of street life.

Women without police records could work at a bordello legally if hooking was a lifestyle they didn't want to leave. Since my time at the Belle Maiden in the sixties, brothels now had legal responsibilities. These facilities were required to be licensed by the state and enforce strict hiring practices. Working girls must be licensed as independent contractors by the state, registered with the County Sheriff's office as sex workers, and of course, pay their taxes. No health benefits or retirement plan packages were offered.

Madams were not supposed to hire anyone with a known criminal history or underage girls. Background checks were completed on all applicants these days. Some places rejected women without class or a good personality. Streetworkers were considered bottom-dwellers in the hierarchy of prostitution. Many were too damaged to work as a high-priced call girl or at a cathouse, especially if they lacked panache.

Social workers like Louise attempted to help women stop hooking and find stable employment elsewhere. They couldn't encourage women to work at a legitimate brothel instead of hustling on the streets, although the work was legal and more secure if the ladies followed the rules. Working in this industry must be the woman's choice and her idea. We couldn't plant that seed. It was illegal to persuade or solicit women into this business; and we wouldn't risk being slapped with a felonious pandering violation. I certainly couldn't say, *See Doris at the Belle Maiden and tell her Penny sent you!*

On the weekends, my team and I visited certain undesirable areas and attempted to speak with the girls directly to ensure they were okay, or ask if they wanted our help to leave the streets.

Many scoffed at our attempts. Some griped in front of others, but kept our fliers and stepped into the shelter on their own, sometimes after an assault—a dangerous wakeup call to receive.

One day, a woman who looked older than her years sauntered in. Her face and features I recognized, but I couldn't quite place her. She stood before me, wearing a pair of jeans and a teal-colored button-down shirt. Her dark brown hair was long and pulled back into a thick ponytail. She wore little makeup, but she grinned at me as if she held a secret tightly.

"Hello, Penny. It's been a long time," she said before introducing herself as Marianna.

No one had called me Penny in years. "How do I know you?"

"You were one of Kenny's girls."

I paused. If I didn't know he was dead, I might have been intimidated. Then I realized who Marianna was. The despicable woman I sarcastically nicknamed "Little Miss Sunshine." The girl who took pictures of me with Kenny that first night I met him. A night that often haunted my dreams still.

She had escorted me to the Montgomery to meet a regular customer, who at the time, I had no idea was John. She looked different now. Softer. Less threatening. More sunshine than despicable.

"That's not a time in my life I care to remember. My name is Sadie. I don't go by *Penny*, ever."

"Sorry, but you were hard to forget. He took a shine to you."

"Lucky me." My sarcasm was obvious. "*A New Beginning* is a program for people who want to help themselves. We help people who want to get off the streets and start a fresh life. If you're here to damage our reputation or start trouble, I'll have to ask you to leave."

"No. I'm here to help."

I was quite certain my surprised brows told her I was shocked.

"Look, I remember that night we met. I was a total bitch. That's why Kenny hired me. To transport broads, excuse me, *women,* to customers. I got caught up in his crazy activities like the porno shots he made me take. I didn't have much choice. Those streets near that motel Kenny stayed at were my home. Kenny gave me a job and a place to crash. Sometimes I'd have to turn tricks for him. I became a victim as much as anyone. Even you."

"You said you wanted to help. How?"

She held up a flier. "These are everywhere. I've seen them before. Seen your posse out on the streets too, before I quit the life, I mean. I moved in with my aunt a couple of years ago. She took me in, and I snagged a regular job as a cook."

"It's good you had family to help you."

"Family didn't matter to Kenny. I wanted out long before. He wouldn't let me leave. He wouldn't let any of us go. When I tried to escape, he beat the crap outa me. Held me down and beat my side, whipped my legs. Didn't hurt my face. Needed me to sell it on the streets."

Shivers flew through my body. "He was a monster."

"Told me he'd let me live if I got back out there. Otherwise, I'd end up like Kitty."

My head quickly spun toward her. "What?"

She stared at me with a blank expression.

"What do you mean, *end up like Kitty*?"

"He claimed he killed her. Admitted it to me with pride. Nobody walks out on him or his business. Kitty tried and failed. His motto became *you leave, you die*. He got meaner when he started using dope."

My stomach ached. Kitty wanted to escape from Kenny's clutches, and the bastard killed her. I knew he was responsible.

"Did you tell the police?"

"The cops? Why? It was just a threat. I didn't see him hurt her."

"Her real name was Rachel Snow, and she was all over the news. Her body was found stuffed in a dumpster."

Marianna lowered her head. She didn't seem to be the same vile woman I met years ago in that cruddy motel room.

"I honestly didn't know. Look, I came here thinking I could help, but maybe this was a mistake." She turned from me, prepared to leave.

My fingers entwined with the strands of the cross necklace once worn by Kitty that rarely left my neck. After a lengthy pause, I shouted to Marianna, "Wait! No. It's not a mistake." I placed a hand upon her shoulder, preventing her from leaving. "We can use someone with your knowledge about street life. You may know how to relate to the people we're trying to outreach. But first, you need to speak to the police and tell them what you know about Kitty's death and what Kenny told you."

"They're both dead. It won't bring Kitty back, and Kenny won't do time. I don't want to be hassled by the cops for not coming forward sooner."

"I have a friend who can speak to you off-the-record. You didn't know Kitty actually died. I want there to be closure in her murder."

Hank arrived at the shelter as soon as he could to take Marianna's statement. She offered a great deal of details, especially the fact that Kenny verbally admitted to murdering Kitty. She spoke about Kenny's biting habit during sex, which was a ritual of his she also had to endure.

Kenny's dead. There'd be no trial for her to testify at. Her statement would be on record, and Hank could speak to the detectives who worked Kitty's case to notify the family she was estranged from. Maybe telling her family her murderer died a slow, painful death would seem like some form of justice.

After that, Marianna became a regular member of our team and helped *A New Beginning* decrease illegal prostitution and homelessness.

Chapter 94

MONEY POURED INTO Tommy's bank account, and I focused on how to use it to improve the shelter and its impact on the community. We enlisted many volunteers now. Enough so that Phoebe, Valerie, and I could take some weekends off for a change.

Jenny, the young rape victim, returned to volunteer. She knew how much we had helped her to move on with her life, and she wanted to support the program and pay it forward to others.

Resources for the shelter continued to expand and some neighborhoods were improving. Las Vegas would always be difficult to clean up completely. No matter how many girls left the streets, there always seemed to be others taking their place.

June 1980, an unbelievable heat wave lurked through Las Vegas. Today was the kind of day an egg could sizzle on the pavement. I attempted to lounge in the pool, but my face and arms began to fry.

I spent the day inside with air-conditioning blasting to keep me cool. Chores needed to be done, beginning with the bedrooms. I turned up the volume of my record player with a Kenny Rogers vinyl playing "Lucille" as I danced around my bedroom with a dustrag.

Tommy had been better at keeping his room clean and picking up after himself. Still, his curtains and bedspread could use some freshening up. While dusting his bed frame, I noticed under his bed was an opened bottle of Jameson, missing a quarter of liquid. I thought he gave this stuff up permanently, but he must sneak a few sips now and then. So much for complete sobriety.

Mom planned a visit in the near future. Whenever she visited, Tommy still returned to my room. We both liked to put on a show for the outside world. Let people believe we had a good marriage. Really, we lived like roommates. On some days, I'd even call us "friends."

A fancy-looking invitation caught my eye on his dresser, embossed with gold calligraphy. I recognized the name of his lawyer, Len Stein. A party was taking place at his home. I realized it had been a while since Tommy asked me to attend a business event with him. However, the invitation implied the party was for couples.

I always wondered how many ladies he had taken up to his suite at the Montgomery. I'd never ask. I had engaged in a few meaningless affairs since Joel left for New York. No one recently, and nothing serious. I felt a little bored with life, hence the reason why I was cleaning today. I could hire help to manage the household chores if I wanted. Tommy's empire filled our bank accounts with millions each year. We're loaded!

Boredom could be dangerous for me. I decided to wash up, forget about cleaning, and take this invitation with me to Len's house and check out this party. I'd see firsthand what my husband was doing, or *who* my husband was doing, should he have a woman on his arm. Now what would I do if I caught him with another woman?

He wouldn't like this, my showing up unannounced. I could be instigating an argument. As I peeked inside the garage, I noticed his yellow Ferrari wasn't in its usual spot. I opened his closet, and his sharpest-looking tuxedo was gone. He left the house with his tux and swanky sports car without telling me about a formal business dinner, local to home.

My walk-in closet was filled with fancy dresses. I grabbed the floor-length sequined gold dress. I caught many an eye when I wore this lavish gown last. I glanced at the clock. I had plenty of time to throw a coat of polish on my nails and curl my hair.

I called for a driver to take me to the Stein's residence. A mansion most likely purchased with the generous salary Tommy paid him. A Lincoln Continental picked me up.

Upon arrival at the Stein home, I asked the driver to wait thirty minutes in case I needed to leave suddenly. Meaning Tommy had some gorgeous mistress on his arm with large breasts that would anger me enough to either tear her apart or run out of there. Maybe both.

This place was unbelievable! A marble staircase to climb to reach the large double doors. Large, squeaky clean windows. Outdoor lighting to highlight fountains, spitting water in a circular motion to the rhythm of classical music. Various roman sculptures were scattered throughout lush, colorful gardens on a lawn clipped to perfection.

Did Tommy attend functions like this often? Instantly, I felt so out of touch with my husband and his world. Why couldn't we upgrade to a mansion like this? Not that there was anything wrong with our lovely English Tudor.

These six-inch heels hadn't seen the outside of my closet in years. I took my time scaling the marble steps to prevent an embarrassing tumble, falling flat on my face.

A man, who I imagined to be a butler, held the front door open for me. Once inside, the detailed architecture looked magnificent. Carvings in the woodwork. Murals painted across the ceiling. Chandeliers shone brightly in the large, open forum. The whitest sparkling walls I'd ever seen.

"Len, hello," I said to the host as he skated past me, sipping a glass of champagne from one hand, a cigarette in the other. "I'm looking for my husband. I wanted to meet him here."

If Len was shocked to see me, his relaxed facial expression didn't show it.

"Sadie! What a nice surprise. Tommy didn't mention you'd be joining him." His eyes glanced around the room. Looking for Tommy perhaps.

"I hope that's not a problem, Len."

"No, of course not. I'm not sure where Tommy wandered off to."

Len signaled a tall man walking down the hallway. A man I remembered meeting years ago. Someone I'd never be able to forget. John and Tommy's friend, Jim. The man who saved my life, ultimately taking the life of Junior Morales. Why was he at this formal event dressed somewhat leisurely in a leather jacket and dungarees?

"Jim, Mrs. Cavallo is looking for Tommy. Can you find him for her, please?"

Jim smiled at me, knowing very well who I was and when we first met. God, would he have told Tommy about that night? I started to perspire just thinking about that possibility.

"Mrs. Cavallo, nice to see you. I'll find Tommy for you. I think he's in the back talking with a business associate. Give me a minute, please, ma'am."

Jim made no effort to indicate he would have relived that night with anyone, not even with me. John and I never offered Jim background details about who Kenny was to me.

Len introduced me to his wife, Wanda Sherman, a woman who, I could tell from the moment she said hello to me, had a big personality. Her eyes were wide and sparkling blue. She seemed so delighted to be hosting this event. She spoke with a thick German accent and began to tell me stories about her time in Germany before moving to the United States. What a lovely and interesting woman. Her laugh was infectious, keeping me entertained for several minutes.

I wondered why Jim was taking so long to find Tommy.

I snatched a delicious-looking puff of pastry off a tray carried by one of the servers dressed in black and white.

Tommy finally approached, looking handsome in his tux. He didn't appear angry at my whirlwind decision to crash this party. In fact, he shot me a smile.

"Thank you for keeping my wife enthralled with your stories, Wanda. May I steal her away for a moment?"

Wanda smiled and nodded. "Of course, Tommy."

"Come with me, *honey*." Calling me honey was ridiculously unusual. Then he kissed my cheek and led me outside. Who was this pleasant, sincere-sounding man using endearing nicknames to reference me?

The breath of fresh air was a relief. I noticed a lovely view of a barn in the back. "Are those horses? Can we walk back there to see them?"

"What are you doing here, Sadie?"

I acted surprised by his sudden rudeness. "What do you mean? I saw the invitation. This party was open to wives."

"So you just showed up unannounced? What is this, some kind of ambush?"

"Ambush? Why would you think that? Unless you've got something to hide."

"Don't you spend your Saturday nights saving people from themselves?"

"Are you mocking me?" I turned my back in anger but soon faced him again. "Why wouldn't you tell me about this function tonight? At one time, you liked having me on your arm."

His hands found their way to his hips.

"You're actually *angry* that I'm here."

"I'm not mad." His hands flopped to his sides now. "I'm embarrassed. My wife shows up alone without me escorting her in front of important clients. That doesn't make me look like a very good husband."

"And you think you're a good husband, otherwise?" Blatant sarcasm in my tone.

He stared with a blank expression. "Come on, Sadie. You're not interested in my business except for the amount of money in the bank. You have your own hobbies."

"You consider my work a *hobby* now? I'm helping people. I'm making a difference in their lives. It's a public service. Sorry if I've not been available to get my hair done and look pretty to accompany you to all of your *snooty* events."

Another couple strolled outside in elegant evening attire. The woman made a point to eye my gold gown up and down before saying hello to Tommy.

He introduced me as his wife. They each shook my hand and smiled. If I didn't know any better, I'd swear they looked confused or surprised. They simply stared awkwardly at me. Did I have spinach in between my teeth from that delightful pastry I sampled?

"Sadie surprised me this evening. I know I normally attend these events alone. You might not have known I was married." He placed his arm around my waist and squeezed me in. He could win an Academy Award for his acting performance.

We stepped back inside for some appetizers and cocktails. Tommy played the doting husband and ordered me a vodka neat, my drink of choice. He introduced me to his business associates and their wives. I had to admit, my eyes wandered the room for a woman without a man on her arm. If he was with another woman this evening, she'd be here somewhere.

He seemed on edge and moody toward me. I slipped a shot of vodka in his club soda. He needed to relax. That opened bottle of Jameson in his bedroom told me he still drank once in a while. Sure enough, within about fifteen minutes, he wore a smile. I fetched him a second and third club soda with a shot of vodka throughout the night as he mingled with others to talk business.

When we returned home, he slept in our bed, and for the first time in a really long time, we had spontaneous, blustery sex. Maybe it was the booze, but I'd like to think there was an attraction between us still. A spark that connected us, triggered by a heated argument.

In the morning when I awoke, Tommy was gone. He left the house bright and early without saying a word.

Chapter 95

BY THE END of August and well into September, I was tired often. My mind was distracted while reviewing Phoebe's quarterly report that highlighted the progress the shelter had made.

Jenny also proved to be good with numbers, so Phoebe taught her how to compile the data in spreadsheets. Phoebe excelled at accounting principles, using those long, thin-lined spreadsheets that made my eyes cross.

Nausea had set in and lingered for several days. It was time to make a doctor's appointment. No fever or chills, but something was wrong with me.

Louise, my friend the psychologist, scurried to the coffeemaker for a caffeine break in between meetings with patrons.

I described my symptoms to her.

She chuckled slightly because internal medicine and gynecology were not her specialties to draw a conclusion. The first idea that entered her mind was if I were pregnant.

I laughed at the notion at first, then wondered for a split second. Looking back at the calendar, June 14 was the night of Tommy's business party. The night we had sex for the first time in years. He didn't wear a condom, and I didn't think about birth control. Considering the abortion I had many years ago, I never thought I'd be able to have a child at this point in life.

Oh my god! I really could be pregnant. I hadn't been with another man for several months before that night with my drunk husband.

Tommy and I might be having a baby, but I needed to be sure. Louise told me about an e.p.t. pregnancy test I could purchase at the drugstore. She believed if I was truly pregnant, the test would return a positive result. This was a better option than waiting several days for a doctor's appointment, or for the doc to stop by for his regularly scheduled visit at the shelter.

Later that evening, I waited for Tommy to come home. I left him messages at the office to call me. I heard his car race in the driveway to a screeching halt at nearly eight o'clock. Usually, he didn't return home before midnight.

He meandered through the front door, briefcase in hand. His eyes gazed at me while settling in the kitchen, searching the refrigerator for a cold beverage.

"What's up with you?"

My hands trembled, nerves were shot, and my stomach rumbled. Uncertain if these jitters were from nausea, nerves, hunger, hormones, or a combination.

He smirked suspiciously while pouring ginger ale into a tall glass.

"Why are you looking all *happy* like that?"

"I'm pregnant." I couldn't wait. I blurted out my news with no warning. No clever remarks to lead up to this moment.

He spat out the ginger ale he slugged in a mist that burst all over the floor. Then he darted to the sink and stuck his head beneath the faucet for some water to minimize the choking fit.

"Are you okay?"

"I know you didn't just tell me you're *pregnant*." He wore a stone-like expression. No smile. Only a blank, hardened stare.

"I am pregnant, Tommy. I took one of those e.p.t. tests."

"What the hell is that?"

"It's a home pregnancy test."

"It can't be right."

"I've been tired and nauseous lately."

"No. No way! If you're pregnant, it ain't my kid."

"What?" I was shocked by his insolent response. "Don't you dare tell me you don't remember that party at Len's house! We created a baby that night. It happened."

He lowered his head. "You got me drunk. I hadn't had a drink in *years*, and you put something in my club soda. I know you did!"

313

"You have a bottle of Jameson in your bedroom, under the bed. Don't tell me you haven't touched that bottle."

"I kept that bottle as a reminder and a test to stay sober. It had been *seven years* since my last drink until you fucked me over! But what the hell else is new?"

"To think I believed this baby might bring us together, but instead you dish out a whole lot of anger and bitterness."

"We didn't plan this. I didn't plan this. Having a baby now is not in the plan!"

"What plan? People don't always plan a family. It just happens."

"That's what got us into this marriage. Jesus Christ!" His hands squeezed his head then combed through his thick brown hair.

"I suggest you get used to the idea. I didn't think I'd ever have a child again after losing the first one. This is a second chance for me. For us. You're going to be a father. If you want to leave, then get the hell out! I'm sure a judge will make sure you support us for the rest of your life."

Excitement combined with sheer tension consumed me, wondering how healthy it would be to bring a baby into this house with parents who didn't use the L word. Sometimes we didn't even like each other. The first time I told Tommy I was pregnant was a huge lie, yet he married me without the seeping emotion of love. I sincerely hoped this baby would bring us love, peace, and harmony.

I paced my bedroom floor that evening, trying to think about how my life would change with a little person in it. I watched my sister manage with Abby. Although, Al appeared to be a supportive husband and father.

Being pregnant with Tommy's child was one hell of an insurance policy. He would always take care of us financially.

The glass door to the bar in the living room popped open. Bottles rattled. The swish of liquor pouring into a glass. I recognized those sounds. Tommy was getting hammered. So much for the sobriety he seemed to be proud of.

Chapter 96

KNOWING THE DATE of conception made it easy to track my due date. I hit the five-month mark.

Morning sickness, they called it. Vomiting multiple times, day and night, had become as routine as breathing. The doctor had concerns about lingering dehydration. Even though I couldn't hold much food down, I had to drink plenty of fluids, which had a habit of resurfacing.

Tommy appeared more accepting of the pregnancy. He brought me ice chips, water, and juice. If I mentioned a craving, he'd drive to the store and buy me that ice cream and fudge. Not pickles and ice cream that you'd hear about on TV. I desired chocolate. Chocolate candy, ice cream, and cake.

The first time I felt the baby kick, I placed Tommy's hand upon my belly. He cracked a smile. Excitement filled his face. This little baby became a reality. I didn't want to jinx this feeling I had, but he almost seemed at peace with fatherhood. Our marriage was far from traditional, but our baby personified innocence.

We started to consider baby names. Daniel John if he was a boy. Mary Lynn if she was a girl. I felt honored to give my son the middle name of his late Uncle John. Mary was Tommy's mother's name. He loved his mother and rarely spoke about her death. But he asked if we could name her Mary.

I was so happy that he discussed it with me. I'd name the baby whatever he wanted if he would try to participate in this event so we could resemble a real family, not just pretend to the outside world—a feat we were accustomed to.

The family beamed with ecstasy when learning about the pregnancy. My friends at the shelter were so supportive, especially because I felt sick constantly. Despite my bouts of nausea and dehydration, I loved talking about this little bundle expected in March 1981, near Tommy's birthday.

Sleep was a rarity for me these days. Between needing to use the toilet often, nausea, and this active little one performing somersaults within me, I was running on empty. I found ways to simplify my life, like arranging for maid service and hiring a painter to transform the baby's room into a tranquil space, colored a soothing shade of pastel green. My new haircut was shorter and far more sensible to care for in my condition.

Tommy bounced out the front door moments ago after checking in on me and bringing a container of apple juice and snacks from the store. He had been so attentive and concerned.

The doorbell chime kept me from napping. I peered through the peephole and saw an attractive brunette holding a clipboard stacked with papers and a few business cards. What was she selling? I wanted her gone, so I could rest. When I became overtired, fifty shades of grouchiness provoked my temperament. But I greeted her through the screened door.

"Hello."

She didn't respond despite the fact that her dark eyes stared directly at my face.

"May I help you, miss?" I spoke up.

"Good afternoon. I'm a realtor walking around the neighborhood. I wanted to leave my information with you, and see if you had a need for maybe a new home, or if you were thinking about selling. You never know when someone may be having a life-changing event. As a female in this business, some men don't think I can cut it." She chuckled awkwardly.

I smiled, pretending to care. I was too tired to care. "Good for you, paving the way for women who want a professional career."

She wore a stylish red dress with heels. Nice taste. Her breasts were much larger than the tiny buds God gave me. Her nails were perfectly manicured with a blush pink-colored polish. A high society woman, I'd bet. She came from money, obviously.

"Would you have a need for a realtor? You have a lovely house. I'm sure you'd get a fabulous price for it if you were to sell it."

I smiled proudly, knowing my house looked lovely. "I doubt my husband wants to move, but you can come inside and tell me what you think." Maybe I was in the mood to show off my home and marriage to a stranger. She seemed so eager to step inside. Her neck could break the way she stretched it out for a closer look. I opened the screen door fully, allowing her enough room to enter.

"You're with child?" she asked, seemingly surprised when those doe-like eyes lowered, focusing on my ever-growing belly.

"Yes, I'm about five months along." I loved talking about my baby and showing my little bundle off.

"My name is Angie, by the way. And you are?"

"Sadie. Sadie Cavallo. You just missed my husband. I've been really sick lately, so he's been checking in on me every day. He's usually very busy." I hoped she got the message that I was not feeling very well. Maybe she'd leave soon. "What made you want a career, Angie? I mean, you're a pretty woman. I'm sure you could scoop up a husband for yourself." Before she had a chance to answer me, I couldn't help but notice the enormous diamond on her finger. "Wow, that's quite a rock. You must have a good man in your life."

She glanced down at the engagement ring and changed the subject, suddenly looking sad. "I suppose I wanted to do more with my life. Not that there's anything wrong with women who choose to be housewives. At least we have a choice to work in a professional career if we want. Unfortunately, men still don't consider us as equally competent in the workforce, and I doubt my salary is as high as my male colleagues."

I couldn't agree more with her. Women worked as hard as men. Maybe someday women would make the same pay as men in all professions. Fortunately, I didn't need to earn money, being married to a wealthy man. I worked hard at the shelter because that cause proved meaningful to me in so many ways.

She followed me toward the living room. She seemed to be taken aback by the large portrait of Tommy and me placed above the fireplace. It was a beautiful picture my sister snapped of us after learning I was pregnant. We were both smiling. We hadn't taken a nice photograph together since our wedding day. I had it enlarged and framed in mahogany. This photo brought positive energy into our home.

"That's my husband, Tommy."

"Yes, very nice. Is this your first child?"

"Yes, and it's about time. We've been married for a long time, and I finally convinced him to have a baby." As if we planned this. Then I recalled the gorgeous mansion Len Stein and his wife, Wanda, lived in. Perhaps a change of address would make a difference for Tommy and me, I wondered. "Maybe if we have more kids, we'll need a bigger place."

She stared at the lovely diamond-studded watch strapped to her petite wrist. "I really need to get going. Sorry to take up your time, but please take my card. And be sure to tell your husband I stopped by to meet you."

A realtor walking door-to-door to solicit clients seemed odd. Since there was no hurry to change our address, she probably didn't want to waste any more of her time. Tommy had a realtor he worked with, so I threw her business card in the trash.

My feet were screaming at me to lie down.

Chapter 97

TOMMY RETURNED THAT evening with Chinese food for dinner, another craving I had. We had been eating together more often. It was nice. We were having a baby. Something in common. Something to talk about. A future to plan.

After dinner, Tommy cleaned up the kung pao chicken and lo mein containers. When he opened the garbage lid, he picked up that realtor's business card from the top of the pail.

"Sadie, what's this?"

"A realtor dropped by to see the house."

"What? Why would she come to see our house?"

"I don't know. She rang the doorbell and told me she was hoping to attract more clients. I probably should've told her you had a guy already. Is something wrong?"

He wore a strange, unfamiliar look upon his face as if perplexed, but his smile soon grew. "No, I don't want to move. I saw this card and thought you were looking to sell our home."

"I like our home. I like it even more when you're here." I kissed him, and he responded.

"I'll do the dishes. You can rest. I know you don't get to sleep much these days." The grin on his face remained.

We were in a better place with this baby entering our lives.

"Why don't you join me?" I solicited, desiring his touch, and hoping he'd return to our bedroom permanently to rekindle the blazing desires we once shared.

"I have some paperwork to do when I finish cleaning. I may actually need to go to the hotel for a while."

"Don't go. I like when we have evenings together like this."

He smiled, his gray eyes neglecting to make contact with mine. He poured himself a glass of Jameson before loading the dishwasher.

It was easy to detect the signs screaming wildly that we weren't quite ready to get back to that honeymoon phase of our lives. My past, the situation with Kenny, my affairs, and how Tommy had been spending his time without me, significantly interfered with our marriage. I hoped to move out of this state of purgatory we lived in. This baby became the perfect reason to reunite in every sense.

I was awfully tired and eventually fell asleep, imagining a fresh start of our life together with a newborn to love.

Chapter 98

ON DECEMBER 1, 1980, we received a telephone call from the hospital, confirming what we had been dreading. Pop passed away after dealing with a persistent fever. His health had declined tremendously. Tommy made time to visit him daily, despite his busy calendar.

I took a ride with my mom to visit Rocky last month when she was in town. The unpleasant aromas in the hospital turned my stomach. Mom said my skin transformed to a light shade of green. It really wasn't good for me to be there, but Mom craved to spend time with Rocky.

Unfortunately, he didn't seem to know who was sitting by his bedside. Rocky's eyes remained shut throughout our visit.

The machine's bleeps and buzzes kept him alive. He'd come in and out of consciousness. Then he'd seem fine again, and the hospital would send him back to the convalescent home. Rocky's health became a vicious cycle of complex care and routine crises that Tommy had to cope with.

I reflected upon the day I told Rocky I was pregnant. He looked so happy, yet surprised. Tommy said he told him about the baby, but his mind wasn't good. Rocky didn't remember, given his condition.

Then he asked where John was. Rocky always asked about his first-born son and why John hadn't stopped by to visit lately.

We always lied, inventing excuses for John's absence.

He was finally at peace, reuniting with John in Heaven. I attempted to remind Tommy of that pivotal detail. His father was not well. He suffered. Maybe he wasn't in pain, but his mind was so lost. There was no quality of life left. He needed assistance to dress, use the toilet, take a shower, eat, and brush his teeth. He couldn't do anything on his own, except die.

To Tommy, Pop was all he had left for family. With a tender touch, I placed his hand across my belly, reminding him he still had family—me and our baby. With the many life lessons Pop taught him about father-and-son relationships, he could carry that with him when our baby was born. Boy or girl, Tommy had a great pop as a role model. If he allowed himself to be open to fatherhood, he could be an amazing father to our baby.

The military funeral Tommy planned was incredible. So many people attended to pay their respects. Some of these people I hadn't seen since our wedding day. Some were important business associates he introduced me to for the first time.

The American flag draped comfortably over the coffin, perfectly centered. A three-volley salute in Rocky's honor caused my body to jerk with each earsplitting rifle shot, followed by a bugler puffing out the melancholic rhythm of "Taps." The honor guards meticulously folded the flag, then presented the Stars and Stripes to Tommy. An eerie silence hushed the crowd, the birds soaring by, and the usual chitter-chatter of nature.

Tommy sat silent and numb throughout the service.

After the funeral, life moved on, seemingly at a slower pace. Tommy was around more often than usual. He'd disappear from time to time, but home early every night. I'd like to think he was putting in an effort to improve our relationship, but maybe his concern was more about the baby's well-being than mine.

He seemed sad and quiet lately. Still grieving Pop's death maybe. But I had a sinking feeling he was hiding something from me. My sixth sense never disappoints. When I asked him if something else bothered him, he calmly replied that he felt *fine*. Jameson bottles were stocked in the bar. Tommy started to drink regularly again. Thankfully, no fists were slammed through walls or glasses smashed. When he drank hard years ago, he could be combative and cruel. I didn't want our child to witness that side of him.

Chapter 99

AROUND THREE O'CLOCK in the morning on March 19, 1981, painful twinges were felt within my side.

Contractions.

Labor pains began.

Tommy still slept in another room, but he checked on me throughout the night every night, knowing the baby could arrive any day, at any time. According to the doctor, I was five days late.

I rolled out of my warm, comfortable bed, which was no easy task these days, and managed to position my plump body at the edge. Sometimes Tommy had to help me up if I called for him loudly enough.

I gained thirty-two pounds, a lot of excess weight for a woman of my five foot height and normally weighing about one hundred five pounds. Thirty-two pounds all in my belly. I understood why pregnant women waddled when they walked. My breasts were filled with milk. I finally had more than a couple of tiny bits, but no sex life for a man to enjoy them.

Clearly, I made so many loud, groaning sounds, attempting to pull myself out of bed, I woke up Tommy. He ran into the room to check on me right when another contraction pinged sharply against my stomach lining.

"Sadie! Is this it?"

"I think so. God, I hope so!" I grunted.

He helped me with my bathrobe then cautiously escorted me outside. His yellow Ferrari blocked the end of the driveway. It looked like I was going to the hospital in style. We forgot my suitcase, so

Tommy had to run back inside to retrieve my bag. I was advised I needed to pack pajamas, clothes to wear home, plus baby clothes for the littlest Cavallo. I packed a pink dress for a girl and a blue jumper with a baseball design for a boy.

Tommy's sports car raced us to the hospital at ninety miles per hour. I was lucky to survive that terrifying ordeal. Once we checked into the hospital and I was settled in my room, Tommy ran to the payphone to call Lisa. Lisa was to contact our parents and Patrick as soon as labor began. If it weren't happening to me, I'd laugh, watching Tommy as nervous as a chicken in a fox den.

Every thirty seconds he'd ask if I was comfortable. I was as comfortable as anyone would be with sharp, stabbing pains jabbing at my side and back, taking over my body every five to eight minutes. I couldn't keep track of how often the labor pains occurred. Tommy was far too jittery to keep track of time.

Finally, a nurse entered the room and began monitoring the contractions.

I had to pee. When I stood to use the restroom, my water broke. A combination of fluid and blood dripped down my legs. I thought Tommy was going to faint.

After nine hours of a mix of contractions, groaning, pushing, and screaming, Daniel John was born. He weighed eight pounds, twelve ounces, and was twenty-one inches long. A beautiful, perfect baby with a mess of wild, dark brown hair atop his little head. He slept soundly in my arms in between alarming cries.

I couldn't wait to watch him grow and get to know his personality. Would he look like the Meades as Abby did, or more like the Cavallos? I was excited to find out.

"Hello there, little one. I'm your mama."

Tommy crept up slowly for a closer look. His cheeks were flushed with soft, delicate eyes, amazed to see the life that had been growing within me for all these months.

"This is your pop." I tried to hand him to Tommy, but he shook his head. He wasn't ready to hold him yet. He just watched intently.

Danny stretched his arms up and out. Then he let out a big yawn, desiring sleep after his grand entrance into the world. As tired as I was from labor, I wanted to absorb every ounce of him. My eyes wouldn't blink, afraid to miss a moment of his movements. The immense love that filled my heart was indescribable.

My parents were so anxious for the birth of this baby. Not nearly as anxious as I was. Swollen feet, headaches, back pain, and nausea. A very uncomfortable nine months. But all worth it now that he arrived. They couldn't wait to meet the littlest member of the family. They had a beautiful, healthy grandson.

Dad shook Tommy's hand, a gesture to make peace. Our family earned this moment of tranquility. God willing, it would continue.

Five Years Later

Chapter 100

EASTER CAME EARLY this year in March of 1986. My folks and Patrick were expected to arrive on Saturday to join in the holiday festivities. We also planned to celebrate Danny's fifth birthday.

Since Danny was born, Tommy spent the holidays at home. We seemed more like a typical family unit and acted like one.

Surprisingly enough, Tommy started to sleep in our bedroom again every night. It didn't take long before we resumed intimate relations. I remained a faithful wife and mother. No more fooling around behind his back. I couldn't say for certain he wasn't bringing women up to the suite at the Montgomery, but my confidence in our marriage blossomed.

I wanted another child. Motherhood came naturally. No one was more surprised than I was to discover that fact. However, Tommy felt he was getting too old to have another baby at this point.

Danny was the reason to get up every morning. Seeing his smiling face, watching him learn, make mistakes, skin his knee, and attempt to catch butterflies, all in one day filled me with euphoria. Each day began as a mystery and ended with him sleeping like an angel. We enrolled him in Saint Francis Catholic School to begin kindergarten in the Fall. I started to take Danny to Sunday Mass when he was a baby. Tommy didn't join us, but it felt right, returning to my Catholic roots and giving my son a religious foundation.

Before the family arrived in town, a trip to the grocery store was in order while Danny played at his friend's house. Another stop at the bakery was needed to pick up a spectacular baseball cake I ordered for Danny. He loved sports, which not only thrilled Tommy but also my dad, who beamed with elation. My father and Danny bonded nicely watching a ball game together.

Soon he'd be able to play baseball at the park nearby with other kids. My dad couldn't wait to watch his grandson play ball. Sure, Abby danced in ballet recitals, which I thoroughly enjoyed. But Dad had been eager to watch someone in our family play sports for decades.

The doorbell rang as I was putting away clean dishes from the dishwasher, listening to the Oakridge Boys singing "Elvira."

I expected the landscaping crew to trim the hedges and mow the lawn before the holiday. But it wasn't the men I had been waiting on, buzzing my bell with fierce impatience.

An Asian man with a crewcut and serious expression stood on the opposite side of the door. He looked like a cop if I had to guess. I opened the door, and sure enough, he flashed a badge my way.

"Good afternoon. Are you Sadie Cavallo?" His voice sounded robotic.

Oh God, I thought, wishing my frantic contemplations weren't displayed across my face. Was he going to arrest me for my part in Kenny's death? Had my past caught up to me after all these years? What would happen to Danny? "Yes," I managed to say with a shaky voice and a crooked grin. "What is this about?"

"Agent Wong with the FBI, ma'am. I need to ask you some questions. Will you please come with me?"

"Excuse me, I haven't done anything wrong." I hoped I sounded convincing.

"No, ma'am. We need to ask you some questions."

"I'm preparing for Easter and my son's birthday party, Agent…"

"Wong, ma'am. And I understand this may not be the best time, but I must insist. You may have vital information about a situation we're investigating."

"Is this about the shelter?" Maybe they were investigating someone we helped, I thought.

"Ma'am, I can assure you, I only have to ask you some questions. We need to talk about your husband."

"Tommy? He's not home."

"I realize that, ma'am. This won't take long."

I went with him, purely to find out what kind of questions he had about Tommy. Why would the FBI be interested in him? Whatever they asked me, I wouldn't turn on my husband.

He drove me to a large building in nowheresville, an out-of-the-way place. From the outside, the building looked like a giant warehouse. Agent Wong opened the car door for me then escorted me inside the desolate-looking building.

There was an empty room to the right of the entranceway. He offered me a seat and a glass of water or canned soda from the machine. I took him up on a 7-Up then demanded he tell me what this was about.

"Mrs. Cavallo, your husband owns many hotels and casinos in the United States, the Caribbean, and in Europe."

I nodded, agreeing he had that information correct.

"Are you familiar with Tommy's business partners?"

The Heavenly Tea Emporium came to mind. I had heard the name come up in conversation numerous times. But I gave Wong nothing but a shake of my head.

He scoffed. "They're criminals laundering money and perpetrating other illegal activities through his hotel chain."

"What? I don't believe it. If his partners are committing a crime, I highly doubt Tommy has any knowledge about it," I insisted, despite the fact that Tommy was involved with all aspects of his family's business and was most likely aware of every detail.

"Look, we're not after Tommy. We want his partners. For years, we've been trying to rid Vegas of mob connections."

"Why aren't you talking to Tommy about this? If he's innocent, and you're after his partners, why question me?"

"As his wife, you have access to business records."

"Aren't there rules about husbands and wives testifying against each other? Why do you think I'd help you hurt him?" I stood to my feet, grabbed my purse, and began to leave the room.

"Wait, Mrs. Cavallo. I'm not asking you to testify in court. I hoped you'd help us out on your own, voluntarily, as a confidential informant. I thought you might need some…*incentive*. Hear me out, please."

Agent Wong was more than polite, which incited a quake in my belly. He opened his hand, suggesting I sit back down. His fingers played with a very large envelope as he continued to speak.

"We had been holding onto certain information about you. You were known as *Penny* at the Belle Maiden Ranch years ago."

Even my best dramatic skills couldn't hide my distress, although I made an attempt. "I don't know what you mean."

"We have photos of you and your friends, Phoebe, Valerie, and Rachel." He flipped a few pictures onto the metal table. They were just photos of me with my friends. He used their real names, not their hooker names. None of his evidence proved where we were or what we were doing.

"Yes, those are my friends. That picture doesn't tell a story."

"Valerie has a record. Several prostitution and loitering charges. Rachel has a much lengthier record with prostitution and drug charges. In fact, there was a warrant out for her arrest before we found her body. We never released that information to the media."

Val never mentioned her arrest record to me before. As for Kitty, I never knew her as Rachel until she died. I was not the least bit surprised she had a record. She was under Kenny's thumb. These street girls were arrested and their pimps often went free.

"Okay, so it's possible my friends lived a different life before we met. Why am I here? If I'm not under arrest, you can't hold me."

"Through a local investigation of two murders, you are connected to both parties."

"What? Who?" They did plan to arrest me for Kenny's miserable life and death, I thought with great concern. An ugly lump nestled in my throat.

"Rachel Snow's body was found in a dumpster in January 1971. Her pimp, Kenny Perez, was found dead in his motel room a year later. A room filled with drugs, appointment schedules, and pictures. Pictures of which you were in."

"That's impossible!"

This shrewd agent whipped out one photo only. He didn't need to show me the others, and I hoped he wouldn't. The picture included that filthy man I hated, mounting Penny, flashing his yellowed teeth at the camera. Clearly, Kenny didn't give me every picture he had per our deal. I shouldn't be surprised. He would have blackmailed me forever. He must have had copies somewhere else in that horrendous motel room. Obviously, the cops found them along with his decaying body.

"Where did you get this?" I managed to ask.

"It was found in the room of a dead man with other photos of prostitutes this pimp controlled. At that time, we didn't know Penny was your alter ego."

"Am I under arrest for something?"

"No, ma'am. I told you I wasn't arresting you. At least not at this time," he stated slyly.

I looked away from the picture. Tried to push it away with the tips of my fingers.

Wong moved the photo into a folder then placed it on top of a file cabinet. He still held that large manila envelope. What other surprises did he have in store for me?

"You've been married to Tommy for many years."

I nodded. "Eighteen."

"Eighteen years? Whoa, that's a long time. Was it a good eighteen years?"

My curiosity was killing me! Why was he dangling this envelope in front of my nose like a carrot to a horse? More information to tease me with a prostitution charge? What exactly did he have on Tommy?

"We've had our ups and downs like most couples," I replied as cool as a cucumber.

"Ups and downs, huh."

"No marriage is perfect."

"Well, you're right about that. But yours couldn't have been very good." He opened the envelope and tossed a pile of photographs on the table before my eyes. Dozens of them.

As I stared at the pictures, I recognized Tommy immediately. He was with a woman. A woman with very long black hair. Every shot was of the two of them. They held hands, walking along a beach.

Another photo revealed them kissing in front of a large fountain surrounded by marble statues. I recognized the location. I'd seen pictures of the Trevi Fountain in Rome before. There was a dinner picture that showed him feeding her a forkful of spaghetti.

I threw them down, incapable of another glance.

"There are hundreds of photos in this pile, Mrs. Cavallo. Your husband has a mistress. Someone very special to him. Someone he took on every business trip for many years. He set her up in a special house in a ritzy neighborhood, a love nest if you will."

"It can't be recent!" I cut his words off, angry at the thought of him being committed to one woman. A woman besides me. I thought we were happy now, or reaching a sense of complacency in our marriage. We had a child together. He started sleeping in our bed again.

Wong flashed one particular picture in my face. A photo of Tommy lying in bed with this woman sitting on top of him, the sheets slightly covering his waist as he devoured her neck with his sultry lips.

"He loves this woman, Mrs. Cavallo. Their affair began in the early part of 1971." He paused, desperate for a reaction.

Could he see the outrage in my face?

"It's possible he's not spending too much time paying attention to the activities of his business partners because his mind is totally focused on this woman."

He pointed to the photo of her in bed with my husband as he uttered those words.

"Maybe he knows more than we think, in which case your husband could be in some trouble."

"Who is she?" I was not sure I wanted to know, but I had to know.

"His realtor. He hired her long after they were involved. He saw her every day and supported her financially."

My head whipped toward him in shock.

"Yes, before she became his realtor, he was her primary supporter. Clothes, shoes, furs, elaborate trips, diamonds."

Diamonds? Realtor? The menacing dots soon connected. She came to my house! That woman with the dark hair showed up unannounced at my doorstep when I was pregnant with Danny, telling me a story about soliciting business. She wasn't there to build up her career. She was there to check me out! Damn her! Damn him!

Tommy acted as if he didn't know her. As my thoughts raced back to that specific moment in time, he found her business card in the trash that night.

"Did she wear a big diamond ring and a diamond watch?" I asked.

"Yes. It's my understanding he plans to divorce you and marry her. He is head over heels in love with her."

The pain I felt must be visible, but Agent Wong didn't care. He had to sense my agony because I felt it oozing from deep within my soul.

Since Danny was born, we became a real family. Why the hell didn't he divorce me? If he really loved this woman, why stay married to me? I gave him plenty of opportunities to leave.

"Let me give you a few minutes." Wong strolled out of the room, leaving the door partially open.

The pictures sat before me. Hard to ignore them. I continued to look through them all. So many. They were smiling, laughing, romantic images captured. Different places, adventures he took *her* on. We never went anywhere after our honeymoon. Granted, I could never fly or ride in a boat, but he wouldn't even drive to California with me. Because of her!

He was with her every New Year's when I visited my parents. And all the holidays he said he was working at the hotel.

I imagined he had meaningless affairs with women, as much as I had with men. But one woman? One woman he *loved*? If he wanted to marry her and gave her a great big diamond to slip on her finger, why didn't he leave me?

One photo, in particular, grabbed my attention. A photo of them making love. Never had he looked at me with passionate eyes and extreme devotion, the way he looked at her. Ever.

I did something I hadn't done in many years. Cried.

When the tears stopped flowing, I became angry. Truly out-raged! I tore the pictures and flung them around the room. I shouted out loud, forgetting where I was.

Maybe he did try to kill me in that car years ago! He wanted me out of the way to be with that home-wrecker!

Wong returned, witnessing my outburst, proud he had broken me. "Mrs. Cavallo, are you okay?"

"I'm more than okay. I'm prepared to cooperate on one condition."

"Condition?"

"No charges against me related to whatever pictures you have of *Penny*. She's a part of my past. I can't have my son learn about that time of my life."

Chapter 101

I AGREED TO help the FBI by snooping through Tommy's business records and mail. The problem was, I wouldn't really know what to look for.

Wong hoped to see contracts, financial records, and written correspondence between Tommy and his partners. If I provided the puzzle pieces, Wong would create the picture, a masterpiece that could destroy Tommy and his Mafia partners while boosting the agent's career.

That bastard was not going to get away with this! I'd respect him more if he threw me out of his house and his life years ago.

When Tommy was home, I tried so hard to pretend to be a nice wife every day. I cooked meals each night since Danny was born. We were eating together as a family. What a joke!

I wondered if his girlfriend liked that he was spending more time at home. If only I remembered her name on that business card. That was nearly six years ago. Too much time had passed for me to recall specific details about our brief conversation.

Wong wouldn't tell me her name. But her name might be found somewhere in his briefcase or files. Tommy wouldn't be stupid enough to leave evidence about her around the house.

I highly doubted I'd make a good living as a spy. Tommy caught me a couple of times in his office at home. I thought I covered myself. He was so sloppy with his paperwork. I merely explained I was tidying up his office space.

Nothing was found in his desk at home or in his briefcase that looked suspicious to me related to his business or his mistress. A few pieces of correspondence and some contracts that appeared harmless to my inexperienced eyes were gift-wrapped for the Feds. I met Wong or his associates to turn over the details I found. I needed to get into Tommy's office at the hotel. More information would probably be found there.

Oh, how I wanted to confront him about her so badly! Could the FBI have lied to me? Were they trapping me as much as Tommy solely to complete their mission?

If Tommy got sent to jail, what would Danny think of me if he learned I secured the starring role in sending his father away? Danny loved his pop.

Chapter 102

SEVERAL MONTHS OF spying on my husband became tedious. Anything suspicious found, I made photocopies of and shared with Wong.

I thought about those business trips Tommy took for so many years. It wasn't merely about business. He mixed business with pleasure. He set his mistress up in a house. Paid her expenses. He probably loved that I was so involved with the church and shelter because I paid no attention to his extracurricular activities.

I was no angel and far from innocent. I had several affairs throughout my marriage because Tommy showed me no love or consideration. I knew he had to have lovers here and there. But he was in love with *one* woman for so many years.

Why did she stay with a married man for so long? For the money? What was her story? I remembered she was very pretty. She looked like a model. A cross between a young Audrey Hepburn in *Breakfast at Tiffany's* and *Charlie's Angel* star, Jaclyn Smith, with large breasts. Thinking about her made me insanely jealous. Not because she was beautiful, but because she stole my husband's heart. A mission I failed.

Did John know? John was angry with me, but he kept my secret. He undoubtedly knew every intimate detail about Tommy's life. John was quite a secret keeper. And he owed me nothing, given the amount of lies I told. Lies I never admitted to.

Tommy's latest secretary took her lunch promptly at one o'clock every day at the Montgomery. Tommy was out of town, probably ravishing that brunette bitch. My stomach rumbled just thinking about it. I could handle bitterness and anger, but this feeling of jealousy wasn't an emotion I was accustomed to.

Since Tommy and his secretary were out, I strolled inside his office and snooped through his desk drawers and safe. I knew his combination. He used John's birthday. Not too difficult for me to figure out. He kept his desk key hidden beneath a vase near the window on the opposite side of the room. He was a creature of habit.

My heart nearly imploded, hearing the sound of the heavy door opening and slamming shut behind me.

"Well, what brings you by my office?" Agitation was detected through Tommy's polite words.

My smile instantly grew so wide my lips hurt. "I'm so glad you're here, Tommy. I wondered when you'd be home from your business trip. Maybe we could have lunch."

"Lunch? Why are you here, rummaging through my safe?"

"I like that red tie. It looks so sharp on you with that gray suit." I approached him playfully and stroked his tie up and down, until he firmly grabbed my hands and removed them from his tie and his body.

"Don't. Don't change the subject, Sadie. Should I guess why you're here?"

I said nothing. He caught me. I had no legitimate reason to be in his office, ransacking his safe.

"If you need extra money, why not go to the bank? There's no reason for you to open my safe. I don't keep much cash in there anyway."

Relieved that he seemed to have no clue of my intentions, my smile remained intact. "I'm sorry. I planned to tell you."

"Actually, I'm glad you're here. We need to talk. It's best we talk here instead of at home in front of Danny." Harshness still sensed in his tone. "Where is Danny?"

"With Lisa and Abby." Unsure what triggered his unusual, intense mood, my mind searched for reasonable rationale. And why was he home early from his trip without notifying me?

Tommy nodded then sauntered to the locked credenza beneath an ornate painting hanging on the wall. The key was looped on his gold keychain, and he unlocked the drawer. He scrambled through a variety of folders then pulled one out, opened it, and studied the contents for a moment. Brazenly, he tossed the folder onto his desk where I stood. "These are for you to sign." He threw a ballpoint pen to me next.

I focused more on Tommy's icy glare than the paperwork. Several pages of a typed document with a title stating *Dissolution of Marriage*.

"Divorce papers?" I asked, confused. That phony smile I wore disintegrated.

He glowered disapprovingly as I studied this document. My eyes saw the words, but my brain couldn't comprehend them.

"I don't understand. After all these years, *now* you want a divorce?" His mistress must have had something to do with this.

"I tried to make this as simple as possible. This agreement spells everything out crystal clear. It's a pretty sweet deal for you."

"Deal?" Anger charged my question.

"If you sign this agreement, you can keep the house and the Cadillac. You'll receive sufficient alimony to cover the household expenses with a generous amount left for yourself. I will also provide child support, because I'll always take care of my son. Danny will never want for anything. If the amount I'm offering doesn't work for you, you can find a job. One that pays a salary instead of all the volunteering you do."

I'd expect this from him years ago, but now? Today? My voice trembled as I spoke. "Why are you doing…"

He interrupted my question. "We will share custody of Danny. I'll take Danny every weekend and will continue to take him on vacations with me when I travel, provided his education isn't disrupted. I figure you can spend more time at your shelter with your friends and the indigents of the world on the weekends."

"Why?"

"Oh, I am on to you, sweetheart."

In all the years we had been married, he never called me "sweetheart." Probably a name reserved for his girlfriend.

"I know exactly why you're here. There's nothing for you to find. I'm squeaky clean. I run a completely legitimate business. Your FBI friends have *nothing* on me."

Crap! He realized I had been helping the FBI. But how?

"What hurts me the most is that you were all set to turn me in. You're trying to send me to jail, away from my son." His tone displayed his outrage with my deception. "You'd take a father from his child out of spite?" His feet crept closer to me as he spoke louder with each syllable.

I never saw him so angry in my life. He had been drunk and outright violent sometimes, but his demeanor at this moment was hideous.

"You gonna marry your girlfriend? That realtor who showed up at our door. Our home! She came to our house! Your whore on the side!" I snapped back.

He laughed. "That's funny. You call *her* a whore? You're the one who lived in a *brothel* for months."

My face surely showed my surprise. Somehow, he learned about my past.

"Spreading your legs for any man with a dollar bill. Do you think I wouldn't have found out? I should have had you checked out a lot sooner, like *before* I married you. That's my fault for not thinking of it back then. You, a hooker, was pregnant, and I was the sucker you hustled into marriage. John was right."

"John?"

"John sensed something was off about you, but my father expected me to marry you, Sadie. Pop knew you were pregnant, and he didn't question the paternity. He wanted me to settle down. I was to *grow up* and *do the right thing*. When you lost the baby, Pop strong-armed me to stay in this marriage and honor my commitment. Even after the stroke, he had me by the balls where you were concerned!"

"What the hell are you talking about? How could Rocky, in his confused state of mind, force you to do anything?"

"The same legal documents that allowed me to control the family business for so many years kept me tied to you and this marriage. Pop was a hell of a businessman, even when it came to my personal life. If I divorced you, I'd lose it all. The business, the money, everything!

"John was smart though. He *begged* me to run out of that church on our wedding day. I never saw him more determined to change my mind about a woman before. I don't know what you did to make my brother distrust you."

John might have kept my secret, but obviously, he still attempted to protect Tommy—from me.

"He insisted I make sure the baby was mine before the wedding. If only that were possible."

"Shut up. Just shut up! And don't talk about that baby!" I screamed. Miles of regret soared through my heavy heart.

Tommy gulped, thinking about the loss of the baby. However, I thought about the actual baby I had created. Guilt consumed me for the decision I made to terminate my pregnancy so many years ago. I'd never admit to Tommy I was never pregnant when we married, especially now.

His moment of silence ended. His rage continued. "Then there was Danny to consider. I could have been a free man when Pop died and his will was activated, but you were pregnant. I wanted my son to have both of his parents full-time. Now he'll have to adjust like other kids from divorced homes."

"You want a divorce, fine. I'll have my own attorney look these papers over. I can't trust what you and your buddy, Len Stein, concocted in this document."

"If you don't sign this agreement, I'll take you to court and sue you for full custody of Danny. I'm sure when the judge hears about your past and the dangerous situations you put yourself in, walking the streets at night to help hookers and junkies, I won't have any problem winning full custody. This agreement in its current state is the best deal you will get. Unlike you, I'm not trying to hurt our son by taking his mother away from him permanently."

"No judge will give you full custody," I insisted.

"What would your parents think about your shady past, selling your body?"

"You bastard."

"Oh, *I'm* a bastard? You tried to work against me and send me to jail. You know nothing about how I operate this business, which is legitimate, by the way. You thought the worst of me and deceived me because you were jealous I found a woman I could actually love. Someone I wanted to be with. Jesus! I still feel the cold steel of the knife you gouged in my back. We didn't marry for love, Sadie. I'll never know if that baby you were carrying back then was mine. But I did right by you, married you, and supported you. Now this betrayal! I'm done! You've got seventy-two hours to sign that agreement, or I'll take you to court and this deal is off the table. You'll be left with nothing if you don't sign it."

I stormed out of his office, unable to listen to his continuous tirade. Tommy's words about Rocky keeping him tied to me and our marriage didn't make sense. Then I wondered if this action was to keep Tommy and me together, or to ensure Rocky stayed connected to my mother. He loved my mother. I saw his love every time his eyes voraciously consumed her. If Tommy divorced me, there wouldn't be a reason for them to spend time together. She was still married to his Army buddy.

Once I found an attorney to discuss my unique situation with, he advised me to sign the agreement. He believed the terms were more than fair. The consequences of not signing this document could be far worse.

I marched past Tommy's secretary and barged into his office, tossing the document, with my signature angrily scrolled across the bottom, at hour seventy-one and a half. Only raging eye glares were exchanged. No words were uttered.

Within a day of my signing the papers, Tommy packed up his clothes and personal items. He moved out, taking Danny with him for the weekend. He wanted to explain the change in living situations with our son without me.

The house was quiet, but in some weird way, I felt free. Tommy wasn't home much for so many years, yet we were tied together in spite of our secrets and affairs. That cord was now broken.

Life After Tommy

Chapter 103

PHOEBE AND MAX were married in the summer of 1987. A beautiful ceremony was held at the Evangelical church. I opened up my home, backyard, and swimming pool for a casual yet lovely reception.

Phoebe reconnected with her mother and siblings after many years. Earning a degree in finance, working at *A New Beginning,* and becoming a bank manager boosted her self-esteem. She took pride in her endeavors as we all did.

Her mother was thrilled to hear from her when she made that initial, nerve-racking phone call. She flew Phoebe and Max to Chicago for a long-overdue visit. Phoebe now had nieces and nephews she met for the first time.

I never knew Phoebe ran away from home when she was sixteen because her stepfather sexually abused her. Her mom swore she had no idea that was happening until after Phoebe left home, he targeted Phoebe's younger sister as his next victim.

According to her mom, she spent a lot of time and money searching for Phoebe after throwing her husband out of her home and into a jail cell.

It was a pleasure meeting Phoebe's mom, brother, and sister, who were thrilled to witness her marry the love of her life.

Valerie found a steady beau named Dimitri from Hungary. He was a homeless immigrant we helped take off the streets. We learned Dimitri was rather handy and skilled in automotive repairs. Val helped him find a job as a mechanic at a nearby garage. The pay was great. Who knew how much money a grease monkey could earn?

They moved in together. He might be the one for my good friend, Val. Maybe wedding bells were in their future.

Hank's wife, Cora, divorced him. She couldn't handle being married to a cop anymore. The long hours and dangerous situations he had been put in was too much. Hank had been hospitalized several times over the years. He had been shot at, stabbed, run over by an assailant's truck, and beaten by gang members. Between his love for the law, *A New Beginning* program, and *me*, his marriage ended.

Yes, Hank and I became more than friends after Tommy moved out. We couldn't deny our feelings for each other any longer. I didn't plan to remarry, but Hank had been a constant friend in my life for twenty years. I couldn't imagine my life without him in it. I always trusted him, even when we first met at the Belle Maiden back in 1967.

When I left that life, I left Penny behind, for the most part. But Penny would always be a part of me.

I never encouraged anything romantic between Hank and me the entire time we worked together at the shelter while he was married. However, after his divorce and my marriage came to such an explosive end, I couldn't help myself. The attraction was always there, pulling us together like a magnet to steel.

Segregation officially and legally ended with the Civil Rights Act of 1964, yet some people still didn't approve of interracial relationships. I didn't care what outsiders thought. People stared sometimes when they saw us together, hand in hand, a black man with a white woman. Then I'd kiss Hank hard on the lips with pride for everyone to see.

I'd say the L word to Hank every single day. And he said it back, every single day.

In the beginning, my dad was not a fan of my relationship with Hank. However, he was vehemently encouraged by me to stay quiet and keep inappropriate opinions to himself. Over time, they made progress with one area of interest in common, besides me. Hank loved sports.

Dad now had someone to talk with about sports stats. The two of them would jest about their football and baseball teams. They really carried on a comedic show when the Patriots took on the Raiders. Good, fun ribbing between the two of them.

Oh, and that delicious-scented cologne of Hank's that I loved was Aramis. I still loved his scent.

Chapter 104

THE FBI NEVER found sufficient evidence that proved Tommy and his partners were committing crimes. Once they discovered I had been made, caught in the act of surveilling him and getting divorced, my collaboration with the FBI ceased.

When my divorce finalized, I only heard from Tommy if he needed to change his plans to see Danny, which was rare. He picked up Danny every weekend and would often take him some weekdays and nights too. Tommy was a much better father than he was a husband.

Alimony and child support checks were mailed to me from his accountant faithfully. I kept the house in Henderson to raise our son. The money I received amply supported the house with extra income for myself, per our divorce agreement.

Tommy showed Danny the world. Every summer, he brought Danny to his hotel in Aruba. Danny would tell me all about the white sandy beaches and crystal-clear water to swim in.

Tommy taught him about culture. He had seen Michelangelo sculptures throughout Italy, tasted delectable cuisine in Spain, and enjoyed Broadway shows in New York City. They were like two peas in a pod.

Danny looked exactly like Tommy. Tommy could never dispute the fact that Danny was his biological son. I always knew it, even if Tommy questioned his paternity. If I didn't give birth to Danny, you'd never know he was mine. But the love I felt from the depths of my soul for my son was astounding.

Danny developed his love for art and culture from Tommy. I introduced him to other qualities of life. He was humble, despite the lavish wealth he'd grown accustomed to. He spent time with me at the shelter and saw firsthand how some people lived when they didn't have a loving family or a good job.

"It's good to give back to the community." I always reminded him.

Tommy bought him whatever he wanted or needed, but I gave him an allowance. Ten dollars a week for taking out the garbage, putting dirty dishes in the dishwasher, and keeping his room clean.

Holidays were never important to Tommy before Danny was born. Each major holiday was spent with my family. Danny adored his grandparents, aunt, and uncles. Abby was like a big sister to him. Lisa had another child, a son they named Jason. Danny doted over him like a big brother.

Family and stability were important. He was reminded every day of his good fortune, and I didn't mean the money.

Besides Tommy, another man who really impacted Danny since he was a tiny tot was Hank. My son didn't care about the color of a person's skin. Hank was his hero. Ever since he met Hank at the shelter as a toddler, he talked about becoming a cop someday. Sure, his father began to show him how to run a billion-dollar empire, but he had a mind for truth and justice, right and wrong. Danny had numerous options. Hotel owner, policeman, or any other profession he might choose when he became an adult. I'd support him in anything he did.

Chapter 105

IN 1992, MUCH to my dismay, Patrick had been diagnosed with HIV. When this awful disease was first identified in the eighties, people were dying. My brother contracted a death sentence.

Fortunately, a treatment plan became available, albeit expensive. Tommy provided me with sufficient funds to manage the house since we divorced, but it might not be enough to help Patrick survive this ordeal.

I knew Tommy couldn't stand the sight of me. I gave him plenty of reasons to hate me. We both made a lot of mistakes in our marriage. But one common factor we had besides our love for Danny was our love for Patrick.

Tommy took Patrick under his wing and gave him job opportunities. He acted as a father figure. Taught him how to defend himself when he was bullied for being gay. He never cared about Patrick's lifestyle. He saw Patrick as a man and admired his passion and ambition.

When I told Tommy about Patrick's diagnosis, he grew silent on the other end of the phone. He said he'd take care of it. Then he hung up on me. Later, I learned from my brother that Tommy agreed to pay for his treatment, and he'd help him in any way possible to ensure he remained healthy. He told Patrick he couldn't stand to lose another brother.

Neither could I.

His disease was manageable with the medication he took regularly and faithfully. And he found love. Patrick and his partner, Will, met at the theater, preparing for an on-stage performance of *Grease*.

Patrick directed the actors in the play, while Will totally nailed the part of Kenickie. Love magically appeared between them.

Someday, if legal, they hoped to be married. A simple dream a man and a woman took for granted was not a privilege for gays and lesbians in the early nineties.

Patrick was able to function managing this despicable virus. He maintained his position as a writer with a weekly column in a local California paper. He continued to act, write, and direct for the theater as well.

As promised, I sat in the front row of every event Patrick starred in. Even our father attended, proud of his son's accomplishments.

Besides Will, only Tommy, Hank, and I knew about Patrick's health situation. He didn't want to worry our parents. He feared if he told Lisa, she'd break down and tell Mom and Dad. It wasn't in her nature to keep a secret from them.

Lisa, Al, and their children were a happy family, or at least that was how their lives appeared from the outside of their home. Patrick and I were far more alike than our practical, brilliant sister.

Like my brother, I held many secrets that I'd take to the grave with me. Secrets that transformed me into the woman I became.

I reminisced about my past often, especially when at the shelter. I recognized myself in some of the young girls *A New Beginning* helped.

The irony about Kenny was, as much as I despised him, if it weren't for him, I might not have achieved success in my benevolent endeavors. After meeting Renee in his hotel room years ago, I realized how sad and dangerous the streets were for young girls, victims of the night. Girls who started off innocent until put in a precarious situation later to turn jaded and isolated from humanity.

With the threat of HIV and AIDS on the minds of society, condom use was mandated at all legitimate bordellos. Monthly HIV tests were now regulated in addition to the traditional, routine medical checkups, since the risk for sexually transmitted infections was high in this profession. However, streetworkers might not be following any specific health and hygiene rules.

A New Beginning volunteers continued to attempt outreaching these ladies working the streets and the johns who strolled, educating them about protection and encouraging visits to their doctor or a local clinic. Most girls wouldn't talk to us. The pimps chased our team away—sometimes with weapons. The johns ran, fearing we were undercover cops, prepared to arrest them.

In spite of the difficulties and sometimes dangerous situations, I wouldn't change what my squad had accomplished through the years. Prostitutes were our initial target population, but any unsheltered homeless person or family were welcome to walk through our entrance for assistance.

I couldn't rescue my friend, Kitty, from the bleak, dismal streets, but I wanted to make a difference for others. And I did.

Thanks to Phoebe's meticulous reports since 1973, *A New Beginning* recorded helping in some way more than 5,000 people every year. Many individuals simply stopped in to use the shower facilities, called their families to let them know they were okay, or to escape miserable weather conditions like days of sweltering heat over a hundred degrees. Others made use of the beds, enjoyed a meal, and met with counselors like Louise, who offered resources to improve their lifestyles, allowing them independence with the potential to lead more productive lives.

The shelter expanded over the years to increase lodging, especially in emergency circumstances. We now had one hundred beds accessible with separate facilities to accommodate families.

Some went back to life on the streets. Others were saved from it. Some success stories returned as volunteers like Marianna and Jenny.

Southern Nevada was identified as having one of the largest homeless populations in the country, with people either staying in temporary shelters or non-sheltered environments like parks, alleys, streets, or beneath bridges. In nearly twenty years of servicing the community, we collaborated with other agencies whose resources were tapped into to support the needs of the unsheltered homeless. Our total numbers of service equated to 118,011 individuals and families who walked through our doors and benefited in some way from our resources.

Committees formed, hoping to create an effective plan to decrease the tragic numbers. Thanks to government funds that financially backed our mission, along with support from members of the community, who made generous donations, our doors remained open.

People with a passion for this cause, like me, ensured conversations continued. News articles referred to me as "the voice of the down-and-out." It took time for me to realize that I couldn't possibly save them all, but I could help those with the desire, courage, and motivation to make essential changes to improve their lives.

Many Moonlights Later
June 7, 2010

Chapter 106

AT MY AGE, my role with *A New Beginning* slowed significantly. Younger people took over managing the program with bigger ideas and financial plans for the shelter and its resources.

The State of Nevada offered funding, which included social workers who were highly educated and trained to help people in need. Through the decades, the needs of the population altered.

Domestic violence incidents became highly publicized to bring awareness to victims through community campaigns, advising that help was available. More people stepped forward now, asking for assistance to escape perilous situations. Unfortunately, some were too afraid to risk leaving an unsafe environment, manipulated by their abusers.

Human trafficking occurred more frequently than I cared to think about. This horrific crime encompassed adults and children forced to work laborious jobs against their will or perform sex acts in exchange for their lives. They had no freedom. They might live in abusive, deplorable conditions, locked away where no one would hear their cries for help. The Las Vegas Metro Police Department was dedicated to bringing local criminals to justice and saving the exploited victims. Hank still had connections with Metro, so he kept me apprised of their success stories.

Programs were in place to ensure children stayed in school. Youth education programs were created to teach teenagers important lifestyle habits, like avoiding drugs and alcohol. Access to a recreation center was available for children and teens to stay active and off the streets. Discussions about the topics of self-respect, abstinence, and safe sex transpired.

We began referring people to a nearby clinic we partnered with for exams, vaccinations, and lab work because the shelter had amplified to an extensive degree. Clinical volunteers couldn't keep up with making regular, on-site visits like my friend, the doc, used to when we first started this program.

The doc passed away ten years ago, shortly after the turn of the century. He managed to enjoy retirement for several years after losing sixty pounds and freeing himself from his addictive smoking habit. The last time I saw him, he had been transferred to hospice, dying from pancreatic cancer. He managed a bright smile in my direction when I reminded him of the difference he made in the lives of so many people. He died the day after my visit.

The doc's services and my crew were good back in the day because our hearts and souls were deeply woven into this endeavor. Today, technology and people with a college education dictated modernized policies and procedures.

I continued to volunteer a few times each month, a fixture to the establishment I founded thirty-seven years ago.

Prostitution was bigger than ever in Las Vegas, outside the legalized brothels.

Police officers turned a blind eye today, having much larger criminal activity to tackle than hookers and pimps using the beard of an escort service. Cops seemingly busted prostitutes only if they robbed or harmed their johns. Escort services were not illegal, and the area brought in more than thirty million tourists annually.

The women today probably made ten times more money than I once did. Despite my efforts, prostitution was still a dangerous career, running rampant in the area.

These miserable contemplations of what some unfortunate people experienced crowded my brain as Hank and I drove to Summerlin to babysit for Danny and his wife, Bianca Warner, at their beautiful home.

Danny and Bianca planned a lunch date today. Recently, they happily announced a third bundle of joy was on the way.

Since Hank retired from the force, he loved spending time with our two granddaughters. Grammy and Grampy, the girls called us.

This day began with a crisp morning blue sky freckled with white fluffy clouds. A few sprinkles of rain fell during the night. The smell of a freshly mowed lawn, combined with a thin layer of dew, sent me back to my life as a girl in Gloucester momentarily. The hot sun was already drying up the bit of moisture in the air.

The prancing of little feet running toward me always put a smile on my face and a skip in my step. I barely had a chance to give the girls a turn swirling them around the living room, followed by kisses and tickles, when the sound of a car door squealing opened and closed in the driveway caught their attention.

"Is that Poppy?" Emma asked, excitement beaming from her blue eyes. Her strawberry blond waves bounced against her shoulders as she hopped about the room. She was the spitting image of her mother, my beautiful daughter-in-law.

She adored Tommy. I noticed from afar the special relationship Emma, at three and a half years old, had with her Poppy. She lit up whenever Tommy was around.

Hearing the name, "Poppy," triggered Kristina to jump up and down, displaying her beautiful, mischievous smile. Kristina favored Danny's looks with gray eyes and wavy brown hair. At only nineteen months, Kristina understood exactly who Grammy, Grampy, and Poppy were.

But it wasn't Tommy.

Gazing through the blue silk curtains in the living room, I monitored Jim walking up the brick path.

Seeing Jim always took me back to the night he rescued me from Kenny. Those memories never vanished completely, as much as I wished they would.

Jim must be in his late sixties. White hair with a perfectly trimmed goatee atop a firm build. He aged nicely and could probably still give a good beatdown if necessary.

I met Jim's wife, Kelly, in passing one afternoon at a restaurant in Spring Valley. I always wondered if she knew he killed a man once. Maybe other deaths were weighing on his conscience. Despite his dubious past, I knew Jim had Tommy's back. That meant Jim would always take care of Danny and his children.

Danny was surprised to see Jim standing at the door unexpectedly. He welcomed Jim inside and shook his hand. "What brings you by?"

I approached wearing a smile, with Kristina now glued to my hip, while Emma twirled in circles, seeking Hank's attention.

Jim nodded at me and smiled at Kristina. "Danny, this isn't a social call. I had to come in person to see you." His voice sounded quieter and more serious than usual.

Although Jim came to speak to Danny, I didn't leave my son's side. A mother's intuition, perhaps.

Jim glanced at Kristina and sent me a look, displaying the seriousness of his visit.

I placed Kristina down and asked, "Hank, will you entertain the girls, please?"

Once the girls bounced out of the room, Jim made a startling announcement. "I'm sorry to tell you this, Danny, but your pop died this morning." Jim placed a gentle hand on Danny's shoulder for a version of comfort I never realized he had in him.

I wanted to pound on my eardrum. Did I hear him correctly? Instinctively, I placed an arm around Danny, who didn't seem to comprehend what we both just heard.

"Do you need to sit?" Jim asked. Then he stared into my eyes and nodded his head, confirming the reality of his somber visit.

How could Tommy be dead? He might have been a thorn in my side, but he gave me Danny, the only good thing that came out of our abominable marriage.

Danny seemed ridiculously quiet. Denial, perhaps. He stared straight ahead with unfocused eyes and said nothing as Jim explained Tommy had suffered a heart attack. His doctor couldn't save him.

"Where's Pop now?" Danny managed to ask with a trembling chin.

"I was listed as his emergency contact," Jim replied. "I notified Len. He'll be in touch with you to discuss your pop's wishes. I hate saying these words to you, Dan, but Tommy's body is in the morgue."

Chapter 107

TOMMY CHOSE TO be cremated. According to his attorney, Len, Tommy didn't want to be remembered by his death. He wished for his life to be celebrated with a non-traditional tribute.

Tommy requested a simple mass at Saint Francis Church. Above the box that contained his ashes near the altar was an older picture of him blown up and placed upon an easel. The photo had been taken after we were married, when he first inherited the Montgomery. He was so handsome.

I couldn't help but reflect upon our past together. There were some good times. Let's face it, Tommy and I simply weren't meant to be married. We could have been friends, good friends, had it not been for my selfishness. I was sorry for the sins of my youth. I hoped Tommy knew that. All our lives would have been different. But that would mean Danny wouldn't have been born.

Friends and employees of the Montgomery paid tribute to the owner at a lively party held in the Buckingham Palace banquet hall in the England wing. Classic rock songs by bands like Lynyrd Skynyrd, the Eagles, Heart, and Aerosmith played at a mild tone.

The bar was open with top-shelf liquor. However, Danny asked the bartender to create a special virgin drink for the ceremony since Tommy stopped drinking alcohol years ago and managed to remain sober. Hot and cold hors d'oeuvres were carried by the wait staff, dressed all in black from head to toe.

My parents flew in for the funeral. I didn't like them driving at their age. In spite of Dad's discontent for Tommy, he respected Danny's loss.

Patrick attended with Will, his husband. The happy couple planned a wedding in June 2008, shortly after California legalized same-sex marriage. Tommy stood by Patrick's side as his best man.

My brother grieved the loss of his friendship with Tommy tremendously. Tommy treated Patrick like his own kid brother. He supported Patrick's lifestyle, health care, and finding a cure for AIDS, contributing financially to the cause. Over the years, scientific research allowed people with HIV the freedom to live a normal life with a treatment regimen. However, there was still no cure.

Many people stood up to an open microphone and told these funny Tommy stories. He had such a large, charming presence that captured the attention of anyone around him. His good looks and powerful body caught many eyes and a lot of women.

One person was missing today, however. That woman Tommy supposedly loved. The realtor he had an affair with throughout our entire marriage. I saw so many photos of her, I'd recognize her if I saw her again, even after all these years.

If he loved her so much, why didn't he marry her? I saw Tommy out with other women after we divorced, but never with his mistress. I wasn't sure what I'd say to her if I saw her.

Most of my anger diminished as time drifted by. The demise of my marriage was not entirely her fault. My transgressions played a significant role. Perhaps I was envious that he couldn't love me the way he loved her, based on the pictures I saw.

Danny stood before a crowded room and thanked everyone for attending the celebration of his father's life. He asked the guests to walk through the casino with him.

We strolled through the corridor like a herd of cattle following their leader.

My brain raced, recalling the image of Tommy and his sexy smirk for the first time by the pool at his father's home in 1966. It was there, near the craps table, where Tommy first put his arm around me when I was lost, distracted by the hoopla of the casino. The old coat room I worked in where Tommy asked me to see Frank Sinatra with him was used as a storage closet.

Hank squeezed my hand, snapping me back to the present day.

Danny stopped us all in our tracks where the carpet ended and the sparkling white marble floor to the grand lobby began.

I inched myself up closer to see what my son was pointing to. An old photograph of a youthful, handsome Tommy, along with a tiny glass casing that held some of his ashes, will be built into a wall at the Montgomery, between the lobby and the casino entrance. A permanent memorial.

"My pop will forever be immortalized here within the empire he built. As long as the Montgomery remains standing, Tommy Cavallo's life and career shall not be forgotten."

Chapter 108

MY TWIN GRANDSONS were born in early December, six months past Tommy's death. Bianca and Danny learned they were blessed with twin sons shortly after Tommy's funeral. They named the boys Thomas and Tyler.

As much as there was love residing in Danny's home, there was stress. Four young babies under the age of five, a career to maintain, and losing his pop unexpectedly was a lot for him to handle. Tommy gave Danny the option to choose his career path. He was still trying to decide if he would help run the Montgomery, the family legacy created by his grandfather, or maintain his current profession as an attorney.

He never shared his distress with me, but as a mother with fierce perception, I sensed it. Deep down, I'd hate for him to let the Montgomery chain go.

I spent a great deal of time at his house, helping with the newborns, or distracting Emma and Kristina to ensure Bianca had a break. Sometimes I wondered if my daily presence added tension.

Danny was far too kind to ask me for some space.

Kristina and I were pressing sugar cookie dough while the twins napped, and Emma was practicing counting to twenty at preschool. Now was the time to ask them if my everyday visits were helpful or annoying. Perhaps I hesitated because I loved seeing my grandchildren so frequently. Maybe I worried they'd tell me not to come around so much.

With Tommy gone, Hank and I were the closest grandparents they had. Bianca's parents, Elliot and Pam Warner, lived in North

Carolina and spoke to the kids through a laptop computer each week. The Warners only visited Las Vegas a couple of times a year.

Before my question could escape my lips, Danny picked up his cell phone and stepped out of the kitchen to call Len Stein. He mentioned that Len had left him several messages over the past week, but my son juggled a lot on his plate these days.

"Grammy, my turn!" Kristina insisted, reaching for the Ariel princess cookie cutter. This little one was pretty demanding. Although I hated to admit that she looked like the Cavallo side of the family, she also inherited my fiery spirit.

"Mom!" Danny's voice shrieked, startling me when he returned to the kitchen.

My body twisted toward him, still pressing out cookie dough with Kristina, waiting for him to tell me what the fuss was about.

"Pop wrote a book! Len told me his book is being published soon."

"What kind of book? When on earth would your father have had time to write?"

Danny shrugged then signaled to Bianca with a turn of his head.

Bianca quickly swept Kristina away from the cookie mix, promising her return shortly, offering Danny and me privacy.

A few tears flowed down Kristina's sweet cheeks as she kicked at her mama, pulling Bianca's strawberry blond waves, angry to be taken away from our afternoon baking activity.

"The reason Len's been trying to contact me is to tell me about Pop's book. He wrote his life story, memoirs. Len warned me that some details could be *sensitive* to our family."

His gray eyes stared into mine, the same gaze of his father's when he was frustrated with me.

"I can't imagine anything Pop would write about me and Bianca that would be harmful. But I'm worried about you." Danny cocked his head, waiting for my response.

I spun my body away to pick up some crumbs of sugar cookie dough Kristina accidentally dropped on the tile floor.

"You don't ever have to worry about me, sweetheart. I'm quite a survivor."

"Ma, I won't pretend that you and Pop had a good marriage. But if there's anything you think I should know before his book is released, please tell me," he pleaded.

Memoirs? Naturally, Tommy still sought attention, even after his death. I wondered what he wrote about me and our marriage exactly. It couldn't be anything good, seeing he carried so much anger and bitterness toward me for so many years after our divorce. Until I read his fable myself, I wouldn't share the most intimate details of my life with Danny.

"Danny, your pop was as eccentric as he was exciting. He had quite an imagination and loved to tell a story with tremendous embellishments. Remember him as the hero you always believed him to be. He wasn't perfect. None of us are. Whatever he wrote may disillusion your perception of him. Maybe it's best you focus on your family instead of some gibberish he created."

I inched away from him as if this news flash was completely irrelevant. I placed the cookie tray into the oven, set the timer, and stepped outside for fresh air, craving a shot of vodka, preferably a double.

My fingers strummed along the crucifix dangling from my necklace. Would Tommy hate me enough to reveal my past working in a brothel? Or share his accusations about my collaboration with the FBI against him? What would Tommy gain from that exposure, especially if it hurt our son?

My mind wandered to that show he put on in front of an audience at his will reading in June, dishing out his wealth like peanuts at the circus. Humiliating me was the main attraction, leaving me pocket change while others were handed millions of dollars, valuable properties, or his prized sports cars.

His mistress walked away with a small fortune in real estate. At least I finally had the chance to tell her what I thought of her that day. I felt a wide smile spread across my face as I remembered yelling aloud that she was a whore for anyone within earshot to hear.

The joke was on Tommy though. I didn't need the mere coins he bequeathed. He dished out a lot of alimony to me over the years because Hank and I never married.

Hank had the heart of a cop but the mind of a businessman. Long before we retired, Hank insisted we invest in stocks, bonds, and CDs. Our main investments through the decades included companies like IBM and Apple. We could live our typical lifestyle off the interest in our bank account alone.

Still, I needed to prepare myself for any bombshell Tommy ignited in his book for the sole pleasure of revenge.

Truth be told, I was scared to death that some secrets from my past would come to light in Tommy's memoirs.

Coming soon from the Entanglements series—*Love Affair: Tommy's Memoirs*. Tommy's tell-all book exposes layers of secrets related to both Sadie and his mistress, Angie; introduces his Mafia connections; illustrates the details of his exhilarating life after his divorce from Sadie; and reveals the extreme events that lead to his untimely death.

The Mistress Chronicles is an Award-Winning, Family Saga Finalist of the American Fiction Awards. If you're curious about Tommy's romantic life with his mistress, this book is available at Amazon, Barnes & Noble, Apple eBooks, Google Play, and other retail stores.

About the Author

Gina Marie Martini is the author of the drama series titled *Entanglements*, honored in 2020 with an American Fiction Award as a Finalist in the Family Saga category for her debut novel, *The Mistress Chronicles*.

She was born and raised in Connecticut, where she lives with her family. With a creative imagination and a love for reading and writing, Gina has been writing short stories since her youth. She earned a Bachelor's degree in Psychology and a Master's degree in Health Administration. Gina maintains a full-time career in the health insurance industry with a background in Behavioral Health and Clinical Programs.

Follow her at www.ginamariemartini.com,
Facebook, Twitter, and Instagram.